SUMMER IN PROVENCE

LUCY COLEMAN

Boldwood

First published in Great Britain in 2020 by Boldwood Books Ltd.

Copyright © Lucy Coleman, 2020

Cover Design by Alice Moore Design

Cover Photography: Shutterstock

A CIP catalogue record for this book is available from the British Library.

Paperback ISBN 978-1-83889-179-4

Ebook ISBN 978-1-83889-181-7

Kindle ISBN 978-1-83889-180-0

Audio CD ISBN 978-1-83889-177-0

MP3 CD ISBN 978-1-83889-721-5

Digital audio download ISBN 978-1-83889-178-7

Boldwood Books Ltd
23 Bowerdean Street
London SW6 3TN
www.boldwoodbooks.com

To Lawrence
Even after all our years together, every single day of my life I still choose
you. You were the one who convinced me it was time to give up the day job
and just write. So, I did. Whenever my confidence has dipped, you've been
there to pick me up. And when it's been time to celebrate, you whisk me
away and make me feel like a million dollars. Love you always and
forever. x

APRIL 2018

STROUD, GLOUCESTERSHIRE

1

THE WIND OF CHANGE IS BLOWING

Is it a blessing, or a curse, to be born with an inner voice... one that pipes up unbidden, filling you with a sense of uneasy expectation?

The situation isn't helped by the fact that my head has been pounding all day. But for the last hour, I've had a familiar shooting pain in my right eye and now it's becoming relentless. It's building, whatever is coming, and the stress of it is making me sick to my stomach.

When it finally reveals itself to me, my instincts are screaming that everything will change. Every little thing I take for granted is going to be threatened.

Change can be exhilarating, but what I feel is a heaviness beginning to descend upon me and I'm fearful about what is coming.

* * *

Buzz. Buzz. Buzz. The phone skitters across the desk, making me jump. I've been trying to read the final page of this report for the last twenty minutes, but the words keep swimming in front of my eyes. I don't want to answer it because it's taking all my resolve to sit here quietly reading, let alone engage in even a simple conversation. Maybe it can wait. It's too late in the day for it to be my boss and I scan around, realising everyone else has already gone home.

I retract my hovering hand, leaning over instead to check the caller ID. It's my sister, Hannah. Instantly I panic and my mouth goes dry as I snatch up the phone, pressing it to my ear. At the moment, she's a constant worry and it's just one thing after another as she lurches from one emotional crisis to the next. Hormones have a lot to answer for, don't they?

My voice is uneven, a gravelly rasp I barely recognise.

'What's up, Hannah?' I pause to clear my throat. 'Is everything okay?'

Thud goes my heart in slow motion, as if it's mechanical and in need of rewinding. I know I should have quit working an hour ago to go home and dive beneath the duvet to ride this out.

'Fern, I can't believe you're still at work. Do you know what time it is?'

The haze of pain around me clears a little as the warm lilt in her tone reassures me she's fine.

'I... I'm leaving soon.'

Closing my eyes to fight the nausea as another wave of pain washes over me – even my teeth are now hurting. I ease back my shoulders to release the tension in my neck, but it doesn't help.

'I'm with Aiden. You need to come home right now. I checked the lottery ticket pinned to the fridge door while we were waiting for you.'

I can hear a jumble of voices in the background, which confuses me as I fight to process her words.

'Ticket?' What ticket?

Oh. The one I bought at the supermarket on Friday. It's... Monday, no, Tuesday. The days roll through my head with absolutely no connection to anything.

'Well?' She laughs, excitement raising the pitch of her voice and making me wince.

'Well, what?' The pounding is now excruciating and I realise if I don't take a migraine pill, I'm going to keel over.

'Fern, you sound half asleep. You only matched one number, but you flippin' won the Millionaire's Raffle!'

My stomach begins to churn and I slump forward, wracked with pain, until my forehead touches the desk.

'Lovely. Tell Aiden I'll be home soon, promise.'

Click.

Why is Hannah at the house? Why isn't she at uni? Then I remember that it's the Easter holidays. It's fine. All I need to do now is to get home in one piece.

* * *

'You look awful, Fern. Are you fighting off a migraine attack?'

I nod, dropping my bag on the floor and gratefully sinking down onto one of the chairs. It looks like I missed a party. The breakfast bar is littered with glasses, two open bottles of Prosecco and an assortment of snacks.

Aiden is staring at me. 'Tea?' he asks, gently.

'Yes please.'

My body feels heavy now that the pain is under control, but the side effects aren't pleasant. My jaw, neck and shoulders feel bruised, as if I've hit something with force. At least my stomach has stopped churning.

'Where's Hannah?'

'She had to head off as she's meeting up with her room-mate for pizza, remember? Your mum and dad popped in to drop off the coat you left at their house after Sunday lunch and they offered her a lift.'

Oh, yes. 'And the drinks?' I nod in the direction of the mess Aiden has begun to clear.

'Georgia from next door knocked to say *hello* when she spotted your parents' car parked on the drive. Hannah had just checked the lottery results on her phone and was buzzing with the news. She texted Steve to join us after Georgia said she'd stay for a drink. It turned into a little celebration and I kept hoping you'd walk through the door.' He carries a mug of tea across, placing it in front of me on the table. 'Sorry about this morning,' he adds, casually, as if wasn't a big deal. But his apology is tinged with guilt and he's avoiding eye contact.

Does he think I stayed away on purpose? In the seven years that we've been married, we've never rowed at breakfast before. In fact, we rarely argue, but recently... I'm beginning to feel I don't know him any more.

'You must be feeling really awful if even the thought of a million pounds hitting the bank account doesn't raise a smile. Have you had it all day?' He wrinkles his brow and his reaction tugs at my heartstrings. I love every little inch of that expressive face; including the silvery white scar on his forehead, a reminder of the boisterous young toddler who drove everyone mad with his antics – or so I'm told. And those hazel eyes and the closely cropped, dark brown hair he daren't grow out as it has a life of its own, is imprinted on my mind. For the briefest of moments, what I see isn't a twenty-nine-year-old man standing in front of me, but how he was when we first met. A seventeen-year-old who thought he was a man already. In those days, he only had two hairs on his chest and now it's in serious need of waxing, in my opinion. The thoughts running through my head make me smile.

'More or less,' I admit.

'You should have phoned. I don't like you driving when you're like this.'

'Like this?' I frown as I look up at him, the effort involved in processing his words is hard work.

Seeing the concern etched on his face triggers a memory from this morning. As he stomped around in a bad mood, I felt he was simply waiting for me to leave. My presence seemed to annoy him, for some reason I couldn't comprehend. All I did was ask him what was wrong.

'In a full-blown attack, babe. You don't always realise your judgement is impaired. Remember the time you got the car wedged up against the pillar as you pulled into the garage?'

It was one incident. Probably five years ago. And yes, that day, I shouldn't have attempted to drive myself home. I'd forgotten my tablets and I didn't want to cause a fuss.

I'd inherited these sick headaches from Dad, who warned me that stress was a big trigger for him. Which didn't help at all. Who can avoid stress?

I remember having to abandon the car before I finally staggered inside. Aiden came back to find me collapsed on the floor in the hallway. The following morning he said I'd scared him, and he made me promise I wouldn't take that risk again.

Well, at least Aiden still cares, so whatever is going wrong between us, that's a comfort, I suppose.

He slides into the chair opposite me, looking sheepish.

'Hannah was right, I double-checked the ticket myself. We've won, Fern.'

Wrapping my hands gently around the mug of tea for a few seconds, I allow the almost scalding heat to shock some life back into me. The migraine pills leave my senses feeling muted, as if there's a slight disconnect – a fuzziness that won't be shaken. As the heat builds, I withdraw my hands and drop them down onto my lap. With fingers tingling, it's good to feel something that pulls me sharply back into the moment.

It's only money: the words jump into my head, unbidden. Money won't fix the fact that something has changed in Aiden and my fear is that he has fallen out of love with me.

'We'll be able to pay off the mortgage. And clear the credit cards.' He draws to a halt. Aiden's tone is gentle and as I watch his expression, I can see he understands it hasn't fully sunk in yet. My brain doesn't seem able to process the words right now, and I look at him blankly. 'Come on. What you need isn't tea, but sleep.'

He stands and, in two strides, a pair of strong arms lift me up out of my seat and steer me towards the door.

'Promise me you won't take that risk again, silly thing. You might be superwoman, Fern, but I suspect even she has an off day every now and again. We all need a little help from time to time and that's what I'm here for.'

I needed to hear that. Oh, how I needed to hear that. With his arms around me, a sense of relief, of being rescued, allows me to let go. Like a balloon deflating, suddenly I feel empty and my husband is in control. My rock is still my rock.

Aiden lowers me onto the bed and helps me undress. As soon as my body sinks back onto the soft, cool surface of the crisp cotton sheet and my head hits the pillow, I'm spirited away. The darkness is like a cocoon and I welcome it.

2

ISN'T IT EVERYONE'S DREAM... A WIN?

Georgia peers at me over the top of her mug of coffee, her eyebrows knitting together in concern.

'What do you mean, it's causing a problem? Figuring out what to do with a considerable windfall requires a lot of thought, but I'm not sure that's a problem, exactly. If it is, it's certainly a problem most people wouldn't mind having.'

She scoops back her mop of ginger curls and those piercing blue eyes search mine.

I sigh. It feels as if Aiden and I have talked about nothing else for the last two weeks. A sudden influx of money, I've come to discover, doesn't instantly magic away all of one's problems. Our family and friends, the people we both work with, all assume we're in some sort of state of euphoria. But the truth is that we aren't, and I know that sounds ungrateful.

'It's complicated, Georgia,' I admit.

She places her mug back down on the table to signal that I have her full attention.

'Come on, get it off your chest. If you can't trust me, then you can't trust anyone. We've been friends long enough for you to know that I have your back no matter what.'

It's hard to put into words and it takes me a few moments to pull my erratic thoughts together cohesively.

'I think Aiden's going through some sort of crisis. Don't they call it burnout these days? You know, when people get themselves into a state of emotional, physical and mental exhaustion. Our life seems to be in limbo, right now. Aiden always feels he has to keep going; what he does is never enough in his eyes, which is crazy because he's running on empty and miserable with it.'

The moment I finish speaking I can't believe I said that out aloud. Georgia's jaw drops, and her mouth hangs open for a second before she snaps it shut.

'I've always thought of him as Mr Dependable, wishing Steve was a little more like him. I didn't give it a thought about how stressful that might be. I know the charity rely on him heavily because he has that ability to motivate others. You know what they say, if you want something done, ask a busy person.'

'I guess it's partly my fault. We'd love to have a baby at some point, but our savings were dwindling. Opportunities were coming up at work and I was in the running for promotion. It was a time to step up and prove I could handle it.'

'Now, of course, money isn't an issue, so you can relax.'

It's a fair enough comment but Georgia doesn't understand it wasn't solely about the money. It was about the recognition and I did what I had to do to make it happen.

'If I hadn't been so focused on where I was heading, maybe I would have noticed it was all becoming too much for him.' This is the first time I've allowed myself to admit my fears. Up until now it's been an elusive worry floating around inside my head. But as the weeks and months have passed, the random pieces have started to come together and what I'm beginning to understand is disturbing.

'This is a bit unexpected, I will admit, although he hasn't been his usually jolly self recently. A bit... preoccupied, perhaps, is what I'd noticed,' Georgia suggests.

I can almost see her mind ticking over as we sit here, glumly realising the signs have been there for a while.

'We no longer talk about the future, it's all day-to-day stuff. We've been married for seven years and I can't help wondering if that has something to do with it,' I admit.

Georgia smiles. 'The seven-year itch? Is that even real?'

'The alleged point at which boredom sets in, apparently. I just didn't think it would happen to us. What a fool I've been, assuming Aiden's silence meant we were still working towards the same goals; he's become withdrawn and that's a warning sign I should have jumped on from the start.'

'He is an overachiever, so I get that bit. But you're the centre of his world, Fern.'

'And he's the centre of mine, but it's always work or family these days. We've stopped bothering to dress up and have a date night, time to just enjoy being together. We come home tired and veg out in front of the TV. And weekends it's either something related to the charity, working on the house or visiting my family.'

'He... um... he hasn't done something stupid, has he? I mean, you do hear of—' Georgia's frown is deepening.

'No. *No.* It's not like that – at least, I don't think he's had an affair, or anything. I'd at least sense *that*, wouldn't I?'

Georgia's eyebrows shoot up, disappearing into corkscrew curls. 'Well, you're a pair of workaholics, which is probably why you've always been so close, because you understand each other. Maybe you need a break, a little holiday to enjoy some undisturbed quality time together.'

'I wish it was that simple, but I fear that would actually tip us over the edge. Being together twenty-four/seven while he's so touchy would be yet another pressure.'

'Ah, I see what you mean. Sort of confronting it head-on because there wouldn't be any distractions. Damn it, this is a bit of a predicament, isn't it?'

Well, she's right there. How can I explain something that's made up of a zillion disparate little oddities? In isolation, they mean nothing; combined they mean something. But what, exactly?

'He's been so grouchy lately that the timing hasn't been right to have a heart-to-heart. So, another week drags by and the gap between us seems to just keep getting wider and wider.'

'You guys always used to have fun together and it was good to see. I feel bad not noticing something had changed. Not much of a friend, am I?'

Now I've made her feel guilty and that's not what this is all about. Aiden has become lukewarm to every attempt I make to reach out to him. What's frustrating is that I can't even pinpoint when the change began to occur. That slip from spine-tingling excitement whenever we're alone into a cosy, almost mundane, existence. I could weep.

Georgia picks up her mug and sips her coffee, mulling over my words. It's agonising.

'Steve and I don't have time to even think about going through a plateau in our marriage, because of the kids. All we can think about is what sleep we can grab and quality time as a couple has become a distant memory. Our gift to each other is a lie-in.' She grimaces.

I can see it's an attempt to lighten the moment, albeit she's speaking from the heart. But this is the last thing she expected me to blurt out and now I wish I hadn't started the conversation.

'This win, well, it seems to be polarising us, Georgia. I just want the old Aiden back.'

She stares at me, shaking her head sadly. 'Now you're worrying me, Fern. You're in HR and you deal with people and their problems all the time. You are a good communicator and you know how to read the signs. If you can't handle this, then maybe it's time to think about talking to a marriage guidance counsellor.'

Before I can react to her suggestion, we hear the sound of the front door opening. Aiden's voice calls out 'Hello,' which makes my stomach flutter, nervously.

Georgia and I exchange a resigned look.

'I'd better go,' she says, brightly. 'I didn't realise it was that time already. It's my turn to cook tonight. My brood will be attacking the biscuit jar and wondering why there's nothing in the oven.' She places her hand on my arm, giving it a squeeze. 'We'll speak tomorrow,' she whispers, and as Aiden enters the kitchen, she gives him a warm smile. 'One in, one out. Catch you later, guys,' and with that she disappears out through the back door.

Aiden approaches, stooping to place a fleeting kiss on my cheek and I can see he has something on his mind.

'Hard day?' I ask, hoping it will prompt him to talk about it.

'Yep.' With that, he turns to grab a mug and carries it across to place a coffee pod in the machine. The noise temporarily puts a halt to any conversation.

I busy myself grabbing a few things from the fridge and begin assembling a salad. Anything to fill the awkward silence that lies between us like an increasing chasm.

My back is towards Aiden, but I hear him pull out one of the dining chairs and the creak as he lowers himself onto the seat.

'We're getting good at avoiding tactics, aren't we?'

His words make me spin around. There's no edge to his voice just a ring of sadness.

'I'm trying not to make it any worse than it is already,' I admit. 'Is that avoidance? I suppose it is, but I don't know how else to handle whatever it is we're going through right now.'

He nods his head in the direction of the seat opposite him. 'Maybe it's time to be honest with each other, Fern.'

His words hit me as forcefully as if I've just been slapped.

'I thought... hoped... we always have been.'

He shakes his head. 'I don't know why I feel like something is missing from my life at the moment, and I know that's not fair on you. It doesn't make any sense whatsoever, but it's affecting everything I do. Or try to do. Suddenly, when I wake up each morning it all feels rather predictable.'

He stares down at his mug, avoiding eye contact.

'Predictable?' Well, I didn't see that coming. Isn't it simply another word for boring?

'Maybe the word I'm looking for is *repetitive*,' he corrects himself, and I feel my shoulders sag in dismay.

'Repetitive?' I repeat, dully. 'If this is about starting a family, then I know we keep putting it off, but it was always in the plan for when we hit our early thirties. If you want to bring that forward, you only have to say. Everything is flexible, Aiden, you know that. But we need to be sure we're ready as it's a huge commitment, darling.'

'It's not that. And I don't think adding yet another pressure right now is a good idea, anyway.' That sounds ominous, to say the least.

'Look, I'm sorry – I was aware that something hasn't been right between us for a while and I should have tackled it head-on. But whenever I approached the issue, you changed the subject and I assumed you weren't ready to talk about it.'

He looks dejected, sitting there in a slump.

'I thought we'd continue to be united by the things that life threw at us.' His tone is now softer and I can see he's making a concerted effort to verbalise his feelings. 'Each step can sometimes feel like a hurdle, Fern, and we know that only too well. We've had some great highs and a couple of massive lows, admittedly, but we've always pulled through it together.'

He's trying to reassure me because he wants this conversation to be over. *Ducking and diving won't help, Aiden – we need to get to the bottom of what's wrong.*

'It's not something we can continue to ignore, though, is it?' I know it sounds challenging, but now we're actually talking openly, there's no turning back.

'I can't seem to find the right words to explain how I feel, so I'm not surprised you don't understand. All I know is that I love you, I really do, and I'm gutted to think I'm upsetting you, babe.'

Eventually he looks up and what I see as our eyes meet is a look of desperation, then it softens.

'Do you remember when we bumped into each other at the school dance and just like that,' he clicks his fingers, 'we knew something had changed? Something big was happening.'

I'm thinking that *collided* would be a more appropriate word. And it wasn't just a dance, it was a full-blown prom. We were all excitable sixteen- and seventeen-year-olds. It was the first time we'd ever spoken because Aiden mixed with the sporty crowd and I was one of the geeks in those days.

I nod, not wanting to interrupt him.

'I remember our first date, three days later, and you phoned me the following day to say that your dad said you couldn't see me again. All because I'd brought you home an hour late and I'd blasted the car horn three times as I pulled away. Lights went on all around the quiet little cul-de-sac that night. But I was showing off because I wanted to impress you and I was wildly happy.'

Back then, I was looking forward to starting an A-level course at the progressive Amersley College in the autumn. Dad, a natural-born worrier, thought Aiden was rather cocky and overconfident, so it wasn't the best start. But, as the years passed, he realised he had gained another son, a man he could trust to take care of his often stubborn daughter.

Aiden continues. 'And you said, "But I don't care, because nothing is going to stop me from seeing you," and you meant it. That made me feel invincible. Nothing in life would ever throw me again because I'd found my soulmate. Two is stronger than one.'

My eyes fill with tears, because while Aiden is a thoughtful and rather romantic man, he doesn't often choose to talk about his emotions. When he does, it's always for a reason and a chill begins to creep up my spine, one vertebra at a time.

'We were headstrong, weren't we?' I admit.

Everyone said it wouldn't last because after A-levels we both hoped to be able to apply for a place at university. Even at that stage, it looked unlikely we would be heading off in the same direction, and everyone knows long-distance relationships don't fare well, in general. But while the thought of being apart was terrifying, we never doubted each other for a second.

In hindsight, what were the chances of staying together through all of that – but we did. It turned out that absence really does make the heart grow fonder and each time we met up it was truly exhilarating.

Aiden scans my face and I wonder what he sees.

'Would you change anything?' he levels at me. 'You've overtaken me career-wise and I realise I held you back. You turned down a dream job offer in London without a second's thought so we could buy this place and finally begin putting down roots. No wonder your dad took a while to forgive me and accept that you had settled for less than you deserved.'

He knows that isn't strictly true. I needed to be close to my family at that time for lots of reasons and putting down roots here was the right thing to do. Is this upset about my recent promotion? I wonder. I hope this isn't about who earns the most as that would be disappointing. If Aiden's ego is that fragile, then I'm doing something very wrong. He means everything to me – more than money, more than a job title and he doesn't know me at all if he thinks those things matter.

Aiden's work role has evolved and he might not have a pile of diplomas to put on a wall, but he has a very marketable range of skills. Skills that come naturally to him because he inspires people to care. That's why he's perfect to motivate the whole team when it comes to fundraising. He's indispensable, but I know he doesn't perceive himself in that way and it saddens me that he undersells himself and his abilities.

I can't avoid answering his question, but it's hard not to sound cross. 'No, of course I wouldn't change a thing. Why would you even ask a question like that?'

Swiping away my tears, a strange mix of feelings stir within me. Is he trying to say I'm the one who has changed?

He sighs and it's a gut-wrenching sound. 'I don't know how to explain this feeling of... *what if?*'

My stomach drops as I stare at him. 'You're regretting the last seven years – the choices we made?'

'No!' The word hurtles towards me at speed, like a bullet shattering the silence. He begins shaking his head emphatically, his hands now balled together in front of him, making a fist.

Aiden stares up at the ceiling and I have no words I can offer because I don't understand what's going on inside his head.

He was emotionally distraught when his grandma died a year ago. But this is different. This is something I have never seen in him before and it scares me.

I'm finally staring in the face of the fear that I have been carrying around with me for nearly six months now. And I don't know what to do, or say.

Aiden leans forward in his seat, extending one hand across the table towards me. Instinctively I reach out and our fingers intertwine.

'I love you, Fern. I always have, and I always will. But suddenly I don't know who I am beneath the outer façade I show to the world... So many different things to different people and yet inside I'm feeling *lost* right now. I know I should just be grateful for the life we have and count my blessings. I tell myself that constantly but—'

But? The silence is painful while I wait, and our fingers slowly drift apart.

'But it doesn't seem to help me make sense of this feeling I have of... it not being enough. As if there's something I'm supposed to do, something that will make a difference, and yet I don't know what.'

'Something better than *us*? I had no idea you felt this way, Aiden – why didn't you say something before now?'

He looks shocked to hear the anger in my voice.

'Fern, I'm just trying to explain something that I'm not sure even I can fully comprehend. This isn't about having regrets and I'm sorry if that's the way it's coming across. You've come into your own and you're blossoming, and I love that. You aren't just a beautiful, intelligent and caring wife, daughter and sister, you can achieve anything you want. You deserve to have someone alongside you who is equally as strong and focused, but suddenly I'm second-guessing everything I do. It makes me feel weak, as if I'm a fraud and I'm taking the easy way out.'

'I feel as if you're punishing me for something, when all I've ever done is put you – us – first. Whatever I do, I'm going to give it one hundred and ten per cent because that's who I am. You know that, Aiden. I'm not competing with you, or trying to prove anything. I just want us to be happy.'

Pushing back on my chair and rising to my feet, disappointment begins to turn into resentment. This isn't the man I married at all.

Aiden leaps out of his seat to stop me from leaving.

'Ever since Grandma died, I've felt as if life is a ticking clock. Every single day that passes is a day I should be moving forward, but I feel stuck. Drained. Invisible even to myself, as if I'm some sort of automaton going through the motions instead of living in the moment.'

'And you couldn't open up to me, your wife? So instead you kept quiet and let it come between us like a growing chasm that gets bigger with each passing day?' His face begins to swim in front of me as tears fill my eyes.

'Don't go, babe, please don't turn your back on me.' His arms around me are comforting and the warmth of his body is reassuring. 'I will sort myself out, I promise,' he whispers into my ear. For one moment, the old, self-assured Aiden is back and it's a relief to know that maybe, just maybe, all is not yet lost.

'I think we both need to do some thinking about where we go from here. I'm struggling because I feel you're pushing me away. It hurts, but I can see that you're as confused about this as I am. That's a good thing, though, isn't it?' My words make him hug me even closer and if I ever doubted his love, his body language is firmly denying that.

'It means I know I'd be lost without you. But maybe to find myself I need to discover who I am outside of our relationship.'

And there is it – the change that little inner voice was warning me was imminent.

The bottom suddenly drops out of my world. He isn't depressed, as I was beginning to fear was the case. No, Aiden feels the life he has is constraining him – he feels trapped! The excitement of the unknown versus the comfort of a relationship spanning thirteen years. The life I knew – we knew – is already a thing of the past. And there's nothing I can do to change that now.

Old words come back to haunt me. My father once said, 'You need to discover who you are as individuals, Fern, before you can take those strengths forward into a relationship. Know yourself first and everything else will fall into place.'

Having three siblings, I knew myself all right. Ours was a noisy house, but we were happy in between the usual squabbles and petty upsets of family life. I was the sensible one, always enlisted to help out and take control of my brother and sisters. Mum said I was a born negotiator and she'd laugh whenever I waded in to break up an argument over who was going to sit on the big chair in front of the TV.

As I grew into my teens, though, surprisingly – as the second eldest – I became the one pushing the boundaries and driving my parents mad. I was so resolute in the belief that I knew best, I often refused to listen to advice. But with their hands full, there were times when Dad would ground me and the cooling-off period often did me good. It helped me to put things into perspective and I needed that.

Aiden, on the other hand, being an only child, was the sole focus for his parents. Did that intensity mean he felt his role was always to please and never to disappoint? Perhaps now he's approaching thirty, he's beginning to rebel at that feeling of having to please everyone around him. And that, it seems, includes me.

That little voice inside my head continues the conversation –

words I simply can't express out loud. *I don't want you to please me, Aiden, I simply want to make you happy; that's what I thought I was doing as we build our future together. Well, I guess I failed the one time it really mattered.* A half-sob rises up within me. *How can I forgive myself for letting you down so badly, my darling?*

3

THE PARTY

'About last night. I didn't mean to—'

Sitting across the breakfast table from me, Aiden's look is apologetic and tinged with guilt.

It took me hours to drift off and I awoke, suddenly, a couple of hours later. As I lay there impatiently waiting for dawn to break, I instinctively knew he, too, was wide awake. With our backs to each other, I'd never felt more alone in my entire life.

'Hey, if we can't be honest with each other, then something is very wrong. I can't pretend that what you said didn't come as a bit of a shock,' I point out, 'but I'm glad you had the courage to tackle it.'

'And you aren't disappointed in me?' Aiden is making no attempt at all to eat his breakfast and the cornflakes are now lying in the bowl in front of him, soggy and unappealing.

I shake my head, scared to utter the word 'no' out loud, fearing it will lack conviction.

'So, how do we play this? You want some thinking time, but I'm not sure exactly what you have in mind.' He'd said 'outside of our relationship' last night, so I'm guessing he wasn't envisaging a three-week holiday for two somewhere exotic.

'I want to widen my horizon and experience things up close that

I've only been able to dream about, so far. The world is a big place and seeing how other people live will put our lives here into some sort of context, for me.'

I've struggled to make things as easy as possible, knowing that Aiden has been stressed. Is he flinging that back at me as if it was the wrong thing to do?

It's an effort not to let out a frustrated sigh. 'What exactly are you proposing?'

Aiden doesn't bat an eyelid as he responds. 'A year apart, doing our own thing. I'll get that travelling bug out of my system, as I know it unsettles you thinking you're holding me back. And you can take some time to nurture the inner you, Fern. You deserve it.'

Words fail me and I stare at Aiden, trying to hide the angry knot forming in my stomach. He's turning this on its head; he's the one causing the chaos in our lives, not me. Or is he simply looking for reassurance and a little time to sort himself out – without which I'll end up losing him?

Maybe my strength has become my weakness – addressing issues head-on, coming up with a viable solution and pulling together an action plan to solve the problem. That's what Aiden is expecting of me now, as if this is some sort of work project. But this has become so much more; it's no longer about simply getting through a rough patch, but being in a position to breathe some life back into our marriage.

Keep calm, Fern. What's a year, if, when you return, your life together is firmly back on track because Aiden's little crisis is over?

'And the party we're planning for the May Day bank holiday, which was supposed to be celebrating our good fortune and Hannah's birthday, will also announce...' I cast around for the right words, which fail me.

'...That we're both taking a little sabbatical. Lots of people take time out to—'

'Widen their horizons,' I jump in, cutting him off. This is a private matter and I want him to be clear that there's no need to worry anyone unduly.

As far as I'm concerned, the sooner it starts, the sooner it will be over. I'm still in shock, but I need to look at this as an adventure. A holiday, from which we will both return and pick back up where we left off. But there's a real chance that it will change us in ways we can't even begin to imagine and Aiden doesn't seem able, or willing, to grasp that fact.

It sounds defeatist on my part, it's not meant to be. But I'm scared. I love my life as it is, and it's always been enough for me. It used to be enough for Aiden, too, and I'm gutted that is no longer the case.

* * *

It's bank holiday Monday and my youngest sister, Hannah, is back home with Mum and Dad for forty-eight hours, before heading off to meet her new boyfriend's family. My parents are stressing over it, of course, as we can all sense this relationship is a little more serious than any she's been in before.

Me? I'm happy to see her smiling and experiencing that first flush of love... which might turn out to be lust in disguise. But she's a confident and discerning young woman. She certainly isn't going to be a pushover just because a good-looking guy gives her some attention. That's my little sister!

My brother, Owen, was hoping to make it home for the party, but he's at the Infantry Battle School in Brecon right now, which is a part of his Combat Infantryman's Course. It's not exactly a picnic and that thought sort of puts our little problems into perspective. He's learning how to become a soldier to fight for people's freedom and here I am, angsting over a little hiccough that will probably disappear as quickly as it appeared.

Our home is heaving with people. Close family, friends,

colleagues and neighbours. Everyone we've invited to the party is here for a reason, because they touch our lives on a regular basis.

'Time for an announcement!' Georgia's husband, Steve, tries unsuccessfully to tap a fork against a glass to gain people's attention. Unfortunately, he hits it too hard and a generous shower of red wine splatters over his white T-shirt as the broken shards fall to the floor. All that remains in his hand is the stem and the base of the glass.

Georgia gives him a look of total disbelief, before grabbing a roll of kitchen towel. The clean-up commences while Steve continues.

'Momentous occasion alert, folks! I'm not exactly sure what's coming, so I'm going to hand you over to Aiden without further ado.'

Georgia is on her hands and knees, glaring up at Steve.

'She worships me, really,' he comments, and everyone bursts out laughing.

I wish I could laugh, but my eyes are on my lovely husband, who steps forward rather nervously. He turns to look at me and I saunter up to him as he reaches out for my hand. It's ironic that as soon as we sorted out what the next step was going to be, things have been almost back to normal between us. I give his hand a reassuring squeeze to spur him on.

'Well, the only person missing today to hear our announcement is Fern's brother, Owen, but he's here in spirit, even if the reality is that he's probably trekking up a mountainside on some sort of endurance course.' A little ripple of laughter does the rounds. 'But to have you all gathered here together today means so much to us both. This party isn't about celebrating our recent lottery win, but the importance we place upon the people who matter the most to us – family and friends.

'We'd like to kick off by asking you all to raise your glasses.' He turns to smile at me, lifting my hand to his mouth and kissing the back of it. 'Over to you for the toast, my darling.'

The look we exchange is one of determination as I gaze back at him. Having made the decision, the change in Aiden is unbelievable.

'It's been a wonderful journey so far and we feel blessed to have such an amazing and supportive bunch of people around us. Here's to you all and a special toast to my baby sister, Hannah, who will be nineteen next week. Happy birthday, sis!'

The response is a loud chorus of 'hear, hear' and gentle clinking of glasses after Steve's little disaster.

'We're both very aware that it isn't money and having *things* that make people happy. Although the lack of it is a problem when you are trying to convince a bank to loan you an extortionate amount of money; we found that out at the start of the long road to buying this place. But with the help of some loving parents,' I tip my glass in the appropriate directions, 'we eventually signed on the dotted line.' I hesitate for a second, then pull myself together determinedly. I agreed to this and now it's too late to back out. 'Being able to pay back what we borrowed, be mortgage-free and have a little nest egg is the dream and we realise just how lucky we are. Sharing is caring, of course, so our three favourite charities will each receive a nice little donation and that means a lot to us both.'

A loud, endorsing 'ah' carries around the room.

'Obviously, Aiden has worked tirelessly for the Merchant Outreach foundation, which offers financial support to families with autistic siblings. It's never been just a job to him and he's devoted a lot of his own time to it; weekends and annual leave when he could have been kicking back, he has been tirelessly fundraising. So, we know what a difference this little windfall will make. The two other charities who will benefit are research into childhood cancers and Alzheimer's. The latter is in memory of Aiden's gran, Daisy.'

As I finish speaking, everyone begins clapping and it's wonderful to know that the general consensus is one of approval.

Aiden holds up his hands, quietening our little crowd of happy partygoers.

'And there's some other exciting news we'd like to share with you all.' He turns to me and I nod, encouraging him to continue – albeit I'm struggling to look enthusiastic. 'This win has allowed us a little self-indulgence. We were in our teens when we met and getting married fresh from university, we jumped straight into work. It's been virtually non-stop and there hasn't been much chance to sit back and relax. So, the other news is that we're both taking a year off. We're having a gap year, a chance for each of us to tick off a couple of items on that list we all tend to have in here,' he taps his head, 'things we'd like to do *someday*. Not exactly a bucket list – more a "before we have kids and get caught up in that" thing.'

There isn't a sound in the room as he continues.

'And we're both excited about the experiences to come. I intend to travel and Fern, well, it's time to take a break from being at everyone's beck and call.' He turns to smile at me with adoration in his eyes and something at my core wilts a little. Aiden is doing a great job of making this sound as if I'm really on board with his idea. Inside, however, I feel I've been backed into a corner and his enthusiasm is beginning to grate on me.

There's a moment of hesitation before Georgia leads by raising her glass and everyone else follows suit. After a raucous chorus of general congratulations, Aiden again raises his hand to quieten everyone down. Maybe the spirits have been flowing a little too liberally tonight.

'Right – that's it, folks. Speeches over and the buffet awaits. Enjoy!'

As people head in the direction of the food, Aiden steers me outside into the garden. We disappear into the shadows as dusk falls around us and this evening is beginning to feel like a dream, one bordering on a nightmare if I'm being honest. Reality is setting in and it sends a cold shiver down my spine.

Over the last couple of weeks as Aiden and I began making plans, we reached a point where it was time to break the news to close family members. Telling our respective parents wasn't easy and I figured that as this was all Aiden's idea, he should do the explaining. There were a few raised eyebrows, but Aiden made it sound so plausible, even I started to relax about it a little.

It was easier to tell Hannah and Owen at the same time, so when she popped in one evening we'd gathered around the monitor and Skyped Owen. The last thing I wanted was for him to feel left out and his reaction had shown a momentary hint of surprise, but it was fleeting.

'Hmm... bold decision. Anything we should be worried about, guys?' he'd enquired, calmly. His words were accompanied by that wicked little grin of his, the one he can't hide whenever he's nervous.

'No, of course not. I'm heading off to Provence, on a little road trip. I'll be spending time in a quaint little holiday village run by a very talented group of artisans. They hold courses in a wide variety of traditional skills. Everything from weaving to engraving, and the man in charge of it all is a renowned artist. I'll be generally helping out as a volunteer working a full day on Monday and then four mornings, so I'll have lots of free time. Aiden wants to travel further afield.'

The truth of it was that I knew Aiden needed to get this travelling thing out of his system. Maybe he wanted to experience a sense of freedom as an adult that he felt he'd missed out on. But how could I possibly stay home, trying to go about life as normal while anxiously awaiting his updates? Heck, a lottery win is supposed to take worry away, not increase it. So, I decided to chase an elusive dream of my own, to keep me busy and stop me fretting over our time apart.

Hannah had raised an eyebrow almost dismissively.

'You're going your separate ways? For a whole year?' She'd stared at me, horrified, and then her eyes had darted across to assess Aiden's reaction. She had no idea, of course, that this was his idea and not mine. 'Free time to do what, exactly?' she'd levelled at me, a tad caustically I felt. How did I get to be the baddie in this? I wondered. Mainly because, in her eyes, Aiden can do no wrong, which has been great up to now, but this wasn't my decision, or my fault. I just couldn't say that as Aiden had enough to contend with, so it was about damage limitation.

'Well, mostly to learn how to draw and paint... but whatever takes my fancy.'

'Fern, you don't have hobbies. You're not that sort of person.'

Naturally, Aiden had jumped in to rescue me at that point. I think he was feeling guilty as everyone else had avoided saying the things that only Hannah was brave enough to voice.

'Fern has spent our entire married life either studying, working or supporting me on the charity side of things. She's always been there for everyone, you both know that. She's never really taken any time for herself.'

It was a cop-out and I'd puzzled over why Aiden hadn't simply told them the truth, that this wasn't about me at all. I was simply falling into line with his plan, in the hope that he'd come back refreshed and ready to move forward together. But the idea of a once-in-a-lifetime break away was growing on me, too. I was beginning to get a little excited about attending classes taught by artist Nico Gallegos.

'I'm just a bit surprised you couldn't find something you both enjoy doing,' she'd declared. 'You guys do everything as a couple.' It was a statement we couldn't refute.

Before I could even think of a response, Aiden took over again.

'Can you see your sister living out of a rucksack? I'll be backpacking and working down that list of places I never thought I'd get to explore. I'm hoping to do a stint of voluntary work to begin with and that, too, won't be luxury accommodation. It's a big old world out there. Change presents opportunity, and this is a one-off chance of a lifetime.'

I noticed that he hadn't mentioned my fear of flying. Or the fact that I could never step foot on a boat. Something over which I have no control and he's had to learn to live with. We've always had driving holidays and Aiden accepted the limitations because he loved me.

Owen had nodded then. 'Well, good luck to you both, guys, and I hope you come back the better for it.'

We knew Owen would understand, being a man of action and few words. But Hannah, well, she wasn't convinced.

'But... but... this is weird. Married people don't take a year off from each other.' She was upset and maybe even a little scandalised.

Inwardly I'd groaned, but thankfully my lips had stayed sealed until something suitable had popped into my head.

'We aren't. We'll be in constant touch with each other. The whole point of this is that we get to share in what the other person is doing, without having to physically be there. A half-hour trip through the tunnel and then it's the open road for me. But Aiden's dream has always been to travel to far-flung places and he deserves to have his trip of a lifetime. I'll also get to see what he's doing and learn about his experiences, but everyone knows...' I'd ground to a halt at that point, unable to find the right words. 'Anyway, I'm looking forward to picking up a paintbrush in earnest.' I'd tried so hard to make it sound convincing, but the person I'd really been trying to convince was me.

'And I'll be getting myself into shape with more exercise than I'd get in a month at the gym,' Aiden had endorsed, his smile and genuine enthusiasm had been abundantly clear.

Hannah had simply shrugged her shoulders, clearly not at all convinced. 'Well, just make sure you keep us all in the loop. You guys are Mr and Mrs Predictable, and to have everyone worrying about you two while you're on your mad adventures is kind of crazy. As the youngest family member, I think I'm the one who's supposed to be causing the angst,' she'd added with a half-hearted smile.

Aiden and I had both started laughing at that point.

'It won't be out of sight, out of mind. We'll keep everyone in the loop, no matter what else we're doing. But I think you can spare us for a year as there are enough people around to keep you on the straight and narrow. Besides, your sister is only a phone call away,' Aiden had replied with mock seriousness.

In the seconds before the Skype session disconnected, a fleeting moment of vulnerability had flooded through me. Was I scared of facing the world alone? I'd thrown off that thought, too worried to consider where it might lead, and had immediately switched into practical mode.

'God speed. And can everyone please take good care of themselves until we're all together again? And for goodness' sake, check in with Mum and Dad so they don't spend every waking hour worrying about every single one of us.' My plea had been heartfelt. There was a moment of silence before we'd been disconnected and I filled it with: 'We love you. Please take care of yourself, Owen.'

Sometimes the next step is as scary as it is exciting, and no one – including me – had thought that Aiden and I would be going in this direction. Dreams are only dreams, unless you choose to turn them into reality. I could only hope that the decisions Aiden and I had made together would turn out to be the right ones.

JULY 2018

BOIS-SAINT-VERNON, PROVENCE

4

SETTLING IN

The leisurely, two-day journey was strangely calming after making some very emotional goodbyes – understandable, given the circumstances – but distance is nothing these days. Loved ones are merely a call away. Or that's what everyone had said whilst studiously avoiding eye contact.

The reality of that scenario, though, is something I will have to learn to come to terms with, because I fear I will get homesick. What if something bad happens and you never get to look into those eyes up close ever again? It's unbearable. It's torture. And the only way to cope with that is to plaster on a smile so no one knows your heart is breaking.

On my first call to Hannah, en route, she managed to put on a brave face because her boyfriend, Liam, was with her. But I could tell that she didn't really want to talk to me and was simply going through the motions. Perhaps she was still cross with me, or maybe she was simply having a bad day.

Liam reminds me of a young Aiden in some ways. But he's less impetuous than the boyish Aiden was, before responsibility began weighing him down.

It did make me stop and think about how much Aiden has

changed since we first met. We went from the excitement of getting married and living together to the harsh realities of having bills to pay and a house to do up. Was it a mistake focusing on the goals we'd set ourselves and that's what ground him down? Did it suck the joy out of life, feeling a constant pressure as our body clocks ticked away... *baby time, baby time*?

The upside to the conversation was that if I'd had any concerns about Liam recklessly breaking Hannah's heart, they quickly dissolved. Liam realises how dependent my sister is on me and he's trying his best to fill the gap, which is touching. There are no guarantees, of course, but they seem committed to each other for the time being. I also think he's a little wary around me, as he senses that anyone who hurts my little sister will have to face my wrath.

The truth is that I really didn't want to leave, but if I stayed, life without Aiden by my side would have been unbearable. Almost as if we had split up. So, I had to pull up my big-girl pants and give myself a talking-to. I can either be miserable and this can be a year of hell, or I can use it to grow. I decided I'd make it about meeting new people and learning new skills. I would return a better person, my life enriched and with a much wider appreciation of the world outside the tiny confines of my personal little bubble.

While Aiden felt he'd held me back in some ways, I, too, had held him back with my phobias. The mere thought of being on a plane and the door closing, incarcerating me for even the shortest of flights, makes me feel faint. I did brave a ferry once and had a full-blown panic attack. It was the same feeling of being trapped and helpless. Aiden admitted it was a frightening experience for us both as he'd never seen me like that before. He's never blamed me for limiting our travel horizon and, in fairness, I can't begrudge him the chance to grab this opportunity. Maybe the lottery win wasn't a mere fluke but fate intervening.

So, here I am. On the last leg towards my own *little* adventure. However, as I pull into the vast forecourt in front of Le Château de Vernon, there is nothing at all *little* about this retreat and my stomach begins to flutter, nervously. Looking at it on Google Maps, it was hard to imagine the scale and I'd expected a cosy little cluster of barns and outbuildings around the main house. This is more like a little village.

I park up alongside an old Citroën and even before I've had a chance to swing the car door shut and stretch my arms, a voice calls out in English.

'Just in time for dinner!' An older woman, elegantly dressed in several layers of very colourful clothing, walks towards me, smiling. 'Welcome, Fern, I've been keeping an eye out for you. Everyone calls me Dee-Dee.' She grins at me and positive energy seems to flow from her.

The accent is subtle, and I can't place it. Her English is perfect, though. She envelops me in her arms as if we're old friends.

'How was your journey?'

'Very pleasant, thank you,' I reply, good-naturedly.

'There's no greater indulgence than the luxury of some time alone to think, is there? A car journey can be quite cathartic, I've always found.'

I nod, grateful for her warm welcome. It helps to calm my nerves and I'm delighted that the first person I meet is someone in whose company I instantly feel relaxed.

'We holidayed in and around the region of Provence several times when I was young. I have some great memories of those days and it's good to be back here.'

Good, the word seems to echo around inside my head, *but not the same.*

'Wonderful. And your arrival is so timely. The next batch of visitors arrive tomorrow, so it's a low-key dinner this evening. We can sort your bags later. It's this way.'

I turn to lock the car and she calls out over her shoulder.

'There's no need to lock anything here. You'll soon adjust to a more relaxed way of living. We're a little too far out to encounter people on foot and you can usually hear a car coming even before it turns into the courtyard.'

Directly in front of the rather commanding château is an old, cobbled forecourt bordered by enormous planters containing neatly clipped evergreen shrubs. I can feel the history as I look around and try to imagine the people who have stood here before me. And the excitement of the owners, when visitors arrived after a long and tiring journey, bringing news from further afield.

I assumed we'd head towards the château, but instead we walk off in the opposite direction, across the courtyard. This much larger area is bounded by property on three sides only. The main house dominates one elevation, with a low wall enclosing the old forecourt. Facing it is an elongated L-shaped, single-storey building, on the other side of which is a standalone cottage. The fourth side looks out across extensive gardens and an orchard that goes on as far as the eye can see. Against the distant backdrop of rising hills covered in dense forest, this plateau feels protected and it's very picturesque.

It's obvious a lot of time has been spent renovating these beautiful stone buildings and their appearance is similar to a terraced row of old cottages. However, the proportions are that of a commercial property, the bonus, I assume, of converting what were probably old farm buildings, maybe even stables. I count six doors in the long run on one side and a further two on the dog-leg.

'It's an interesting arrangement of buildings,' I comment, increasing my pace to keep up with Dee-Dee.

'Yes. Originally it was a hamlet, but several of the old buildings were beyond repair and have been levelled. They had everything here, including a bakery, a blacksmiths and a store for fruits and vegetables. Of course, now they've been turned into individual studios. The internal layouts vary. Over there, beyond the fruit trees,' she points to the far corner of the square, 'is the forge. Our blacksmith, Bastien, isn't a talkative man, you'll come to discover, but don't let that put you off. He's a good listener and very reliable. Anyway, let's introduce you to the team first of all and then, after dinner, we can settle you in.'

This environment is going to be more of a shock to my system than I thought it would be. I don't know what I was expecting, but now I'm here it's all rather surreal. I think longingly of home and the daily routine I thought would never change. A lump fills my throat and I cough to clear it.

Don't be silly, Fern, I tell myself. *You're a grown woman.* But I've never been this far away from my family before, well, not on my own. I consider myself to be a strong and capable woman, but I suppose we all experience situations in which we feel vulnerable. *Take a deep breath.*

Dee-Dee swings open one of the latched oak doors and the sound of laughter greets my ears. Inside, there's a long, stripped pine table that could easily seat thirty. However, at the moment there are only five people in the room and they are all clustered around one end. Immediately as we walk in, the laughter comes to an abrupt halt and everyone turns to look in my direction.

'Hi, Fern.' One of the men stands and walks towards me with his hand outstretched. 'I'm Nico. Welcome to the Château de Vernon Retreat.'

The man standing before me has wavy black shoulder-length hair and the darkest brown eyes I've ever seen. So dark, they are mesmerising. His neatly defined beard is close-cropped and suits him. I was expecting an older man from the tone of the emails we exchanged, but Nico Gallegos is probably in his early thirties. If it wasn't for the faint Spanish accent, he would be well cast as Mr Darcy.

There's something instantly magnetic about this man and I realise I'm staring at him. His olive skin and muscular physique make for a powerful first impression and Nico takes the word *smouldering* to another level. But there's something else lurking there. Something rather sad – sorrowful even – that unwittingly adds to the overall mystique.

'Thank you, um, it's good to be here,' I force the words out rather nervously as he takes my hand. But he doesn't shake it, instead he holds it in both of his and stares into my eyes.

'You're not quite what I was expecting,' he replies, as if he's literally taken the words out of my mouth.

It's good to meet everyone, but tiredness makes me excuse myself early as it has been quite a day. My adventure has begun.

* * *

As I begin unpacking my things, I lay them out on what looks to be a very comfortable bed. My room in the château must be three times the size of the bedroom at home. The beautiful oak floor, which runs throughout, creaks underfoot as I move around. I don't think I've ever stayed in a building as old as this one before and now that I'm beginning to relax a little, I can at least appreciate the setting.

It's quite spartan and the only other furniture is a large armoire, a huge chest of drawers and a chaise longue; the latter being a well-worn and decidedly shabby antique. Either side of the bed are nightstands, on top of which are two very elegant and ornate table lights with cleverly arranged and entwined metal leaves. Graced by a large white globe, one stands a good thirty inches tall and the other is a smaller, almost identical version. I place my phone on one of the tables, then begin carrying the neat piles of clothing across to place them in the drawers.

Stark white walls contrast beautifully with the dark brown of the furniture and floorboards. I like the simplicity of the overall style, it's restful. But what really stands out, dominating the entire space, is the enormous painting which seems to leap off the wall. The vibrancy of the colours is breathtaking and the riot of different shades of green, which up close are comprised of very crude brushstrokes, form an enchanting forest when viewed from a distance. It's clearly the Bois-Saint-Vernon, but the signature isn't Nico's, it's by someone named José.

I place a few items on coat hangers, marvelling at the beautiful carving on the front of the armoire. As I close the door, I run my fingertips lightly over the inset panel of little acorns and flower heads, appreciating the detail and the skilled tooling.

Suddenly, a short rap on the door interrupts my reverie and I call out, 'Come in,' watching as the door slowly eases open.

A head appears around the side of it. It's Ceana MacLeay, the woman who oversees the extensive garden and grounds.

'Am I interrupting?' The Scottish lilt has a warmth to it that matches her sunny disposition. Ruddy-cheeked, this wiry, energetic woman is deceptively strong. She's all muscle and I can only look at her enviously. Why do the pounds begin to creep on with every passing year? I wonder. My waistline is a good couple of inches bigger than it was just two or three years ago.

'No. I'm nearly done, actually. Come in.'

'I have a big favour to ask.'

I look at her in surprise because I can't imagine what I can do that Ceana can't sort for herself.

'Fire away,' I reply as I perch on the bed and indicate for her to take a seat on the chaise longue.

'This is a gorgeous piece of furniture, isn't it?' she remarks. 'Dee-Dee keeps saying she'll whisk it away and work on it as one of the projects in her textiles workshop. The fabric is too moth-eaten to rescue. When we were all in here painting last week in preparation for your arrival, I nearly pinched it for my room.' She chuckles.

'Is every project around here a group thing? I don't mean the teaching sessions with visitors, but when it comes to the property itself?'

'More or less,' she confirms. 'Nico doesn't charge us for accommodation, only a contribution towards the cost of our meals, but we all receive an equal share of the income. In return we help out in any way we can, in addition to running our individual sessions, of course.'

'That must help him a little as it's a big place to maintain.'

She nods. 'He has injected a lot of money into bringing it back to its former glory. We sell surplus produce to the locals in summer, which brings in a little additional income. But money isn't an issue for him. If he gets stuck, he simply sells another painting. His father left him a lot of canvases and his own work is growing in popularity. Have you heard of José Gallegos? Sad story, but his work only began to increase in value after his death. Nico's work is very popular, though.'

I shake my head. 'What an awful shame. That can't have been easy for the family, but wonderful that Nico inherited his father's talent.'

'Oh, they didn't get on and he says it's only money. He's the last of the family line and he has no children himself.'

Only money and money doesn't bring happiness. The words have a familiar ring to them.

'Anyway,' Ceana continues, 'Anton usually cycles up from the village to help out with the weeding every day. Some of our visitors prefer to do something simple and enjoy the fresh air, so he keeps an eye on them. It's an easy task but necessary. Not everyone who comes here is eager to learn new skills and when that's the case, something simple to do, a friendly face and a few kind words go a long way. Anton is good at that and he's an excellent gardener. His wife is poorly at the moment, so Nico suggested I approach you to see whether you'd mind stepping in for him? Just to supervise a couple of our visitors for the morning session until he's back. I'd really appreciate it.'

A sense of relief washes over me. 'Of course. I can, at least, weed,' I laugh. 'Well, and supervise people weeding. When you talk about the guests, or visitors, what can I expect?'

'Great, thanks for that. It is a retreat, but not to worry as it isn't some sort of halfway house set-up. Nico advertises it as five days of hands-on activity. We don't run classes at the weekends for people who opt to extend their stay, but they're free to use the facilities. It's very much aimed at people who need a break away from their everyday lives. Most folk battle some sort of stress, and I jokingly say this is the holiday for those who don't want to go down the yoga route. Well, at the moment, anyway, but that might change in the future.

'You end up getting similar health benefits because it's an active week and a lot of it is outdoors. It's all about recharging the batteries. We all believe it's important to ensure no one feels out of place, or pressurised into joining in if they need quiet time. It's okay here to just go off for a walk or sit and chill beneath a shady tree. That applies to tutors and volunteers, as well as visitors.'

'Well, that's a relief. When I found this place online and clicked on the tab about becoming a volunteer, it hadn't occurred to me a *retreat* had more than one connotation. It just fascinated me, with so many different and interesting workshops on offer. The area, too, drew me in. I love the forest and I thought I'd feel a sense of peace here. Hopefully tinged with the familiar, as one of the holiday cottages we stayed in several times when I was a child is only a couple of miles away.'

It was the perfect solution for me. Free meals and accommodation in return for helping out. I told Aiden that I didn't want him worrying about exceeding his share of the budget we'd allowed ourselves for this year. There are still bills to be paid to keep the house ticking over while we're away. At least I feel I'm doing something constructive and not just frittering away our nest egg on a whim.

Ceana stands. 'I can understand that. It's quite a change in lifestyle for you, I should imagine. But Nico is very easy-going and I think you'll love it here, Fern. We can usually tell from the outset if someone will fit in.' She gives me an encouraging smile. 'New visitors arrive by coach mid-morning every Monday. We do get the odd guest who arrives by car, but most fly in and are picked up at the airport. They settle in, grab a quick lunch and then do a short afternoon session. There are always a couple of newbies who opt for some gentle weeding rather than one of my horticultural teach-ins.'

I burst out laughing. 'Sorry. My mother would be so impressed with me. She spends hours pottering in the garden and for much of my childhood I was her unwilling accomplice, so I've handled a weed or two.'

Ceana grins. 'Well, we grow most of what we eat. Bastien is in charge of the livestock, as well as the forge. Taylor is our fisherman and there's a lake in the woods if you ever fancy helping to catch dinner when fish is on the menu.' She heads over towards the door, placing her hand on the embellished, cast-iron doorknob before turning back to look at me. A moment of hesitation passes over her face. 'Nico is a lovely man, very passionate and fiery at times. Moody, too. When he's not approachable, it's usually best to leave him be, if you know what I mean.'

'Oh, thanks for the heads-up, Ceana. Much appreciated.'

'Sleep well,' she says as she steps out onto the landing. 'Breakfast is at eight.'

I watch as the door closes, reaching out for my phone to check if Aiden received my text. He's on his way to Australia to begin his adventure as it's a country he's always longed to visit.

Glad you arrived safe and sound, babe. Another hour before I board the plane for the final leg of the journey. Sleep well. Love you. Miss you.

His reply was sent only twenty minutes ago. Maybe he couldn't get a connection before that, who knows, but it's strange not having that instant interaction. We're apart by choice, but the choice was Aiden's. I can't let go of the feeling that he has let me down.

I lie back on the bed, looking up at the vaulted ceiling, and watch as a tiny black speck works its way around the large, suspended light fitting. The little spider is on an epic journey and I know exactly how it feels.

5

FEELING MY WAY

After breakfast, everyone heads off to prepare for the visitors. I stay behind as Nico wants to talk to me about my work schedule. He's going to give me the general tour, but he received a call a few minutes ago and had to dash off to sort out a problem. So, I'm left all alone, loitering, as I await his return.

The inside of this stone building is mostly open-plan. Looking up to the rafters, it's partially boarded on one half, which houses some rusty-looking lifting equipment. I'm guessing it's a former hayloft. The flagstone floor is well-worn, but there's nothing shabby about the interior, it's rustic. Simple. Clean. Well kept.

I wander over to the back of the room; the huge dining table is dwarfed by the amount of space. A scattering of assorted chairs of all shapes and sizes, together with several sofas, help to soften the acoustics.

In one corner, there is a library of books and magazines, next to which is a small table with tea- and coffee-making facilities. In front of me are two doors. Opening the first one, I see a toilet and shower room. The second one leads into the kitchen and I'm surprised to see a cheerful, smiling face peering back at me.

'Ah, the new lady.' A rather portly French woman, dressed all in black, is loading up one of two dishwashers. She smiles across at me.

'Bonjour. I'm Fern, Fern Wyman,' I introduce myself, and she stops what she's doing for a moment, half turning to face me.

'Margot Bressan. I hope you eat most things?' She looks at me in earnest.

'Oh, yes, I'm easy to please.'

She nods. I wish my French was better, but I've learnt from the past that if I offer more than a few words of French, then it gives the misleading impression I'm fluent. In fact, I can't keep up as most French people talk very fast and I generally only manage to pick up snippets. And that's not an easy way to conduct a conversation.

'I'm here if you need anything special. Except pasta. I leave that to the Italians. But most English dishes. I cope.'

Scanning around, it's a pretty average-looking commercial kitchen. All stainless-steel workbenches and equipment.

'I saw from the website that you hold cooking demonstrations throughout the week.'

She rinses her hands in the sink, stopping to wipe them on a towel before walking across to me. 'Yes. I like teach people.'

We exchange grins.

'Well, I'll pop in if I'm not needed anywhere else. I'm not a great cook, if I'm being honest, and it would be fun to learn.'

That makes her laugh. 'I will teach you best croissant and bread making. I promise.'

Suddenly a voice interrupts our conversation. 'Ah, Fern, there you are.'

Nico steps in through the doorway and begins talking to Margot in French. I can only understand part of what he's saying but enough to grasp that he's agreeing mealtimes for today. When they finish talking, he turns in my direction, his eyes sweeping over me for a second before meeting my gaze.

'Come, let's walk and talk.'

I say goodbye to Margot and follow Nico out into the morning sunshine.

'My apologies for the delay, Fern. There's always an issue to demand my attention. Today it's the van, which has broken down on the way to town to drop off the fresh produce. Hopefully the local garage will sort the problem quickly. I trust you slept well last night?'

He leads me across into the centre of the courtyard.

'I did, thank you.'

Those eyes are so intense, dark and full of mystery. My senses are telling me that this man has demons which lie very close to the surface. For such a young man, his face has deep-set lines and he frowns more than he laughs.

'Taking a year off from such a busy job is quite a big decision to make. I hope you find what you're looking for here.'

As our eyes connect, I can see that he isn't simply curious, he's genuinely interested in my motives. I'm not ready yet to explain my situation, so I go with the safe option.

'It's time to reconnect with my creative side. As a child I loved drawing, but it's something I've never had time to really explore as an adult.'

I can see he isn't fooled, but I also think he won't press me.

'Well, there will be plenty of time to get you started again. In your emails you seemed quite interested in a few of the different skills on offer. And Ceana was delighted you were prepared to help her out in the garden until Anton returns. Looking after the land and making it productive is central to our lifestyle here and that's why we encourage everyone to get involved during the summer months. I firmly believe that fresh air and nature is restorative.'

For a Spaniard, his accent is very subtle and I'm guessing it's been a while since he lived in his homeland.

'In this setting I do believe you're right. At home, well, getting out into the countryside is usually only a weekend pursuit. But while I don't know much about tending plants, I'm willing to learn.'

He draws to a halt and half turns to face me. I feel as if he's trying to figure me out, in the same way that I'm curious about him.

'Good. I'll put gardening duties on your morning schedule for the first week, then. I think you will do well spending some time working closely with Ceana to begin with, anyway. In the afternoons, I will look forward to seeing you in the art sessions. We'll soon discover where your skill and interests will take you and then I will coach you on a one-to-one basis. During your stay you will be regarded as a member of the team and I hope when your time here is over, you will feel you have gained much from taking part in this programme.'

'Thank you, it's an amazing opportunity and I intend to work very hard to prove worthy of it. I'm sure there must be lots of people who would love to be able to walk away from their day-to-day lives for a whole year in order to explore a hidden yearning. I can't promise I have any actual skill, but I always felt happy whenever I was able to take time out with a pencil and a sketching pad. Art lessons at school were scary, if I'm honest with you. It rather put me off at the time, but I doodled a lot when I was at home alone.'

He shakes his head, his eyes blazing. 'How it annoys me to hear that. No one knows what they are capable of until they are given the chance to explore their creativity. That should never be stifled. Every eye perceives reality in a slightly different way. Art is about capturing that uniqueness and preserving it.' Nico's tone is curt as anger rises up within him at what he perceives to be an injustice of monumental proportions. 'A true artist works first and foremost from their heart, not merely seeking to impress or please a client in return for money. Commerciality often kills originality. I know because I've travelled that road.'

'It must be a pressure, working to deadlines,' I empathise. 'Creativity isn't something you can just switch off and on, is it?'

'No. However, we are about to explore your inner muse and most people find that liberating, Fern. I'm sure that's what you will discover, too. Painting for pleasure is a wonderful way to relax in the busy world out there. Sometimes it becomes more than simply a hobby, but only time will tell.'

I'm entranced. And inspired. Nico is a passionate man, but that sort of determination and drive, while inspiring others, can also be a hard taskmaster. Ceana said he has no one, no remaining family, to give him a sense of belonging, so I wonder if his work and this little community are now his sole reasons for being? It's almost as if he's shut himself off from the world and the chance of building a life with someone. I wonder why?

I'm filled with an overwhelming sense of sadness for him, as I sense a life of pain and possibly regret. If Nico notices my spontaneous reaction, he doesn't show it and, thankfully, it's fleeting, albeit unsettling. That's the downside of being intuitive; sometimes you feel you are invading someone's privacy without their permission. Like a voyeur.

'You've seen the kitchen and day room – the first of the converted barns in the L-shaped building. The other sections as we work along are woodworking, run by Taylor Hamilton. He also uses one of the two open barns in the orchard; the other barn houses Bastien Caron's forge.'

I scan the long row of doors, moving my eyes along the entire length of the building as Nico talks.

'Next to that is Odile Moreau's pottery room and kiln, then we have Dee-Dee's textile studio. Beyond that is our craft centre, and Dee-Dee oversees that, too, at the moment. The art studio is the double unit in the bottom corner. Some of my workshops are held there, but in the warmer months I often take the class down to the lake or into the woods to draw and paint.'

The sound of an approaching vehicle carries on the air and the exhaust is clearly blowing. A white van pulls into the courtyard, parking up near the entrance and, when the driver gets out, he waves across at Nico, who puts up his arm in acknowledgement before turning back to me.

'At the far side, the next two sections and the detached building a few metres away are all accommodation. The tutors have rooms on the second floor of the château, as you know, except Bastien, who has two rooms in *la petite maison*, which everyone refers to as the cottage. My suite of rooms is on the ground floor at the rear of the château.'

I haven't had the full tour of the château yet and I'm rather curious about it.

'Do guests ever stay in the main house?'

'Rarely these days, although we have eight rooms available on the first floor. There are sixteen rooms in total in the courtyard, but I can't remember the last time we exceeded that number. It's a fine balance between offering a personally tailored, interactive experience and making sure we earn enough for everyone here to make a living. We shut for three weeks over the Christmas period and our tutors tend to stagger their holidays throughout the year so we can remain open.'

That's quite a weight this man has on his shoulders. Maybe the château is his sanctuary. And I can understand even the other tutors wanting their own personal space to relax in at the end of each day. After all, this appears to be their permanent home, too.

'It's an inspiring set-up, Nico. And such a beautiful setting.'

One look at his face and I can see that he wants to draw our little talk to a close. He keeps glancing across at the van and the driver, who has now disappeared.

'Why don't you go across and wander around the studios? Familiarise yourself with the layout and the facilities.' With that, he turns to walk away.

With most people his departure could be construed as a rather abrupt ending to a conversation, but with Nico it's easy to see that he's constantly juggling things in his head. Having ticked off one item on his mental list, he's on to the next. Right now, it's all about finding out what's wrong with the van and checking that the produce was safely delivered.

Curiosity makes me head straight towards the art studio in the corner. Raising the latch, the door opens into an enormous space, but this one doesn't have a vaulted ceiling like the day room and kitchen unit. There's a small staircase off to the right, heading up to a mezzanine. As I walk up the stairs, the sound of my footsteps grate on the silence.

At the top is an informal arrangement of chairs and easels arranged in a semicircle around a small table. It's draped with a dark blue silk cloth, not spread out flat as one would expect, but rumpled as if it's been thrown down. The irregular folds mimic the effect of rippling water. Standing slightly off-centre is a bowl of lime-green apples and soft yellow pears, no doubt from the orchard. One of the pears still has a portion of branch with several leaves attached to it. Nico has placed it so that it spills out over the white ceramic bowl. His eye for detail in all things is evident everywhere you look. I wonder, though, if that sort of intensity is also a source of compulsion.

Compulsion. A word that, now it's in my head, unsettles me for some reason. What is it I can feel here? Is it paranoia because my life has been turned upside down and everything around me is a totally new experience? This... year of discovery, as Aiden phrased it, seems to me like opening a door on a whole new world. I don't want to turn the handle because I've always felt complete. Satisfied. Is that so wrong? We can't all be adventurers and it's not that I've settled, unless being happy with what you have is now regarded as no longer enough. As if, in some way, it's a failing.

'The world is going crazy!' I cry out aloud, my voice echoing around the empty building.

It's the general air of must have, must do, must be something *more* that could end up tearing my husband away from me for good.

I yank the phone out of my pocket. Still no new messages, so I begin typing.

Today's update: I'm standing in an artist's studio and I can't wait to sit down with a brush or pencil in my hand and a blank piece of paper in front of me. The journey has begun.

My fingers automatically continue typing to tell him how much I'm missing him, but I stop mid-sentence and delete the letters, one by one. If Aiden has outgrown me, outgrown our love, then that's something I'm going to have to deal with. How exactly, I can't even begin to comprehend because he is everything to me. He is the centre of my world and the reason I get up every morning. Now he's no longer by my side, it's like a part of me is missing.

* * *

The buzz of activity after the coach arrives is frenetic. People, suitcases, hand luggage, a cacophony of sounds... everyone pulls together though, and I simply follow the directions I'm given. After helping to carry some of the surplus bags as people head off to their allotted rooms, I walk back to the dining room to lend a hand in the kitchen.

Margot is busy setting out a buffet on the long table and several of the tutors are here helping, too. Ceana sidles up to me, leaning in to have a quick word as I move platters aside to make some more room.

'Nico mentioned there's a young girl named Kellie among the arrivals. I don't know if you noticed her. Pale girl, with all the bracelets and the dragon tattoo on her arm. She's eighteen years old and he asked if we'd keep a special eye out for her.'

She raises her eyebrows and I nod. 'I carried one of her bags; she's staying in the cottage.'

'I'll put her with you this afternoon, if you don't mind. There's another woman, Patricia, who might join you, too. She's a very reserved lady, rather shy. Kellie isn't very talkative, as you might have noticed, so I think that's a good pairing. Don't worry if Kellie isn't responsive, just get her started and let me know if you have any concerns.'

I nod. 'It's a pity there's no one else in the group who is nearer to her age. It could be quite isolating for her,' I add, wondering why a retreat of this nature appealed to a teenager.

'We often find age doesn't matter when people come here. They connect in a different way when they are taken out of their normal routine.'

'Ceana, can I ask you a personal question?'

She deposits the cheeseboard she's carrying into the space I've made on the table.

'You can ask me anything. I don't have any secrets,' she half whispers.

'I know you're a gardener, but what else do you do?'

She straightens to look at me directly. 'My background is in mental health and well-being.'

I nod as she heads back into the kitchen.

Why, of all places, did fate bring me here? A buzzing against my hip sends me scrabbling for my phone.

My first update: I'm here and I'm fine. I've hooked up with a couple of guys who are going opal mining. I'm going to check it out for a few days but might not be able to get a signal. Enjoy your drawing lessons. Will be in touch when I can. Miss you, babe. Love you.

I stare at the words, disappointment flooding through me. Opal mining? That's how Aiden is going to work through whatever his problem is? Has he lost his mind? The only thing I know about opal mining in Australia is that it can be dangerous.

I'm torn between feeling anxious and angry that the man I love is capable of making such a stupid decision. And he's with strangers. Anything could happen and how would I know if he was in trouble?

Aiden is trying to make sense of his life, a life he felt has become mundane, and I just let him go. I should have talked him out of it instead, knowing he's been under a lot of stress and pressure. Stress doesn't simply throw the body out of kilter, but the mind, too. No wonder my senses are jangling like wind chimes in a heavy storm.

6

ACCEPTANCE

While everyone is eating, Ceana shows me where the gardening tools are kept, in preparation for the group's first session of the week. We wander down through the orchard and beyond, where I get my first real glimpse of what looks like a very commercial market garden. Row after row of vegetables cover an extensive area, making it look rather daunting, if I'm honest.

'I had no idea it was going to be on this scale. Where will I start?'

She laughs. 'Don't worry, you'll be working on the herb garden. Follow me. It's over here.'

As we head off towards a small collection of wooden sheds, I can't shake off the gloom I've felt since reading Aiden's text. How can I throw myself into this when my heart and head are somewhere else?

Ceana turns to look at me, seeing my frown. 'It's not as bad as it looks, you know. The beds are raised, and you simply start at one end and work your way across with the hoe. It's a laborious job but satisfying. We keep the tools in here and that's pretty much all you will need today, anyway. Just make sure the ladies are clear about what's a weed and what's a plant. I'll run you through the various varieties.'

It's a good job she does because there are a couple of things that look too straggly to be useful, but Ceana explains that herbs don't grow neatly like many other plants. Some like to grow in clumps, while others re-root themselves as they spread and that's why they are planted in raised borders.

'Mint will take over an entire area if it's left to its own devices. The wooden shuttering stops the spread and contains the roots nicely. Are you happy?'

I nod. 'Yes. It should be fine.'

'You're not fine, though, are you?'

I shake my head, miserably.

'In my former profession, I always found that sharing a problem generally helps. Sometimes a worry is coloured by perspective. Anything we discuss is in confidence, Fern. You can trust me.'

'It's not a case of trust, Ceana, it's more a case of not knowing what's happening in my life any more,' I admit, sadly.

She says nothing, and I find myself tugging away at a straggly weed and then another.

'It's my husband. His job is very demanding. He works for a charitable organisation and he takes his responsibilities very seriously. Work spills out into what should be relaxing quality time. The stress has taken a toll on him, both mentally and physically, I'm afraid. He's off travelling, but that isn't my thing so—' I grind to a halt.

Ceana scans my face for a moment. 'So, you decided to take a break and reassess your feelings?'

'No. We decided, well, *he* decided we should take a year's sabbatical from work. The gap year we couldn't take when we were younger because we both went straight from university to earning money to pay the mortgage. We had a little windfall recently and Aiden thought – oh heck – the truth is that I have no idea why he had this crazy idea to go off and do his own thing. He said we should take some time to explore ourselves. Whatever that means. But he wanted to travel, and I've never flown, and I'm no better over water, either. It's the thought of not being in control of my surroundings which makes me go into panic mode. It restricts the list of destinations we can visit. And now, he's backpacking in Australia and hooked up with some guys who are going opal mining. Opal mining, for goodness' sake!'

My voice cranks up a notch out of sheer frustration. It actually feels good to have blurted that out, although I wonder if I've shocked Ceana. I don't want her to feel that I've come here for the wrong reasons. The truth is that I've always longed to explore the artistic streak that I've had to suppress because it felt too indulgent, I suppose. Working, studying to gain my HR qualifications, sorting out the house – there were never enough hours in the day. What was left was taken up with spending quality time with Aiden and my family.

The pile of weeds I'm dumping on a bare patch of soil is growing as I continue to snatch away at them.

'I have one word for you, Fern, and that's *acceptance*. Think on it while you're out here working this afternoon.'

She turns and I reluctantly follow her. Acceptance? I don't think being dismissive of someone's problems makes for a very smart counsellor, but maybe it's a shock tactic.

* * *

'Grab some gloves, ladies, and if you haven't seen one of these before, it's called a hoe, apparently.' I grin at them both in a friendly manner.

Patricia and Kellie stare back at me with a little less enthusiasm than I'd hoped.

'We're going to do a couple of hours weeding in between the herb borders. I did a little patch earlier on, as you can see, and for the most part it's easy to identify the weeds. Do either of you recognise any of the plants here?'

I'm simply trying to get some interaction going, but Kellie looks on, sullen and unwilling to contribute. Her offhand attitude is unsettling Patricia, who is a very private, reserved lady by the look of it. I glance at her, but it's more of an appeal and thankfully she speaks up.

'I should be fine because I grow a few things in my garden at home. Mainly salad stuff in the summer and a few potatoes. I think I recognise most of the herbs here.'

'Great. How about you, Kellie?'

'Yep.'

Just *yep*. Right.

'Okay, well if you each choose an end, I'll work the middle patch.'

Kellie grabs a hoe, ignoring the gloves, and walks off to the lower end of the raised bed. Far enough away that she's out of earshot, so I'm assuming that means she wants some alone time.

I look across at Patricia and see she's been watching me watching Kellie.

'Sad little thing, isn't she?' Patricia remarks.

I nod. 'Maybe the fresh air will perk her up,' I reply, keeping my voice low. I'd hate Kellie to think we are talking about her, but any fears I have are soon cut short as Patricia begins working away in silence.

Surreptitiously glancing in Kellie's direction, I'm surprised at how enthusiastically she throws herself into the task. It's quite fiddly as, unlike the vegetables, which are in straight rows and easy to drag the hoe down between the plants, the herbs grow in an irregular pattern. Some of the rosemary plants are more like little shrubs, beneath which the weeds seem to enjoy the shady spots, and the lemon balm has flopped, probably flattened after a heavy rainfall. But, give the young woman her due, she isn't looking to cut corners and is every bit as diligent as Patricia and me.

At four o'clock, we down tools and pack away for the day, and as I lead them back to the courtyard, it doesn't feel right walking in silence.

'I'm new here, myself, actually. I arrived yesterday. It takes a while to settle in, doesn't it?'

Wondering if there will be any takers, to my surprise, Kellie jumps in.

'I noticed a guitar in the day room. Music wasn't on the list of workshops, which is a real pity.'

Hmm. Interesting.

'That is a shame. But if there's a guitar, then I'm sure someone here must play. I'll find out, if you like.'

'Thanks. That would be cool.'

I notice Patricia's wearing a little smile. I'd say that's a result for just one afternoon's work.

* * *

'Hey, Fern, how're you doing?'

It's Owen. I lie back on the chaise longue, closing my eyes and picturing my brother's cheeky grin.

'Good. It's great to hear your voice. How's training going?'

'Relentless but the end is in sight. And now I have abs, would you believe.'

My bro, and they're turning him into a soldier. Only the tough survive the training, but he's always had determination – he's just taken a while to find the right thing to fire him up.

'Amazing! I hope they're feeding you well,' I add, wondering if I'll recognise the fitter version of the former computer-obsessed game player when we next meet up.

'To be honest, I'm always so hungry I'd eat anything they dished up. It's not bad, though. We're off to Salisbury Plain for a few days and I wanted to check up on you before I left. I expect it's all a bit strange, being away from everyone.'

I know that Owen is worried about me, but it's not his style to admit that.

'It's wonderful here actually. I've spent the afternoon gardening with two of the new arrivals. Tomorrow I'll be working in the garden again, but in the afternoon, for the first time in years, I will be sitting in front of an easel. How exciting is that?'

He laughs.

'What's so funny?'

'Just trying to imagine you doing something *you* want to do for a change. It's about time, I'd say.'

Hmm. I'm doing it because I'm here. If I was at home—

'You're a nightmare, Fern. Promise me you will relax and enjoy this time, please. Don't waste it pining over Aiden and fretting about what the rest of us are doing. We can all look after ourselves – well, to varying degrees. Hannah hasn't phoned you back, even though she said she would, because she's helping Liam decorate his flat. I called her just now and she wasn't very receptive. That poor guy has no idea what he's getting himself into with our little sister.'

I sigh. 'I guessed she still hasn't forgiven me for heading off to France. And she's not so little now, in case you haven't noticed. It's time to start treating her with a tad more respect,' I add, sternly.

'Well, she's still a bit up in the air about it all as she'll miss Aiden, too, but she'll always be a royal pain in my book. Youngest kids always are,' he adds, rather unfairly. I'm sure that isn't true in every case, although he might actually have a point when it comes to Hannah. 'She'll come around,' he continues, 'but I wanted to reassure you that she's fine. I know what you're like, too.'

It's ironic that my tough, action-man brother is the empathetic one and my little sister can only handle emotional issues by refusing to dwell on them.

'That's thoughtful, Owen. And appreciated. I guess one of the lessons I'm going to learn on my gap year is that it's time for me to step back and be less involved. But you do know that I'm here whenever you need me, don't you?'

I don't want to labour this because I hope he never needs me, well, not for an emergency. I want – no, I need – to believe that he can handle this new career he's chosen and that he'll be both sensible and safe. He's always had a positive attitude, but the army is now backing that up with the physical stamina to endure anything.

'There you go, worrying already and you've only been gone a couple of days. Look, I have to go, there's a bunch of mates hovering and I'm holding them up.' There's loud jeering in the background and he stops to call out, 'All right! I'm done!'

'Go on, don't let me stop you. Text or call me when you're back from Salisbury. And thanks, Owen. Great advice, by the way. Love you and take care.'

'Will do. Bye, Fern.'

Click.

Suddenly the air around me feels lighter and brighter. My younger sister might not be talking to me properly still, but it sounds like she's happy. And my brother, well, he's always been my biggest supporter. One day, hopefully, he'll find a woman who is worthy of him but in the meantime at least he has a good head on his shoulders. I keep forgetting that Hannah has now turned nineteen, so she's only a year older than Kellie.

At twenty-four, Owen seems so much more mature than her, but then she hasn't been at uni for very long. Mum and Dad are always around and eager to listen to all of us, but it's the things you don't want to share with your parents for fear of worrying them that mean a sibling comes in handy at times. At least you get honest, impartial advice.

There's just time to Google opal mining in Australia before I head downstairs for the evening meal. But as I open up a tab, something makes me type in the word *acceptance*. I've been mulling it over all afternoon. I know what the word means, but not why Ceana levelled it at me as if it was a solution.

> Acceptance in human psychology is a person's assent to the reality of a situation.

Okay, I know that. I cursor on down the screen.

Synonyms jump out at me – *receiving, embracing, approving.* Then I drop down to the antonyms. *Disagreeing, rejecting, denying* are the ones that draw my eye and they pretty much accurately reflect how I feel.

I'm a woman who is used to being in control; I manage people and situations at home and at work all the time. How can I simply become accepting of a situation that makes no sense at all from anyone's perspective? Aiden can't explain why he feels the way he does. My family, and probably everyone else we know, think that taking a year off and not spending it as a couple is ridiculous. We're more likely to grow apart than closer together, surely?

My head begins to ache because this is an almost constant conversation I'm having with myself every time I'm not occupied doing something.

I type in *opal mining in Australia* and begin reading. Then quickly wish I hadn't.

7

THE DRAGON TATTOO

I didn't expect to enjoy myself last night but after a worrying session online, it was a relief to immerse myself in the company of a large group of people. Nothing brings strangers together more amicably as simply sharing a relaxing meal at the end of the day. Afterwards, Nico began an around-the-table short and sharp introduction. One sentence that would give everyone a real sense of who we were.

It was interesting as most people found it quite hard to sum themselves up in that way. It was like the creeping death for some as we worked around the table and several asked for more time, so there was some skipping around.

I kept it simple. 'My husband and I are taking a gap year of self-discovery, before beginning the next stage of our life together.' Admittedly, there were a few raised eyebrows, but then it was on to the next person.

Kellie, who happened to be sitting next to me, said: 'I'm searching for something, but I don't know what until I find it,' and her honesty felt raw.

Nico's description, too, was troubling.

'I'm an artist battling to control what he creates without killing off the spontaneity.'

Afterwards, we lingered over coffee and then a few headed off for a walk; some went to their rooms and that left a small group scattered around the day room. Kellie made no attempt to move and I didn't want to leave her on her own, even though I was tempted to retire to my room for an early night.

She asked me if it was difficult leaving my family behind and I could see she was genuinely interested.

'Yes, but it isn't as simple as that,' I'd explained. 'My husband, Aiden, is backpacking as he's always wanted to travel to far-flung destinations, but I don't fly unfortunately. My brother, Owen, recently joined the army and is about to complete boot camp. My younger sister, Hannah, went off to university in Cardiff last October. She shares a house with three of her fellow students and they all have part-time jobs in and around the city. So, the time is right for me to do something I know I will enjoy and I'm eager to pick up a paintbrush.'

Kellie looked genuinely surprised. 'There must be a lot of trust between you and your husband. My parents loathe each other but are too lazy to do anything about it. Splitting up is a hassle and staying together—' she'd paused to reflect on it for a moment, 'is a hassle, too! Life, eh?'

'That must be tough on you. It's not easy being around a relationship that isn't working, I should imagine. It's hard enough when people get on well.'

'It's living hell, actually. I try to switch off when they're arguing. I put in my earphones and turn up the iPod. I have two brothers, but I'm the youngest and the only one still at home.'

We didn't get to take our conversation any further as someone suggested playing cards. Before we knew it, we were part of a small group assembled around the table.

Kellie didn't seem put out, so I joined in too. It was just after eleven when we all headed off to bed and I suddenly remembered that I was going to find out about the guitar. Something tells me that music is important to Kellie and I made a mental note to make enquiries in the morning.

I remember my head hitting the pillow and uttering a sigh, then nothing.

* * *

'Nico, before I head off with my little weeding group this morning, can I ask about the guitar in the day room? Kellie mentioned she's into music and she spotted it, so I'm guessing she plays. I was wondering if any of the tutors had any musical experience?'

He looks at me in surprise. 'Taylor is pretty good. He's into country music, I believe. I play a little but not enough to coach someone else. Do you want to see if you can fix something up with him? I'm sure he won't mind.'

I nod, gratefully. 'Will do, that's great, thanks.'

We exchange brief smiles before I go in search of Ceana, to see who she's assembled together to join me this morning. I instantly spot her when I step out into the courtyard.

Today I have four people, two guys who I played cards with last night, Kellie and Patricia.

'And here's Fern, my assistant, who will sort you out. Have a fun morning, all.' Ceana's words make me smile. So, I'm her assistant now. A promotion already!

Glancing at them all, I can see that Kellie looks okay, but Patricia is standing on the edge of the group, nervously. I give Ceana a nod.

'Right, follow me. It's a beautiful morning, that's for sure.'

Immediately the two guys fall in line either side of me, leaving Kellie and Patricia to bring up the rear. It's impossible to take this walk without your eye being constantly drawn to something you haven't noticed before and there's little chatter as everyone scans around.

'This is quite something,' Quin remarks as I turn to look at him.

'To me, the hills and mountains in the distance are so representative of Provençal,' I reply. 'I know many tourists perceive the towns as the real heart of the region, but here, on this little valley plateau, every breath I take in seems to contain that hint of perfume from the lavender fields and the olive groves around us.'

'It's so inspiring,' Patricia adds. 'The delights of Provence really do show nature at its best.' And she's right. That's why so many artists found their way to this region to experience something unique. The light, the colours and the sheer variety of nature's splendours and challenges, in sharp contrast. Often on a turn in the road, or an uphill climb, one vista is exchanged for something totally different but equally as awe-inspiring.

I turn to smile at Patricia, thinking how at ease she looks right now. 'Every view, whichever way you turn, is postcard-worthy, isn't it? But here, in amongst the little villages where time seems to stand still, family, farming and festivals are the very essence of life – it's truly authentic.'

We stop for a moment as I point towards the backdrop in front of us.

'It's impossible not to be awed at the ruggedness as the land rises up. Remote communities perched up high and seeming to defy all logic, as the buildings cling on to the rocky ledges. From a distance they don't look safe, but when you're up there, it's another matter entirely. They were built in times when defence was crucial, I should imagine, but now it's a photographer's dream.'

As we continue walking, I point in the direction of the two barns and the forge, then the lake way off in the distance. When I lapse into silence, I can hear Patricia asking Kellie about her dragon tattoo.

'It's a Celtic dragon. It symbolises strength and they were supposed to have magical healing powers. The red is the fire and the passion. The wings are in the style of a Celtic knot, which represents the Holy Trinity.'

'It's beautiful, Kellie,' I hear Patricia say, and I find the gentleness in her voice touching.

The dragon covers virtually all of Kellie's right arm, from the edge of her shoulder down to her wrist, and she wears a series of silver and black bangles on both arms. They extend upwards for several inches. Patricia, by contrast, is a very traditional-looking lady, old-school even, and when I heard her mention Kellie's tattoo I wondered what she was going to say. It is a piece of art and the fact Patricia could appreciate that is heart-warming.

'Right, everyone. Let's head into the shed to grab some gardening gloves and hoes. The first of the herb borders was done yesterday, but there are four more to work on. Feel free to spread out, or stay as a group if you like, whatever you're comfortable doing.'

I hand out the tools and when we step back outside, I suggest the men follow me so I can just run through the process with them. It turns out they both seem to know their plants and after a little chat I leave them to it.

Walking over to Kellie and Patricia, who, I note, are working less than a metre away from each other, I'm delighted to see that they are content in each other's company.

'I have an errand to run, but I'll be back shortly,' I explain.

Heading off in search of Taylor, judging by the sounds coming from one of the open barns, he's in the middle of doing a chainsaw demonstration.

I join the other three people standing around him watching in awe. Taylor slices into a huge offcut of tree trunk, stripping off the bark as if he's cutting into butter. Within just a couple of minutes, he's stripped the top two thirds and has carved the outline of what looks like an animal's head. He releases the handle and silence reigns. We all start clapping as that's quite a feat.

'Okay, folks. Demonstration over. Let's head into the back area and get you started with a chunk of wood and some chisels. Feel free to pick something out of the wood bin. Think about what you'd like to create, then focus on the shape. So, for a bird, you will need a stocky offcut. If you're gonna do a decorative spindle on the lathe, then think elongated.'

As everyone wanders off in search of the perfect piece of wood,

Taylor places the chainsaw back on the rack and turns to walk over to me.

'Hey, Fern. How you doin'?'

He's such a laid-back, friendly guy but the sort who, unless he's teaching, only speaks when spoken to. He has powerful arms and he's really tall. He looks down at me, smiling.

'Good, thank you. That was quite something,' I add.

'Like anything else, it's all about practice. I learnt it from my Pa.'

'Well, it was very impressive. But I've come to ask a favour, actually. Kellie noticed a guitar in the day room and she was wondering if anyone here played. I talked to Nico and he suggested I have a word with you.'

He puts his head back and laughs. 'Well, I only do country and western, but, yep, I strum. So, little Kellie is into music, then?'

'Yes. I think she already plays guitar but maybe would benefit from a little encouragement.'

His hand travels up towards his chin and he rubs his fingers down his jawline, taking a moment to think about it. I try hard not to look at the scar that extends across his right cheek from below his eyebrow to just above his earlobe. It's an old wound that, I'm guessing, for whatever reason, wasn't attended to properly. It's jagged and raised, adding a ruggedness to what is a very handsome face.

'Well, I ain't no tutor when it comes to music, but we could have a session or two. I'll crack out my guitar and Kellie can grab Nico's. Yeah. Why not. Set something up for this evening, okay?'

I give him a grateful nod. 'Thank you, Taylor. That's really good of you and I know Kellie will really appreciate it.'

'The lyrics of some songs hold a lot more sense than the words a lot of people spout, I've found.'

I raise an eyebrow. 'I think I can agree with you there. Enjoy your morning session and I'll catch up with you at lunch.'

'Will do, m'am.' For a young man he certainly has a charming way about him. He's smart, but his charm lies in his little 'ole American, small-town country style. I think Kellie will be safe in his care because I'm guessing he's travelled around and seen a fair few things.

As I leave him to it and walk back out into the open, a slight breeze catches my hair and I stop for a moment to take it all in. This is my life now for the next year unless I tire of it and decide to move on, and already the newness is wearing off and I'm settling in.

Knowing that each batch of visitors will only be here for a week, I have to guard against getting too close to anyone. However, Kellie reminds me a little of Hannah, who is now determined to demonstrate she can cope perfectly well on her own. But we need other people or risk isolating ourselves and becoming withdrawn. Kellie, I fear, at some point chose to withdraw and my aim this week is to ensure she has fun without her knowing I'm keeping a close watch.

'Hey, Kellie. Wow, you two work fast.' I sidle up next to her, surveying the now neatly hoed, weed-free expanse.

'It's easy once you settle into a pattern. And the smell is great.' She turns, wrinkling her nose and smiling. The air is filled with the heavy scent of mint and thyme as her hoe continues to work along the top layer of soil in a succession of little stabs.

'I wondered if you fancied having a guitar session with Taylor this evening? He's into country music and is up for it. He has his own guitar and you could use Nico's, the one you spotted in the day room.'

She stops what she's doing and stands upright.

'Seriously? That would be awesome. Thanks, Fern, I appreciate it.'

My eyes wander over the red dragon as it clings to her arm and she follows my gaze.

'He's called Laoch.' She pronounces it as 'Laok'.

'I'm presuming that's a Gaelic term. What does it mean?'

'Warrior.'

'I like that. The artistry of the ink is incredible. Simple, yet he has great character.'

She nods, staring down at him and when she raises her head back up to look at me, her gaze is forthright.

'I'm a survivor,' she says firmly. 'I always will be, but I doubted it for a while. Never again.'

I reach out and place my hand on her shoulder, giving it a gentle squeeze. Some secrets aren't easy to share and I understand that.

'I'll tell Taylor you're up for a session tonight after the evening meal. I think you'll both enjoy it. It beats playing cards,' I add, and that makes her smile.

'It was a bit boring, wasn't it?'

I bite my lip and she laughs. It's genuine and rises up in her without summoning. Even in the last twenty-four hours I'm seeing a change, like a weight has been lifted off her shoulders.

'Time I grabbed a hoe, I think, and joined you. Those weeds certainly flourish in the sunshine.'

8

A DAY OF DISCOVERY

There are five of us seated in front of the easels, all anxiously looking at Nico as he talks in length about techniques and brushstrokes. He has a small stack of canvases leaning up against a wall and when he's finished talking, he begins hanging them from hooks on the rough stone wall behind him. The riot of colour against the stark white-wash is dramatic. The theme is nature, but there are a wide variety of differing styles.

'This first painting is by a professional artist friend of mine whose work sells for tens of thousands of pounds. Fortunately, I purchased it at the very start of his career when he was struggling to afford to buy paint and on the verge of giving up. Everything else here has been painted by people sitting where you're sitting, some of whom were picking up a brush for the very first time.'

I can see we're all impressed by that. All of the canvases are inter-esting; admittedly, two are in a style that is quite traditional and although they are very good, they're not something I'd hang on my wall at home. But the others are good in a different way, more thought-provoking.

'The point I'm making,' Nico says with gusto, 'is that there is no right or wrong when it comes to art. There is only what is in the eye of the artist and once you commit to that, what will flow from your fingertips will be what is in your heart. You cannot – and must not – concern yourself with the eye of the beholder.

'The role of the artist is to express what is within. Like reading a book, the beholder who engages with your vision as the creator will appreciate and understand it. Others won't, but some artists perceive that as a failing. However, one school of thought is that pain is a necessity, anyway, when it comes to producing great art. That is true in some cases and with great talent often comes a great burden, which, as we all know, isn't specific to this form of self-expression. Look at Kurt Cobain, or John Belushi, for instance. Both very talented in their respective fields, unique yet troubled.'

He smiles and looks at each of us in turn. I find myself holding my breath, captivated by the strength of the emotion in his words.

'When you pick up the brush, I don't want you to hesitate. Take that sense of uniqueness lying deep within and go with it. The fear is always "Will I be good enough? What will other people around me think of my work?" and that very natural reaction is what will hold you back. It will stifle your creativity if you let it.

'You will notice that the positioning of your easel doesn't allow you to see anyone else's work. If, after this afternoon's session, you don't want to share what you've done with the group, then that's fine. Simply unclip your painting and take it back to your room.

'Some of you might be picking up a brush for the first time, only to discover that paint isn't your medium. But what I'd like you to do is to trust me. Don't think about what you're doing, just do it. Today we are working with acrylic paint and heavyweight paper. It's water-soluble. You will obtain the best finish if you apply a thin coat of primer first. Drying time is about ten minutes for it to be touch-dry.'

Nico walks over to the nearest easel and grabs one of the pots, holding it up.

'It helps stop the paper warping with the moisture content in the paint and also makes the surface a little smoother. However, if you want that slightly gritty texture, then skip the primer. If you need to start over again, there is a pile of fresh paper over on the table in the corner, but try not to give up on a painting too soon. And, most of all, have *fun*, guys!'

Suddenly I can't wait to get started, and even though I'm happier with a pencil in my hand and a little sketch pad, that bowl of fruit is so fresh and colourful I'm going to give it a go.

I look around at the other visitors and when Nico turns back to the wall to begin taking down the canvases, one of the guys catches my eye. He grimaces, picking up his brush and holding it awkwardly aloft, and I almost burst out laughing. Well, here goes!

* * *

The day unfolds in many different ways – interesting, challenging and rewarding. Unexpected. So many different emotions and new experiences are coming at me from every angle. In the rush of new things, my problems have been parked to one side and I'm now fully invested in what's going on around me. And that's the biggest surprise of all.

This evening I introduced Kellie to Taylor and left them to their own devices as they headed off into the courtyard to find a quiet room, guitars in hand. Patricia is still on the edge of everything, not really approaching anyone unless they talk to her first, so I spent most of the evening with her. It turns out she's a chess player and while I need to think quite hard about what the various pieces do, we managed to have a few light-hearted games.

Throwing open my bedroom window, I look out, not realising how late it is and no idea why my brain doesn't seem to want to switch off tonight. I spin around to look at the painting I brought back to my room this afternoon.

Glancing up at the wall and that vibrant forest scene, I try to compare the two. When I first walked into the room, the painting captivated me. And even now, it's still catching me unawares and drawing my eye. I'm a detail person but the crude brushstrokes are so clever, so inspiring, that it is a revelation.

Staring down at my own painting, I'm rather shocked at myself. It isn't at all what I expected to create. The picture looks colourful but a little obscure. I grab a pillow off the bed and place it on the chaise longue, jamming it upright against the wall. Then I carry the sheet of paper across and lay it against the angled surface so it doesn't slip off. I turn and walk across the room, almost fearful of turning back around. But when I do, what I see fills me with a feeling of elation. Up close, I saw rough blocks of colour, but stepping back it's clearly a bowl of fruit. I'm happy. In fact, I'm amazed and feeling rather proud of myself.

A sudden noise outside draws me back to the window and I peer out into the gloom. Something, or someone, has fallen over and I can just about make out a shape next to one of the garden tables.

Quietly, I tiptoe down the two flights of stairs, trying to remember which of the treads creak the loudest. Being careful where I step, I keep the noise to a minimum to avoid waking anyone up until I know what's going on. If it turns out to be an intruder, then I'll be screaming at the top of my lungs.

The front door is locked and I head through into the kitchen to find that the back door is wide open. Rushing over and stepping outside, I hear a loud groaning sound, but the mound on the floor doesn't move. As I approach, I see that it's Nico and I kneel down next to him.

'What's happened? Nico, it's Fern. Can you stand?'

After a moment, he opens his eyes. 'Ah, Fern. I missed my footing.'

The smell of alcohol is so strong that I recoil a little.

'Nico, you need to stand up. Let me help you back inside.'

He lifts his head and I pick up his left arm, placing it around my shoulders so I can help lever him up. It's not easy and it takes several minutes to get him back onto his feet. Nico leans quite heavily on me and it's difficult steering him back towards the château.

'It's a night for reflection,' he slurs the words.

'Just keep putting one foot in front of the other. I'm not sure I can hold you up for very long, Nico. You have to work with me.'

We shuffle forwards rather perilously, but I grit my teeth and keep going. Once we're inside, I'm not sure where I'm heading.

'Nico, where is your bedroom?'

He grunts, lifting his arm and pointing, but that sends his body into a tilt and we end up teetering sideways and crashing into the wall. The sound echoes around the hallway. I hold my breath, listening out for any sounds, but there's nothing. Only Nico's raspy, drunken breathing. He shifts his position and I yank him back into a standing position.

'Walk, Nico. Walk. You have to help me because you're too heavy and I don't want you to fall.'

He rallies a little.

'*Mi hermosa*, Fern. You are my beautiful angel.'

I shush him, surprised to hear him speaking in Spanish and calling me beautiful.

'Quietly, Nico. Everyone is asleep. Here, lean against the wall while I open the door.'

'My muse left me, but now you're here. She said you would save me.'

'Shush!! You must be quiet, Nico. Please.'

I hope he doesn't slide to the floor, because if he does, then I'm going to have to get some help. However, he takes a deep breath to compose himself and, as I throw the door open wide, he starts to stagger through without my assistance. I follow close behind.

He manages to get over to the bed and collapses onto it, face down. I can't possibly leave him like that and I kneel beside him to slip off his shoes. Almost instantly he's snoring softly and I feel a little panicky. I can't sit here watching him all night, so I try to get him to roll on his side and, after a few minutes of arm flinging and resistance, he's in a safer position.

Grabbing two pillows, I put one behind his back and one alongside his front, hoping it will anchor him. He's too drunk to know what he's doing and I hesitate for a moment, not quite sure what else to do. Then I remember the recovery position from the first-aid course I did at work and I push one of his legs up, so it's bent. Reasonably happy that he's in a safe enough position until he's slept some of the alcohol off and is more aware, I make my way back upstairs.

When I walk into the room, I see my partially dry painting must have been top-heavy because it has folded over upon itself. As I scrabble to gently open the fold, it appears to be stuck together. A gentle tug confirms that it's too late to save it, and for some silly reason I feel tearful.

* * *

Nico isn't at breakfast and I'm not sure what to do. I can hardly go to his room to check on him, so instead I go in search of Ceana.

'Have you seen Nico, this morning?' I ask, breezily.

'Yes. Briefly. If there's anything you need, it will have to wait, I'm afraid. He's dropping the van off at the garage as the new exhaust has arrived. He's getting a lift back, but he'll be about an hour. I'm heading out to set-up his class this morning.'

'Oh, no problem, then. It's not urgent.'

I can't tell from her expression if she knows what state he was in last night, but I'd guess not. I don't know whether I should mention it, but I don't feel it's my place to do so, even though something tells me that Ceana looks out for Nico. Not because he's in charge, but because she knows him rather well.

'You had your first lesson with him yesterday, how did it go?' she asks.

I raise the corners of my mouth, a satisfied smile beginning to creep over my face, unbidden. 'Surprising,' I say before I turn and walk away.

This morning I have very mixed feelings. Having a longing to create is one thing, but then suddenly being able to tap into that is a rather scary thing. I'd accepted that I'd have to wait a long time to be able to indulge myself in my little daydream. The one where I imagined myself in a field of flowers, sitting in front of an easel. And it isn't just a lottery win that has made this happen. The irony is that this is only happening because of Aiden. Yesterday's session unleashed the desire I've had to push away for so long and now... I'm nervous. What if I don't have any real talent?

'You're deep in thought,' Patricia falls in line with me as I head down towards the gardening shed.

'Oh, hi, Patricia. How did you sleep?'

'Well, thank you. The best I have in a long while. Have you seen Kellie? She's in good spirits this morning too. I think that little session with Taylor went well last night.'

'Oh, I'm so glad. And relieved. It's funny, Ceana did say that on a retreat like this, people tend to be drawn together for many different reasons. A love of music is a wonderful reason for a connection and hopefully they'll share it with us all at some point.'

Patricia purses her lips. 'Now, wouldn't that be something!'

I'm still puzzling over what it is that would help Patricia get the most out of her week here. She hasn't really connected with anyone except me, although she has a soft spot for Kellie.

'What's on your agenda for this afternoon?' I ask.

'Oh, I thought maybe I'd tag along with Ceana's group. I think she's giving pruning tips and demonstrating how to take cuttings. It might come in useful, although my garden is mostly grass with only two borders. No trees, but a couple of climbers and a large collection of prize-winning rose bushes.'

Somehow, I worry she isn't really getting into the spirit of things. It's as if she prefers to watch rather than join in.

'I noticed there wasn't anyone down for Odile's pottery class this afternoon. If I wasn't already committed to the painting group, I'd switch, but it's only day two and I don't want Nico to think I'm giving up already,' I joke, dropping a big hint.

'Oh, I didn't realise. Maybe I could give that a go instead.'

'Why don't you talk to her at lunch, find out what's on offer?'

'I will, thank you.'

It's not long before Kellie and three others join us and, this morning, Ceana has moved us across to begin weeding one of the vegetable patches. The rows extend out seemingly endlessly and it's already getting very warm, so it's going to be hot work.

Everywhere around us is filled with the sounds of buzzing bees and birdsong; summer is a busy time and every little creature has a full agenda, it seems.

'Can I just remind everyone to take frequent breaks in the shade? I'll pop back up to the kitchen and grab one of the cool boxes so there's plenty of water on hand.'

They're a cheery bunch this morning and already there's a little banter going on. I think two new faces will make a big difference. You only need one chatty person to encourage everyone else to join in and create an air of camaraderie. John isn't someone I've really spoken to, but he has a natural sense of humour and it's good to hear a little laughter.

As I'm walking back to the kitchen, my phone begins to ring. I yank it out, glancing at the screen, but it's too bright to see anything.

'Hello?'

'Fern, it's me! God, it's good to hear your voice!'

I stop in my tracks. My stomach does a somersault.

'Aiden. Oh... same here, darling.'

'We're in town picking up some supplies. As I finally have a decent signal, I just wanted to... I mean, you're on my mind all the time.'

He sounds distant, not in miles, but as if he doesn't quite know what to say to me and yet he made the call.

'I've been worried.' I shouldn't have said that.

'It's all good. Fun, surprisingly, and I can see how people get hooked once they find a piece of rock with some twinkling colours in it.'

After a creaky start, at least he sounds a little more relaxed.

'Are you still with those guys? It's not underground mining, is it?' I've done it again.

'No. I've been manning a bulldozer, exposing the bottom of a rocky incline. We found our first vein of opal.'

I can hear the buzz in his voice now and I close my eyes. At least he's not in some hand-hewn tunnel somewhere far beneath the ground.

He said 'we'. 'You sound like you're enjoying it. Any plans to head off somewhere else?'

'Not sure at the moment, babe. Anyway, I must shoot off. I just wanted to check you were okay and settling in. How did your first art class go?'

'Illuminating. And you're right, it is fun.' I'm desperate to make the few words I say sound upbeat and not judgemental, even though I have concerns, I don't want to alienate him in any way. 'It's a wonderful set-up here and the first group are very friendly.'

'Is everyone all right at home?' he asks.

So, he hasn't been in touch with anyone.

'Yes. Mum and Dad are doing well; Mum sends me all the gossip by email – you know what she's like. They're restyling the garden, but it sounds like a lot of work when there wasn't anything wrong with the old layout. Still, it's keeping them busy. And Owen rang. He's spoken to Hannah and says she's fine.'

'Oh, she still hasn't forgiven us, then.'

'Not quite.'

Us? You're responsible for this, Aiden. Not me.

'And you're well? And safe?' There I go again. I can't hide my anxiety and he'll know that from my tone.

'Everything's just great. Send me some photos and I'll do the same. Sadly, my lift is about to leave and the line is beginning to break up.'

'I will, promise. Love you.'

There are a bunch of voices in the background and it's getting hard to hear him. One of them calls out his name. It's a woman's voice.

'Love you, more.'

Click.

I let out a huge, depressed sigh. Temptation is everywhere when you're in the middle of a crisis. I know Aiden slept with someone before me, but he's my first and my only.

It isn't until I hear Nico's voice that I even realise he is walking towards me.

'Problems?' he asks, concern in his tone as his eyes scan my face.

I try to turn my anxious look into a smile, but I don't quite manage to pull it off.

'No. Just a family call. We're in different time zones which doesn't help.'

He gives me a sheepish look. 'I came to apologise for last night. And for anything I might have—'

'It's all right, please don't feel you have to explain. I was just glad to help.'

He idly kicks the toe of his trainer against a tuft of grass. 'It was the anniversary of my father's death. Even from his grave he continues to haunt me, it seems. I, for one, should know better than to let the past drag me down, but it caught me unawares. Your discretion is appreciated, Fern. I mean it.'

With that, he turns on his heels and strides out purposefully in the direction of the art studio.

9

STILL WATERS RUN DEEP

Lunch is a low-key affair today. Margot was in early making up pack lunches for everyone and then she disappeared. Apparently, she won't be back until late afternoon as she had a full-on day yesterday. Regretfully, I missed the late afternoon session where she demonstrated how to make croissants, but those who sat in on it said she made it look easy. Next week I'll make sure I don't miss out.

'Is it okay if I join you?'

I peer up, squinting. Standing there, the sun's rays are uncannily like a halo effect around Kellie's head. I nod and smile back at her.

'Of course. I only came out here because I had a long email to read and I wanted to send my husband some photos, but I'm done. My mum is keeping me up to date on all the latest news at home and she doesn't leave anything out,' I say, unable to hide the amusement in my voice. 'But that's my mum and I love her for it.'

'You must miss them all. It's a big change being here, isn't it?'

I adjust my position as the rough bark on the tree begins to dig into my back.

'Yes. But sometimes being taken out of your comfort zone is a good thing. It can give you a slightly different view of life. You didn't fancy a fishing expedition, then? I bet it's nice and cool down by the lake beneath the canopy of trees,' I reflect.

Kellie lowers herself down next to me, screwing up her face.

'I like the idea of fishing, but catching something on a hook seems cruel. I mean, I'll happily eat the fish tonight after Margot's cooked it, but I'm a bit squeamish. If I stop to think about where my food comes from, I end up living on chips. I went through that stage for a while a few years back and it wasn't much fun,' she admits.

'You came through it, though. That's all that matters. And I agree with you, but the food chain is what it is and we need to eat to live. I hate waste, but I don't have qualms about what I eat.'

We lapse into silence as I tidy away the wrappings from lunch and snap the lid back on the plastic box. Kellie bites into an apple and we both stare out over the orchard.

This is bliss. At home it's either too wet, too cold, or too hot. Here, even when the temperature soars, as long as I can find a little shade, it feels therapeutic. It warms from the outside in and lifts the spirits. The air is fragrant and that adds to the sense of well-being. I wonder if it's because I associate that with other holidays, or whether it's a part of the charm of Provence? Maybe everyone has a special place with which they connect and this is mine.

'Can I ask your advice about something, Fern?'

'Feel free, but it will only be my opinion, remember.'

'I'm thinking that I'd like to extend my stay here if Nico will let me. My parents can afford it and I think they'll be relieved not to have me hanging around for another week or so. I love working on the garden and Taylor's pretty cool. He thinks I play quite well and he's very patient.'

'It sounds to me like you've already made up your mind. I'm sure Nico will be fine about it, but you might have to change rooms. So, why are you hesitating?'

'I wanted to ask if you're here permanently. It's just that I know Patricia is leaving on Friday and you're the only other person, besides Taylor, I feel really comfortable around. But I know you aren't a tutor, as such.'

Ah. That touches my heart.

'Yes, I'll be here for the foreseeable future.'

'You said your husband is travelling around and maybe if he gets to really miss you, he'll fly back to the UK early. You know, you might both get homesick.'

I draw in a long, slow breath. She's an intelligent young woman and deserves an honest answer.

'We've known each other a long time, Kellie, as we met while we were still at school. Fortunately, we've grown together over the years, but this break is allowing us to explore our different interests. So, while we do miss each other, naturally, this is a time of self-discovery for both of us. Time we might never get again. I have a creative side of me clamouring for attention, but family commitments and work mean time is always at a premium. With Aiden, he longed to travel further afield and my fears have held him back. He sacrificed his sense of adventure because he loves me. We will get homesick at times, I know I already have, but this is a once-in-a-lifetime opportunity. No one wants to live their lives regretting the things they didn't do.'

She ponders on my words for a little while. We are both content to take in the ambience of the leafy setting around us. The myriad shades of green at every turn and the sound of rustling leaves over-head, as the breeze disturbs them, is restful. Time seems to have been temporarily suspended and I can't help wondering if Kellie is feeling as at peace as I am.

'You sound concerned that he will resent what he gave up for you. But you don't seem to regret what you gave up for him.'

I'm shocked at her perception, because she's spot on. I can feel her eyes as she stares at my side profile. Raking my fingers over the spiky grass, it feels good against my skin: grounding. My old life hardly seems real any more; already it's like a distant memory.

'It's not as easy as that because I know he understands it's extremely difficult to overcome a deep-seated phobia. I appreciate that and I'm happy with my life, so what's to forgive?'

'I've never felt that sort of love for someone. I hope I do, sometime in my life. I'd hate to settle for what my parents have. They never put each other first and never will. Sounds like you'd do anything for Aiden. Well, except jump on a plane.'

I swallow hard.

'My eldest sister died in a plane that went down over the Mediterranean Sea in 2010. Sixteen out of the thirty-nine passengers and crew lost their lives.' The words seem to come from someone else; matter-of-fact, almost devoid of emotion because, right now, it doesn't feel real.

'Oh, Fern, I'm so very sorry. I didn't mean to pry. I wasn't thinking—'

I reach out and squeeze her arm, comfortingly. 'It's fine, really. I rarely think about it these days. I've learnt to accept that some things in life are outside of our control, even though they still influence the way we live our lives. I shared my secret with you because I want you to know that I'm here if there's anything you ever want to share with me.'

She looks at me with tears in her eyes and I lean in to throw my arms around her shoulders.

'I don't know how you knew, but when I'm ready... I'd like that.'

The sound of voices draws our attention to the trees beyond the allotment. The fishing party is returning.

'Are you taking the art class this afternoon?' Kellie asks.

'Yes. You?'

'I might have the afternoon off and head down to the orchard to read a book. It's one I picked up in the day room last night and I stayed up till midnight because I couldn't put it down.'

'What's it about?'

'A woman whose life is rather messed up and she runs away to start over again. It's quite sad in parts, but there's also a lot of humour. I can't wait to find out how it ends. We're all looking for that happily ever after, aren't we?'

I thought I had mine and I hope when I return home the new reality won't have changed that.

'I guess we are,' I reply, softly.

We stand, exchanging an empathetic smile as we part company. I feel I did the right thing confiding in Kellie; it was strange, though, hearing myself say the words because it's been a long time since they passed my lips.

I traipse back to the courtyard in a little world of my own, startled when a hand touches my shoulder. I turn to see it's John. He's the joker of the group and a Londoner.

'You whipped your painting away yesterday before I could get a look at it.' He leaps forward to hold the studio door open for me.

'Thanks, John. Well, it was my first ever attempt and a bit of a disaster. It's in the bin, but I'm looking forward to today.'

'Ha! Did you see mine? Couldn't tell what was apples and what was pears.'

I start laughing. 'Oh, I thought it was rather unique; Picasso eat your heart out.'

He tips his head back and laughs with gusto. 'Ain't put off, though. Never 'ad so much fun.'

'What do you do for a living, John?'

We head up the stairs, walking side by side.

'I'm a retired painter and decorator, so I'm used to being plastered in paint. Thought I might get a bit creative, but after yesterday I think maybe not. Nico says we're drawing today. Might 'ave a better chance with that.'

It's hard not to laugh. 'Well, good luck to you, John.'

Nico looks across, catching my eye for a moment as I settle down on one of the chairs he has set out in a semicircle. On each is an A4 artist's sketch pad and a small tin, which I place on the floor by my feet.

'Okay. Today we're going to explore the art of sketching. If you open the tin, you will find a range of six different graphite pencils and a sharpener. You will notice that the blacker the pencil, the softer the lead. The rule of thumb is that for detailed work use one of the H pencils – you'll see the scale printed on the side just here.' Nico holds up a pencil to indicate. 'If you want to create texture and tone, then you choose a pencil with B on it. The most popular ones for general sketching, and to begin with, are HB and 2B.'

Nico's demonstration makes it look easy and, fortunately, instead of asking us to draw something from real life to experiment, we simply start with 3D shapes to see what each pencil does. It's fun without being a daunting challenge.

'Right. Practice time over. Now I want you to head out and find something to draw. It doesn't matter what, but if this is your first time I suggest you choose something simple. A single leaf, or flower head for example. For the more adventurous, have a go at maybe one of the sheds down in the garden. It's easier to focus on one thing, rather than to make it complicated.

'Sketching can be like taking notes. A small drawing that at some point will inspire a much bigger work. Maybe divide your page into four for this afternoon's task. Above all, make it fun, and I'll be around if anyone needs any help or advice.'

We all stand and walk off towards the staircase when Nico motions for me to hold back.

'I know you enjoyed yesterday's session and I wondered if before you make a start, you'd like to see what a working artist's studio looks like up close. It's messy, I can promise you that.'

I'm intrigued, but then I can see he knows I will be. 'I'd love to, thank you.'

As we walk up to the château, Nico tells me a little about the history of the house. Originally, it was his grandmother's parents' home. When they died, his mother was living in Villacarrillo, in Andalucia, and had been for many years, having met his father while on holiday there. It fell into decline because she rarely came back here. It wasn't until Nico's father experienced financial problems that they came here to live. Nico was settled into school and his mother, Viviana, began working part-time as the local notaire's secretary, who, he explained, was a legal specialist. She kept the family going.

'He was almost penniless at the time; a typical impoverished artist living on dreams. After he died, eight years ago, my mother returned to Spain and I remained here. As difficult as he was to live with, it broke her heart and two years later she succumbed to pneumonia. Life was never the same for her; it was easier without the worry of his turbulent moods, but she lost her zest for life.'

'How sad. I'm so sorry to hear that,' I reply, gently.

Nico leads me through the long corridor, past his bedroom on the ground floor, and I try not to recall the image of him slumped up against the wall.

'It's through here.'

I follow him into a large room that overlooks a walled garden. It's filled with a mass of different hues, from white through to opulent purple. So unlike the orderly allotment, this feels instead like nature has taken over. Several huge rambling roses spill over the walls and there's a real sense of the beauty of a garden doing its own thing. But the colour isn't just outside. While the end wall is mostly glass, the rectangular, elongated room – which has two enormous tinted skylights – is also a riot of colour.

There are stacks of varying sizes of canvases leant against two of the walls and I do a double take. Each one would have taken weeks, months, or even longer, to have completed.

The third wall, which is bare brick, has several tracks running along it at three different heights. Extending well in excess of forty feet in length, there are five partially completed paintings.

'My goodness, that's impressive!' I exclaim.

The floor is covered with almost as much paint as one of the canvases I'm staring at, and the smell is heavenly. That intense prickle as it hits my nose and I breathe in a wonderful whiff of oil paint. A sense of excitement wells up within me – it's intoxicating.

'I didn't realise you painted in oils too,' I declare, walking towards a huge canvas which is ninety per cent complete. It's a village scene and so beautifully detailed I find myself wanting to reach out and touch it because the leafy scene looks so real. 'I just love this smell, it's heavenly. I could live in this room. This is quite something.' I lean in closer, marvelling at the way he's captured the light. It seems to jump out, it's so vibrant, and yet there's hardly any white paint to be seen. The light and shade has been applied in such a subtle way that all the eye sees is the overall effect.

'It's where I was born,' Nico says with a catch in his voice.

It's then that I realise few get to step inside this room and see what I'm seeing. It instantly brings a lump to my throat.

'I don't have a problem with alcohol,' he says, flat out. 'I felt I owed it to you to make that clear. My father, however, was an alcoholic. It was a stupid thing to turn to a bottle of whisky in an attempt to obliterate some memories that aren't pleasant. But it's because of him that I usually manage to keep on an even keel. I saw what his frustrations did to him and it destroyed him in the end. He thought he was misunderstood. And he was, because who can really judge what is art and what isn't? He painted what he saw through his own eyes and that's not wrong. But allowing himself to become isolated and desperate was wrong, and that's why I run the retreat.'

I spin around to look at Nico as his eyes bore into me.

'The painting in my room is your father's and I find it inspiring. It grabs at something in here.' I hit my chest with my hand. 'That's a gift and he passed it on to you.'

His face freezes and I feel I've touched a raw nerve. But he shirks it off and, feeling embarrassed, I turn and walk along the line of partially completed works. Stopping for a few moments to marvel at each one in turn, I'm inspired.

'I never realised artists worked on more than one piece at a time,' I comment, making my voice sound more cheerful than I feel. I'm gutted that I inadvertently said the wrong thing.

'It's all about being in the right mood, Fern. Each day is different.'

'I can see that,' I add, smiling and hoping to lighten the moment. 'Do painters have days where one colour is more meaningful?'

He starts to laugh. 'I see what you mean, but it wasn't intentional. My blue mood first, then a green day as you go along the row... but, no, it's just the way I work. Sometimes it's the sky that catches my attention and I want to experiment to find that perfect shade. Other days it's the forest beyond the orchard that calls me. Or the walled garden and the profusion of pinks, reds and purples.'

'Your father struggled, you say?'

He nods. 'So many unfinished works. He battled with drug addiction for the last few years of his life as well. With great talent comes great passion and he was a man obsessed with detail. The truth is that he had a different reason for hating every single one of his paintings. I remember as a young boy taking his lunch into him in the studio and he was stabbing at a canvas with a knife. He was mutilating it because he couldn't capture the light and shade to his satisfaction. Weeks of work destroyed in minutes.

'What I saw in his eyes scared me. The pills he began taking seemed to take the edge off the pain, but it was a downhill slope. One day he swallowed a whole bottle and that was it.'

He isn't looking for sympathy and I say nothing. What can you say to something like that?

Nico has led me over to a stack of canvases leaning against the wall in the corner of the room and pulls off the cover protecting them. He lifts the first canvas and turns it, placing it on one of the tracks. It's about four feet square and it's a young woman sitting on a chair, looking out of a window. But it's so unlike the painting in my room; this one is intricate and precise.

'Can you see the flaws?' Nico watches as my eyes travel over it.

'Well, it's beautiful and the face is so true to life that the eyes seem to follow me as I move a little closer to the painting. I feel I could reach out and actually touch her skin, but there's something not quite right. I can't tell you what, exactly.'

He stands back, gazing at it. 'The neck is a little too long and the angle of the window distorts the perspective ever so slightly but enough for the eye to register and that detracts from the overall aesthetics.'

'But it's still a very beautiful work of art, Nico.'

He nods. 'I agree. However, my father didn't. After he completed this portrait of my mother, she wouldn't allow him to reuse the canvas, which he often did in those days. That was before his drug phase. It only survived because of her, but it has never been hung on a wall, because to him it represented his inadequacy. For me, it's a fond memory of my mother, but it also reminds me of his madness.'

His pain is so real, it seems to envelop me.

'That's so sad, Nico. What incredible skill he had and yet he could only see the tiniest of flaws that probably exist in every painting. But at least he had the satisfaction of seeing some of his work sell before he died.'

Nico turns to face me and I can see the anguish in his eyes. 'Yes, but that ended up being the reason he killed himself.'

10

'Hi, Fern. How was your afternoon?'

'Good, thank you, Patricia. I have a couple of pages of little draw-ings and learnt a few things about perspective. How was your session?'

I move along the bench so that Patricia can sit next to me, avoiding a rough patch of splintered and peeling, sun-bleached wood. It's a nice quiet spot and after another of Margot's tempting dinners in which I ate a little too much, I feel rather drowsy. If I'd stopped at the main course, I would have been fine. But who can resist a traditional *tarte aux poires*? Not me, anyway.

'To my surprise, it went very well. I actually managed, with a little direction, to throw quite a nice little pot. Odile has filled the kiln and the pots are firing overnight. We get to glaze them tomor-row. I'm so glad you suggested it. I had a very interesting chat with Stefan, too, and he was very helpful. Nice man, actually.'

I can hardly believe it. I don't think I've seen Patricia talk to anyone other than myself or Kellie. She's certainly beginning to open up and looks very relaxed this evening.

'Kellie is staying on for another week, maybe two. Did she tell you?'

Patricia shakes her head. 'I didn't know that. Oh, I am so pleased for her, though. She's getting on so well with Taylor. I noticed she was one of his little group this afternoon.'

I look at her, rather surprised, and she raises her eyebrows, indicating that Kellie's news isn't entirely unexpected.

'Oh. That could be a bit awkward. He's a good ten years older than her, I reckon. Do you think I should mention it to Nico?'

'Maybe, but Taylor is such a reserved and polite young man. I haven't spoken to him directly, but I just happened to be within earshot of them yesterday. I took a little walk down to the allotment early evening after they'd taken themselves off to the orchard with the guitars. It all seemed very innocent.'

And I thought I was a mother hen, keeping an eye on everyone.

'I do wish I could stay on, but there are things I have to do back at home. This little break is wonderful, though. And a blessing. Nico is a very interesting man. I suppose all artists are a little temperamental, but he seems quite intense.'

'I suppose he is, but running this place demands a lot of his time. I imagine that can be rather frustrating when his work is calling him,' I reflect.

She takes a deep breath in, gazing out over the low-level shrubbery in the sweeping border that edges the lawn. Behind it are some standard rose bushes.

'I love roses,' she says, nostalgically. 'My husband, Fred, has spent his life tending our collection, but this year they haven't fared so well.'

'That's a shame and what a pity he couldn't take this little trip with you. It sounds like his idea of paradise.'

A frown knots her forehead. 'He isn't well. It's been a tough year, but my brother insisted I take a break.'

'Oh, Patricia, I'm so sorry to hear that. As a carer it's vital to be able to step away for a while. My heart goes out to you.'

'He's been an avid gardener all his life and can spot a greenfly at thirty paces! Can you smell the perfume in the air?'

I sniff and then sniff again, savouring that little floral hint that hadn't even registered with me.

'Yes, I can, now you mention it.'

'One of life's little bonuses. Thank you, Fern,' she says, turning to face me.

'For... what, exactly?'

She laughs. 'For being you.'

'Me? Really?'

'You put me at ease. I feared I'd make a mistake coming away on this trip, alone and at a low ebb. But it was important to me for all sorts of reasons I can't put into words. And I'm so glad I didn't go with my instincts to simply head back to the airport. Cold feet,' she explains, winking at me.

It makes me chuckle.

'Well, I'm glad you stayed, too. And I know Kellie is; I think she felt the same way you did on Monday and you encouraged her.'

I glance at Patricia, who nods her head.

'Ahh. Anyway, I must go. Nico is heading in this direction and he probably needs to talk to you.'

With that she jumps up and walks off in the direction of the orchard. How strange that felt. It was almost as if she wanted to tell me something, then changed her mind.

'I wondered where you were. I owe you yet another apology. Seems I keep making a habit of it with you.'

Smiling up at him, he looks very relaxed this evening in an open-necked white shirt and navy blue, denim jeans. He's wearing a cologne that has a citrussy edge to it and, judging by his damp hair, he's freshly showered. Our eye contact is easy, comfortable, and he indicates towards the bench.

'Can I sit, or was the lovely Patricia heading off because you wanted some quiet time? I didn't chase her away, did I?'

'No, not at all. She's just a little shy. Please, take a seat.'

'How did the sketching go?'

I can feel his eyes scanning the side of my face; the bench is small and we're sitting very close together. It's a little bit unnerving for some reason. Nico adjusts his position, the seat being a little too low for his long legs, and he stretches them out in front of him. He half turns towards me again, flinging an arm over the back rail.

'Good, well, I think. It's funny though, yesterday's session blew my mind a little and that was a complete surprise. I never imagined myself as being a dauber, but that's what I did yesterday when I picked up the biggest brush on the table and went for it. Today it was all about the intricate detail and I thought that was where my interest would be, but I'm itching to get my hands on a brush again.'

He smiles and the white of his teeth against his beautiful skin makes me feel a little nervous. How utterly ridiculous I'm being; he's curious about one of his new students and that's only natural.

'I saw your painting before you finished it yesterday, but then you disappeared and took it with you,' he says, frowning.

'Well, it was my first attempt. Sadly, I dropped it on the way to my room so it ended up in the bin, I'm afraid.' It just seems easier to make light of it, as I don't want to make it sound like I thought it was any good. 'I was inspired by the painting on the wall in my room. That's not plagiarism, is it?'

This time his laugh is throaty as he continues to look at me. For my part, I continue to avoid his glance as I scan the view in front of me.

'No. Your personal style is just that and you seem to lean towards the abstract. It reminded me of the work of Michele Tragakiss, an artist whose work is very popular right now. You surprised me, Fern. What I really wanted to ask you this afternoon was whether you'd like to have a go at painting on a proper canvas. The door to my private studio is always open and it bothers no one. I often end up there late at night if I can't sleep. I usually paint for a couple of hours until the brush is about to fall out of my hand. What do you think?'

A little bubble of excitement leaps up from my stomach into my chest at the tantalising thought of that next brushstroke.

'That's very kind of you, Nico, but I simply wouldn't know where to start. I'd hate to waste a perfectly good canvas when I have no idea what I'm doing.' It's the truth, but I'm also afraid of messing up and embarrassing myself in front of him. It's not like me to feel so vulnerable, and yet I do.

'Well, it didn't look like that to me. Besides,' his smile drops suddenly as I force myself to look at him, 'I need to ask you a big favour. I was rather hoping the temptation of access to my studio would mean you wouldn't refuse me.'

Now he's piqued my interest.

'Hmm. I'm tempted before I even know what I'm getting myself into,' I confess.

'Ceana has to return home for a few days because her cousin is getting married. She'll leave at lunchtime on Friday but won't get back until Tuesday afternoon. She acts as my deputy, as you've no doubt already discovered. We get our heads together when the new visitors arrive and try to pick out those who are a little more reserved. The aim is to buddy them up with someone, although it doesn't always work. Just for the first session in most cases, although sometimes it instigates genuine friendships.'

I nod, having seen her in action.

'Ceana checks in with all of the tutors every day to make sure there aren't any problems and is generally my eyes and ears. I need someone to step into that role while she's away. Plus, we have three visitors here over the weekend to keep an eye on in case they need anything, so it would really help me out. She says I walk and talk too quickly and that's why it's not easy for me to sidle up to people and check they are okay. Intense is the word she uses.' He grimaces, and I burst out laughing. When he's relaxed, it's like talking to a different man.

'So, I would just check in on the people staying here and make sure the cleaners don't have any problems. After that, I help assess the new intake on Monday? Generally circulating and reporting back to you?'

'Yep. Don't forget to check that the mid-week linen change has already been delivered and that we aren't low on towels. That's about it. Low-key but necessary to keep things ticking over. And in return you get to create your very own masterpiece. Think of all those tubes of paint... just waiting for the touch of a brush.'

He makes it sound almost sensual.

'Enough! I'm sold. You knew I would say *yes*, didn't you? Although, I have to admit, I think I'm benefitting the most from this deal.'

Nico smiles. 'That's because you're a lovely lady. It's in your nature to nurture, so you don't see it as a chore.'

I glance at him, caught off guard by his observation. What else has he noticed? I wonder.

'My family are rather demanding at times. There's always someone to look out for and a problem to help solve. People's well-being is also crucial to my work, so it's ingrained in me now.'

He studies my face and I watch as his eyes flick over me.

'You care about people, Fern, and sometimes that can end up being a burden. But here you are, alone and stepping outside of your comfort zone to discover new interests. That's a bold move for anyone at any time in their life.'

I shrug. 'I think it's my husband who is the bold one. We accepted that for our year off work we wanted to do different things. It's an opportunity we're lucky to have, but perhaps it's foolish. We won't know until it's over, I guess.'

'Things weren't going well between you?' Nico's frown is genuine; he's trying to understand my situation.

'Maybe we'd grown a little complacent. We rely upon each other and I suppose, with hindsight, that is a form of complacency because it can lead to taking each other for granted. Knowing you are there for each other whenever, whatever happens. I don't see that as a bad thing, but maybe absence does make the heart grow fonder.'

'So, it's a year of brave new discoveries which is also a huge risk for you both.' His words are unsettling. I miss my normal routine; my normal life. But each day here is bringing with it something new and I'm realising things about myself that are surprising, as I begin to understand how strangers perceive me. And now Nico is prepared to put his trust in me, which is a confidence boost I wasn't expecting.

'And an adventure; one neither of us may ever get to experience again. Which is why I'd love to accept your offer, Nico, if you think I'm up to it. Thank you.'

'Great. I'm glad you're prepared to step outside your comfort zone. How about we head up to the day room as Ceana has talked Taylor and Kellie into playing a couple of songs. After that, we can get you set up in my studio.'

I nod in appreciation.

'How did she manage that, I wonder?'

'As a man from Montana, he couldn't resist a little Fourth of July Celebration. She thinks of everything.' He chuckles and his eyes sparkle.

'You're going to miss Ceana when she flies back to Scotland,' I remark.

'I will, but she said if I could talk you into it, she'd go off feeling I was in good hands.'

Those intense eyes smile back at me, gratefully, and I hesitate, wondering if this isn't such a good idea after all. But what excuse could I possibly conjure up when he's doing everything he can to encourage my creativity?

* * *

'Hi, deserter,' Hannah's voice trills down the line. My heart almost stops in my chest, so great is the joy I feel now that she's finally reaching out to me. 'I can't stay mad at you for long. Besides, Mum and Liam have been on my case. Apparently, I'm being selfish.' Her tone is apologetic.

'You have a lot going on and I don't want you worrying about

Aiden or me. We're fine, really. Sometimes it's good to allow the people we love the freedom to discover more about themselves. Besides, you're off doing your own thing now, so popping in for a chat most days was already a thing of a past.'

'I know, but I miss you. And that's why I feel bad for giving you a rough time, but you're so far away, which makes it worse somehow. If you hadn't bought that lottery ticket, I can't help thinking that none of this would have happened. You'd still be back home with Aiden and everything would be on track. You guys are as much of an institution as Mum and Dad are.'

I roll my eyes but say nothing. Even big sisters sometimes need to put themselves first and stop worrying about what sort of role model they are. Anyway, I wouldn't be a very good one if I was sat at home worrying myself sick about Aiden, now would I?

'I love the fact that you have your freedom now and I'm proud of you. This is a time for grabbing every opportunity that comes your way, and enjoying each and every moment. Don't get bogged down worrying about things that might never happen. For you, or for anyone around you. Accept that life is all about constant change.'

She gives a little laugh and I can imagine her pulling a face. 'All right, all right, big sis. Guess I'm about to add another little worry to your list. Liam and I are engaged. Don't go panicking; you haven't really missed anything. We won't celebrate properly until you and Aiden get back, but I am wearing the most gorgeous ring. He took me out to dinner to thank me for helping him do up his flat. Suddenly, a violinist appeared and Liam got down on one knee! Honestly, Fern, I nearly died of embarrassment, but I'm so happy.'

I screw up my eyes in desperation, wanting so much to be there with her. But another part of me is crying out: *Don't rush into things, Hannah, because if you don't experience that sense of real freedom first, it might come back to haunt you. As it has done for Aiden.*

What *it* is, I don't really know. A sense of adventure lost for some, maybe. A sense of... what, for me? Decadence? Selfishness? You can't recapture the exhilaration of being young and free when you are facing thirty and life is all about responsibility.

'If that's what you want, Hannah, then I'm happy for you both. And when we're all back home together we can have a huge party to mark the occasion.'

My mind is in turmoil. I did this to my parents and now my sister is doing it too – falling hopelessly in love at such a tender age and rushing headlong into it. But she sounds so happy and I can't voice my concerns as that would make me a hypocrite. I want the best of everything for Hannah, and Liam is a wonderful young man, but it's so soon. She's experienced nothing really in the grand scheme of life. I didn't understand that at her age, either – who does?

'Thanks, Fern. I kinda thought you might give me a hard time as you aren't here. I texted Owen, but he's off doing some sort of special training thing. He replied briefly and said he'd phone me when he was back. How's France?'

I can't shake the sadness I feel at the distance between us. I wonder how Mum and Dad reacted when Hannah broke the news. I know they will be concerned that she's following in my footsteps, but we are two very different personalities. What we do have in common is that we're both rather stubborn; it's Owen who is more amenable and I guess being bossed around by his sisters, he learnt to be a little more laid-back.

'It's wonderful. Sunny. Friendly people and I'm feeling more relaxed than I have done in a long time.'

'That's awesome. You needed to chill out a bit.'

I remember only too well the invincibility I felt as a teenager and truly believing those who disagreed with me weren't living life to the full. An age thing, I remember thinking, whereas I was young and full of eternal optimism. Nothing was going to spoil my dream of the perfect life stretching out before me.

'I've discovered that I'm an abstract artist at heart, so be warned. There will be changes when I get home as I'll be swapping those mass-produced, chain-store pieces with the real thing.'

'Wow. And I thought Aiden was being the brave one, heading off to far-flung destinations. Now I discover my sister is turning into one of those artsy folk. I hope Aiden's prepared for all this when you get back.'

As we say our goodbyes, I can't help agreeing with her sentiments.

11

A FRISSON OF EXCITEMENT

'That was very good. Aside from a few nerves at the start, Kellie and Taylor sounded like a real duo. Do you think Kellie sings?'

Nico swings open the heavy oak door to the château and holds it ajar for me. As I step through, I remember my phone is switched off and I quickly turn it back on.

'I'm guessing she does, but whether she'll let down her guard enough to give it a go, who knows? She was very comfortable playing, though. It was good to see and everyone enjoyed it.'

'You didn't want to stay for the karaoke?' Nico gives me a sideways glance.

'Um, let me think about that for a second... that would be a *no.*'

He laughs. 'I don't think you're in the mood, anyway. You seem a little down tonight. Missing home?'

Nico stops to push open the door to his studio and I walk on ahead, immediately taking a deep breath in. Little prickles begin to run up my spine. It isn't just the overwhelming smell of the paint, but the reality hits that I'm going to create something that will, hopefully, end up on a wall at home.

'I'm fine, really. I was wondering how easy is it to get canvases sent over to the UK?'

'It's not a problem. I ship them to the UK as well as most of Europe. I only exhibit in Spain, but I sell quite a bit from my website. There are customs forms to be dealt with, but the easiest way, if you're going to do quite a few pieces, is to roll the canvases and transport them in tubes. Much cheaper and you can have them stretched and framed as and when you want.'

Suddenly my phone begins to buzz.

'Sorry, it's my sister, I need to get this.'

Nico nods and rather diplomatically heads down towards the far end of the studio.

'Hannah, what's up?'

'Obviously Aiden still hasn't managed to reach you, then. He rang me to say he'd tried calling you as there's a problem, but I struggled to hear what he was saying. The signal was awful, so I said I'd get hold of you. Guess you haven't been on his Facebook page, either. Who the heck is the woman in the last photo? I'll send you a screenshot. I don't know what's going on, but you need to call him, like now.'

'Photo? Hang on, give me a moment.'

I pull the phone away from my ear and see I have three missed calls. There are also two texts. They're all from Aiden. Damn it, why didn't I think to switch it back on immediately after the performance?

Hannah sends through the screenshot and, glancing at it, I have no idea who the woman is, the only person I recognise is Aiden.

I open the first message from Aiden.

Trying to call you. We have to leave pretty sharpish as there's a problem and we can't stay here. I'll try you again in a while.

We?

The second text doesn't tell me much more.

I'm safe and travelling with two other people. We've found someone willing

to take us to Adelaide for a reasonable fee, but it's a long drive from
Coober Pedy. My battery is almost dead. I'll phone you when I can, but
there might not be many places to stop by the sound of it. Speak soon.

'Hannah, I have no idea what's going on, but Aiden's text says he's
safe. I had my phone switched off as there was a musical thing going
on here. And I haven't seen any of his posts.'

'He put up four photos earlier on, about an hour before he called
me. Aiden sounded panicky because he couldn't get hold of you,
Fern. There was so much noise, like a fight going on in the background.' I can hear the fear in her voice.

'Listen, whatever has happened, Aiden says he's safe and he's
with two other people heading towards Adelaide now. Take a deep
breath and calm yourself down – my phone's back on now and I'll
keep monitoring it. I'm sorry this scared you. Aiden knows how to
take care of himself and he probably panicked in case I tried to get
hold of him and couldn't get a response, that's all. As soon as I hear
anything, I'll let you know. Okay?'

'Okay. It was a bit of a shock with all the noise in the background
and he sounded... scared. At least you're in a safer place, I mean,
what harm can you come to in a lovely little château in the French
countryside?'

I glance towards Nico, who has slipped off his cotton shirt and is
pulling a T-shirt over his head. I avert my gaze, thankful that his back
is towards me.

'Aiden can handle himself, Hannah, and I'm sure he'll be fine.
Now go do something to take your mind off it. It might be a while
until I hear from him as he said it's a long journey and his battery
was almost dead.'

I feel bad playing this down when it's tying my stomach in knots.
But Aiden and Hannah have always been close and I know that on
the few occasions I've fallen out with her, she always turns to him for
advice.

'All right. But as soon as you hear from Aiden, you will ring me, won't you? Doesn't matter what time it is, right? I just want to know he's okay.'

'Promise. Now stop worrying and don't breathe a word of this to Mum and Dad. There's no point in everyone losing sleep when it seems the crisis has already been averted.'

As I'm about to slide the phone back into my pocket, I remember to turn up the volume to full. The next call I receive could be important.

Glancing back at Nico, I see he's been watching discreetly and he walks towards me.

'You look like you've had a bit of a shock. Bad news?'

I nod, then shake my head as I think about it and end up shrugging my shoulders.

'I don't really know. It's Aiden, there's been a problem. Ah, I forgot, my sister said he'd posted some photos, I'd better check.'

As I yank the phone out again and open Facebook, Nico disappears. Aiden has posted four photos in total. The first one is clearly the mine as there's an old, weathered sign, although I can't quite make out the name. The next two are shots of the area which is just rough terrain. There's nothing much to see except a moonscape of tumps, some low-level scrub and, in the background, several huge mounds of earth. The last one is of Aiden, standing in between a youngish man and a woman with dark brown hair tied back in a ponytail, the one Hannah sent me. There's another man in the background who is carrying a pick over his shoulder. They're all laughing and pointing at a sign that says *Cook's Kitchen*. It's no more than a shack in the middle of nowhere.

'Here, it looks like you need this,' Nico says, holding out a glass half filled with red wine.

I take it from him and he cradles his own in his hands, not sure what to say.

'I don't know what's happening. I had some missed calls and two short texts. Aiden says he's safe but on the road, and he's with two other people. He was at this opal mine in the middle of nowhere. I doubt I'll hear anything further tonight. His battery was almost dead, but he told me that they've managed to get a lift to Adelaide. I think that's more than a day's drive, and I have no idea what the roads are like.'

Taking a big gulp of wine, I quickly lower my glass, wondering if Nico should be drinking. He senses my concern.

'As I said, I'm not an alcoholic, Fern. Everything in moderation,' he adds, tipping his glass in my direction.

I smile, half apologetically, not wanting Nico to feel I don't trust him. 'Well, I doubt whether Hannah or I will get much rest until we hear from him. It's all my fault as I shouldn't have missed his calls and now my sister is worried sick, too. It's so frustrating not knowing what's going on.'

'I have the perfect solution.' Those dark eyes seem somehow a little softer under the studio lighting. 'Here, hand me your glass. Now, let's get you all set up. If you aren't going to be able to sleep, nothing is more relaxing than painting, I promise you.'

Nico sounds enthused, but that little lift I had when I first entered the room has dissipated and he can see that.

'I only buy linen canvas and I've stapled one to a board and prepared it for you with two coats of Gesso. It primes the surface ready to take the paint. Once it's finished, I can make up the wooden framing and stretch it for you, if you prefer. Or you could simply store it rolled so it's easier to transport.'

Nico lifts the large board with ease, but the width is the span of both of his arms almost fully extended.

'It's enormous!' I gasp as he lifts it onto the bottom track, which is only a couple of inches off the floor. He shows me how to secure it with a special clip either side.

'I'm going to suggest you work with acrylic paint, simply because it dries much quicker.'

He stands back, joining me to gaze at my very own blank canvas.

'Where will I start? What do I paint?' I feel almost overcome with a mixture of fear and excitement.

'Well, begin by sketching out a few ideas.' He walks over to a large cupboard with floor-to-ceiling doors and effortlessly slides one across. Lifting out a flip chart on a stand, Nico carries it across. 'Of course, you might prefer to paint something from a photograph or try a still life. I could set you up a small table. The painting in your room is a view out over the forest from the courtyard.'

You can do this, Fern, that little voice inside my head reassures me.

'Great. It might take me a while before I can actually pick up a brush, though. I don't want to waste a perfectly good canvas.'

Nico throws back his head and laughs. 'You are surrounded by stacks of canvases that will probably never go anywhere. Never destined to grace a wall but only to lean against one. And then there are those which seem to soar from the very first brushstroke. Here, grab this.' He bends down to pick up a folded cloth draped over one of the rails. 'If you don't want me to see your work until it's finished, then simply cover it with this muslin. I won't cheat, I promise. Now, let me show you the one I cannot finish at the moment because my muse has temporarily deserted me, it seems.'

That instantly transports me back to the other night. Nico was muttering something about that, but I can't remember his exact words. Muse, yes, he mentioned that and – oh, he called me an angel.

When I turn, as he gently lifts the drape of fabric away from one of the canvases, my jaw drops. I thought the partially finished street scene that he said was his home town was amazing, but this is something very different. Elegant, painted with love in every single brushstroke. But only a third of the canvas is covered. The background has already been brought to life, but there is only the outline of a face and the form of a woman, without any real detail. It stares back at us hauntingly, the emptiness as distracting as a gaping hole in the canvas.

'It's the lake here, isn't it? But that isn't the lady your father painted, I mean it's not your mother and yet it's in his style.'

He shakes his head. 'No, it's not her. Although she was the one who inspired the setting for this piece. She often disappeared when my father's moods became unbearable and I'd always find her sitting down amongst the long grass, looking out across the water. She said it was her little slice of heaven.'

'It's beautiful, Nico. But why are you having problems finishing it? It couldn't be more perfect.'

He stares at the canvas for a few moments in total silence.

'This woman often comes to me in my dreams; the angles of her body as she sits, legs curled up, are in here,' he taps the side of his head, 'but when my brush touches the canvas, it simply doesn't happen. I need a model. Ceana sat for me once, but we both knew it wasn't going to be quite right. I sketched her in several poses but came away without inspiration. This is one painting where I have to take my time because it's my homage to the breathtaking beauty of a woman, both inside and out. So, it sits, patiently waiting for my muse to appear.'

I'm holding my breath, such is the intensity of the emotion attached to his words. And, somehow, I understand. Doesn't every artist have a muse?

'You and Ceana are very close. Have you known each other a long time?'

He busies himself for a moment, turning away to straighten one of the canvases.

'Quite a while,' he calls over his shoulder. 'I went through a rather depressed period a number of years back and she helped me through it. It feels like a lifetime ago, now.' He turns back to look at me. 'Because of that we will always be friends; that often happens between counsellor and patient. Now we share a common goal, borne out of our respective experiences in life. We'd like to expand the business here to include a well-being centre. A place of healing. Ceana's background as a practitioner of mindfulness and holistic healing gave us the initial idea. The dream is to enlist another professional to help take it forward.'

'That's a wonderful idea, Nico. There's something about this place that is so welcoming and comforting that it's easy to settle in. To take that a step further is a natural progression from what I can see. Even among the people here this week, everyone seems to have something sad in their lives they are holding on to, maybe without even realising it. I'm surprised you haven't already ventured there.'

Nico eases his shoulders downwards in a circular motion, stopping to run a hand across the back of his neck. His arms are powerful, and I find myself watching his every move. He's beautiful to look at, like a painting. A man so vibrant and with such big dreams.

'It's down to money. My work sells well, but if I don't invest the time, then I simply don't have pieces to send to the gallery. I'm running behind, but the summer months here are demanding. It's not simply my own income on the line, but everyone else who has bought into this dream.'

The distant sound of voices in the hallway filters through for a few seconds before fading into silence.

'My muse will return and the paint will flow,' he says, turning back to gaze at the portrait of his mystery lady. Nico throws the flimsy cover back over the painting. 'It has to, because until it's complete I can't rest. Anyway, this evening you are here to think about the beginning of your own creative journey.' He throws the words at me with bold enthusiasm.

'I think this might be a purple phase,' I reply, then begin laughing. 'I only have to turn my head and glance out of the window to find my inspiration.' The deep, purply-red of a climbing rose drips decadently over a stone wall, an entrancing waterfall of colour.

'Well, you had better take a snap quickly because the light is beginning to change. But you have a good eye, because I often think the garden is at its most vibrant just before dusk descends.'

I feel a sense of exhilaration as I head towards the window, until I pull out my phone to take the photo and I think of Aiden once more. *Please, God, keep him safe.*

12

FINDING MY COMFORT ZONE

It was a long night. Nico and I worked in silence, for the most part. I did discover that the village scene of his home town is a commissioned piece and his top priority at the moment.

I spent several hours going around in circles and every now and again Nico would appear at my shoulder, giving me little hints and tips. Sheet after sheet on the flip chart lay crumpled on the floor as I rejected every rough draft and I was becoming disheartened.

Eventually, Nico suggested I send him the photo I took earlier in the evening. When he returned from his workroom, he had with him a colour printout which leapt off the page.

'Here. Pin that alongside your canvas and pick up a brush. Too much thought is a bad thing. It can stifle the flow. Your first attempt may frustrate you, as much as it fills you with elation as you finally get to express what you see in here,' he'd tapped his head. 'Just do it so I can relax and get back to work.' His glance had been firm and I knew he was right.

And so I began.

When suddenly, at shortly after one a.m., my phone pinged, it shattered the companionable silence in which we were working.

Pit stop. Trouble now a hundred kilometres behind us. All good. Exhausted though. Adelaide here we come. Will ring you when we get there some time tomorrow. Love you, babe, and sorry if I panicked you.

If? He didn't only panic me, he panicked Hannah. I sigh as I call her, feeling angry with him.

'Aiden's safe. He'll reach Adelaide some time tomorrow but I'll have to work out the time difference to see roughly when that will be.'

'This isn't easy for you, is it? It's agony not knowing exactly where he is and what's happening. Aiden's supposed to be sightseeing, not getting himself into trouble. I feel for you, Fern.'

She sounds relieved on one hand, but cross on the other. As I am.

'Well, I think we can relax now and get some sleep.'

'What are you doing? Reading?'

'No, I'm painting and it's going to be hard to put the brush down.'

'Wow, Fern! That's really good to hear, although it is a little late. Sleep well. Hopefully tomorrow won't be quite so fraught.'

* * *

I'm late down to breakfast, but when I finally dropped into bed in the early hours, I was asleep within moments, so this morning I feel well rested.

'Hey, Fern,' Ceana appears behind me as I load up my breakfast plate with croissants and jam. 'Nico says you'll help out when I head home. Thank you. It means I can go off without having to worry about anything.'

I can see she's genuinely pleased.

'It's my pleasure. It's nice to feel useful.'

Bastien appears in the doorway, calling out Ceana's name to attract her attention.

'Oh dear. Looks like we might have a problem. I'd better see what's up.' She gives me a weak smile and dumps her plate on the side table.

Bastien is the only tutor I've not really had a chance to talk to, but that's mainly because he's rarely around. I hear him – well, I hear the sound of a hammer on metal as it reverberates around the little dip in which the barns are situated, but that's about it.

I head over to the far end of the table where Kellie and Patricia are deep in conversation.

'Morning, ladies. I hope you both slept well.'

'Fine,' Kellie looks up brightly.

'Very well indeed, thank you,' Patricia adds.

'I won't be gardening this morning, Fern,' Kellie continues. 'Patricia suggested I have a go at the pottery workshop. It sounds like fun. I've already committed to Taylor's woodworking class this afternoon. We're learning how to use a lathe and having a go at turning mushrooms. Sounds like a cookery class, doesn't it?' She's excited, happy and I can see a playful smile hovering around Patricia's lips.

'Great, it will be interesting for you to try something different this morning as well, Kellie,' I add, enthusiastically.

I'm sure Odile will be delighted to have another pupil and hopefully it will give Kellie a chance to chat with some of the others. Her guitar performance seems to have given her confidence a real boost. That hard-edged, aloof attitude she had when she first arrived is softening nicely.

'And we have a new recruit joining us on weeding detail,' Patricia says, looking across at me rather gingerly. She takes a small bite out of a piece of brioche and it's a moment or two before she continues. 'Stefan said he'd come along this morning to help out.'

I try hard to contain my smile. That's great news and he will be wonderful company for Patricia. My little team of newbies have found their feet and soon it will be time to say goodbye to one of them. I can't believe it's Thursday already. But I feel like I've been here for a long time, as if I was destined to be one of the team. How ironic that I seem to be having a better time on my little adventure than Aiden is on his. This is therapeutic, and I feel that I'm recharging my batteries.

* * *

'Sorry, I didn't mean to disturb you.'

Nico's eyes connect with mine and I'm worried I've interrupted his flow. I had no idea he was still in the studio.

He glances at his watch. 'I'm going to be late for lunch and I have some prep to do for my workshop. I didn't realise it was that time already.'

I move closer, studying the small area on the canvas that he's been labouring over all morning.

'How long will it take to finish it? The sense of depth really draws you in and I can imagine walking along that dusty pavement, past the flower shop and the park. Lucky person who gets to gaze at that every day.'

He raises an eyebrow, his face quite serious. 'A wealthy patron and a Marquesa, too. She's a wonderful benefactress I feel blessed to know. This commission will help fund the new venture here. But it won't cover all the costs and I need to sell a few smaller paintings this summer, too.'

That's quite a pressure Nico is under.

'Can't you simply sell one of your father's paintings?'

There are so many canvases here and I remember Ceana saying his father's work increased in value after his death.

Nico picks up a small piece of cotton cloth and begins to wipe his brush.

'The ones he didn't mutilate are unfinished. I have to rely upon my own resources now.' He glances at me, rather cagily.

'But the one in my room is truly amazing. That would surely fetch a lot of money, wouldn't it?'

Nico tips his head back, rotating it in a circle, and I hear his neck click from the tension of several hours of pure concentration.

'I keep that to remind me of many things, but mostly the pitfalls in life when someone loses their way.'

I can see his discomfort as he speaks. He's clearly on edge and I wonder if he regrets taking me into his confidence. Naturally, I'm touched by his trust, as it must be so hard to talk about it, still. Obviously, it's devastating when a father commits suicide, but it was hardly Nico's fault. Sadly, mental illness and addiction often go hand in hand and it's a battle many people lose. I return his gaze and it occurs to me that maybe he needed to hear himself say those words out loud.

'I'd be more focused if I could finish the portrait by the lake first. I need to capture the form that is woven into my dreams and yet continues to elude me. I can't help wondering if fate has sent me a new muse, Fern. You have that simple grace which I need so badly to create. Would you sit for me?'

I take a long, slow breath in. From his sketch, it's clearly a younger and very beautiful woman, but it's also a nude portrait. She sits partially hidden by the long grass of a lush meadow next to the rippling waters.

The outline of her seems to call out to me, as if appealing for help. Nico isn't doing this for money, but for his own sanity as this unknown female seems to haunt him. I wonder if she represents the one elusive element of his great passion in life. In the style of the old masters, this is about achieving his personal dream in a way that his father would have understood. It's as if he feels he has to prove to himself that he can do it, once and for all, before moving on.

'I need to think about that, Nico. Forgive me, but I can't say *yes* to you at the moment.'

He closes his eyes for a second or two, nodding to acknowledge my hesitation.

'Of course. Please, take your time. There is no pressure and I realise it's a big ask. But, as an artist, I know that with your help I could finally put an end to the dream that seems to fill my head each night. Like a restlessness that won't go away until the task is done. Right, that's it for this morning. This afternoon it's time to teach.'

For a moment I feared this conversation might have pulled him down, but his mood is light and it's good to see him looking so content after his morning's work.

I scan around, waiting for him as he pulls off his old, paint-splattered T-shirt and grabs the crisp cotton shirt hanging from the hook on the wall. I suppose in this context the body is just a form, whereas to me I instinctively want to cover up. It's not that I'm ashamed of my body, but maybe deep down I'm a bit of a prude.

How can I possibly pose nude in front of a man I hardly know, even in the name of art? A part of me wants to do it because I understand the enormity of the request and what it means to Nico. But no man, aside from Aiden, has ever seen me naked.

I study Nico's back, those firm muscles as he slips on his shirt, and he turns, catching my gaze. But I don't feel embarrassed as he gives me what I can only describe as a soulful look; one of acceptance. I envy his skill, as I would dearly love to capture that strength of body and character on canvas. I've never met anyone who is so *alive*, in all senses of the word. To see everything through the eyes of an artist is to see a very different world indeed.

'I'm hungry, how about you?' His tone is teasing. Is he flirting with me now? How would I know – it's been a long time since I've really studied another man other than my husband, looking for the telltale signs.

'Starving,' I admit as we make our way out into the sunshine.

Walking towards the day room, Ceana approaches, walking quickly.

'Nico, an animal got into the forge last night and did quite a bit of damage. Dee-Dee and I have been helping Bastien, but we both have sessions this afternoon. He needs to make the back wall good, but he can't finish it off by himself.'

Nico frowns and I immediately interrupt.

'I'll help out. I bet John would join in, too, if I asked him. That means two less in your class though, Nico.'

'If you're sure you don't mind, that's fine by me.'

Ceana looks pleased. 'That would be amazing, Fern. Thank you. If I can leave that in your hands then, I promised I'd help Margot in the kitchen.'

I watch as she studies Nico's face for a moment and then glances across at me, a fleeting look of curiosity in her countenance. I hope she doesn't feel I'm trying to usurp her position in any way, because I'm not.

To ensure there's no misunderstanding, I follow her into the kitchen and work alongside her as she helps prepare a huge bowl of salad. We exchange some small talk and when she asks how things are at home, I tell her briefly about Hannah phoning to say she's engaged. Then Aiden having to flee goodness knows what in the wilds of the Australian bush.

'It's hard when family are so far away, isn't it? I get the same pulls. My mother is eleven years sober, but it's still one day at a time. Childhood memories never seem to dull and every time the phone rings I fear what I'm going to hear. My father hasn't been well and he's the one who keeps her on track. But there's not much I can do, other than be a listening ear. At least I'll get to spend a little quality time with them. My cousin is getting married and it will be wonderful to have a good old Scottish celebration.'

The fact she has confided in me takes away my concerns. What I don't know is how she feels about the time Nico is spending with me, but I have nothing to hide.

'Of course,' she says, leaning in towards me, 'I'm not at all prepared. And a gardener's nails aren't really something anyone would put on show.' She laughs.

'Well, that's something I can remedy. I have a manicure kit and some gel polish. We could sort that tonight, if you have time.'

'Really? That would be amazing. Hair I can handle. One twist and it's up on my head, stick in a sparkly comb and I'm wedding ready. Thanks, Fern. Now all I have to sort is the right thing to wear.'

Margot looks across at us. 'Salad finished, ladies?'

We focus on the task in hand, giggling like two schoolgirls who have been caught out.

'We have hungry people waiting,' Margot points out, as if we didn't know.

13

HARD WORK IS GOOD FOR THE SOUL

'Hi, Bastien. John and I have come to help. Just tell us what you need doing and we'll have a go. And Margot made up this lunch box for you. She isn't too happy that you didn't stop to eat. I really couldn't understand the message she was giving me to pass on, but I'm sure you can guess that it sounded like a stern telling-off.'

He shrugs his shoulders, probably relieved that she didn't deliver it in person.

'Merci, Fern. She is a tough woman, but kind. Like a dog, yes?'

John and I start laughing as Bastien steps forward to take the box and smiles appreciatively. I think we get his meaning. A good heart and a dispenser of tough love.

'Is problem that is not easy to solve.' He walks us over to the gaping hole in the back wall of the half-open barn. The farm building is enormous, like a light aircraft hangar, and was probably used to store hay bales in the winter. The other side of the central dividing wall is the woodworking unit. 'The sheep pen backs onto here, this wall. Maybe fox, or deer, wandered into forge and sheep in the pen got spooked. They kicked down planks here and wall collapsed.'

Looking out through the hole, the sheep aren't in the lean-to pen now, so I guess he's moved them to safety.

I watch as John wanders along the back wall, tapping on it with his fist at regular intervals.

'The framing and braces are sound, but a few of the cross members have been knocked out,' he says, giving Bastien a nod. 'I see what you're doing, but in my opinion it's going to take several days to put that pile back together and some of it is beyond repair.'

We all stand gazing at the heap of splintered wood which has been neatly stacked up ready for reuse. Bastien has made a start, but it's a huge task. Suddenly, Taylor walks up behind us and lets out a loud, 'Jeez. What a mess!'

'I think the only answer is to replace the cross members and see if there are any other materials hanging around you can use. This stuff came down easily because it's not in great shape.'

Taylor seems to agree with John.

In the end, Bastien and Taylor go off in search of some sheets of corrugated metal, leaving me to be John's assistant. It doesn't take him long to get organised and we sift out the chunkier bits of wood into a separate pile.

'Right, Fern, I'll just grab that ladder and move it over here. Then, if you can get ready to pass me the hammer and some nails, we can make a start.'

He doesn't seem at all fazed by the old, albeit stout-looking, ladder and in no time at all he's pointing at pieces of wood for me to hand up to him.

'We'll soon have this frame sorted. If they can find eight sheets of something substantial, we can be done in time for dinner.'

'Not bad for a painter and decorator, John,' I reflect, looking up at him in awe.

He chuckles. 'I lost me wife a few years back. Grand old soul she was, but she liked to keep me busy. Said I couldn't get into any mischief if I always had a job to do. Renovated the whole house together, we did. Side by side. Then we built a summer house in the garden and a tree house for the grandkids. And, you know what, she was good with a drill that one. Not faint-hearted, for sure. Miss the old girl, every single day of my life. She made me the man I am.'

'What a team you must have been, John. True soulmates.'

He nods. 'She's still with me. I sense her around me all the time. Keepin' an eye, like.' He winks at me.

We plough on and when the guys return, they're carrying a large metal panel.

'Lots more where these came from,' Taylor confirms. 'Shouldn't take us long to carry them across.'

I help wherever I'm needed and there's lot of banter. John is such a happy man, always joking. I'm not sure Bastien's English is good enough to understand some of John's more obscure cockney terms, but he laughs in all the right places.

Suddenly my phone begins to ring and it's Aiden.

'Sorry, guys, back in a minute. Aiden, can you hear me?' I hurry outside and scramble up the grassy bank to get a better signal. There's lots of static. 'Aiden, can you hear me?'

'Fer—'

'Aiden.'

'Fern. That's better. Where are you?'

'I was in a big barn down in a dip, but I've just clambered up a steep slope to get a better signal. More to the point, where are *you*?'

Wherever he is, there's a lot of background noise but, thankfully, it sounds like general traffic.

'We've stopped for gas on the outskirts of Adelaide. It's just after midnight. Bit of an interesting journey, but everything is fine now.'

His voice is so clear it's hard to believe how many miles there are between us.

'What happened?'

He grunts. 'Turned out the guys I hooked up with didn't own the land but leased it last year. This was their second season, but they began mining before the new contract had been agreed and signed. A truck full of men turned up and shots were fired. It's pretty rough territory and isolated. One minute everyone was working and the next it was like a war had broken out. It wasn't what we signed up for, that's for sure.'

I close my eyes, grateful that at least he's in one piece.

'You said *we*?'

'Oh. Yes. I'm travelling with new friends called Eddie and Joss, now. Eddie's been backpacking for a couple of years, but Joss was the cook at the mine.'

Joss. She must be the woman in the photo.

'Well, I'm just glad to know you got away without getting hurt – I don't want you putting yourself in danger. At least you now have companions and there is safety in numbers. I don't like to think of you going it alone, Aiden, and this incident proves that you must be vigilant at all times. What are you planning next?'

Someone calls his name in the distance and he shouts out, 'Okay. I'm there.' Then he says, 'Look, babe, I've gotta go. We need to sort a place to stay tonight and it's late. I love you and I miss you. Even more so now that I've heard your voice. Take care and I'll be in touch when I know where I'm going from here. Bye.'

I quickly blurt out, 'Love you, too,' but I don't think he heard me. 'And I'm fine. Really. Thank you for asking,' I mutter as I make my way back down to the barn. 'France might not be as scary as an opal mine,' I continue through gritted teeth, 'but there are still surprises coming at me from every turn.'

* * *

'Are you too tired from your hard afternoon to take a stroll with me down to the lake?'

Patricia catches me gazing into thin air. My head is trying to deal with a wide range of thoughts that seem to be bombarding me from every angle.

'No, not at all. Just a bit achy in a few places. I'm discovering muscles I didn't know I had,' I admit.

Pushing back on the chair, I quickly scoop up my plate, mug and cutlery. Placing them on the trolley, I pick up my phone and follow Patricia outside.

'You were deep in thought and frowning. I wondered if you wanted to talk about whatever it is that's troubling you,' she enquires as we amble out across the courtyard.

'I'm just irked. You know when someone disappoints you, someone you trust? You start looking at them in a slightly different way. Then you begin to see things you maybe didn't notice before.' I pause, realising I sound like a moaner. 'Oh, ignore me, Patricia. I'm feeling cranky. I'm used to a routine and... well, I function best when I know that the people I love are doing okay. And now I have no idea what's going on with any of them from day to day. Just snippets when we briefly have contact. They seem fine at the moment and my brother, Owen, is safely back from his little excursion to Salisbury Plain, so it's all good; but there have been a few panicky moments already. It's hard when there's nothing I can do to jump in and help out.'

'Ah,' Patricia gives me a sympathetic smile. 'It's not easy for you. I'm sure they're all thinking about you, too, and how you're adjusting to life here.'

'Hmm. Some maybe, but not all of them. Oh, I don't mean that they don't care, but I'm the sensible one. I'm the worrier and it's not in my nature to be the person other people worry about. In fact, I don't think anyone has had to worry about me since I was a teenager – well, until now. And that's only because of the distance between us all. My parents were horrified when I broke the news to them that Aiden and I intended to get married.' I begin to laugh, softly. 'And I did say it just like that. Bold and to the point. He hadn't even asked me formally at that stage, but we both knew that was the first thing we would do once we had our degrees.

'Of course, everyone assumed we'd break up while we were away at uni, but we survived and even managed to get a small nest egg put away. But it was tough studying and working evenings and weekends. That's the reason we never got engaged, as it was a luxury we couldn't afford. I still only have just my wedding band.'

Her eyes light up. 'I think that's a lifetime of worry right there.'

'I know. But I'm sensible, and I always do the right thing. That was the right thing, even way back then and I have no regrets at all, but maybe I've become a little too complacent as the years have passed. I loved my life the way it was, but things change and there's no point in pretending that isn't the case. The problem is that now I'm beginning to feel a little unsettled. My husband is off doing things that are out of character and that's worrying.'

We saunter past the two barns and begin to climb the grassy mound. I offer Patricia my arm when she begins to struggle a little.

'It's a bit slippery. Grab hold.'

'Thank you, my dear.'

At one end of the lake, there's an intricately carved, albeit rather rickety, wooden bench beneath an old willow tree. We make our way over to it and once we're seated Patricia turns to look at me, pointedly.

'Are you saying you think he wasn't content with your old life, and that's becoming more apparent now that you are apart?'

'He hasn't said anything quite that blunt, but he's different in some way. For example, Aiden rang and he didn't ask me how I was and it didn't occur to him I might have my own issues. I know he's not having an easy time right now, but it made me feel unimportant. Taken for granted, if you like. I assumed we'd share every little detail of our respective journeys, but our calls are always cut short and he never emails, only sends one-liner texts.'

'From what you've told me about him, it sounds like perhaps he's floundering a little. I think most people reach an age where they stop and look back, as well as forwards, for the first time. In the spring of your life, it's all about tomorrow. In the summer phase, it's often about being so caught up with family demands and working, there's hardly time to take stock. But there comes a point when suddenly there's another crossroad and big changes that affect the rest of your life. It's a period of adjustment and people cope in different ways.'

I know what Patricia is saying, that this is about Aiden finding himself and to do that requires a lot of introspective thought, with no outside pressures. It's not about being one half of a couple – well, until he returns.

'What if I discover that there's a different *me* buried deep down inside, too? Some unknown me who isn't simply a wife, a daughter, a sister or a friend?'

Patricia stares at me for a moment and I wish I hadn't blurted that out, because her look is one of real concern.

'People can come to regret the mistakes they don't make, as much as they regret the mistakes they do make.'

I'm stunned. That wasn't at all what I was expecting her to say. This rather refined, very gentile lady is such a surprise in so many ways. I can't help feeling that Patricia's life is complicated, too.

'*If only* is such an emotive phrase, isn't it? I've spent my entire adult life so far, being sensible and cherishing every single moment spent with the ones I love. They are my reason for being and if they're happy, I'm happy,' I confess.

'It sounds perfect. But life is rarely that, I've discovered. And somewhere within that is you – never forget that *you* are equally as deserving of "me" time, as anyone else.' Her face reflects a sorrow that can only come from within. I have no idea what troubles Patricia has had in the past, but I can see something is weighing heavily upon her. She's waiting for me to continue, unable or unwilling to share her private thoughts. I wonder if I open up to her, whether she'll change her mind about that.

'I had an older sister, Rachel. She died in a tragic accident in 2010. A loss of that magnitude changes how you look at everything. We rarely talk about her because my parents have never let go of their grief. I felt I had to step up and take over her role while missing her so much, because she wasn't just my sister, she was my best friend. A truly beautiful soul.'

'I'm so sorry for your loss, Fern, that can't be easy even now.' The empathy is real and I give Patricia a tearful smile.

'I wonder now what would happen if I stepped outside the lines I've drawn for myself, for a while. Would I simply be content to cross back over again and lead a life that has always given me everything I wanted? Or would I, like so many other people out there, become dissatisfied and ruin what I have? Rachel would be disappointed in me if I did that.'

Patricia reaches out to place her hand on my arm, gently giving it a squeeze. 'I think you are a sensible enough woman to make the right decision for the right reasons, Fern. Wherever that leads you. Human beings aren't perfect and we all make mistakes. But the human condition includes forgiveness, as well as reminding us of our mortality.'

I feel my eyes beginning to well up with tears as she stands, and I ease myself upright to take her arm. Tears for Rachel and tears for Aiden.

Suddenly Patricia looks very tired and I realise this conversation is done.

'Time to stroll back. I'm painting this evening.' My voice isn't quite as bright as I'd like it to be, but Patricia gives me an encouraging smile.

'Ceana was telling me, in confidence, about the plans they have for expanding the facilities here. I think it's a wonderful idea, don't you?'

I'm not surprised Ceana has taken Patricia into her confidence about the proposed changes if she was looking for an unbiased opinion. Judging by the way Patricia is looking at me, Ceana also told her that I'm aware of what's going on.

'I think that a lot of people would benefit if they can pull it off. What I like about this place is that it isn't solely about profit. Nico doesn't just care about the visitors but he cares about the people who work with him, too. It's like an extended family. In this day and age, that's refreshing.'

As I help Patricia down the grassy slope, her voice is full of admiration. 'I thought so, too, Fern. It restores one's faith in mankind. Despite what we read in the papers and see on the news, there is a lot of kindness in this world.'

14

EMOTIONS RUN HIGH

With Ceana heading off to Scotland feeling – as she declared – like a new sparkly version of herself, it marks the start of a string of good-byes today.

After a group breakfast, with everyone appearing more or less on time for a change, this morning's gardening session was spent harvesting fruit. It was a team effort as everyone had been enlisted.

Despite a tinge of sadness in the air, there was a lot of chatter and laughter, too – the culmination of a pleasant stay and the creation of some great memories. Stefan, I noticed, wouldn't let Patricia wander far from his side. He hooked the branches, pulling them down within her grasp so she could pluck off the firm little plums to place in their wicker basket.

Margot, too, sat with us for lunch and we lingered over it for a couple of hours. Everyone seemed happy to join in, even Bastien was a little less reserved. And, to our great surprise, after a little prompting from Nico, he sang a song. It was in French, of course, but his deep baritone voice was a joy to hear.

Inevitably, the final parting of ways was tearful for some. Hearing Kellie promise Patricia she'd keep in touch as she tried to pin a smile on her face was very emotional. I could see they both had tears in their eyes. Patricia is one of a kind, a gentle spirit with a good soul. Whether Kellie will bond with any of the new arrivals on Monday is a real concern for me. I fear that it will push her closer to Taylor, rather than encouraging her to make an effort to make new friends. Especially if there's no one she feels comfortable being around.

As Patricia released her arms from around me, she whispered, 'Go with your heart, Fern. Paths cross for a reason. Like spotting a shooting star, sometimes you find yourself in the right place at the right time and you get to experience that moment of pure joy. This has been my moment, thanks to you, Kellie and Stefan.'

* * *

Turning the handle and entering the studio, Nico turns his head towards me, the brush in his hand poised mere inches from the canvas in front of him. 'I thought you'd turned in for the night. Can't sleep?'

I nod. 'My mind won't switch off. Bit of an emotional day. I don't want to stop you, though, so say if you'd rather be alone.'

'What I'd love is a cup of coffee to keep me going,' he replies, his eyes pleading as he raises his eyebrows. 'There's a kettle through there in the workroom. Everything you need is on the shelf.'

As I step through, it's more like a big cupboard and it has no windows, just one of those annoyingly bright overhead lights. I switch on the kettle and grab two mugs.

'Is Kellie okay?' Nico calls out.

'She was a little upset, but she spent the evening with Taylor again.'

As I carry the drinks through, Nico turns to look directly at me.

'You're worried about them?'

'She's eighteen, Nico. He's old enough to have seen a fair bit of the world already. What if they fall into something and it all goes wrong?'

Nico grabs a cloth to wipe off his brush. 'Come, let's take these outside.'

He accepts the mug and concertinas the glass doors back with ease.

Outside, it's a balmy night and the silence is only broken by the chirping of the cicadas, which never ceases, and a group of bats swooping back and forth, performing one of their elaborate dances in the dark.

Rising up in the distance, blending into the darkening sky as if it's the work of an artist's palette, are the mountains which many refer to as Europe's Grand Canyon. In daylight hours, it's the bordering forest slopes which stand out. At this time of the night, the eye is taken up towards the lightest part of the sky, and it's the silhouette on the distant horizon that becomes the focus of attention.

This is a far cry from the view I'm used to seeing and I still find it a little incongruous that this is my temporary home. Even though, for some reason, Provence has a comforting sense of familiarity to it for me. Is it possible to feel you belong somewhere simply because you've been uprooted and are desperate to make the best of an uneasy situation?

Nico indicates for me to take a seat at the little bistro table. The air carries with it a blend of floral notes, but somewhere close by there is a profusion of jasmine, which is quite dominant tonight. It eclipses the fragrant perfume of the wonderful roses even.

It's very private here, mainly because of the height of the shrubs and the wildness of the garden within the three stone walls. A tranquil place nestled within a forest, protected by the mountain ranges.

'This is a beautiful little oasis, Nico. I bet it drives Ceana mad, plants tumbling over each other in unorchestrated chaos. But it would be such a shame to tame it.'

He smiles, a dimple in his cheek turning it into a rueful look. 'At the end of the summer, she'll appear with shears and I have to look the other way. The plants repay her kindness and hard work in the spring.'

I tilt my head, looking up at the night sky once more and as my eyes adjust I begin to notice the stars. I can feel Nico watching me.

'Kellie is a troubled young woman, I can see that, but she has a mind of her own. It's a strong and determined one. And I know Taylor well enough to vouch for the fact that he would never take advantage for the sake of it. He's had his heart broken in the past, so you can relax. If anything develops between them, then it will be because they have feelings for each other. That's not wrong, is it?'

I stop looking up and turn to face Nico. He stares back at me anxiously, as if it's important that I agree with him on this.

'No. But she's very young and fragile.'

'No more fragile than Taylor, Fern. He bears the scars of his biggest regret as if it's his penance. But he didn't commit a crime. Is your concern stemming from something closer to home? Kellie is a similar age to your sister, I believe?'

'Yes. But they are two very different personalities and it's not about that. As for Taylor, how sad that the jagged line on his cheek is a constant reminder of a bigger hurt than just the physical pain.'

'That's life, Fern, you don't get to choose the hand you are dealt. And you know full well that you cannot shield the ones you love from life's troubles, or make their decisions for them.' His voice takes on a factual tone, almost totally devoid of emotion now.

'Sometimes a word of caution is prudent,' I reply.

'I disagree. The time to solve a problem is when it presents itself, and then take action based on the information you have. You can't live your life worrying about things that might not happen. Or inflict that upon other people.'

He can be as infuriating as he can be charming, at times.

'I think maybe my reactions are born out of experience, Nico.'

He laughs, but it's perfunctory. 'With age comes wisdom, Fern?'

I feel that he's being purposely challenging, almost goading me.

'Knowing people will get hurt because they are making bad decisions is soul-destroying to watch, whether you are close to them, or not.'

'Are you trying to save the world, or save yourself?'

I glare at him angrily and he throws his hands up, palms facing me.

'Sorry, I take that back. I'm in an argumentative mood tonight for some reason and I apologise. You are the very last person I want to alienate as I know your intentions are nothing but good. I'm taking my frustrations out on you and that's unfair of me. I'll have a general conversation with Taylor when the moment presents itself and see if he's comfortable and in control of the situation.'

'Thank you. And I owe you an apology, too, Nico. It's not my place to express concerns and I didn't mean to imply I was doubting your judgement in any way.'

We glance at each other sheepishly, before sipping our coffees. Nico's eyes seem fixated.

'Don't move. Not one muscle.'

He dashes off, back into the studio, but I'm a little freaked. If he's seen a giant spider or something, I hope he would have warned me so I could run, too. Instead he returns with a sketch pad and pencil.

'Good, continue drinking, but keep the mug up in the air if you don't mind.'

I flash him a look of mild annoyance but do as he bids.

'So, any news from home today?' he asks.

His pencil skims over the page with ease as I focus on maintaining the pose, conscious of the experienced models Nico will have worked with in the past.

'All's well. You said there were three visitors here this weekend,' I reply, changing the subject promptly. 'John, of course, and Ceana mentioned a lady named Ellie, who is stopping off to break her journey and explore the area. Who's the third person?'

'Mmm,' he nods, distractedly, so I remain silent. And still.

After a minute or two, he replies.

'An interviewee coming to take a look at the set-up here. It's a pity Ceana isn't around as he's a friend of one of her former work colleagues and comes highly recommended. I'll spend some time with him, but he's only staying one night and will fly back to the UK on Sunday morning.'

'You're pushing ahead then?'

'Creaking ahead. I doubt I can offer him a position until the New Year. I've been turning down bookings for October so that we can look at repurposing the cottage. The ground floor will be turned into the holistic centre with individual treatment rooms. The craft studio will be fitted out with mats and wall mirrors. We intend to offer meditation classes, as well as installing a few pieces of standard exercise equipment at one end – two treadmills, maybe two static bikes, a CrossFit machine and a multigym with weights.' He smiles to himself, flicking shut the sketch pad and placing it on the table. 'Thank you. Perfect pose and the perfect light to catch those shadows. I couldn't resist.'

His bad mood has evaporated as suddenly as it began and I feel we've cleared the air between us.

'Time to get back to work,' Nico says, tiredness giving his voice an edge.

Studying him for a moment, he stares out blankly at the garden. I feel a sadness descending over me as I watch him summoning the effort to ease himself up off the chair. He's moody because he's exhausted; a man so passionate about his beliefs and his goals that he doesn't listen to what his body is telling him.

'Nico, when was the last time you ate? You weren't at dinner tonight.'

He blinks, a small frown wrinkling his brow and accentuating those deeper lines. 'Earlier.'

'Just as I thought, you don't know, do you? I'm going to pop over to the kitchen to make you a sandwich. If you want to keep going you have to take care of the basics, or your body will rebel.'

The little smile that creeps over his face is annoyingly smug.

'It's a long time since anyone fussed over me, Fern. Be on your guard because I could get used to it.'

15

A MOMENT TO REFLECT

Margot isn't here at weekends, so mealtimes aren't set and food is self-service. When I wander into the kitchen to grab a yoghurt and some fruit for breakfast, Dee-Dee is there prepping veggies for tonight's dinner.

'Ah, just the person,' she says, looking up. 'Anton, our gardening assistant, is back and already hard at work. His wife is much better, he informed me, and judging by the fact that he's turned up at the weekend means he's in need of a little quiet time.' She raises one eyebrow as she peers across at me.

'Oh, right. Yes. Of course, it's his domain. I think I've pulled enough weeds for one week, anyway. So that means a change of itinerary for me next week, then.'

'I'd love some help if Nico can spare you. We have a bumper crop of visitors due on Monday. Quilting and weaving is a popular option, but that means keeping a close eye and it's a stretch if there are visitors in the craft room, too.'

I look at her aghast. 'Um, I will warn you that I'm not very hands-on in that department. I've never made a bracelet or decorated a wooden box, and I wouldn't know where to start.'

'Oh, bless you! There's no right or wrong way when it comes to crafting.' She laughs at my reaction. 'I have a full range of PowerPoint presentations on my laptop. There's a list of ten different activities, from making greeting cards to scrapbooking, and everything in between. You only need to talk to the visitors and find out what they'd like to do for each session. It's all set up, you just press a button and sit with them in case there's a problem and it stops working. I can show you where the different activity packs are kept and once the tutorial is over, you hand out the relevant one. Sometimes people will ask for additional items, so just make sure you're on hand. It's nice to join in, if you can, and have a go yourself.'

'Oh, right. Well, that seems simple enough.'

'I'll pop in as often as I can, but I don't think you'll have any problems at all. It's been difficult not having a craft tutor, but I don't think Nico has had time to think about finding someone. So if you're happy, I'll talk to Nico. Thanks, Fern.'

That means Dee-Dee doesn't know about Nico's future plans for the craft room, then. I hadn't realised it wasn't general knowledge amongst the group and I'm glad I didn't put my foot in it by saying something.

'Great. Have you seen him around this morning?' I finish my yoghurt and pop the spoon into the dishwasher.

'Yes. He's gone to the airport to pick someone up. I don't think he's going to be free today as he'll be showing his guest around when they return. What are you planning to do?'

I lean back against the counter as I pick up one of the plums, choosing one that is the least green. 'Well, I felt obliged to do some weeding, but now I can paint instead, which suits me just fine. I wouldn't admit that within earshot of Ceana, of course, because she's been wonderful. But I'm rather glad Anton is back.'

'Ha! Ha! I did wonder. But give you your due, lady, you've done well. It feels like you've always been here, Fern. Volunteers come and go, but you're a real team player and you fitted in from day one. And Nico appreciates that you've been able to take some of the pressure off Ceana. You know, keeping a general eye out.'

I'm flattered and it means a lot to hear Dee-Dee say that. She's a straight-talking woman and I like that about her.

'There's always something happening here, and you never know from one minute to the next what you'll get pulled into,' I reflect, biting into the plum with some difficulty, wondering why they are so hard.

'Yes. Like weeding and picking not-quite-ripened plums, ready for Margot's chutney-making class on Tuesday.'

It's too late and my face puckers up as the tartness hits my taste buds, making me shudder. I walk over to the bin and toss it in, half tempted to spit out the piece in my mouth. Dee-Dee is trying her best not to laugh.

'Hmm. I did wonder why they were so hard. You can tell I'm no gardener, although it was a lovely way to end the week. Guess I'll head off and get some paint on that canvas then, unless you want some help with that?'

'No, it's fine. Odile has written instructions about how to reheat the rabbit pies Margot left prepared for tonight's dinner and I'm almost done here. Enjoy having some quiet time while you can. You've earned it.'

'Thanks, Dee-Dee, see you later.'

Walking back to the château, I wave to Kellie and Taylor, who are wheeling bicycles. They wave back and I watch as they mount up and cycle out of the courtyard. Guess it really is going to be a quiet day as everyone seems to have disappeared.

As I head inside, a jangling sound comes from my pocket. It's a Skype call and I yank out my phone, eager to see who it is.

'Aiden, what a surprise. I thought it was going to be Mum.'

'We're in a motel with good Wi-Fi, plenty of hot water and reasonably comfortable beds. It's basic but feels like luxury after the last week. What are you doing?'

'Just heading into the château. Take a look.' I reverse my phone and pan around slowly.

'Hey, that's impressive. I didn't realise it was such a big place.'

'I'm heading into Nico's private studio to do some painting. Do you have a few minutes?'

'I'm all yours. The only thing on the agenda is going in search of a big steak in a little while. Then a few beers.'

'Great, you can get a quick glimpse at where I'm spending a lot of my free time. You look well, I'm just relieved you don't have sunburn after working outside.'

I head down the hallway and try to keep panning around so Aiden can get a feel for the beauty of this place.

'The temperature was quite comfortable, around nineteen degrees, and the rainfall is negligible in Coober Pedy. They only get about six inches a year, but the ground is so dry that when it does rain, it's a big problem as it can turn a track to mud. In January and February it's unbearably hot and the temperature soars unbelievably, apparently. No one could work in it. It's in the middle of nowhere, a legend of the outback, and the nearest town is Roxby Downs, over two hundred and seventy kilometres away.'

'That sounds like a real adventure, Aiden. Any regrets?'

I swing open the door and head inside the studio.

'Not really. It was a once-in-a-lifetime experience, but in a way I'm relieved to be moving on. I was talked into it but had no idea how remote it was. No need to worry, it's out of my system now.'

I laugh at him and wish I could reach out and touch that face I know so well. Just to have contact again, skin on skin. He needs to know that I want him to enjoy this time, even though it's a constant worry.

'I'm relieved to hear it. You're supposed to be having fun, which is something Hannah said to me, but you really scared her, too.'

He at least has the grace to look a little embarrassed by his poor decision-making. 'I think most men have a secret desire to jump into something exciting and be Indiana Jones for a while. Lesson well and truly learnt. The plan is to do a bit of sightseeing here, while trying to sort out some sort of voluntary work for a while. Not even sure where, but I'm researching that at the moment.'

There's a loud tapping sound. It's quite insistent.

'Hang on a second, Fern.'

The angle of his laptop doesn't allow me to see the door, but after he disappears from view, I hear low voices speaking in the background. Seconds later he returns, looking excited.

'Joss is speaking to one of the aid agencies at the moment and she wants me to sit in on the call. So sorry, babe, but this could be the next leg of the journey. Great studio. Next time maybe you can show me what you're painting. Love you. Miss you and take care.'

Bing. The call ends.

'Miss you, too,' I croak and my words echo around the silent room.

I feel alone and deflated. I so wanted to share this with him, right now.

Heaving a big sigh, I tap contacts and click on Georgia's name. It rings a few times and then the screen opens up.

'Hi, Fern! How are you, my lovely friend? Oh, how I miss your company. Steve has been unbearable this week. Seriously, it's like I have three big kids and not just the two.'

Just hearing her moaning about Steve instantly cheers me up.

'I'm good, thank you, and it's so wonderful to hear your voice, too. Although, I will admit I've settled in really well here.'

'Is that a huge painting behind you I can see?'

I spin around, glancing at the now finished village scene. 'Yes, it's a commissioned piece which the artist who owns this retreat has just finished. It's an oil painting so it will take a while to dry.'

'It's very beautiful, Fern. I didn't realise you were going to be spending time with a famous artist!' she exclaims, her eyes lighting up. 'Is he there now?'

'No. I'm here alone. It's very low-key at the weekends as the courses only run Monday to Friday. Nico is collecting someone from the airport and giving them the tour of the facilities today.'

'Nico. Ooh, tell me more.'

'I'll show you instead.'

Her face looms closer to the screen as she tries to get a better look behind me. I rotate the phone and give it a panoramic sweep around.

'That's incredible. And he allows you to wander around when he's not there?'

'Better than that. Take a look at this.' Spinning around, I crouch down a little and, holding the phone at arm's-length so that I'm in view, stand next to my own little project. 'This is my very first canvas. There isn't much to see at the moment as I spent ages sketching before I felt confident enough to make a start. But it's so exciting and I'm loving it.'

In fairness, it probably only looks like a biggish splodge in the middle of a stark white sheet, but every brushstroke is a learning curve and I seem to be learning fast.

'It's very purple,' Georgia admits, raising her eyebrows, and I can't help being a little disappointed by her reaction.

'Well, it's early days. It's taken about seven hours so far. That will give you some idea of how long it takes. Nico has been working on this street scene from his village for months. His patron is a Marquesa.'

'Oh, he's Spanish, then?'

'Yes. He's from Andalucia.'

'And you're spending quite a bit of time with him as his... student?' She cocks an eyebrow.

'Officially, I'm a volunteer, so every morning I help out. My first week was spent mainly in the garden supervising a small team. But I also got involved in helping with a repair to one of the barns. Next week, I'll probably be assisting in the craft room. In the afternoons, I can attend any of the classes that I choose, so I only get to paint in here at the end of the working day, really.'

I can see from her face she's rather surprised.

'And how's Aiden?' she asks, rather pointedly.

'He's been opal mining of all things! You obviously haven't seen my mum, then. I'm sure she would have told you all about it, although Hannah didn't tell her until after we were sure Aiden was safe. They ended up having to leave at short notice due to a dispute over the lease and it got a bit nasty. He's in Adelaide now, figuring out his next move.'

Her face has dropped. 'For goodness' sake, you two. This was supposed to be a fun-filled year, not a bloomin' game changer. Will I even recognise my old neighbours when they get back home?'

'Less of the *old*.'

'I was speaking figuratively. Was this the intention all along? Because it looks a bit like you guys are going your separate ways. It's good to see you looking so perky but, hmm, that's quite an experience you're having there, too. I'm just rather surprised by it all, to be frank with you.'

Now I wish I'd ignored my fleeting moment of homesickness.

'Aiden's always yearned for a little adventure. Me, I've always yearned to sit and draw, although it turns out I'm happier with a brush in my hand. And, Georgia, it's a truly wonderful feeling. Like nothing else I've ever done before, you know, just for me. I've found my guilty pleasure at long last.'

I almost find myself whispering the words and her eyes open wide in surprise.

'As long as it's the painting that's your guilty pleasure,' she replies, as I give her a wry look, 'then I suppose I'll get used to this new artsy side of you. Who would have guessed it?'

'Look at the garden, Georgia, it's the inspiration for my first canvas.'

'Gosh, that's beyond beautiful, Fern. You know, you look so relaxed and happy. I can't believe you aren't stressing over Aiden and the family like you usually do. I haven't seen any comings and goings at your place, yet. Are they all doing well?'

'It would seem so. I've had a few phone calls and texts and constant emails. Mum and Dad are changing the layout of their garden, apparently, so I suspect they've only been able to pop in briefly. You'll know when they arrive to do a big clean, because you'll think they're taking up residence. You know what my mum's like.'

'I do. If only she'd pop in here first, I'm sure she'd get this place sorted in no time,' Georgia replies, wistfully. Cleaning isn't her thing.

'Oh, and Hannah says she's engaged. I'm not even sure Aiden knows yet as we've had such little time to talk. Him going to the outback first was a bit of a mistake. At some point, though, we will catch up properly with all the news, I suppose. Owen is back from a training exercise on Salisbury Plain. He seems to be enjoying it, although he's lost some weight.' It ends up sounding a bit wistful, even to my ears. I can't hide the fact that a little piece of my heart is with each of them, always.

'Well, just a couple of weeks ago you were the average family. Now look at you all! I miss not being able to pop into yours and have a good old moaning session. I'm having to actually talk to Steve now, out of sheer desperation. I'm even thinking about getting a part-time job. See what you two have started? Where will it all end, I ask myself?'

As we say our goodbyes, Georgia is laughing and I join in, but it's half-hearted. I'm well aware that her words merely reflect that niggling little concern I'm trying so desperately to push to the back of my own mind. Where *will* it all end?

16

A DEEPER CONNECTION

Nico and his guest are nowhere to be seen when I head into the day room to grab some lunch. I wonder if he's taken him into town so they can talk and eat in peace. Odile, aided by Bastien, is putting out platters with an assortment of cheese and fruits. There are chunks of baguette and baskets of savoury biscuits, perfect for scooping up the freshly made tapenade – an olive dip with capers, anchovies and garlic. Alongside them is a tray of fougasses – baked flat breads covered with *fromage de chèvre* – with thinly sliced courgettes. What I love about the meals here is that the ingredients are so fresh, the flavours singing the delights of Provence. Even the herbs are packed full of flavour and something simple, like a little scattering of freshly picked and chopped tarragon, can elevate a dish to another level.

Kellie appears and saunters over next to me to grab a plate.

'Did you enjoy your cycle ride?' I ask casually, wondering where Taylor has gone.

'Yes. It was very pleasant. Are you sitting outside to eat?'

There's something in her tone that makes me think it's a request, rather than a question.

'Yes. I thought I'd wrap this in cling film and wander down to the lake to enjoy it. I'd love some company.'

She looks pleased. 'Okay. That would be great.'

Minutes later we begin our stroll and for once I don't really have to focus on keeping the conversation flowing. Kellie seems happy to chat away about how pleased she is to be staying on and that her mother is on her side. I wait until she's finished to ask a question.

'Your father isn't happy that you're here?'

Kellie shakes her head. 'I'm always in the middle of them. Out of sheer principle, they never agree on anything. Mum usually takes my side, so Dad does the opposite. He says if Mum hadn't cosseted me —' She pauses, mid-sentence, and a look of anxiety passes over her face. 'Well, he thinks my problems are because I'm spoilt,' she finishes. But I can tell that wasn't what she was going to say in the first place because her unease is very evident.

When we reach the bench, we unwrap our lunch plates and I pass her a napkin. She asks how the painting is going. I tell Kellie how nervous I was the first time my brush touched the canvas and how vulnerable it made me feel.

'It was both thrilling and scary, creating something visual and having to accept that not everyone is going to like what you do. Beauty is in the eye of the beholder, as they say.'

'I should imagine it's a bit like being told you have an ugly baby,' Kellie replies, giving me a sympathetic smile.

'I Skyped my neighbour this morning and showed it to her. Of course, I've only just made a start on it, but she didn't look at all impressed.'

'It's hard to be brave when that's not how you feel inside,' she admits.

I nod.

We eat in silence for a while, but I notice that Kellie is only toying with her food. She keeps playing with her bracelets, and they softly jangle as she eases them back and forth.

'I like Taylor,' she says, quietly.

'I know.'

'He likes me, too. But he said he's not ready to get close to someone.'

A part of me is relieved, although I can see she is upset about it.

'Do you know the story behind his scar?' she asks.

I shake my head.

'It was a few years ago. He and his girlfriend were in the back seat of a car which ended up rolling over into a ditch at speed. Taylor's girlfriend drowned and he was badly injured. He told me that he feels guilty because she didn't deserve to be the one who died. How awful is that, Fern?'

I'd sensed whatever he'd been through had been life-changing, but that's so terribly, terribly sad to hear. No one should have to spend their life thinking they shouldn't have been the one to survive in a situation like that.

'It's good to be honest with each other, but it's heart-breaking to hear that, Kellie.'

'He understands what it's like to feel desperate at times and I think that's why we hit it off from the start. When you're broken inside, it takes a long time to heal and only another sufferer can fully understand that pain.'

I'm unable to eat, a growing sense of anger banishing my appetite as I consider how unfair life can be. Placing my plate on the bench next to me, I throw some of the bread onto the grass. A little group of birds has been watching us, flitting in and out of the branches above our heads.

The only other sounds are the leaves rustling in the warm breeze when it gusts and a cacophony of birdsong, with the usual accompaniment of chirping cicadas. Often, there's the sound of wood being chopped, or metal being hammered at the very least, so this relative peace is bliss. We sit quietly for quite a while, just watching the little ripples on the surface of the lake. There's an odd *gloop* sound every now and again as a fish suddenly jumps to catch one of the bugs sitting on the surface.

'I wear my bangles to disguise this,' Kellie states, suddenly.

Holding out her right arm, she tugs the bangles upwards, exposing her wrist. The cut is straight. It was clearly deep.

Instinctively, I want to throw my arms around Kellie and hug away her pain. With no siblings, she has only her parents and, from what she's said, they don't seem to understand her. But she isn't looking for a reaction, she's staring into space quite blankly. I sense that what Kellie really needs isn't sympathy but someone to listen. Someone not to judge, or question.

'School was horrible. Every single day of it. I didn't fit in. Always on the edge of things, always different. Then the bullying started. I eventually told Mum and she did take me seriously, but I didn't want her to do anything about it. I simply had to share it, to hear someone say it wasn't right. I made her believe I was handling it and that the head of year knew.'

A magpie squawking in the tree high above us suddenly decides to swoop at the bread. The temptation is strong and he lands, his head tilted as his beady eyes scan around for danger. He pecks at the largest piece of bread and is soon joined by a partner. They are the tree bullies, scaring away the little grey wagtails who usually flit in and out of the olive trees.

'One for sorrow, two for joy,' Kellie mutters.

'I'm surprised you know that old saying,' I reply.

'My nan says it all the time. I miss her. That's Mum's mum, of course. My other grandma is just like my dad.'

I shift position reluctantly as I don't want to break her train of thought, but my left leg is going to sleep. She turns to look at me face on for the first time since we sat down, then she returns her gaze to the magpies. The look is one that sends a shudder through me. Isolation. Despair.

'When it escalated and I couldn't hide the bruises, Dad got involved. He went to the school and let rip. Sounds positive, doesn't it? But at home he made it clear he thought it was all my own fault that I wanted to be different, because I was trying to prove something. Mum and Dad rowed about that, of course, and it became all about them and not the bullies. Then, one day, I'd had enough. I thought I had the perfect solution and I welcomed it. But I even managed to mess that up. I chose a day when Mum happened to pop home mid-morning because she'd forgotten some important papers. She's a solicitor. I don't think she'll ever forgive me. She spends her days dealing with broken people and realising she had a broken daughter made her feel like a failure as a mother. What a stupid, stupid mess. But Taylor knows, and I wanted you to know. It matters to me what you think.'

I feel a little overwhelmed to be taken into her confidence, but the last thing Kellie needs now is banal sympathy.

'Your strength is amazing, Kellie. You are one strong woman who has been through hell. If you can survive that, you can survive anything. But I'm guessing the problem is where do you go from here?'

Her head tips forward and she stares at her feet, shuffling them back and forth for a few seconds.

'You got it. I can't stay here forever. It's tempting though.'

For the first time, her voice sounds brighter and a huge sense of relief washes over me. I said the right thing. At the right time. I don't care whether it's luck, or judgement; I just care to see that smile on her face and hear the lift in her voice.

'They made me see a lot of counsellors and doctors, but I'm not depressed, Fern. I'm embarrassed now by what I did, but I was at my lowest point. This break was to prove to myself I could mingle with strangers and not be regarded as odd. You and Patricia reached out to me, then Taylor. And Nico has been brilliant, too. I've only spoken to him a couple of times, but when I told him I wanted to stay on, he said he'd talk to my parents. I've spent my whole life being constantly judged by my parents for not quite fitting in, but here I feel a sense of freedom and it's liberating. Aside from my nan, who thinks I can't do anything wrong. Now, she does spoil me.'

'So, your future is a blank page. Exciting.' My enthusiasm is real, because I believe there is no going back for her and the danger has passed. But the next steps are going to be vital to her recovery.

'Yes. And after talking to Taylor, I'm not going to rush my decision about what happens next. I might stay on for a couple of extra weeks if I can get my parents to agree to another extension. Taylor is a bit of a loner, too, and I want to help bolster his confidence. Like you've done with me, Fern.'

'I'm not a counsellor, Kellie. I just happen to have a younger sister who is only a year older than you. The world can be scary at times and we don't always know what to do next. Life is all about trial and error, which can be a painful process. But we all need someone to confide in and it helps when that someone has had similar experiences.'

'Your sister is lucky. I hope she appreciates having you around. Can I see your painting? I know you've only just started, but can I take a look?'

It's an afternoon of sharing and by the end of the day I feel positive. There's a natural source of healing here, in this place. It's something I don't fully understand, but Kellie feels it too. So does Nico. And Ceana.

My year here is not going to be wasted. What Kellie taught me today is that I have two skills I've never considered to be of any particular merit. One is that I'm a good listener; the other is that my natural instinct is to be a source of encouragement and optimism. Maybe that's why I ended up working in HR. It's all about the complexities of human nature and the importance of communication to solve the problems that arise along the way.

If only I could solve Aiden's problem. In our case, communication seems to be making things worse, not better.

* * *

'How was your day?' I enquire, passing Nico a mug of coffee. He takes it, gratefully, setting it down on the table next to what I refer to

as his *green* canvas. It's an explosion of summer foliage and reminis-
cent of the orchard.

'Mixed. I received some news I didn't want, but on the other hand
I might just have found the right guy to join us.'

'Well, at least there was some good news in the mix. Actually,
before you pick up your brush again, there's something I'd like to ask
you about, although it might mess up your plans.'

He looks at me, pulling a face. 'Problems?'

'No. Not really. It's about Kellie.'

His gaze sharpens. 'Should I be worried?'

'No. Everything is fine with Taylor and you were right. I had no
idea what happened to him, but he's confided in Kellie. What draws
them together is what they've been through, not some unrealistic
and transient passion. But Kellie is looking for something; a place
where she can find her feet, I think. Her home environment is a
battlefield by the sound of it. I know she's young, but she understands what it really means to survive when something in your head
is telling you to give up. Am I making any sense here?'

He shrugs his shoulders. 'Continue.'

'It would help her if she could stay on here for a while in some
capacity. I know you intend on turning the craft studio into a gym
and meditation centre, and I agree it is a wasted space. But I
looked through Dee-Dee's PowerPoint presentations this afternoon;
she's going to ask you if I can assist her next week. I think it's a
useful module to offer if you can find an alternative location.
There's something for everyone and it's easy to turn a session into
a group activity to encourage less able people to participate in a
fun way. The origami has great potential for some big disasters, I
will admit. Kellie and I both had a go and ended up giggling like
schoolgirls. But I can imagine the results would generate a lot of
interaction in a very light-hearted way. Kellie could run those
sessions with ease. And if Taylor feels comfortable with Kellie,
then maybe some of your new visitors would make that connection
too.'

Nico is perched on the edge of a stool, one leg thrust out in front of him, but his eyes haven't moved from my face.

'On one condition. You supervise her. Dee-Dee is too busy, and I've known that for a while. Perhaps next week you and Kellie could partner up and see how it goes.'

I could cheerfully hug him. Instead, I simply raise an eyebrow, very casually, and give him an acknowledging nod.

'Now, is it all right with you if I get back to work?' he asks, talking to my back as I'm heading over to slip the muslin off my own canvas.

'Feel free. I'm in the mood to paint.'

Before he can respond, his phone lights up and begins to buzz. I turn, glancing in his direction, and he checks the screen before raising it to his ear. Then he saunters off into the little workroom.

It's not that I'm eavesdropping, although I move slowly so as not to make any noise. He's talking in Spanish and he sounds totally different. His voice is so smooth, and the words sound almost poetic. There's laughter in his voice, too, which surprises me.

I'm in need of a clean rag, so I tiptoe down closer to the door. Nico's leaning against some of the racking, facing away from me, but I'm pretty sure he's smiling as he talks. I can hear the inflection in his voice. The conversation sounds like it's coming to a close.

'*Eres demasiado amable, mi bella Marquesa.*'

So, I'm guessing that last bit was probably my lovely Marquesa. *Amable...* nice, kind? It's good news then, but the way he's talking to her... his voice is soft, almost seductive. Intimate. Sexy.

Edging backwards quietly, I don't take my eyes from the door until I'm back in position. Then, quickly grabbing a brush, I start fussing around with one of the colours on my palette.

Hearing his footsteps behind me, he doesn't say anything, and we work in silence until well after midnight. Eventually my eyes begin to feel heavy and I start tidying up. Standing back, though, I'm pleased with what I've done tonight. Up close, it's still vague, but from a few feet back, it's clearly a mass of roses dripping from an intricate network of intertwined stems, fastened to trelliswork on a brick wall.

I glance at the photograph which I can now see is just a flat piece of paper, whereas my canvas is starting to come alive. It has texture, it has form and it's beginning to have depth. But it also has feeling, and I've been able to communicate that without any conscious effort.

'Nico?'

I turn to look at him and he glances across at me, frowning.

'Tomorrow night, can you show me how to get that little glint, you know, on the tips of the petals. Where the sunshine catches them. I'm happy with the shading and I think I've nailed that velvety finish so far. But I'm sure you're going to tell me there's a technique and I can't just soften a titanium white and go crazy.'

He laughs. 'Ah, the pupil isn't quite ready to dismiss her mentor yet, then. I was beginning to feel a little redundant.' Although he's probably every bit as tired as I am, he's in such good spirits tonight.

'Why don't you quit now and get some rest, too?'

'I think I will, in a bit. It's been a tiring day. But a good one. Productive, and I've had some good news. My benefactress is pleased with the photographs I sent her of the painting. A large transfer of funds will be in my account tomorrow.'

I can't hide my smile. 'That's wonderful news, Nico. You've worked so hard to get that finished. How long will it be before you can ship it? It's good to receive the payment so promptly, though.'

'Yes, I'm fortunate indeed. A few weeks, the longer the better. Although in this weather, the paints dry quite quickly, but I never like to take a risk. We know each other well – very well, actually. As I said, the Marquesa is very kind, although she is ultimately an astute businesswoman. If all goes well, my work will appreciate in value, so to her it's an investment. The not-so-good news is that the van isn't going to last much longer. That's an expense I hadn't factored into the budget, but that was more wishful thinking than facing the inevitable.'

'Don't let that take the shine off the fact that you've sold another painting, Nico. Your mother would be very proud of what you're achieving. And of what you're doing here at the château.'

He shrugs. 'Let's hope I can keep it all together, then.' With that, he picks up his brush, tilts his head forward and begins to dab very tentatively at the leaves. From where I'm standing, with the soft glint from the inset lights above us, they seem to shimmer as if they're moving. I realise that I'm watching a genius at work and the inspiration comes from deep down within him. That thought makes me catch my breath.

There's passion in this life and then there's *passion*. One is transient, sexual, shallow. The other is all-consuming and affects every single thing you say, touch, do or think. And that's something I was never able to appreciate, or understand, before I met Nico.

I walk away as quietly as I can, shutting the door behind me. My heart is pounding in my chest. The excited knot I can feel in my stomach is exhilarating. Nico has awoken something in me and I can only hope that it's merely a dormant desire to create and nothing more.

But what I'd give to sketch him while he's painting. Inside my head, I can already imagine the brush against the canvas as the sketch is turned into something alive and vibrant. Like a living flame, I'm a hapless moth dazzled by his brightness.

DECEMBER 2018

17

TEAMWORK

As the winter chill starts to bite, first thing in the morning and late at night, there's a real buzz in the air. The days are still quite mild, given the temperate climate here, and the sun is keeping the daytime temperatures very ambient. The retreat has only been closed to visitors for the last four weeks as the bookings kept coming in. We all knew that Nico needed the funds, because we've had to draft in two local builders to help with the conversions; so, it's been a period when everyone had to work even closer together and we've become more than a group of peers, we are a family.

Every one of us has turned their hand to tasks that, quite frankly, none of us ever expected we'd have to tackle. I've climbed ladders to paint ceilings and also learnt how to spin wool so I can help Dee-Dee. Her textile workshops have been centre stage this autumn. I've also learnt how to bake bread and make chutney according to Margot's strict guidelines.

The screen on my laptop lights up and it's Aiden, Skyping me. We talk every Saturday morning as that's when he has a few hours off, but we rarely text these days. Sure, we send photos back and forth as little updates, but we've both been so caught up with what we're doing.

'Hi, darling. You look tired.' The words tumble out of mouth before I can stop them. Tired, but content, I see, and that cheers me a little. He's in south-eastern Mexico on a twenty-four-week internship at a Save the Children Centre in Playa del Carmen. Volunteers pay to enrol on the programme and are involved in the continuing education of vulnerable and special needs children. They also assist local veterinarians as it's part of a wider community project that fits with the United Nations Sustainable Development Goals. It can be harrowing at times, he's told me, but Aiden has thrown himself into it with great enthusiasm. At night he studies Spanish and he seems happier, more fulfilled.

We take a moment to just look at each other and I place my fingertips on the screen. Aiden does the same.

'I've been helping to build a new boundary wall. A labourer's job is physically demanding. Owen would be proud of me. I feel like I've completed the poor man's boot camp.'

'I can identify with that a little. I feel so trim these days because I rarely get to sit still. Even when I'm painting, I tend to stand and pace back and forth. There's always something to do here and now everyone is beginning to get in the festive mood.' My upbeat tone evaporates as it reminds me that we are facing our first Christmas apart since we exchanged our wedding vows.

He pulls a face. 'I know. But your parents will be over in Wales at their holiday cottage and Owen will be sampling the delights of Newquay with his mates. Hannah is flying off with Liam and his family to ski in Austria. It was always going to be a very different celebration for us as a family this year, anyway. My parents might even have invited themselves over from Greece to keep us company.'

He gives me a sardonic smile. Aiden's parents took early retirement and sold up in the UK to live on the island of Corfu. They'd holidayed there at least once a year for more than twenty years and had gained a lot of friends in that time. They joined an expats club and now have a hectic social life, which is lovely, but whenever Aiden has flown over for a short visit, it certainly hasn't been a rest.

Joss walks behind Aiden, turning to give me a brief wave.

'Hi, Joss,' I call out.

She never stops to chat and that bothers me. Not because it's rude, but because... well, I guess I can't help thinking she's avoiding me. She's probably trying to give Aiden some privacy as he usually calls from a communal room.

'We can have our Christmas in July when we get back,' I continue. 'Hopefully we can get everyone together for at least a long weekend and I'm sure your parents will be eager to pay a flying visit. Mum and Dad will want to hold an engagement party for Hannah and Liam, too, so maybe we can tie that in at the same time. It's going to be all go.'

He chews his lip and I know how he feels. It's hard to talk about going home when it's still such a long time away.

'You're right, but we'll cope somehow. How's the painting coming along? Any new canvases?'

I give him a mirthful look. 'Incredibly well. I'm ordering paint and canvas every other week. The problem is that I don't know what I'm going to do with them all. I need to sort out and discard the ones that turned out to be a painful part of the learning process. But I'm pleased with my little collection, Aiden. And I'm finding inspiration everywhere.'

His smile comes from his eyes. 'I'm glad you've managed to release your inner muse. I've never seen you so... well, you're glowing. No more wrinkled brow and pinched nose. You've learnt to relax and not to worry all the time. I like that.'

Muse. I wish he hadn't said that word. Nico hasn't mentioned it again, but it hasn't gone away. The request continues to hang in the air between us like a half-finished sentence. Sometimes I catch Nico looking at me and I know he's thinking of the unfinished painting languishing in the corner.

'Have you decided where you're going when your time in Mexico draws to a close in January?'

Aiden swivels in his seat to see what's going on behind him and waves to a small group of people gathering near the doorway to the recreation room. He spins back around, giving me a sober look.

'Our permits only give us a couple of days' leeway before we have to leave the country. It means making a decision really soon so we can get it all sorted, but the Mexico trip has been costly – the internship alone cost five grand. I'm thinking Thailand, but I have to look at the finances. This volunteering lark isn't cheap and with flights, visas and the cost of a few excursions, it mounts up.'

He's still saying *we* all the time. I know he hates anything to do with paperwork, but can't Joss go off and do her own thing? It's not rocket science, and I'm sure Aiden could figure it out. It makes me feel so sad and... a bit forgotten. Aiden and I used to be the only *we* in his life and now another woman has taken my place. I try not to dwell on this subject, because it will serve to make me even more paranoid and needy.

Lots of people go backpacking on their own and team up with people they meet along the way. It's safer and that should be my main concern, I keep telling myself. Safety in numbers.

'Well, don't let the cost deter you, darling. The money we set aside is a shared pot and I certainly won't be spending anything like fifty per cent of it. Even if I come back with a trailer load of rolled-up canvases. I want you to return to the UK feeling you packed in as much as you could.'

The background noise is growing.

'Okay. Thanks, babe. It sounds like our transport has arrived. A group of us are going to help out in one of the animal shelters today. Have you spoken to the family this week?'

'Yes. Mum sent another long email and Hannah and Owen are busy, but fine. They all send their love. I rang your mum, but it was only a quick chat as they were just heading out to a supper party. Honestly, when I get back I'm going to feel like I haven't missed a thing.'

Aiden leans closer to the screen, trying to blot out the escalating noise coming from behind him and having to raise his voice. 'Well, for me it's going to feel like a dream from which I'm just waking up, I suspect. I can't imagine getting ready for work again and our big adventure will be a dim and distant memory from the past. But it's helping me to put life in general into perspective and that's a good thing for us, Fern.'

Is he saying that just to reassure me? His direct contact with everyone is patchy and it has been noticed. I keep making excuses for him, which I hope are real. *'He's out of signal,'* I say, or *'His workload is demanding and he can't simply walk away when people are suffering and your efforts make a difference.'* Which is true.

But Aiden sounds nostalgic today and I wonder if he's a little homesick for our old, familiar life together. I'm hoping it's a good sign that he's already starting to think about picking life back up again after our adventure. I know how much I miss just being in each other's company, aside from the physical aspect. Simply to have Aiden's arms around me, to feel his body pressed up against mine and the softness of his kiss, is a tense longing I can't shake.

And I hate all the goodbyes. When we disconnect, my heart sinks for a moment. It's always the same, whether it's with Aiden, my parents, Owen or Hannah. I want to hang on for one more second, the old me kicking in and that awful 'will I really see them again?' feeling comes back to haunt me. But I'm able to look at life a little differently now too. I've discovered that learning about other people's lives helps to put your own into perspective.

It's important to appreciate the gift of good health and understand that happiness is a state of being. Learning what lifts your spirits, rather than focusing on what you can attain, or measuring yourself by other people's standards, is key.

There's a real satisfaction that comes from knowing Aiden and I have always worked together as a team – well, up until now at least. But what I hadn't quite grasped was that there are so many people whose childhood, tragically, scars them for life. Sometimes, through no fault of their own, or the people looking after them. That's humbling because my family are so very lucky in many ways and maybe we tend to take that for granted.

'Hey, am I interrupting anything?' Nico appears in the doorway of the day room, dressed in that tired, old, knitted jumper that looks like something not even worthy of a jumble sale.

'No. Just finished a call.'

'Ah, I wondered why you were in here all on your own and didn't pile into the minibus with everyone else.'

'I wasn't being unsociable, but Saturday mornings always leave me feeling a bit sad.'

'Actually, I've come to take you out to lunch. No arguments. It's my treat and I've booked a table in my favourite restaurant on the outskirts of Figanières. Bring a coat and wear some comfortable shoes as there's a bit of a walk involved; it could get a little windy.'

I gasp and splutter. 'Are... are we celebrating something?'

He looks at me with a gleam in his eye. 'We are. All will be revealed. Fifteen minutes?'

'Fifteen minutes.'

I pack up my things and march off to my room. A quick brush of my hair, change of jumper, squirt of perfume and a slick of lipstick and I'm done. But when I slip into the old Citroën, I notice that Nico has made an effort. He's wearing cologne and a shirt, beneath his padded jacket.

'Wow. This must be a momentous occasion,' I remark, wishing I'd changed out of my jeans. Admittedly, they are my dressy weekend jeans, not the colourful, paint-splattered ones, or my working leggings.

'It is and I will reveal all when we arrive at *Chez Lucien*. It's up in the hills, on the slopes of the village. I think you'll enjoy the scenic drive and you get a much better view of the mountains beyond, the higher we climb.'

The Provence-Alpes region is referred to as the gateway to the Côte d'Azur. Obviously, people celebrate the beautiful sea views of the renowned French Riviera, but inland, and just beyond le Bois-

Saint-Vernon, the deeply wooded mountains are truly a sight to behold. While the forest around the château was glorious when it was wearing its autumnal coat, now it's looking sparse in places. Only the pockets of evergreen trees give a flash of colour.

But up in the mountains, that's reversed. The large variety of fir trees extend for acre after acre, interspersed with small swathes of deciduous oak trees that are simply swallowed up. The mass of green has a bluey tinge and even as a distant backdrop from the château, I keep finding myself striving to catch a glimpse at every opportunity.

'As we climb it gives you a real feel for the terrain.' Nico inclines his head in my direction. I find myself staring at his hands as he lovingly grips the steering wheel. To me it's just an old Citroën, but it's clear he loves this car.

'You've had this car a long time?' I ask, and that raises a little smile.

'*Cette vieille dame*? This Citroën GS came with the property and belonged to my grandmother in the day, way back in 1978 when she had her from new.'

'That accounts for the colour then,' I reply without thinking, and his head tilts back as he begins to laugh rather softly.

'After the psychedelic 60s, the colours of autumn were the symbol of the next decade, apparently. They called it burnt orange. Anyway, lots of manufacturers offer this colour now, so it's back in vogue.'

In vogue. I doubt that would ever worry Nico – he's a man who loves vibrant colours, anyway.

'I'm not a car enthusiast, but I'm pretty sure she counts as a classic now – if I can keep her going, of course. The local garage has replaced just about every working part on her over the years.'

He reaches out, placing his hand on the dashboard and patting it affectionately.

As the journey continues, I can't help marvelling at the scenery. Nico winds down the window a little, letting in a gentle breeze and the air is filled with the smell of the fragrant pine needles and cones.

The floor of the forest is carpeted with them and they're nature's own, very abundant air freshener.

The road winds rather dramatically and even amongst the towering trees it's easy to catch the odd glimpse of a number of beautiful villas set back from the road. A kilometre or two further on and we're passing a large cultivated area: row upon row of grapevines indicating there will be a cluster of buildings somewhere close by. And then I see the sign for the vineyard.

'I recognise that name. You serve this wine back at the retreat. I love their rosé.'

'Yes. I've known the owner for quite a long time. The soil here is good and it reflects in the quality of the grapes. And, of course, Provence is famed for its wonderful olives and oil, apricots and the lavender fields. But you're no stranger to France.'

'I've been to Provence before, but not quite this far to the east. We did the lavender trail in July once, but that was in the Luberon. It was the first time I'd heard it referred to as *blue gold*. A trip to *Les Agnels Distillerie de Lavande* included a tour of the processing plant and fields. The depth of the colour is imprinted on my memory as if it was yesterday. It was an endless glow of deep, purply-blue extending out over a vast plain, with the smoky-grey mountains on the horizon. It was unbelievable.'

He smiles to himself. 'The artists' trail, they call it. The colours and light of Provence and the Côte d'Azur inspired so many – Picasso, Matisse, Chagall, Van Gogh. It was a pilgrimage.'

I turn to look at Nico, studying his side profile intently. It's obvious that driving this car gives him great pleasure. Maybe it triggers old memories, I can't tell, but he looks content, carefree even, as he continues talking.

'Figanières itself is a small, picturesque, medieval village sitting on a hillside ridge, but it's high enough for the surrounding views to be spectacular. Personally, I think this area has it all. Fine weather, timeless architecture and natural beauty. Who could ask for anything more?'

The landscape is already beginning to change again as the incline levels out. We're now passing endless orchards of evergreen olive trees and the leaves flashing past the window are like a waving stripe of soft, muted green. A ribboned scarf of colour floating in the breeze. It's much brighter now, without the tall trees towering over us and closing in on the road.

'My mother always complained the twists and bends of the snaking roads made her sick to her stomach. But really she was an impatient traveller, like a child who is only interested in how soon they will arrive at the destination. That was a great pity, because the scenery is spectacular and deserves to be savoured.'

'I suppose the forest is full of boar and deer?'

'Yes. Predominantly red deer, the smaller roe deer and wild boar. But a little walk will send foxes, hares and rabbits scampering for cover. Occasionally, there is an accident when one of the larger beasts is in chase and vaults across the road. The boar tend to amble along the verges grazing, as if they are waiting for the right time to cross, but a collision with either a boar or deer could be catastrophic.'

A few kilometres further on, the view changes once more and now dense, Mediterranean shrub land with steep, rocky cliffs rises up. To our left, though, tantalising glimpses of turquoise blue sea, way in the distance, meet a cobalt-blue sky on the horizon and seem to blend into one. The magical vista comes and goes in gaps between large runs of shrubbery.

'Beautiful, isn't it?' Nico reflects, a sense of pride in his tone.

'That purplish red of the cliffs is vibrant – stunning, but I'm trying hard not to worry about how steep it is, or how high up we are going.'

'It's not far now. There's a bit of an uphill trek after we park, but it's well worth it, I assure you.'

Eventually we pull into a loosely gravelled car park at the bottom of a long run of steps. As Nico locks the car door, I wonder if I have the stamina for this. Ahead of us, a steep, winding slope seems to stretch out forever. Elongated, cobbled steps, two paces deep for my stride, help to ease the going under foot. But it's tiring and surprisingly quickly my calves begin to tighten, the gradient taking a toll.

Nico, on the other hand, seems not to notice, so I try my best to keep up a reasonable pace as he follows behind me. The stout, rustic stone walls either side rise up high above us, punctuated only by stone archways with solid, dark oak wooden doors. Tumbling over the walls is a profusion of intertwining stems; many have shed their leaves, although a few still linger and some sport dark red, winter berries.

There are rambling roses still in bloom and, the further we climb, I notice winter-flowering jasmine and the splashes of colour are delightful. I can't help but imagine what it must look like in spring and summer, when everything is burgeoning. Honeysuckle, climbing hydrangeas and the sturdy framework of a very old wisteria cover large areas of the walls.

I stop for a moment to catch my breath, tilting my head back. A church spire looms up, partially obscured from view by the high walls. Its tapering profile is visible enough to show that it's a fine example of the rustic chapels of the area.

It's not possible to see any roofs at ground level, but as soon as we turn the first corner – which I'd assumed was at the top of our walk – the lane opens out, and the incline is much easier to handle. About fifty metres in front of us is an open gateway. The hand-hewn, oblong stones of the staunch pillars support two oversized stone urns. Either side the top of the walls slope away from the pillars in an elegant sweep. Peering through the entrance, a very old stone-built manor house stands on level ground.

As we step through into the immense, flagstoned courtyard, the gardens around us are surprisingly formal and manicured. This beautiful setting has an air of exclusivity and elegance, rather than rustic charm. It's a hidden treasure for sure, but so far off the beaten track I can't imagine that anyone would stumble across it. No, people who come here are either regular patrons or have heard about its reputation.

'This is amazing.' I turn to face Nico, who is now standing next to me, eagerly watching my reaction.

As we approach the entrance to the restaurant, he holds open the door for me, leaning in as I pass. His voice is low and his eyes are playful.

'I keep this in reserve for special occasions. And for special people. I've taken the liberty of ordering a rather good bottle of wine. Unfortunately, I'm only going to be able to join you for one glass, but I want you to relax and savour the moment.'

'Nico, you should have warned me. I would have made more of an effort if I'd realised this was an important day for you. And now the suspense is killing me. What is this all about? Have you sold another painting? Oh, my, you have!'

A satisfied little smile makes his lips twitch, but he says nothing.

I know the purchase of the upgraded van put a big dent in his bank balance, but it was a necessary investment. If his good news means that it's covered, then that is indeed cause for a toast.

The sprawling restaurant is on two levels, reflecting the nature of the site. We are led down to the lower level and a quiet table looking out over a terrace. As the land falls away, I gaze out at the bell tower of the old church, which rises up to our right, and at the far-reaching views ahead.

'Parfait, merci,' I mutter, as the waiter pulls out a chair for me. He proceeds to lay a white linen napkin on my lap with a flourish.

Scanning around, all of the tables have a white church candle in the centre. It sits on a wooden plinth within a glass sleeve. In addition, on our table there is a posy of electric blue, winter-flowering irises in a small, cut-glass crystal bowl. Next to it, a bottle of red wine has been opened and is breathing.

'Is it your birthday?' I ask Nico, thinking that some thought has gone into this today.

The waiter returns with the menus, distracting Nico. They

exchange a few words in French and there is much smiling and nodding of heads. When we are left alone, my patience runs out and I peer at him intently.

'There must be a big cheque coming your way, Nico?' Maybe enough to pay for the building work and materials for the recent renovations, I hope.

'This isn't about the retreat, or me, Fern. This is about *you*. Now, focus on the rather excellent selection of food on offer. All will be revealed very soon, I promise.'

It doesn't take me long to make my choice and Nico indicates that we are ready to order. The very charming waiter dispenses a taster of wine for Nico. After a ceremonious sip, savouring the flavours, Nico nods his head appreciatively. Pouring an inch of the rich, red liquid into our glasses, the waiter retires, and Nico immediately raises his glass for a toast.

'What are we toasting?' I ask, quizzically, as I hold my glass aloft.

'An offer. I sent photos of some of your canvases to the Marquesa and she agrees that you have talent. In fact, she has offered you space in her very prestigious gallery in Seville.'

'What?' My hand starts to tremble and I place the glass back down on the table, for fear of spilling the contents.

'Three pieces. The choice is yours, but she is definitely taken with the purple rose garden. That's quite a compliment. But I know your first piece is always special. Sometimes you cannot let it go. I need a decision from you by the end of February, at the very latest, as that's when the next crate of paintings is due to be sent to the gallery.'

I'm speechless, so I simply stare at Nico, unable to process his words. His reaction is to break out in laughter.

'What? You didn't think you had talent? You didn't realise I saw that the instant your brush touched the canvas? I've mentored a lot of students in my time, but none compare to you, Fern.'

To my horror, I burst into tears. I don't know what to say.

It's a meal I will never forget and an afternoon that will stay with me forever. Tears and then laughter and then exhilaration. Nico warned me there are no guarantees; some paintings sit on the walls of the gallery for their allotted time, only to be taken down unsold. Others sell within hours.

'It's rather like life itself, when everything suddenly comes together in the right way,' he'd told me. 'Right painting, right buyer, right time.'

I'd studied his face and saw how much it meant to him, because he knew what it meant to me. I was no longer some hapless dauber. A gallery owner, who looks at art as an investment, was taking me seriously. None of this would have happened without my mentor, the man who saw something in me and gave me the confidence to fly.

Fern Wyman, an actual artist. A woman who was able to pick up a brush, daring to show the world what she saw through her own eyes. I felt a surge of emotion so incredibly empowering that I could barely contain myself. I wanted to jump up and scream at the top of my lungs, 'Yes, I did it!' but I didn't, of course. I sat there, discreetly wiped away my tears and smiled brightly back at Nico. The tender look on his face had been one of pride and immense satisfaction. And when Nico reached out for my hand, all I remember was the warmth of his skin as our fingers touched.

18

SANTA ARRIVES A LITTLE EARLY THIS YEAR

It's delivery day. A whole vanload of new kit arrived this morning. The treatment rooms and fitness centre are now complete, all that's left is to do a final clean through and sort out the furniture and furnishings. So, the former craft room is now stacked high with boxes, all waiting to be unpacked and put in situ over the next few days.

One week today the first visitors will arrive to test out the new facilities and we have to be ready to welcome them. I still haven't had a chance to chat to the new guy, Pierce Mansford-Smythe. Shortly after he arrived, Pierce, who hails from Ireland, and Ceana, headed off together to attend a four-week course in London. They aren't due back until the weekend.

Staring at the mountain of boxes, the task ahead is daunting.

'It was bad enough helping to carry these in, let alone move them again,' Kellie declares. 'Some of that stuff is heavy. I suppose there's more space to unpack it in here, though, and half of it will be staying, anyway. What's next, Fern?'

In Ceana's absence, I'm in charge of the day-to-day organisation as we plough forward. Everyone is standing around looking to me for direction.

'Well, if Taylor and Bastien would like to begin unpacking the exercise equipment, I'll mark out the floor where it's all supposed to go. If Dee-Dee and Odile are happy to carry through this stack of supplies, perhaps you and I can make a start on getting the new craft room sorted, Kellie. Is everyone okay with that?'

Taylor's head suddenly appears around the side of a tower of boxes, catching my eye. 'Fern, it might be a good idea if we moved these lightweight boxes back against the wall. They're bulky suckers and we're going to need a lot more floor space when we start assembling the equipment.'

I survey the mound of boxes and realise he's right.

'Good point, Taylor. Probably a third of them are the interlocking floor mats, anyway.'

He grins at me. 'Are you saying they need to go down before we erect these extremely heavy pieces of equipment?'

There's a little ripple of laughter.

'Um... and that's a *yes*, sorry,' I smack my hand to my forehead, dramatically. My brain has been going at a hundred miles an hour trying to relieve some of the pressure from Nico. He's been number-crunching for the last two days, hoping that now the bills are in he will be within budget. His absence has been worrying and whenever I have caught sight of him, he's been frowning more than he's been smiling.

Since Ceana left, this whole thing has come together more by luck than judgement, because I've had to think on my feet. As an ardent planner, it's fallen into my lap piecemeal and I'm being reactive, not proactive, which is the least effective way of getting anything done.

'Listen, you look frazzled, Fern. We've got this, haven't we, guys?' Taylor declares, firmly.

There's a mutual nodding of heads and a chorus of, 'Of course!'

'You haven't stopped since Ceana left. Why don't you take the afternoon off and disappear into your artist's cave? We'll begin work in here and Kellie can make a start setting up the new craft room in the cottage on her own. Can't you, Kellie?'

I turn to look at her and she beams at me. 'You bet.'

You bet? They're spending so much time together she's starting to take on Taylor's accent and mannerisms. I smile to myself. But I'm touched that Taylor can see I need a break, because I do. It's been a roller-coaster of concern. I worry that Nico is taking on too much and that, coupled with the anxious excitement of choosing the final of my three paintings to send off to the gallery, has been tough. I've agonised over the decision and at times it's driven me to tears. Plus, Ceana leaves a big hole because she keeps everything running smoothly and, unwittingly manages to make it look easy, even when it isn't.

'All right!' I hold up my hands in mock surrender. 'I get the message and I'm grateful, to you all. I'm thrilled about this gallery thing, but it's just come at the wrong time.'

'No,' Kellie says, firmly. 'It has come at the right time, Fern. You deserve this, and we can pull together to sort out a pile of boxes. It's going to take a few days, but we'll have everything looking perfect before next Monday.' Then she stands back, surveying the enormous mound and grimacing. It's enough to make everyone laugh.

'Well, good luck. Some of the boxes have flat-pack furniture in them for the treatment rooms. That huge box is a professional massage table, so we can leave that for Pierce to sort out. But if you can trolley it across to the number one treatment room in the cottage, Taylor and Bastien, I'm sure he'd be very grateful and it would be one less box in here.'

'No sweat.' Taylor looks in Bastien's direction and he nods, flexing his muscles to make me laugh.

'You're all going to feel like you've had a good workout at the gym by the time this lot is sorted,' I throw over my shoulder.

* * *

I love painting when it's still daylight outside. Sometimes the artificial light at night exaggerates the colours on the palette. The bulbs in the studio are supposed to mimic natural daylight, but it's not the same. Until I picked up a brush, I had no idea of the difference it can make.

The final canvas I've decided to paint in preparation for the exhibition, is an abstract piece. Crazy, because it's my first attempt at just letting go and following my instincts.

Nico has shown me how to prepare my own canvases now, and is going to teach me how to stretch them, once they're finished. But when it comes to painting, it's not like taking a class, as he doesn't believe that an artist should be influenced by someone else's techniques. So, he simply observes me from time to time. We might end up having a whole conversation based around the angle at which a brush is held to build a lip on the outer edge of each stroke. It has the effect of creating its own natural little shadow and discovering that was quite a revelation for me.

Tackling an abstract painting simply reflects the fact that I'm still discovering who I am, when it comes to finding my preferred style. So today, I'm going to be working with cartridge paper and watercolours, because Nico said that's the best way to experiment. He asked me whether colour was going to be my lead, or shape, or texture? Or all three? I'd looked at him as blankly as the sheet in front of me is right now. It's an exciting moment, for all that, and I don't intend to hesitate.

Time passes quickly. I have no idea how late it is, but it's already twilight outside when there's a knock on the studio door. I turn in surprise, calling out 'Come in' and wonder who it can be.

Dee-Dee pops her head around the door. 'Sorry to bother you, Fern, but you have some visitors.'

I stare at her, wrinkling my brow as I wonder if it's another delivery. 'Visitors?'

'They asked for you by name. I took them into the day room as I wasn't sure you could just walk away from, you know, whatever paint you've mixed up there.' She glances first at my mixing palette and then at the array of paint tubes scattered all over the side table. The floor is littered with more than a dozen sheets of paper, most of them already dry.

'Oh, it's fine. I'll just clean my brushes up, though, and pop the lid on. I'll be ten minutes, tops. You said *they*, did they say what they wanted?'

'No. Sorry, I didn't like to ask any questions in case it was personal. I did say you were working and might not be able to break off. I know Nico has a *do not disturb rule* when he's in here. Look at you, working away as if you've done this all your life.'

I feel myself colouring up; my cheeks warming as I smile back at her.

'I'm still feeling my way along. Should I change?' I glance down at my old T-shirt, which is now almost as paint-splattered as the ones Nico often wears.

'No. It might be referrals wanting to know more about the retreat. I'm sure a bit of paint isn't going to put them off and it does make you look like the real thing if they're artsy folk.'

Dee-Dee hangs around while I clean up, wandering up and down to stop and stare at each of the canvases in turn. Then we head across the courtyard together, the lights of the day room glowing out into the gathering darkness. The cold air hits me and I shiver as I struggle to pull on my jacket.

She turns to look at me for a moment.

'Okay, I'll leave you to it. And don't forget to grab something to eat. It's really not a good idea to work through dinner. I expect Nico will be back soon, too, so maybe you two can eat together? The others have gone into town for a late supper and I'm about to sink into a relaxing bubble bath. Catch you tomorrow.'

Glancing at my watch, I see it's just after eight p.m., but the dark nights make it feel much later and I realise that I am hungry. Looking across to the parking area I make out the shape of a car I don't recognise. I'm cross with myself for not grabbing the iPad in case I need to check availability, but I know we don't have any vacancies until the middle of April at the very earliest. As I push open the door to the day room and step inside, my stomach drops to the floor and zips back up into my chest, threatening to knock me off my feet.

'Surprise!' Hannah shouts, hurrying forward to throw her arms around me. Owen isn't far behind and Liam stands behind them both, looking a little unsure, despite my obvious delight.

I draw in a sharp intake of breath and then expel it at force, so it comes out like a half-sob, half-laugh. 'What on earth are you all doing here?'

Hannah, Owen and I are hugging, our smiles lighting up the room. I wave my hand for Liam to join in.

'This is so amazing. I simply can't believe it!'

'Well, the mountain wouldn't come to us, so we decided to go to the mountain. Besides, we come bringing a whole pile of presents from Mum and Dad. It would have cost them a fortune in postage,' Owen declares, rather lamely. And we begin hugging all over again before I reluctantly peel myself away to stand back and gaze at them in astonishment.

'Oh, it's beyond good to see you all. It's wonderful. Amazing. Unbelievable.' I throw a hand up to my forehead, hitching back my hair as I try to take it in. 'I feel like I'm dreaming,' I add. 'Sit down. I want to hear everything, about... everything.' I know I sound like a crazy woman, but that hit of unfettered joy makes me feel like I'm going to burst.

Hannah holds up her hand and I glance down at her ring.

'Oh, Liam, that's perfect. I'm sorry Aiden and I weren't there when it all happened. But we will make it up to you both, I promise.'

There's a bang as the door clicks shut. We all look up to see Nico standing there hesitantly, looking as if he might turn and walk straight back out.

'Nico, this is my family, come and meet them.'

He breaks into a genuinely welcoming smile and strides across.

'This is my brother, Owen.'

Nico shakes Owen's extended hand, vigorously.

'Always a pleasure to shake the hand of a soldier,' Nico says. I can see that Owen is surprised and pleased.

'This is my sister, Hannah, and her fiancé, Liam.'

There's more handshaking and Nico congratulates them on their engagement.

'Have you all eaten?' he enquires, glancing at each of them and finally at me.

'No, we came straight here. It was a spur-of-the-moment thing. Owen has five days' leave and only arrived back home yesterday,' Hannah replies, smiling. I turn my head to look at her, askance. 'My tutor was fine with it, honestly. I explained the situation and said I'd be back in on Thursday. Liam offered to drive and his dad kindly let him take a few days off.'

'Well, this is just the tonic I needed. Thank you, lovelies, for making the trip. And what a long drive you've had.'

Nico slips off his coat and I follow suit.

'I'll go rustle up some food for us all. Then we'll sort you out some rooms.'

I glance at Nico, flashing him a look of pure gratitude. This is so unexpected, and I could understand if he baulked a little at the sudden arrival of three unexpected guests. But he's clearly delighted for me.

'We set off in the early hours and shared the driving, so we've all had a few hours' rest. We were hoping to find somewhere locally to stay for two nights. We don't want to be a bother.' Owen gives me an anxious look, but Nico intervenes.

'Of course, you are all very welcome to stay here. We're in the midst of some upheaval after a little building work, but your timing is perfect. Our next visitors don't arrive until next Monday and Fern has some free time.' He didn't have to say that and I'm touched he's doing everything he can to put them at ease.

Making eye contact with him surreptitiously, Nico raises an eyebrow and nods his head in the direction of the kitchen.

'Come, Fern, let's get some food on this table.'

We head off, leaving them all to slip off their coats and settle down. Once the kitchen door is closed, I turn to Nico, apologetically.

'It's a wonderful surprise and it's so good to see them, but there's so much happening here, Nico. I need to be directing operations tomorrow.'

'Well, I'll make myself available to help out and I'm sure they'd all love a tour of the buildings and the grounds. I can do that after breakfast while you sort everyone's work schedule for the day. When we get back from that, simply tell me what you want done and I'm on it. I want you to enjoy your family's visit, Fern. Clearly, you've been missed and it's quite something when loved ones go out of their way for you like this.'

I can see that he's touched by the gesture and suddenly I feel sad that he's alone in this world without a family to support him.

'Okay,' he says, striding across to swing open the fridge door. 'Let's see what we can find to feed your hungry crew.'

19

A BITTER TRUTH

We linger over our meal and there's a lot of bantering and laughter as Owen regales us with stories from being on exercise. I hardly recognised the man he is turning into, as he seems to have reinvented himself. The short haircut, lean, muscular body and a new air of confidence gives him a certain swagger. I try not to let the change in him bring a tear to my eye, as it's been threatening to do all evening. It makes my heart swell to see him so happy and know that he has finally found his vocation in life.

Hannah was a bit reserved in Nico's presence at first. She seemed suspicious of him and kept glancing back and forth between the two of us. I know it's strange for her, seeing me in a totally different environment and without Aiden by my side. But eventually she relaxed a little and spent a lot of the evening gazing at Liam as they discreetly held hands out of sight beneath the table.

Nico was brilliant. I was surprised that he'd remembered so many of the little things I'd told him about them all. He engaged each of them in conversation, drawing them out in such a natural way, making the evening entirely about them. My family.

It's just after eleven o'clock when we finally take our leave, and Nico and I head back to the château after sorting out their rooms.

'Are you working tonight?' he enquires, shutting the front door behind us.

'Yes. You?'

We exchange knowing little smiles.

'Of course. The bills don't pay themselves.'

'But you seem happier this evening. Lighter.' It's been very evident, so something good must have happened.

'There's still money in the bank, thanks to the way everyone has pulled together. We did it, Fern. *Le Havre de Paix à Bois-Saint-Vernon* is born. The retreat becomes *The Haven*.'

'Oh, I love that name. It's so peaceful here. It's perfect, Nico.'

'We could actually be in profit if bookings continue to stream in, instead of it being a constant struggle to break even. This is what I've always dreamed of, Fern. This place has a spiritual connection and it would be wrong of me to ignore that. But this year has been tough, and it has taken almost everything I have just to keep going. Now, I feel optimistic again and, hopefully, when the next batch of paintings go off, one or two will sell quickly and I will have my safety net back.'

As he swings open the door to the studio and I pass through in front of him, our eyes meet for a brief second. I can see how relieved he is and how crucial what we've all been doing has been to the viability of this place; for everyone to whom this is home for the foreseeable future.

'I'm thrilled for you, Nico. No one could have done more to make this a success, and everyone is excited about the new direction you're taking it in.'

'The people here are my family, Fern, and I know you appreciate how important that is and the sense of responsibility that comes with it. But the changes will be huge, and I hope everyone will be happy about that and regard it as a positive move forward.'

The look that passes between us, before we begin to peel off our coats, is one of acceptance and understanding. As Nico changes his shirt, I discreetly turn away to take the lid off my palette, then I head into the workroom to get some water.

'There's only one cloud on the horizon now,' he admits. 'The paintings my father sold in the year before his death, Fern, were mine. As is the one on the wall in your room.'

I've just stepped back across the threshold and I stop dead in my tracks. I don't understand. The one in my room clearly says *José*. I stand here, staring rather awkwardly at him and frowning.

As our eyes meet, what I see reflected back at me is a sense of anger, quickly followed by embarrassment. He runs a hand roughly across his forehead, kneading it with the tips of his fingers as if to relieve a stabbing pain.

'I was very prolific when I first began painting. For me it was merely practice; I never signed anything because I was just learning my craft. I notice you, too, have yet to take that step and it's a big one, isn't it? A meaningful moment when a line is crossed.'

I nod, scrabbling around for something to say to break the heavy silence between us. 'Yes, it is. I still don't feel comfortable referring to myself in general conversation as an artist. But to put one's signature on someone else's work, Nico – that must have been an act of sheer desperation for him.'

Nico's head bows as he stares at the floor in front of him for a moment, fleeting memories no doubt jostling around inside his head as he relives the shocking moment of discovery.

'At last my father was actually finishing canvases again and not destroying them in a drunken rage. My mother said a prayer to thank God for saving us all. Then he sold another and a couple of months later, another. When I eventually discovered some of my canvases were missing, I tackled him about it and he swore me to secrecy.

'I couldn't face breaking my mother's heart if she had discovered the truth. We needed the money to survive, but she would have thrown it back at him if it had come to light. I should have told her, but it was impossible to do so because she believed it was divine intervention.' His laugh is jaded and when he raises his eyes to meet mine, all I see now is sadness and love; empathy tugs mercilessly at my heart.

'What a terrible position he put you in, Nico. The guilt isn't yours to carry, though. He made his own decisions and, as his son, what could you do? You were so young and who would have listened to you?'

He shakes off my words; he isn't prepared to forgive himself for what he seems to perceive as his part in this web of lies.

'The painting in your room is the last one he signed fraudulently. If I sell it, then I'm perpetuating his dishonesty. I've spent several years tracking down those pieces and buying them back at market value. I have them all, except one. While that remains in a collector's hands, the truth is that I'm a party to fraud, which is a criminal offence. I chose to do nothing when I discovered that he'd been signing my paintings; bearing his signature, and not that of an unknown, he sold them for more than they were worth.'

'But that's appalling, Nico. You had no say in what he did, no intention of committing a crime,' I blurt out, feeling angry on his behalf. 'It's unfair you could be called to account.'

'Until I realised what he'd done and from that point onwards, I chose to do nothing. So, it appeared to my mother, and the world at large, that he died just as his work was being appreciated. The truth is that he was on the verge of bankruptcy, but every painting of mine that he sold destroyed another little piece of his soul. He did it so that we could live, but it killed him in the process.

'There was a hint of genius in his work, but he was his own worst enemy. Nothing he did was good enough; he felt as if he was constantly failing. So many great pieces destroyed needlessly and so many others unfinished. He discarded them as if they had no value, when in truth they could have been masterpieces.'

I shake my head, sadly. What a mess.

'Unfortunately,' Nico continues, 'his tragic suicide added a premium to the pieces out there. The worry about his deception being discovered has weighed increasingly heavily on me as the years have passed. I have an agent who has been working on my behalf to track down the owners via the auction houses.'

I can't take this in. 'But that can't be easy, Nico,' I say, letting out a huge breath.

'No. It's all above board, but it has cost me dearly. Obviously, I can't share the real reason with him, so the story is that I'm trying to bring my father's paintings together as one collection. And I've almost succeeded in doing that, but they're locked away in a storeroom and will remain there forever. It would have destroyed my mother had she discovered the level to which he had sunk; she was a strong and proud woman who put up with so much in her lifetime. For her sake, I refuse to let him bring shame on our family from his grave.'

I'm horrified. I can tell that this has been an almost unbearable burden for Nico to shoulder. It must be hell living with a secret like this. And he values my friendship enough to trust me with it now.

'Does Ceana know?'

He shakes his head. 'No. I've told no one except you. Until I successfully purchase that last piece, I honestly live in daily fear. My agent has been in negotiation with the current owner, who is – unfortunately – in declining health at the moment. There's a likelihood it could turn into a lengthy process. Every single piece of my work that I sell increases the risk of discovery. That last elusive canvas of mine with a *José* signature is probably displayed on a wall in a home. If some art expert happens to see it before it's in my hands again, they could make the link. It's ironic that the more successful I become, the bigger the worry, but people here are dependent on me and I can't let them down.'

'But if you've bought all the other paintings back, doesn't that prove you are trying to right a wrong?' I interrupt.

'Internationally, art fraud and forgery are taken very seriously, as one would naturally expect. The police wouldn't simply take my word for how many of my paintings my father sold under his name. Even his early works, which sold for next to nothing, would come into question. Artists often paint in more than one style and, at first, his canvases didn't sell for much because he hadn't tapped into his real strength. I would argue that he never really allowed himself to do so.'

He looks tired and dejected. Almost beaten.

'His style was very different, though. An art expert would be able to distinguish your work from his, surely?' I can't believe a father would inflict this on his own son. A wrong has been done, but it isn't Nico's fault.

'Ironically that was the root of the problem. He saw himself as a classical painter, whereas at heart he was more of a Cézanne, who was the true father of modern art. That post-impressionist movement which laid the foundations for the move away from the nineteenth-century endeavours, to the new and exciting twentieth century. Art isn't just about painting something that could be a snapshot, a photograph if you like, of reality. It's about what each artist sees in here.' He stabs at his temple with his forefinger, angrily. 'The reality is that, time and time again, he came back to the classical style; but many of his paintings were a lot less formal. If a major investigation was launched, my reputation could be ruined overnight. Investors would panic at even a hint of the validity of a painting they purchased coming under question.'

I'm sickened at the way Nico's body language is reflecting his sense of humiliation and desperation. Without thinking, I throw my arms around him and he sinks into me. His pain is tangible and it's heartbreaking.

With some reluctance, we eventually draw apart, a moment of awkwardness rearing up – unbidden – between us.

Nico breaks the silence. 'I won't give up, Fern, I simply have to be patient. Painting is my life and it's the only thing I know how to do. If I fail to right this wrong, then my career, too, is in jeopardy. I wouldn't simply lose all credibility, I'd end up losing everything I have. He won't only have destroyed himself, but also his son.'

'You can't think like that, Nico. You were the one who said to me that you can't worry about a problem until it arises. The important thing is that you are doing everything you can. You must think positively.'

'I know. I believe that too, and I am trying my best to do so. We're waiting on a reply to the last email communication and that's about all we can do right now. But I'm so close, Fern, so close, and yet it feels as if this horror will never end.'

'Everything ends in the fullness of time,' I reply, emphatically.

We hold each other's gaze for the briefest of moments before turning to begin work. The unspoken bond between us is now impossible to ignore and it's growing with each day that passes.

I find myself staring at the blank canvas, knowing I'm finally ready to unleash the explosion of emotions that are tumbling around inside of me right now. Nico's passion is heart-stoppingly real. Anger, on his behalf, mixed with exhilaration at knowing my family is so close by is a painful juxtaposition. They are safe and sound and happy. But Nico is in a permanent state of torment.

And yet, tonight was truly wonderful, a special family evening – the irony of it being that Nico was there, when it should have been Aiden.

* * *

After breakfast, Nico takes Owen, Hannah and Liam on a tour of the facilities and they eventually catch up with me in the old craft room. They are all in high spirits and I've never seen Nico so relaxed and upbeat. Clearly it was the financial pressure he's been under that has been weighing him down in recent weeks and now he's free of at least one of his major worries.

I think he couldn't face the prospect of having to tell everyone there was no future for them here, because that would have made him his father's son. A person who let his own personal torment eat away at him to the extent that it affected everyone around him. Nico isn't simply an artist and mentor, he's a motivator. Someone who can't bear to see anyone not fully utilising their natural-born skills. He has created a home for a group of people who were seeking something that would give their lives back some meaning, and he has done that organically.

He understood that need because it mirrored his own situation and the universe has an inherent ability to draw like-minded people together. That's why I found my way here – this has become my temporary home and, right now, I feel I belong here, too.

Nico could have an easy life, spending his days painting and selling fewer pieces if he only had his own needs to consider. But what he's been through, and continues to suffer, has drawn those kindred souls to him. What he has created here is bigger than any one individual; bigger even than his immense talent as an artist.

'I'm handing our guests over to you, Fern. Maybe head into town to do some sightseeing, or venture up into the hills,' he suggests, but Owen interrupts before I can reply.

'Look, there's a lot of work to do here and I don't know about you two,' he casts a glance at his sister and her fiancé, 'but we'd like to help. The more hands available, the quicker it will get done, it seems to me.'

Nico and I exchange hesitant glances.

'But this is a little break for you all,' I reply, adamantly.

However, all three of them are scanning around and look keen to help out.

'I'm good with flat-pack furniture,' Owen throws in. 'Dad sells enough of it and I always assemble the pieces for the displays.'

He casts a glance at Taylor and Bastien, who are knelt on the floor with a partially-built carcass that could be the bare bones of anything at all. Alongside them, lying open, is an incredibly thick instruction booklet. Next to that are about a dozen piles of different nuts, bolts, screws, washers and small wooden dowels.

'We wouldn't say no to some help,' Taylor admits, scratching his head as he stares at the screw in his hand.

Owen and Liam immediately walk over and kneel down, leaving Hannah looking at me enquiringly.

'What can I do to help?' she asks.

Nico looks at me for direction, too.

'Okay. Hannah, come with me. Nico, when Dee-Dee and Odile have finished cleaning the floor over there, maybe the three of you could unpack the rest of the interlocking mats? It's that entire stack of boxes against the wall. You'll have to lay a few rows at a time, clearing a space and cleaning the floor as you go. I'll take Hannah over to the cottage to help Kellie begin setting things up. Nico, there are still a lot of craft boxes to be moved out of here.'

'Great. I'm on it,' Nico replies, giving me a wink.

He's like a totally different person today and it's good to see him so eager to press on.

Hannah and I head over to the cottage and I'm feeling content.

'Kellie is a little star. She came for a week and stayed on. There hasn't been a craft teacher here for many months and Dee-Dee's textile class is so busy she doesn't have time to cover both. I stepped in briefly, but it's not my thing. Kellie has a lot of patience and will give anything a go.'

Hannah nods, taking it all in. 'How long will she be here?'

'Well, I don't think Kellie is planning on leaving us for a little while, but her term here depends on a number of things. She's been through a lot recently, and I think she'd really appreciate a little company; someone of her own age. You know, relatable.'

Hannah gets my drift.

'It's not at all what I'd imagined, Fern, but I'm so glad you found this. It's very *you*. Backpacking isn't your style and now I can see why you and Aiden decided to do your own thing. We are going to see one of your paintings before we go, aren't we?'

I smile at her, taking in every little nuance of her face. She's relieved that I'm settled and has satisfied herself I'm okay. It's strange knowing that Hannah is worrying about me now, when it's always been the other way around.

'We'll see,' I laugh. 'I'm still a little hesitant to show anyone my work, but my confidence is growing daily. Anyway, it's wonderful of you all, pitching in to help out. And much appreciated. Everyone's livelihood here depends on this exciting new phase. They are a bunch of good people genuinely wanting to do good things.'

'What sort of visitors come to stay?' she asks, genuinely interested.

'All ages, all backgrounds. Not many couples, to be honest. People looking for an activity holiday that isn't too physical, if you don't count gardening as heavy manual work. But from next week The Haven will come into its own, with a whole range of holistic treatments on offer. From meditation, to Reiki and, very soon, an introduction to a personal fitness trainer. All in addition to everything from art classes to woodworking and pottery. Cooking lessons, too. It's a long, long list,' I explain.

'So, it's not a holiday they're looking for, exactly?' she asks, puzzled.

'Well, not really, although that might have been the case in the past. Visitors come here to get away from their crazy lives. In future, it will be to learn coping techniques to de-stress and give them the tools they need to survive modern-day living, I suppose. It's an exciting new venture for everyone involved.'

Hannah stops and when I turn towards her, she throws her arms around me and we hug. 'I've missed you, sis,' she whispers. 'I'm happier now I've seen where you are, and I know Aiden will be fine now he's back to his usual, sensible self. I mean, opal mining – what was he thinking! I wasn't sure you would cope, being on your own when it wasn't really your choice. I was worried you'd be lonely without a family you feel you have to check up on all the time.'

'You know me so well, Hannah. Please don't worry about me, though, because I'm fine. And I'm thrilled about you and Liam. Love happens when it happens, and you can't do anything about that. As long as you each put the other person first you can't go far wrong, in my opinion.'

'Like you did, indulging Aiden when it was clearly the last thing you wanted. But, ironically, it wasn't quite so daft an idea, after all, because even Mum and Dad thought you were in need of a little time for yourself. I know we don't talk about Rachel very often, but you kept us all ticking over. So, enjoy every moment of your time here, please, Fern, because we all want what's best for you.'

I smile at her, softly, the emotion contained within her words is better than a hug. 'Maybe you're right, but I was happy with things the way they were. This is something Aiden needed to do, Hannah, and I support him. We miss each other, of course we do, we've hardly ever been apart since the day we married. But I want him to fulfil all of his dreams, even though I can't be with him to enjoy this one. Losing Rachel changed my life in so many ways, not least the way I look at everything. And here, at least, I still feel my contribution really counts for something. I live my life wanting her to be proud of me.'

'She would be very proud, Fern, as we all are, but don't make this totally about other people. Indulge that artistic streak of yours, and I'm sure Nico is an excellent teacher. It's just a shame he's so darned attractive, but a good thing I have the most level-headed sister in the whole world.' The look she gives me as she arches an eyebrow, catches me off-guard and I feel the heat begin to rise in my cheeks.

Linking arms with her, I toss my head nonchalantly.

'I hadn't even noticed,' I reply. 'Come on, I'll introduce you to Kellie and then I'm off to let Margot know she has three extra people for lunch, as well as dinner. She'll cook something special,' I add. 'She loves a reason to show off.'

20

MORE GOODBYES

It feels like the last supper. Owen is going off on his first overseas training exercise in a few days' time. Hannah is going back to move in with Liam. And I'm fast approaching the six-month point in my time at the retreat. Aiden could be heading off to Thailand next month and then goodness knows where after that.

'I can see a lot of you in both your brother and your younger sister, Fern,' Nico says, leaning in as we watch them all dancing away.

I nod at him and smile, loath to take my eyes off them as they will leave early tomorrow morning. It's like watching a ticking clock and knowing that each second is one nearer to departure time.

The meal was wonderful, and Margot stayed on to join us, which was touching. She's had a glass or two of wine tonight and Taylor will drive her home later.

'How was your family Skype session earlier on? Good enough signal?'

I make a face. 'It kept freezing and Aiden was obviously disappointed. We had to give up in the end.'

'That's a pity. You told him the good news about exhibiting your paintings, didn't you?' Nico enquires, looking like the proud teacher celebrating his pupil's first triumph.

'I didn't get a chance as we were only getting one word in every three at this end,' I admit.

'Come on, Fern. You can get up and join in. And you, Nico,' Hannah shouts across at us.

I look at Nico and he looks at me, then shrugs.

'Okay. If you will, I will. But dancing isn't my thing,' he warns.

Before I really have a chance to think about it, Nico pulls me up and off we go. Even Margot eventually joins us, flinging her arms in gay abandonment over her head. It's wonderful to see her enjoying herself, although I'm pretty sure the wine has something to do with it.

It's been a while since I've seen Owen dancing and it's wonderful, because he's lost that self-consciousness that sometimes held him back. As he dances with Dee-Dee, who is twice his age, he has the biggest smile on his face. They're shouting at each other over the loud music, chatting away like old friends.

Feigning the need to sit down to catch my breath after several dances in a row, I'm delighted to look up and see Liam approaching. His excuse is that he needs some water, but when he sinks down next to me, he places the untouched glass in front of him.

'Hey, Liam. I don't think I've had so much fun in a long time. My stomach hurts with laughter.'

Nico is now teaching Margot, so it appears, the rudiments of flamenco dancing. He strikes a good pose and Margot is tiptoeing around him, pretending to have castanets in her hands. It's hilarious.

'We needed to come and visit,' Liam says, quite seriously. 'They were all concerned you were pining. I told them that although I've only met you twice, you'd find something worthwhile to do because that's in your nature.'

I turn to look at Liam and I can see that he's a thinker. I didn't get that from my first impression of him, maybe because he was nervous. It was a strange time, anyway, for the whole family.

'I will look after Hannah, you know. I appreciate you probably feel it's too much, too soon. But I'm miserable whenever I'm not with her, although I know that sounds crazy.'

His words transport me back to those early days after I first met Aiden. It hurt not to be with him, too. Even when I knew we were going to see each other that same evening, getting through the day was my sole focus, because all that mattered was when we would next be together.

'No. It doesn't, Liam. It's something you can only understand if you've felt that way yourself.'

He chews his lip. 'This year you are both taking away from each other must be hard? But I can sort of understand it. Please don't let her know I've told you this, but Hannah wanted to give up uni. She wanted us to get married next year. She'd get a job so we could buy a house together, rather than share my flat. I said *no*. I want us to be together, but I don't want her to sacrifice anything that she might regret in the future. Can you understand that?'

I nod. 'Yes. And I appreciate that you are thinking about Hannah, putting her first, because as the youngest member of our family she's had a lot of people protecting her. But I'd be a hypocrite if I said I didn't understand how loving someone changes everything.'

I'm glad Liam is happy to confide in me, especially as I might not get a chance to talk to him again until after my time here is over. It's sweet of him trying to put my mind at rest.

'Hannah is worried about you and Aiden. She thinks the world of you both, you know.'

'This year off isn't because we aren't happy together, Liam. I'd hate anyone to think that. I don't want Aiden to have any regrets because I can't share in his dream to travel. While this break isn't something I'd choose, I will admit, it's turning out to be a wonderful learning experience for me, too. As I see it, that can only enrich our lives as we go forward.'

Looking at Liam, I wonder if he can understand. He's so young still, but even the few years he has on my sister is more life experience gained. He seems very clear about where he's going and what he wants out of life.

'I hope Hannah and I can face whatever problems life throws at us in a constructive way, too. I believe it's important not to take anything for granted, as I've seen how quickly a relationship can unravel when assumptions are made. Taking a risk is infinitely better than doing nothing at all.'

'If you can survive the tough times, the good times will be so amazing it will blow your mind.'

He grins at me. 'Your sister blows my mind every single day. She's a bit of a whirlwind at times and she can be very stubborn, but I think that might be a family trait.'

My eyes open wide as my forehead lifts. 'Oh dear, and I thought I was the only one bestowed with that! You're in for a roller-coaster ride with our family, then.'

'And I wouldn't have it any other way, believe me.'

A voice pipes up. 'Are you two talking about me?' Hannah enquires, one eyebrow raised in disdain.

'Of course we are,' Liam replies, and we all burst out laughing.

* * *

Partings are tough. But what this precious visit allowed me to see is that Owen and Hannah don't need their big sister as much as they did in the past and it's time to recognise that fact. They are living their own lives and doing a good job of it; and, yes, we all miss each other like crazy, but when we get together, it's like we've never been apart. The break has allowed me to reset my thinking, though, and I wonder if that's why Mum and Dad didn't really have much to say when Aiden and I told them about our plans.

Just then, the door to the studio opens and one look at Nico's face tells me it isn't good news.

'I've just had confirmation from my agent, Fern. Negotiations for the purchase of the final painting have drawn to a halt. The last email said that the owner does not wish to proceed with the sale. No reason was given and, stupidly, I'd convinced myself that it would all be over very soon. It's hard to accept.'

My left hand instinctively flies up to my face, covering my mouth. 'Oh, Nico, I'm devastated on your behalf! You were so close to freeing yourself from the worry.'

Stepping closer to him, his pain seems to radiate outwards from his core. It's a tough blow to accept there is nothing more he can do.

'My agent's hands are now tied. He has no choice other than to wait and see what happens, and whether in the fullness of time they will approach him to start negotiations again.'

I have no words I can offer.

We work through into the early hours and I know that Nico's mind is as full of conflicting emotions as my own. It's not my place to console him in the way that I instinctively feel he wants me to. The closer to him I get, the more I'm pulled in and there's a line I simply cannot cross. But whatever this connection is that we share, it doesn't always seem to require words. Just being in the same room is a form of comfort. Can silence, too, be deemed an act of betrayal if it's meaningful?

I stay until I simply can't lift the brush any longer and leave Nico calmer, more accepting of something he cannot change.

21

A SURPRISING TURN OF EVENTS

'Fern, there's something I've been meaning to say to you. Well, a couple of somethings really. Do you have five minutes to take a little stroll? I know it's rather cold this morning, but I want to say this where I know I can talk without being overhead.'

I frown. This is serious, and I have no idea what Kellie is going to say; I can only pray it isn't bad news. I'm pretty sure her relationship with Taylor is still only platonic. Unless I'm misreading the signs.

I nod, grabbing my jacket off the back of the chair, and follow her to the door of the day room.

'Problems?' I enquire. Casually enough, I hope, not to hint at my concern.

'Yes. No. Not really.'

'Well,' I smile at her, 'that seems to cover just about anything and everything in between.'

She laughs. 'Okay. I need a favour and I also want to share something that I was asked in confidence, which is a little awkward. Oh, and to thank you. I'm not sure what order in which to tackle it all, though.'

As we leave the courtyard behind, the grass crunches satisfyingly crisply underfoot. Provence is beautiful in all of the seasons, of course. But on a day like this, being outside is a reminder of how sheltered we are here, nestled at the foot of the huge mountains in the distance.

'In your own time, Kellie,' I reassure her, adjusting my bobble hat.

She begins to giggle.

'What?' I ask, as she straightens her own.

'Dee-Dee is wonderful, truly wonderful, but these hand-knitted hats make us both look like pixies.'

I turn to look at her and suddenly we start belly-laughing. It's not the style, so much as the fact that Dee-Dee used up the *oddments*, as she calls them. So, the hats are rainbow-coloured, if rainbows ever had forty different colours to them. The pom-pom on mine is pale blue and on Kellie's it's purple.

'Who cares?' I shrug, and Kellie takes the words out of my mouth.

'It's the thought that counts!' She pauses for a brief moment, before picking back up. 'Okay. The favour is quite a biggie. I've told my father I don't want to go back. Not forever, but for the foreseeable future. I need you to approach Nico about that in case it doesn't fit in with his plans. I don't want to do it myself as he might feel awkward about it if he doesn't think it's a good idea.'

I draw to a halt and Kellie does the same, but the air is damp with the intensity of the cold, and you can feel it in your bones.

'Come on, let's shelter beneath one of the barns.' We speed up our pace. 'Here, help me move this bench out a little and we can sit for a moment against the wall.'

With only three sides to the barn, it's still cold, but there's protection from the elements.

'Of course I'll do that for you. But I know Nico would love it if you wanted to stay on. You've been wonderful, taking on the craft lessons and being so chatty with visitors in general. And honest, when the occasion has warranted it.'

'Ah, you mean about cutting my wrists. Well, that's another thing

I wanted to get off my chest. When I came here, it was either this place or being under constant scrutiny at some facility, or other. Or worse, Dad getting in a nurse and keeping me at home. I'm ashamed to say that initially it was my intention to do a better job of it next time around.'

Her face is stony as my jaw drops and tears begin to prickle behind my eyelashes. Before I can pull myself together enough to express my concern, she continues.

'What I wanted you to know is that I don't feel that way any more. I've discovered that I can do something that makes me feel good about myself. I fit in here. And this is the first place I've ever been able to say that. You know that it was you and Patricia who gave me back a vestige of confidence, don't you? And it's grown from there.'

'Oh, Kellie. You are so full of empathy, compassion and love, it's breathtaking at times. How can you not know that? You are an inspiration and your maturity and patience is well beyond your years because you are a survivor. I hope you've noticed the change in Taylor, recently, because that's down to you. And Bastien, too, is so much more sociable because you've taken the time to include him whenever you can.'

'We are a bit of an odd team, though, aren't we? The Three Musketeers,' she chuckles, hoarsely, then coughs to clear her throat. 'The bad news is that my dad wants me back where he can *keep a close eye on me*, as he puts it. He said this is a cult and I'm being brainwashed.'

My eyes spring open wide. 'He said *what*?'

'His words. Literally. If Nico says *yes*, then could you ring my dad, please? I mean, I'll be next to you, but you'll know what to say when he starts kicking off.'

I shake my head, unable to understand her father's reaction. That's an outrageous accusation to make. 'Of course. I'll do everything and anything I can to help, Kellie. I'll talk to Nico tonight. He was singing your praises only the other day, actually.'

A little smile of satisfaction twitches around her lips for a moment. 'That's nice to know, Fern, thank you. Okay, so now the awkward bit.'

She looks down at her feet, scuffing them along the compacted dirt floor of the barn. That's not a good sign, avoiding eye contact.

'When your sister, Hannah, was here, she asked me if you were having an affair with Nico.'

My mouth goes dry and I have to swallow hard to force out some words.

'Why would she think that?' I wonder, letting out a low groan of disappointment.

Kellie shrugs her shoulders, uncomfortably. 'Because you two are close and he's your mentor; that's rather special. We all know it's a working relationship, but Hannah was… shocked – maybe *surprised* is a better word. It was in confidence, Fern, but if I were in your shoes, I'd want to know so I could set my sister straight.' The way she looks at me, I wonder if it's a question Kellie is posing, too.

'I really appreciate that, Kellie, and of course I will do that in a way where she won't realise we've spoken about it. I'm horrified she thinks that, though, and it's not fair on Nico, either.'

She nods. 'I guessed as much. But I owe you, Fern, and Hannah is stressing over it.'

I flounder for something to say to change the subject to ease the air of tension. 'How's Patricia?'

'Darn it. I still haven't told you! Doh – I keep forgetting, my head's so full of stuff at the moment. She's going to be popping in to say hello. She'll be on her way to a holiday cottage her and her husband own, about twenty kilometres further south, I think.'

'When?' I ask, excitedly. 'It will be so good to see her again.'

'The twenty-third of December, but I'm waiting on Patricia to confirm that date. She wanted to surprise you, but I didn't want you making plans and missing her visit as it's a Sunday.'

'You two are very special to me. You arrived on my first official day here as a volunteer.'

Kellie grimaces. 'You were thrown in at the deep end, then.'

'And look how far we've come. Anyway, let's head back and get warm. I can't actually feel my toes!' I exclaim.

'Me, neither. I think this calls for Margot's special hot chocolate.'

'Definitely.'

* * *

'Hello?'

'Fern, it's me. Just a quick call, I needed to hear your voice, that's all. Nothing's wrong.'

I hear Aiden's words, but I don't believe him. His general demeanour is odd, so I know something has happened but not why he won't share it with me.

'Oh. Right. That's unusual for you, darling.'

Why ring if he doesn't want to discuss whatever is unsettling him? I can't help feeling a little cross; we've always shared everything.

I can sense that he's already regretting making the call and my stomach begins to churn. He says nothing, just sits there not even looking at me but fiddling with some papers next to his laptop.

'I had a chatty email from your mum, and Hannah texted to say she had a long chat with you. Have you heard from Owen?' I ask.

'Yes, to both. Guess it made me a bit homesick. They both said how well you looked and how content. France suits you, it seems.'

Oh, so this is what... regret? Or mistrust because I should be miserable without him? A little nerve at the side of my eye begins to twitch, as feeling mildly cross begins to turn into full-on annoyance.

'God, there are moments I wish I'd never started this,' he admits, his words coming out in a rush. 'Sorry, Fern, I've had a bad day, that's all. And with Owen heading off on his first deployment abroad, I know your parents are anxious. If we were still at home, you'd be there to—'

He comes to an abrupt halt. I feel like returning a quick retort about making one's bed and lying in it, but that would be mean. I know my anger is irrational and I'm shocked at the strength of my reaction, but I don't know why we can't simply talk through whatever has happened. I decide, instead, to change the subject. 'How are the plans for Thailand coming along? Any news?'

He sighs, a tired edge to his voice indicating that maybe he's been overdoing it and now my guilt begins to kick in. He must witness a lot of the harsher realities of life on a daily basis, things I can't even begin to understand. He's not holidaying but helping a community where everyday problems can quickly escalate out of control. It's even tougher when kids are involved, and I know that will be hard on him. Whatever he's witnessed, he's taken it to heart.

'Good. It's all coming together, and the flights have now been booked,' he confirms. *Flights*? As in several legs to the journey, or more than one person flying?

'That's great.' Well, maybe it is; or maybe it's not.

'You know, Fern, one thing I've realised is that you've always been there to smooth things over for me. Even through the rough times, you just stepped up. You know, when it all went wrong, and I lost us everything we had. And a year later, when your sister died in that tragic accident, I didn't know how to handle it. Now I wonder whether you ever felt that I didn't man up, that I let you down on both occasions?'

My stomach tightens, and my throat constricts a little. He's raking over the past, the things we haven't referred to in years. Why now?

'We got through it and that's all that matters, Aiden. That was over eight years ago, so why are you bringing this up now?' I'm not challenging him but the timing of this conversation. 'I've only ever done what I felt was right for us all. It wasn't your fault the business went bust, but the downturn in the economy at the time. You always did everything you could within your power, no one could have asked for more than that.'

He pauses for a moment. 'I should have acknowledged how amazing you were during those tough times, though, before now. I'm sorry I didn't. Anyway, I have to go, I'm afraid. Duty calls. Hannah said it's busy at the retreat. Well, she said you were really caught up with this painting thing.'

Painting thing? If you took the time to ask me about it, I'd tell you everything, but you've switched off, Aiden, and I don't know why. 'Yes,' I admit. 'It's all good, though. I wouldn't have it any other way.'

There's a pause that stretches out across the seconds, awkwardly.

'Right. Um. Anyway, next Saturday on Skype?'

'Yes. Speak then.'

'Miss you, babe, love you,' he adds, emphatically. 'And thank you.'

'For what?'

'For being there for me every single day of our married life.'

And then I realise what day it is, and I berate myself.

'Happy anniversary, darling. Miss and love you, too.'

As the line goes dead, I can't believe I forgot. Eight years ago today, we tied the knot with a simple ceremony at the local registry office. The wedding party consisted of thirty people and afterwards we headed to a local hotel for a slap-up meal. Then back home to the house we'd been renovating for almost a year but which had been on hold since the death of my sister some four months prior.

It was our first day living there together, as unfinished as it was, but it marked the start of our future. Before Rachel's death, the anticipation was like experiencing a dozen Christmases all at once and it filled us both with a sense of exhilaration. But in the aftermath of what happened, it was hard to celebrate, knowing that she should have been there and feeling angry that she'd been taken from us.

When Aiden and I parted for our break, though, we agreed not to dwell on being apart for special occasions during this year. Instead, we'd make next year's celebrations more memorable. Bigger parties, bigger gatherings. But I should have remembered our anniversary. The fact that Aiden appeared maudlin means something has lowered his spirits. Maybe because he's never had to cope on his own with the fallout from any major upset, that's what triggered his call.

And the fact that I'm not there to fold my arms around him feels wrong, very wrong.

I sigh. I need to talk to Hannah about Nico, next. I don't suppose she unwittingly said anything in conversation with Aiden that added to his worries? I touch the blank screen with my thumb, tempted to call him back. But what would I say? Instead, I text him.

If you need me any time – night, or day – just call. I'm always here for you. x

* * *

'That's good, Fern. Are you pleased with how it's going?'

Nico appears at my shoulder, watching as I sweep the brush upwards in a gentle curve.

'I think I am. I'm going to call it *Solitude*, I think.'

He continues to study the canvas, tilting the angle of his head and then leaning in to inspect the brushstrokes up close.

'Good choice. My initial thoughts were along the lines of *Separation*, or *Loneliness*,' he replies softly, straightening to look at me. 'The way you've portrayed the light working out from the centre gives it a feeling of depth. This here represents a person?' He indicates to the shape in the centre of the mass of colour.

'Yes. It's the soul. The layers are like veils, which need to be peeled away if one wants to connect with one's true self.'

'Hmm,' he nods his head.

Then I begin laughing. 'On the other hand, it could just be a very yellow smattering of paint that would brighten a wall and be a conversation piece.'

He chuckles. 'It certainly draws the eye, and the longer you look, the more you see. Cleverly done and not easy when you're working with such a limited range of tones. That's impressive.'

It's hard not to feel pleased with myself, hearing his words of endorsement. I've enjoyed every single brushstroke. I think the colour alone has brightened my spirits, despite the fact that it hasn't been a particularly easy day.

'Do you know, Fern, having you here and seeing you so engrossed in what you're doing has been very satisfying for me. It's been a long time since I had the pleasure of mentoring someone over a prolonged period of time. It's a humbling experience because it reminds me of my own early years.'

I swish my brush around in the clean water pot and dab it on the rag.

'I wondered if it was actually rather frustrating, watching someone and wanting to constantly correct them. Even now, I look back just a couple of months and I can't believe how much I've learnt in that time.'

'You're a good student. And you watch and learn, too. But what's important is that you take away with you what works best for your personal style. No two artists are the same. That's what makes each painting unique. Are you packing up, already?' he asks, as I swish another brush in the water.

'I think so. I want this swathe to dry before I add a little shimmer of white. Just to give it the illusion of a curve.'

Nico raises an eyebrow then edges back a couple of feet. 'Stand here. The perspective opens up the further back I go. It's almost like that soul is inside the sun; as if it's being swallowed, encapsulated.'

I join him, and he's right.

He raises both eyebrows this time. 'And it is very yellow. Time for a glass of wine?'

I nod.

As Nico disappears into the workroom to do the honours, I dim the lights and walk down towards the glass doors. The wind tugs at the leafless skeleton bushes and shrubs. The evergreens are swaying gently, their denseness allowing them to fight back.

'I bet that's a bitingly cold wind,' Nico says, sidling up to hand me a glass.

'Yes. Sometimes winter just seems to go on and on.'

I watch as he sinks down to the floor, leaning his back against the wall. Following suit, I sit facing him as we both gaze out over the garden. The low-level lighting creates a backdrop of shadows, which move as the plants and bushes sway in the breeze.

'It's funny how as a child you look out and you see something quite different. Simple shapes become looming monsters that turn darkness into a frightening place,' I reflect.

'Hmm. I was thinking the same thing. Even as an adult, the mind can play tricks. My father and I went out with a group of locals truffling on a night like this, once. Black diamonds, they call them. We ventured deep into the woods with only lanterns to light our way.'

'I didn't realise you could harvest truffles in winter.'

'June to August, and November through to March, are when you often hear the baying of the hounds late at night.'

I swirl the red liquid around gently in my glass, releasing the flavours before sniffing and then taking a sip. 'At night, in the dark? Wouldn't it be easier in daylight?'

'Yes, but there are secret locations, you see. The tubers grow just a few inches below the surface, which protects them from frost and snow. It's slow-going if the ground is a little hard, though.'

It's the first time he's mentioned doing anything at all with his father, so it must be a very special memory.

'It was freezing, with a wind as biting as the one tonight. He was reasonably sober that night, not wanting to let himself down in front of the other men. It was when he was still functioning, on his good days, that is. As we headed out, he started to talk about the past for some reason. When I was a small boy, he often took me out exploring and it was strange, hearing him talk about that with a genuine fondness. I realised then that he harboured a real sense of regret for what might have been. The life he could have had, I suppose, if he'd gotten his demons under control.'

Nico lays his head back against the wall, one leg out straight in front of him and the other bent. His arm rests on his knee, holding his wine glass. He's deep in thought, and not wishing to disturb him I say nothing but turn my head, looking up towards the heavens.

And then I see it.

'A shooting star!' I yell, and he jumps, spilling wine down the leg of his jeans and laughing at me. 'Did you see it, too?' I ask, hoping he did.

His smile is broad. 'I caught it. Make a wish, quickly – but don't tell me what it is.'

I smile, nodding. The words were on my lips the moment I first saw that little flash of light making a perfect arc against the almost pitch-black sky. *Keep everyone safe and take us where we are meant to be.*

'I'm not sure I believe in that,' I admit. 'But you never know, I suppose.'

'Do wishes ever come true? For most of my childhood and teenage life, all I longed for was that my mother would feel a sense of peace. When my father died, I thought her life would be easier, but she crumbled, a lonely and disappointed woman who felt an acute sense of having failed. Looking after him had become the driving factor which kept her going; it was all about getting through each day as best she could. Suddenly, there was this emptiness, a void she told me. I thought that was the saddest thing I've ever heard. How can you miss someone who was so selfish and abusive? Someone who stole her life, like a thief.'

It's incredible to think a parent would put their child through something like that, let alone a partner.

'You must have missed her when she returned to Spain,' I remark. My voice is low as I monitor Nico's reaction. He wrinkles his brow, staring down into his glass.

'I knew her time was running out, but I didn't know how to handle it. I didn't want my mother to go, but it was the right thing for her. She spent her last summer surrounded by those who knew her in happier times and that was a blessing for which I was grateful.'

I can't even begin to imagine what it must have been like for Nico at that time. Alone, grieving and having to piece together a new life for himself.

'And that's how the retreat began,' I find myself saying out loud.

He nods. 'Loneliness is an awful thing. For a while I didn't think I could stay here, but Margot convinced me to offer bed and breakfast. She stepped in to sort me out after my mother left, fearing I'd starve.' He looks suitably embarrassed.

'But you can cook, I've seen that for myself.'

His laugh is throaty. 'Only what Margot has taught me over the years. She became my housekeeper at first, sorting the breakfasts when I had guests here. Bastien was one of the first to arrive and we just hit it off. I needed someone to repair some fences and he was looking for some temporary work. Within a year everything seemed to fall into place, so I can't really take any credit for it. It was fate.'

Fate. *And fate brought me here, too.* What purpose am I supposed to fulfil in Nico's life? I wonder. It seems out of kilter with the path I'm following, like a detour. But Aiden created this little deviation to the plan and our life back in the UK has nothing at all to do with Provence, or Nico. I'm feeling confused and trying hard to keep any emotion and empathy I feel for a troubled artist, a man I've grown to respect, in check. All I can offer is words of comfort, even when it's clear how much he's hurting and how deep his wounds go.

If Nico's mother was here now, she'd be so very proud of him and what he's achieved because fate doesn't hand anything to you if you aren't prepared to put in the work. This place obviously meant a lot to her and she instinctively knew that this was where Nico was supposed to be. She distanced herself from her son to ease the impact of her passing and that's the true sign of a mother's love. True love, I reflect, is all about sacrifice.

22

STEPPING IT UP

With only four days to go until our first visitors arrive at The Haven, Ceana and Pierce return amidst much excitement.

Nico arranges for everyone to get together for a celebratory lunch and then formally reveals the new name for the retreat, handing around the redesigned advertising materials.

'I'll get a batch of these sent off to several clinics in Ireland and the UK, Nico,' Pierce immediately steps in. 'Ceana and I handed out a pile of business cards on our trip. There was a lot of interest and I think we should see the enquiries begin to roll in quite quickly.'

I think the rest of us are a little taken aback at Pierce's proactive approach. He's very business-orientated and it feels a little out of step with how things have been run in the past.

'Great, thank you both,' Nico replies, sporting a big smile. 'Fern has been organising everything in Ceana's absence and she's done an amazing job of directing us all. There isn't much left to do. We didn't unpack the things for the treatment rooms, Pierce, so maybe Fern will help you get that all sorted. You can draft in additional help as needed.'

There's a lot of nodding heads around the table, more than willing to help if required.

'Great. Have you decided yet on the maximum number of places that are going to be available? It's something that needs to be finalised with some urgency as it will impact on everyone and, in particular, I'm thinking about the catering side of things. I know the first couple of weeks will be lighter as we test everything out, but places are going to fill quickly. Once we're confident we have a chance of hitting our targets, we can look for some additional help.'

Pierce has only been back here a couple of hours and already he's putting pressure on Nico, but Nico seems unfazed.

'I am conscious we're placing a lot on both your and Ceana's shoulders, Pierce. I'm hoping Ceana and I can work through the accommodation issues together and look at the logistics.'

'I have a few ideas, Nico, and I'm sure you do, too. It will probably mean a little reorganisation, but if we look at that later this afternoon, then we can run through the changes with the group after dinner tonight, maybe?' Ceana is our acknowledged organiser, but suddenly even she sounds more business-orientated. The course and her time away with Pierce have been extremely productive, it seems. I am surprised that his attitude has rubbed off on her, though, as it's a very different approach, albeit one that's probably what was needed.

Glancing around the table, I don't think I'm the only one who didn't realise the arrival of one new person could change the dynamic of the whole group. I can only hope that's a positive development and Nico doesn't end up stressing as his original dream morphs into something quite different.

* * *

The guys had carried everything across to the new treatment rooms in the cottage, together with some boxes that Pierce had brought with him. He hadn't had time to unpack them before he left with Ceana.

'You've all been working very hard, I see,' he comments as we enter treatment room number one on the ground floor of the cottage.

'Everyone works as a team here. If we need to switch any of the larger boxes between rooms, then either Taylor or Bastien will be happy to help out,' I remark, hoping my guesswork wasn't too far wrong on what was going where.

'We're fine. I'm used to lugging stuff about. Between us we'll manage, I'm sure. Thank you for sorting the cupboards and desks. I realised afterwards I should have roughed out a plan for you, but there wasn't time. The focus has to be on filling places and getting the word out amongst our peers. Courses are great networking events, but Ceana needed to bring herself up to date on a few things. The sessions I ran went well, and I've honoured my outstanding commitments. It's wonderful to be back here with just the one agenda, now.'

I didn't realise he taught, as well as being a practitioner. In fact, as the day goes on and we begin unpacking his things, we part-fill the wall above his desk with his diplomas and certificates. This man is a perpetual student, it seems, even though he has a vast wealth of experience spanning in excess of twenty years. Everything from a sports masseuse, to bereavement and grief counselling, accredited by the UK College of Holistic Training.

'I'll miss running courses for them,' he says, suddenly appearing next to me as I rub a duster over the frame of the last certificate. 'But Nico is very persuasive. It's unusual for someone to be more focused on the quality of delivery than the money rolling in.'

That remark has cheered me up a little. Maybe this man isn't quite the table-thumper, with pound signs in his eyes, that I assumed him to be.

'Your approach is very different to the way it's been here in the past, if you don't mind me saying, Pierce.'

He purses his lips. 'Not at all. I believe everyone should speak their mind and not bottle things up. The Haven has to turn a profit, Fern. This is a major change of direction and the holistic elements require everything to be cohesive. The plan is that all staff members will receive basic training, so they are fully aware of what will be on offer. Experiencing something first-hand is the best way of understanding the overall concept.'

It's been good spending this time getting to know Pierce. His heart is in the right place and he's going to take a lot of pressure from Nico's shoulders in moving things forward. I realise that Pierce is still talking and I tune back in.

'... And Ceana is going to organise that as quickly as possible. I will be interested in sampling some of the other workshops on offer, too. But, to protect Nico's investment and ensure a long-term future for us all, advertising is crucial. However, that costs money, which has to be found. Nico has put everything he has into this, so we must rise to the challenge and get everything working smoothly. We want visitors to go home feeling we haven't simply met their expectations but exceeded them. Creating that environment is down to each and every member of the team. Personal recommendation is everything these days, as are good reviews on the website.'

It all sounds rather daunting. 'Is the intention to eventually replace people who don't have the necessary skills?' I think of Taylor, Bastien and Dee-Dee – skilled artisans, but will they still fit in here, as time goes on?

His eyes narrow. 'You're suspicious about my motives. Don't be. And the answer is *no*. Some of the people who will come here will need appropriate guidance and we will be adding at least one more professional to the well-being team. I have a personal trainer and fitness guru already lined up for that, but he can't join us until March at the earliest. So, use of the gym equipment will be recreational only, at the individual user's own risk, until then. But a big part of the attraction is still going to be based around visitors being able to learn new crafts and skills – or at least have a go. Hobbies are an important part of learning how to de-stress, as is doing something physical, or meditating. On that note, Nico suggested I approach you about becoming my assistant for the first couple of weeks.' Staring back at him with a surprised look on my face, he grins at me. 'Hey, I'm not asking you to go in cold. I'll talk you through the meditation process one-to-one so you feel comfortable with it. I just need an extra pair of eyes and ears. As I'm conducting the sessions, it would be great if you could circulate and check everyone is happy. I can't demonstrate and floor-walk at the same time, I'm afraid.'

'Okay,' I sound hesitant, because I am. 'I think I can handle that if you are very specific about what you want me to do.'

'Oh, I will be most specific,' he retorts. I don't doubt that for one moment.

'I'm not sure I'm the right person, I will be honest with you,' I reply, almost without thinking.

'Ceana says you are intuitive, and I think you will be able to spot someone who is struggling, or outside their comfort zone.'

'Intuitive?'

He stares at me, blankly. 'You didn't know she was psychic?'

'No. And you?'

His smile is humble. 'Sadly, not, because I envy her that quality. I live my life according to my ethos.'

'Which is?'

'Live as if you only have one life; but I believe we have many. Celebrate the good qualities in people, but always lead by example. And finally, good deeds often go unrewarded, but seldom unnoticed – it would be a better world if everyone kept that in mind. Simple.'

Pierce is anything but simple. How that will change things here, I have no idea, but we're all about to find out.

* * *

'Hi, Mum and Dad.' Kellie stares at the screen, nervously.

I reach across and squeeze her hand.

'Exciting things are happening here, and I really do want to stay and be a part of it. Fern is here, she's Nico's assistant, and I thought if you have any questions, now's the time to ask them.'

I feel it would be polite to introduce myself properly. 'Hello, Mr and Mrs Preston. My name is Fern Wyman. I'm a manager of a Human Resources department back in the UK, but I'm taking a year's sabbatical to work as a volunteer at the retreat. I'm halfway through that year as we speak. It's only natural there are things you'd like to ask as I have a sister who is about the same age as Kellie, so I understand your concerns. So, please, feel free to pose any questions you have and I'll do my best to answer them.'

There's no eye contact between them and the body language is non-existent. Their chairs are a couple of feet apart.

'Kellie, it's time you came home,' Mr Preston says, totally ignoring my little speech.

'I agree,' his wife joins in. 'Strangers don't have the same level of interest and concern as family, Kellie. I don't see why you need to stay any longer.'

Considering Kellie has shared the fact that they seldom agree on anything, they seem united on this, at least.

I can see Kellie beginning to panic, her face has frozen.

'We all want the best for Kellie, I can assure you of that. The change in her since she's been here is incredible. You have raised one very determined and capable young woman,' I acknowledge, hoping to foster some goodwill.

'Well, it's easy to say that glibly, but she's fragile and we've seen that with frightening results. This was supposed to be a little holiday for her, Ms Wyman, nothing more. It's time she came home.' Her father looks adamant.

Kellie stares at me, the colour draining from her face.

'Your daughter has recently taken over the role of the craft tutor. It's something she enjoys doing and in which she demonstrates a natural ability. It requires patience and leadership skills, both of which she has in abundance. I believe this is just the sort of positive, reaffirming environment Kellie could benefit from and she's keen to stay. To pull her away now would be a step backwards, in my opinion. Her confidence is growing daily and I'm proud to be working alongside her.'

Mr Preston snorts. 'I bet you are. Living there for bed and board with no salary is slave labour. Kellie needs looking after and pretending she's fit to help other people is a big mistake.'

If I'm horrified by that remark, how must Kellie feel? I can't even look at her because I'm so angry. 'That sort of negative attitude is precisely why Kellie's confidence dropped to such a low level. Desperation results in people acting out of character and Kellie's reaction demonstrated how unhappy she was at the time. Here, she's in a very supportive and positive environment, and now she's teaching other people a whole range of creative hobbies. That's some achievement, Mr and Mrs Preston, and if you don't believe me, then you are very welcome to come here and witness it for yourselves.'

That changes everything.

'Oh, I can't possibly get away from work to head off to France with Christmas looming,' Mr Preston says sternly. 'This is all nonsense and we should never have agreed to her leaving the UK in the first place.'

Kellie's eyes flash. 'I'm happy here. Doesn't that mean anything to you?'

Her mother leans towards the screen, finally she has something to say.

'Happy is good, my love, but you're being used. They don't care about *you*, or your situation.'

I glance at Kellie and she looks ready to burst into tears. No wonder her life is a total mess. Sorry, *was* a total mess. Suddenly, her head jerks back.

'I'm old enough now to get married and pretty much do what I like. What I want is to stay here. I'm right, aren't I, Fern?'

Well, that's a surprise.

'Yes. You are officially an adult, Kellie. It's not always easy for parents to get used to that fact and let go, but you are a free agent.'

Mr Preston almost chokes as his words erupt, vehemently. 'Are you a fool, Kellie? Cheap labour, that's all this is – you work for a bed and three meals a day. It's shameful!'

I reach out to restrain Kellie as she moves to stand, and presumably flee.

'You and your wife underestimate how valued a member of our community Kellie is; as a volunteer here, we all work under the same terms and conditions, I can assure you of that. While we are here, this is our home. It's a wonderful way to learn new skills and grow in confidence. I think Kellie has made her decision.' I turn to look at her and she nods firmly. 'You can turn up at any time, unannounced, to inspect the facilities here and see up close the work we carry out. We have nothing to hide. Now, if you would excuse us, we have a lot to do before the end of the day. There's nothing quite as satisfying as building something as a part of a team. But each member is key and that includes Kellie. Lovely to meet you and I do hope to see you in person very soon.'

With that, Kellie presses end call and we both let out a shriek.

'OMG – did you see my dad's face?' She throws up her hands to cover those blazing cheeks. 'He looked like he was going to explode!'

Her eyes are glowing, and I can see that she's delighted with the way the conversation went.

'You know, Kellie, when I leave here, if you're ever stuck for somewhere to live, then I'll always have a bed for you. You must never let someone else's negativity pull you down or make you stop believing in yourself. And I mean that, sincerely.'

She sucks in a deep breath. 'Aww... thank you, Fern. It means a lot to know that, but just hearing you stand up to him makes me feel that at last I'm free. I have choices. My parents could never understand what's going on here. Maybe the changes to come will mean I don't quite fit in, but while I do, I'm so happy to be a part of this. As for the future, well, I'm more than content to take it one day at a time. Although, at some point, I'd really like to focus on something, maybe go to college when I've found what really inspires me. I'd like to help other people in some capacity.'

'When you're ready, have a chat with Pierce. His skills are very diverse, and he would certainly be a good place to start if you have specific questions.'

She does a fist pump in the air. 'Ha! My dad was so not expecting that!' It's telling that she rarely talks about her mum, it's always her dad.

Independence brings with it the challenge of taking full responsibility for your actions. As I watch Kellie celebrating what she perceives as an important triumph, I realise just how much she has changed. The moody, introverted character she was has completely disappeared, and now look at her. I do believe that she's ready to take on the world and will quickly learn from any mistakes she might make in future.

23

ALL CHANGE

After lunch, we spend an hour in the gym as Pierce leads his first meditation session and I'm pleasantly surprised. I thought maybe I'd end up sitting here, wondering why everyone else gets it and I don't, but it isn't like that. He talks us through a walk down to a beach and for a while I feel I'm actually there, the imagery is so tangible. I can even sense someone with me, as if they are inside my head, but I have no idea who that person is – or whether I even know them.

'Right, everyone. That's part one of the exercise completed. Now, I need you all to pair up as you're going for a little walk in the fresh air to get the blood pumping.' Pierce looks way more enthusiastic than the rest of us. I feel ready to take a nap.

As we stand, Ceana makes a beeline for Bastien and, naturally, Taylor and Kellie were lying next to each other on their mats during the session. I hesitate for a moment as Nico stands back and it's obvious Odile and Dee-Dee are going to feel more comfortable together.

'Guess that narrows down your choice,' Nico leans in to whisper, with a mischievous glint in his eye.

'No one wants to partner up with the boss,' I declare. 'I think we were all surprised Pierce managed to drag you away from your work.'

Pierce raises his hands, calling us to order as now everyone is talking at the same time. 'Okay, folks. This should take no more than an hour to complete. Grab one of these sheets and follow the instructions. There's a short feedback form I'd like each of you to fill in with regard to the two sessions and I'd be grateful if you could let me have those back when you return. Enjoy your little stroll and having a go at the list of tasks. Great job, guys, and I appreciate that for most of you these workshops might involve you stepping outside your personal comfort zone. But what doesn't kill you makes you stronger.'

Pierce's joke heralds a lot of laughter and it helps to dispel a little awkwardness we've all felt. Well, aside from Ceana, to whom none of this is new.

The group splits up and Nico and I head off to grab our coats. It's really cold again today but not icy and the wind has dropped, so it could be a lot worse.

As we all traipse down the lane leading into the woods, there's a point at which we start going off in different directions.

'Have you read this list?' I ask Nico, trying hard not to frown as I look at the tasks we've been given.

'Yes... it's a bit outside the box for me, I will admit.'

'Well, in that case you should go first.'

He looks at me and grimaces as we draw to a halt.

'Do you trust me not to look?' he asks.

Task number one is to close your eyes and let someone lead you forward while you talk through what you're experiencing.

'Pull your beanie hat down just in case you get tempted,' I tease.

'Well, that's hardly a confidence-building start, considering you're asking me to put my trust in you.' He flashes me a cheeky grin and I bat my eyelashes at him in feigned annoyance.

'Let's just get on with it, shall we?'

Nico does as he's told and I push the sheet of paper into my pocket.

'Ready? Now, I'm going to lead you forward very slowly and you tell me what you're feeling.'

Standing next to him, I place a hand firmly on his arm and the other around his middle. It's a bit of a stretch as he's wearing a padded jacket, but I feel I can steer him safely and off we go.

'Well?' I ask, when we're several steps ahead.

'It's strange. I keep thinking I'm going to trip over something.'

'I won't let that happen. What else?'

His initial couple of steps were faltering, but he's beginning to relax now and walk forward more purposefully.

'I hear an airplane somewhere in the distance. And voices, someone is laughing. I can hear you breathing. Are you nervous?'

'No. Just making sure I'm doing a good job of making sure you don't fall over your own feet.'

He stops. 'It's your turn.'

As we swap over, he yanks my bobble hat down over my eyes.

'Hey, I had no intention of cheating, believe me,' I tell him, firmly.

As he slides his arms around me and we move off, I feel safe. I don't hesitate to take that first step because I know Nico wouldn't let anything bad happen to me. He's already gained my trust, implicitly.

'Well?'

'Um... the floor is crunchy beneath my boots. The twigs make it a little uneven and I can hear something moving, it's very close.'

After what feels like several minutes of me tentatively putting one foot in front of the other, Nico suddenly yanks off my hat. 'Over there,' he whispers, 'a rabbit.'

The little guy is up on his hind legs and appears to be eating something, probably an acorn. He nibbles away, his eyes firmly fixed on us as we remain still. Even when a bird flies overhead, he continues eating until he's done. Then he turns and disappears into some thick bushes, seemingly content we pose no threat whatsoever.

Easing my shoulders back, Nico releases me rather awkwardly, clearing his throat. We're going through the motions but neither of us is really taking this as seriously as Pierce intended.

'I think we can tick that one. This is a sensory thing, isn't it?' He looks at me and I nod in agreement. 'Okay. Number two. Shall we take a seat over on that huge log?'

'If you like.'

It's sad to see what was at one time a sturdy tree, now lying on its side. Whether it was hit by lightning, or the roots failed because of rot, it's hard to tell. But it's been here a long time and the trunk rises a good three feet off the ground.

Nico gives me a boost and I sit astride it as he hauls himself up.

'Eyes closed then. You go first. This is a test of your sense of smell,' he says.

'Ugh, rotting wood, for sure – that's very strong. Mushrooms. Ooh... woodsmoke, do you get that?'

'Hmm... yes, it's getting stronger. Someone's only just lit a fire. Burning leaves, I think. I'm getting that earthy smell, I wouldn't say mushrooms exactly, more like well-composted peat. As for rotting wood, I think that smell is wild garlic that is going over. It has a bitter, dank odour to it.'

'Oh, I didn't know that. It's a bit fishy, too.'

Nico laughs.

'What's next?'

We open our eyes at the same moment, and he gives me a warm, intense smile.

'It makes you stop and think, doing this, doesn't it? The things around us we take for granted and cease to notice.'

His eyes are combing over me and I feel a little uncomfortable, so I look away, pulling Pierce's instruction sheet from my pocket.

'Point out a natural feature that looks like something else.'

We gaze around for a few minutes.

'See that tree trunk over there?' Nico raises his arm, pointing. 'There's a big knot on the left-hand side just before it branches up. It looks like a witch's face. Two eyes and a long, beaky nose.'

It takes me a moment to see what he's talking about, but once I've got it, he's right.

'Ooh, I'm not sure I like that. It's a bit spooky, actually. Now, let me see... Over there, by that group of tall, skinny trees. There are some weird little branches sticking out of the side of one of the trunks. It looks like—'

'Antlers,' Nico replies in a hushed voice.

Nico puts a finger to his lips, and we watch in fascination as a deer forages around amongst some low-level shrubs. The tiniest of sounds catches his ear and his head shoots up, ears straining. He turns this way and that, head cocked – his eyes fixed in flight or fight mode. Seconds later, all we can see is his bobbing white tail as he runs off.

'It's a roe deer, *un chevreuil*. He'll shed his antlers soon.'

'Well, it was worth coming just to catch a glimpse of him.'

Nico jumps off our perch and extends his hand to help me down. My left foot slips and I end up almost pushing him over; only a pair of strong arms and a taut body saves us from landing in a heap on the compacted earth floor.

Nico stares down into my eyes. 'Your hand is cold; you should have worn gloves. We'll whip through the last few things and get back.' His voice is uneven and my heart begins to pound.

Berating myself for my stupid reaction, I say the first thing that comes into my head. 'You don't find this all rather fascinating? I thought it would be something and nothing, but it makes me realise we walk around all the time not really seeing what's there. If we switch off the whirling thoughts we carry around in our heads, then maybe we'd all begin to see things differently. It's liberating, isn't it?' I disentangle myself from Nico's arms with a brief 'thank you', but I can still feel his eyes on me while he's considering my question.

'Sometimes people are liberating,' Nico mutters, as he turns away to read the next task on Pierce's list.

'People?'

He turns to look at me once more, but it is with a sense of reluctance. 'Whenever I'm around you, Fern, I find myself looking at things differently. My eyes have been opened and the world seems a better place with you in it.'

Nico holds my gaze for a few agonising seconds. It isn't only the deer that has been startled on this little walk and I have no words to explain how that statement makes me feel.

* * *

As I head back to the château in the early evening, Nico is in the hallway with his arms wrapped around a large box.

'Just in time, Fern – can you get the studio door for me? It's rather heavy, thanks.'

I traipse along two steps behind him and when he comes to a halt, I lean forward to swing open the door, then follow him inside.

'You've been busy, I see.' Glancing at the canvas he's been working on, I marvel at the difference as some blossoms I hardly noticed before are now jumping out at me. I'm surprised he was in the mood to paint after our walk in the forest. 'Beautiful shading, Nico. I wish I had your level of skill.'

He reappears from the workroom, leaning against the door jamb to look at me.

'It all comes with practice, Fern. Patience is everything. Pierce seems to be winning you around, I'm glad to see. I noticed that he stopped to glance over your feedback sheet the minute you handed it to him.'

I admit that my first impression was that Pierce is rather over-powering, but I accept that I might have been wrong.

'Maybe I was a little quick to judge him. I realise there's a serious business side to the changes being made and perhaps we needed reminding of that. But I think today was a turning point for several of us, when it comes to understanding some of the techniques he uses. The whole team is committed to making this work, Nico, on every level.'

He nods, appreciatively. 'It's about time we began generating enough income to guarantee a long-term future here for everyone. That means offering something more than a basic salary and the ability to cover the running costs. If we can't achieve that target, the fear is that either I'll run out of money or we'll lose good people who can earn more elsewhere. It all began in a very low-key way, which has been fine until now. But volunteers are few and far between these days, and those who regard this as their home deserve to be recompensed accordingly for their skills. It's only fair and to do that we need to get serious. Pierce doesn't just bring his expertise, but he also has that sound business acumen which could be the difference between success and failure. It will allow me to step back from a role I was never really very good at, anyway.'

It's heartening to hear Nico sounding so delighted about delegating some of the workload; maybe this means he will be able to spend more time in his studio in future. I hope he's proud of what he's achieved here, though.

'You were good enough, Nico, to set this up and bring together a group of like-minded people. Without that start, The Haven would be nothing more than a dream. Don't underestimate your abilities.'

His smile is lopsided; I've embarrassed him a little, but I can see he's pleased by my words.

'There's a place for you long-term if you want it, Fern. There's no time limit, the offer is open-ended.'

I drag my eyes away from his face, reluctantly. 'Thank you, Nico. But I don't think my future is destined to be here. The thought is lovely on one hand, but to stay would mean my life had fallen apart. This will always represent a very special time for me, though. And I'm glad to be a part of this new phase, until my year is up at the end of June.'

It seems strange being at the halfway point in my stay. A year felt like a long time to begin with, but now it seems to be speeding along.

'Are we dancing this evening?' he asks, and I laugh.

'Yes, we're dancing.'

It's been a good day, much has been achieved, so why wouldn't we?

* * *

Ceana calls for quiet as Nico begins speaking. 'Before we set up the karaoke and let off some steam, can we just run through our proposed plan for revising the accommodation under the new regime?'

Quiet descends around the table as everyone is keen to know about the final changes.

'This was a tough decision, guys, and I don't want you to think it was taken lightly. In order to justify the increased rate we're going to be charging to guarantee a reasonable income for all, we have to move the guest accommodation back into the château. That means the two courtyard units will, in future, be the staff quarters.

'Bastien, my friend, that includes moving you out of the second floor of the cottage, too, I'm afraid. It doesn't increase the number of places we can offer, which will stay at sixteen rooms in total, but it frees up a couple of additional practice rooms in the cottage.'

Nico pauses, glancing briefly at Ceana, who takes over.

'One of those will be turned into a consulting room ready for when our final staff member joins us, hopefully early in March. Then all of the nine staff bedrooms in the two units will be occupied. So, we've gained our new quiet rooms and utilised all the available space in the most productive way. Offering bedrooms in the château again is going to be a big part of the overall package and that will get us the premium we need.'

Nico looks around to check everyone's reaction. 'Feel free to speak your mind. I know it's been a tough few weeks.'

Bastien leans forward in his chair. 'You mean I get to bump into these guys on the landing? What's the world coming to?'

Everyone begins to laugh.

'No problems here,' Taylor jumps in.

'Show of hands? Those in favour?' Ceana asks.

One by one the hands go up, and both Nico and Ceana look relieved.

'Pierce and I are in discussion with our accountant about revised pay scales that will come into effect in January, to reflect the increased course fees. We won't be offering volunteer status any longer, so we need to look at how that will affect Fern and Kellie going forward,' Nico confirms. I wasn't expecting that, and I don't think Kellie was, either.

'We have no idea how many weeks of the year we'll run at our target eighty-five per cent occupancy,' Pierce explains. 'The intention going forward is that we agree, as a group, set holiday weeks when we close The Haven. But what Nico tells me has traditionally been the quieter time has turned out not to be the case this year and you all kept going. At the end of the first year, a staff bonus will be paid to reward your hard work and commitment.'

Everyone is stunned, but Pierce continues. 'Nico is very clear about that. It never was simply about making a profit for the sake of it, but building something we can all be proud to be a part of. However, the financial burden on Nico in the past has been phenomenal and it's up to us now to grow our reputation to ensure that's no longer the case.'

Kellie looks so happy, her smile lights up her eyes, but I'm beginning to wonder if, when I leave, I will feel like I'll be letting the team down. As my mind starts to process Pierce's words, Nico begins talking.

'Pierce is now the official general manager of The Haven, and Ceana will become the supervising team manager. Anton will be joining us on a full-time basis as our head gardener and we will be drafting in help during our busiest months in the garden. Ceana will still teach horticultural lessons, in addition to some well-being classes. I will continue to run art classes, but the plan is to change the emphasis so we attract people who already have some level of experience. Now, let's stop talking work and uncork the wine – we did it, guys. I think a toast is in order and thank you all for helping to make this happen. I feel privileged to be working alongside each of you.'

There's a unanimous round of applause and Nico raises his hand to quieten us all.

'Since the château was handed down to me, I always felt it deserved to be given a purpose. It is my home, but over the last few years it has become our collective home. I didn't want it to become a sad, empty place in which one man shut himself away from the world. You all give it life and I couldn't ask for any more than that.'

The air is filled with a chorus of noise and air punching. It's been a long journey and I've only been a very small part of it, but I'm delighted for this wonderful group of people.

As chairs are pushed back and the music begins to play, Nico heads over to me looking bashful.

'No pressure for me to stay, then?' I quip, mockingly.

'Sorry. I knew the timing wasn't right for you, but you are one of the team and you've contributed since your first day here. It's a fact. We might have to pay you a fee as a consultant, but our accountant will sort all that and go through it with you. You feel so much a part of this, it's going to hurt when you leave. You're irreplaceable, Fern.'

I smile up into his eyes. 'Somewhere out there is someone searching for something they haven't yet found, and they will find their way here – to you. I'm sure of that. I don't need paying, Nico. This year off was funded courtesy of a lottery win.'

'I don't make the rules now, Fern. All of that is handled by our very capable management team. It's a huge weight off my shoulders and it feels good. Change can be positive and sometimes you simply need to roll with it.'

He knows I can't do that. But tonight it's about celebrating together and as he grabs my hand and pulls me into the crowded space, we're celebrating big style.

This has become my second home, I reflect, unable to deny it. But it can never be my first home and that's something Nico must accept.

24

The last two weeks have flown by and tonight, although both Nico and I came to the studio to work, neither of us is in the mood to paint. And that's something we seem unable to hide.

There's only so long you can mix colours and prevaricate, instinctively knowing that if the brush touches the canvas when you're not inspired, you will regret every single brushstroke, and hate yourself for it. I know Nico's been watching me out of the corner of his eye for a while and that tells me exactly how distracted he is, too.

The changes that have been going on here are positive, if a little unsettling in some respects. How ironic that I came here to escape the changes going on in my own life, only to be reminded that it's one of life's givens. Nothing stays the same way forever.

'What is it?' Nico calls out as he begins to clean up. It's only just after eleven p.m. which is early to call it quits for the night. 'Your mood is affecting me.'

'I could say the same thing to you,' I retort. I won't let him pin this on me when he's clearly not himself, either. We're bringing each other down with the negative vibes in the air.

'There's little point wasting our time, Fern. This isn't happening tonight, is it?'

I nod in agreement. 'My head is so full of stuff right now.'

'With Christmas just two days away, it must be hard for you. Is this the first time you haven't been together as a family to celebrate?'

I dip my brush in the jar of water and swish it around, extracting it and mopping up the moisture vigorously with the rag. Tonight, we ought to feel jolly; the second batch of visitors left yesterday, and it was another successful week under the new regime. We're closed until the seventh of January now, albeit there are going to be some in-house training sessions. Even Ceana opted not to go home to Scotland for the holidays.

The snow hasn't helped, although it isn't too bad here, merely a light dusting over the sheltered forest plateau. Further afield, though, travel has been a real problem. Maybe one or two of the others would have made an effort to be with their extended families, but no one seemed unduly upset about it. This is where we feel comfortable right now.

'Yes. Hannah is in Austria and Owen is back from his two-week stint overseas and on holiday in Newquay with a group of his army pals. Aiden is counting down the days until he heads off to Thailand. Mum and Dad are snowed in with relatives in Wales, which wasn't a part of their plan, so even if I was at home, I'd be on my own. But it doesn't seem real somehow.'

Nico eases himself up off his stool and beckons me. 'For a natural-born worrier that's a harsh lesson to learn – that the people you love can function without you fussing over them. They might not be quite so comfortable having to sort themselves out, but they'll cope. Come. I have something to show you.'

I pull the baggy T-shirt over my head, careful not to get any fresh smears of paint on my pristine jumper. Smoothing down my hair, I walk across to follow Nico out through the studio door and into the hallway.

It's so quiet and dark, he uses his phone to light our way, tapping it whenever it begins to fade. Suddenly he diverts into the kitchen, rummaging around to find a candle and some matches.

'Candlelight? There are no guests at the moment, remember?' I muse.

'We need our eyes to be accustomed to the dark. You'll see why, in a moment. Here, we'll take one each.'

He slides a slim, tapered wax candle into the centre of a cup-shaped metal holder sporting a sturdy handle. I wait as he lights a second candle and then hands one to me. It's an antique and quite heavy.

'This way,' he calls over his shoulder, before heading out the door.

I wonder if he feels unnerved now the guests have gone and with everyone else lodging in the courtyard accommodation. It must seem strange. The château is large; the wood creaks and the pipes groan at night, as one would expect from an old building.

Even by candlelight, the shadows seem to stay close as we continue up to the top floor. There's a lot of history in this building and it weighs heavily upon me at times, almost as if I can feel a presence, but it's elusive. I wonder if Nico feels that, too?

We pass my old room and head towards the end of the corridor and up the flight of stairs to the second floor. There's a narrow door I can't say I really took note of before, but then I never walked along to this end of the landing. Nico swings it open and ahead of us is a steeper set of stairs rising up into the eaves of the building.

I hesitate for a moment.

'It's fine. The treads are a little narrower, so make sure you hold on tight to the rail as we go up. It's worth it, I promise you.'

If I thought the landing was dark, the stairs seem to close in around us even tighter and the candlelight flickers wildly in the confined space. But when we're at the top, it opens out again and I can see the whole attic is boarded. There are a series of interlinking rooms which are mostly empty. With a few boxes stacked in one corner of the first room and several items of furniture set back against a wall, it's a cavernous open space with only a fine layer of dust that flies up, tickling my nose as we walk.

Heading on through into the next room, Nico suddenly draws to a halt, gazing upwards. I join him, and we stand together, bathed in the soft glow from the candlelight.

He places his metal holder on the floor to go off in search of something and returns with a couple of thick blankets. There is a distinct chill in the air, away from the warmth generated by the old heating system in the main part of the building. Any heat up here will dissipate quite quickly as it's shut off and not designed for habitation.

I watch as he throws two of the blankets on the floor and then raises his candle up towards his face to blow on it. I follow suit.

'Here, pull this over you,' he instructs as he sits on the floor, waiting for me to join him.

We lie back staring up at the navy-blue sky framed in the large skylight. In the murky-grey darkness, it looks like a painting. As my eyes continue to adjust, the night sky is studded with a trillion stars.

'It's beautiful, Nico. A living canvas.'

He turns his head, but I can't really gauge his expression, just noting a little gleam as the moonlight makes his eyes sparkle, indicating that he's smiling.

'I come here whenever I can't settle. It reminds me that there must be more to life than what we know. The universe is too vast for us to assume our little planet is it and there is no other life out there. It's a rather arrogant assumption anyway, isn't it?'

I keep scanning the heavens, as with every passing moment it's like peeling away the layers and the longer I look, the more I can see. The flatness begins to open up, revealing depth and perspective in a way I've never witnessed before. Almost like the light at the end of a long tunnel, focusing the eye and extending one's view.

'It's a scary thought, though.' One I tend to push to the back of my mind. 'How many shooting stars have you seen?'

'A couple, over the years,' Nico confesses with a rueful smile. 'But then I do a lot of sky watching. Enough to know that if you see one, it's special. You're the first person I've brought up here. This was my mother's secret hideaway; we used to creep up very late at night to lie back, chat and marvel at God's creation.'

He expels a few deep breaths, as if he's following one of Pierce's relaxation exercises.

'So, why are you feeling unsettled tonight?' I ask, wondering if it's because the château is a lonely place when Nico is here on his own. Do old memories come back to haunt him?

'There's been another email about the last painting.'

I turn to face him, hoping it's going to be good news. 'That's a positive step, isn't it?'

'Not really. My agent decided to do a courteous follow-up, hoping to recommence talks. He was informed that the gentleman died shortly after our last correspondence and his family don't wish to discuss the sale of the painting. It's over, and that was made very clear to him.'

I close my eyes, feeling his distress. 'Maybe they can't bear to part with it because it's a prized possession. Doesn't that mean it – and you – are safe, Nico? If they were going to sell it, to have someone eager to purchase it knocking on their door would surely mean they'd have named a price. Don't see this as bad news; it's just not quite the result you were hoping for.'

He rolls on his side and I turn in to face him. We're no more than two feet apart, close enough to make eye contact now, even in the gloom.

'Things don't always work out as we want them to, do they?' he murmurs. 'Did you love your husband from day one?'

It's a strange question to ask, but I guess he's just curious.

'Yes,' I admit, 'with all my heart. People are cynical about instant attraction, or at least say it won't last when two young people fall so madly in love. But it can if you nurture it and don't take each other for granted.'

Nico is studying my face. 'But he let you go for a whole year. That's a big risk; why take it?'

It's so hard to explain to someone else because most people won't understand. You have to live our life to comprehend how we got to this place we're at right now.

'It was a bigger risk to look back in years to come and wonder "what if?" Or feel resentful about the things we didn't get to do. Neither of us wanted that. We needed to know for sure whether we were strong enough to get through another big change in our lives that would take us in a new direction. I didn't go into this willingly, but I've learnt so much about myself. I will freely admit now that, as tough as it's been, it has been worth it. I had no idea my creative side had been stifled and was clamouring to get out.' I can hear the optimism in my own voice as I speak.

Nico adjusts his position, moving his arm up and sliding it beneath his head so he can see me better. I do the same. I can feel his breath on my face and as I breathe in there's a note of citrus from his aftershave that seems to wrap itself comfortingly around me.

'I suspect that because you've always put everyone else before yourself, Fern, there never was time for *you*. You've changed so much since that first day you arrived here. Nervous, uncertain and so obviously outside of your comfort zone. What if when you go back it no longer feels like home? Would you come back here and be a part of this going forward?'

My heart thuds in my chest as a sadness washes over me. Sadness for Nico, and sadness for me being unable to answer his question. What if he's right? Haven't those exact words passed through my mind on several occasions? I keep pushing it away, because I have another life and people are expecting me to return to it. I'm not here because of divine intervention. None of this was supposed to happen and it would be so very wrong of me to take it as a sign or regard my time here as meaningful; or worse, life-changing. I've seen the results when people make silly mistakes and live to regret them.

'I'm tired,' I admit. 'Too tired to think.'

'I'll walk you back across the courtyard when you're ready. Life without you here is going to feel... lacking in some way. Different.

And, rather empty, I'm afraid. I'm sorry if that's not what you want to hear, Fern, but for me it will be a day I will never forget, when I am forced to watch you drive away.'

Neither of us make any attempt to get up; we both roll over onto our backs and continue gazing upwards, contemplating what lies beyond what we can see with the naked eye. When eventually our bodies begin to ache, we head downstairs in a companionable silence.

We're both in a sombre mood and yet, in less than twelve hours we have a special visitor coming and everyone is looking forward to it. Patricia is a very reserved and quiet lady, but she managed to get to know each and every one of us during her stay here.

Let's hope that after a few hours' sleep both Nico and I feel more festive. There's no point dwelling over things we are powerless to change and maybe it's time to accept that fate already has a plan.

25

THE UNEXPECTED CHRISTMAS PRESENT

Margot is like a sergeant major, directing us all as we trim up the day room ready to complement her festive French buffet. The guys have been out gathering greenery and Pierce volunteered to help Bastien cut down a fir tree.

'Um... it's a little lopsided,' I inform them, as they stand holding it upright in front of me. 'But it will look absolutely perfect if you can turn it a little bit that way,' I direct, pointing to my right and hoping the sparse section will be hidden in the corner once they ease it back into position. 'Yep. You've nailed it, well done.'

They both look rather pleased with themselves, their faces still red from the exertion and the sting of the bitingly cold wind.

Ceana is already unpacking the decorations and laying them out on the sofa. Behind her, Kellie, Taylor and Dee-Dee are working from a trestle table, assembling small bunches of holly, ivy and mistletoe. Nico is at the top of a ladder busily hanging them from the large oak beams as Odile hands them up to him.

It's wonderful to see everyone working together, and hear their banter.

The door to the kitchen opens and the smell of meat roasting in the oven makes my stomach grumble.

'No music?' Margot calls out as she walks across to the table to lay out a couple of platters.

Bastien jumps up, pushing the last rock into the bucket to stabilise the tree, while Pierce gingerly holds it in place.

'I'll sort that now, Margot. Do you need a hand?' Bastien enquires, always the kind-hearted one, first to offer help.

'Please. There is much to be done.' Today she's dressed all in black, as usual, but she's wearing a little blue scarf, tucked in at her neckline. That's a sign that she intends to let down her hair and dancing will ensue.

The clock is ticking, but as I scan around, the ambience is truly wonderful. Christmas starts here, now. Everyone has switched off from work and it feels like the festive holiday has finally begun.

I'm so happy that Patricia is dropping in to see us, because everyone is putting in that extra little bit of effort in her honour. When she was here, I worried when she shied away from some of the group activities, but on an individual level she made time for everyone. It will also be a real pleasure to meet her husband before they head off to their holiday cottage for a relaxing Christmas. She'll no doubt be relieved that he's well enough to drive, and that's a blessing.

'I'm just popping into the garden to see if I can add some colour to the table centre,' I say, leaning in to Ceana. She gives me a brilliant smile and it's clear she's feeling the festive vibe. 'I won't be long and then I'll help you decorate the tree. There are still a few roses in bloom, nestled back against the high wall to the rear. I'm sure Nico won't mind me rescuing them for us all to enjoy.'

'Great idea,' she muses. 'A little pop of colour in winter is a treasure.'

We exchange nods and suddenly it strikes me how much brighter she's been since Pierce arrived. Why hadn't I noticed that before? He's also much more easy-going now, but then I've come to understand that he's a man who lives by his ethos. *Order in everything* is his favourite mantra and until that has been achieved, he can't relax.

I can't help wondering whether Ceana's happiness is because she's grateful to Pierce for taking a lot of the pressure away from Nico, or whether it's personal. It would be wonderful if there's a spark developing between the two of them. Loneliness is a terrible thing, and these two are workaholics who would both benefit from being with someone who can empathise.

I text as I walk, just quick responses to Owen and Hannah's one-liners. Aiden was very subdued again yesterday morning on Skype. I think as the days pass, he's feeling torn about leaving the project. He's grown very close to several people and one family in particular. Having helped rebuild their house after a fire, I sense he feels guilty about heading off to travel simply for the fun of it. But the community development internship in Mexico is for twenty-four weeks, and that's driven by the Mexican Immigration Laws; the voluntary workers visa applies to those undertaking non-remunerated work and if he stays on he'll be in breach of that.

But what I fear most is that his relationship with Joss is changing. He never mentions her, but she's always hovering in the background. Maybe I'm being a little paranoid as they are part of a much larger group now, or maybe he feels awkward about their friendship.

I let myself out of the back door of the château to traipse around in the garden with secateurs in hand. My stomach is churning as I think of Aiden. Nico asked what would happen if when I return it's not the same. What if the man I married is different; so different I don't feel I know him any more. I thrive on having people to take care of; that's the role I've carved out for myself – daughter, sister, wife and homemaker. But they are all surviving without me fussing over them and when I go back it will be just the two of us trying to pick back up where we left off. Will Aiden and I feel like strangers for a while as we get used to being a part of a couple again, or the lovers we used to be?

The impression I get of Joss is that she's a free spirit, living her life to the full on a daily basis. Which is fine, because she's free and single, from the little Aiden has said about her; she doesn't have a husband and responsibilities at home to put first. Life is easy when you only have yourself to please.

I wonder if Aiden finds that energising and exciting. He's been in a committed relationship for all his adult life and I wonder if anything has changed in him since we've been apart.

At last I stumble across what I've been looking for in the garden. Still partially hidden and tucked away in the far corner where the two high, stone walls meet is a little cluster of colour. Brushing aside the overhanging winter-flowering jasmine, I snip away gingerly until I have a little posy of deep red blooms. The smell is wonderful against the sweet jasmine and I stand for a moment, enjoying the floral notes as I suck in the cold air. It jars on my teeth, but it's invigorating.

Is my life about to change forever? I wonder. Does my old life even exist any more? I can't imagine a day passing, now, without wanting to paint. Will Aiden understand how important it has become to me? And how will he settle back into our cosy little life together, after being exposed to such a wide range of new experiences? From poverty and desperation, to the wonders of the world – then back to domestic bliss. It sounds crazy when I think about it like that.

Until our adventure is over, we won't know for sure, but I miss him so much. I'm getting used to the separation, but it still doesn't feel natural. It's as if a part of me is missing and I won't feel complete again until we're together once more. Or am I kidding myself it's as simple as that?

* * *

When a rather smart-looking, black motorhome pulls into the car park, Nico and I make our way across the courtyard to welcome our visitors. But, to our surprise, it's Stefan who is behind the wheel. As he steps out to walk around and open the passenger door, I wave out to Patricia, who is beaming back at me.

Hanging back while Stefan offers her his arm, she steps down and then hurries across to hug me.

'It's so wonderful to see you and to be here again, Fern. Fond memories, for sure! Oh, Nico.' She releases me and turns towards him.

He leans in to kiss her on alternate cheeks three times, French style. 'You look well, Patricia.' He smiles at her and I can see she's a little embarrassed at the fuss.

'And Stefan,' Nico thrusts out his hand, 'what a lovely surprise. I thought you were back home in Germany.'

I never really got to know Stefan, so I hesitate, but after a quick shaking of hands he gives a little bow of his head. Patricia looks on, amused.

'Come, let's get you both out of this cold wind,' I interrupt, and Patricia links arms as we make our way back towards the day room.

When we enter, there's a flurry of hellos, hugs and introductions, as Pierce brings up the rear. When Kellie and Patricia hug, there are tears in their eyes. Patricia seems happy, but I can't wait to find out what Stefan is doing as her driver. I'd assumed it would be her husband, so this is a total surprise – I just hope it isn't bad news.

'Ah, you are here!' Margot barrels in, heading straight to Patricia, and we all step back. 'Oh, another surprise. Stefan, alors! If I had known, I would have made your favourite *bouillabaisse*. No one tells me anything. Lunch is ready. Come, take off your coats; it's time to eat.'

I have no idea what's going on, but the atmosphere is jolly and everyone is more than happy to begin filling their plates.

From the assorted charcuterie, the potato salad with aioli sauce, the taboulé, to the goose stuffed with prunes and dates, it's a feast. And in pride of place is the Bûche de Noël – Christmas Yule Log – at which Margot has excelled herself.

With the music turned down a touch, it's hard to hear it at all above the chatter and ensuing laughter.

I'm not sure anyone other than myself is aware that Patricia has a husband, so the question isn't raised, but I'm curious. Stefan simply explains that he's touring the UK and stopped off to visit Patricia. She's selling her holiday cottage over here and he couldn't resist offering her a lift. 'Any excuse for a trip to France,' he adds.

'Are you staying in France for a while?' Kellie asks.

Stefan looks across at Patricia, who duly answers.

'Maybe a week. I have a few things to sort out and take back with me; Stefan very kindly offered to be my transportation. There isn't much, just a couple of boxes of personal effects before the property goes on the market. It will be rather nice to experience one more Christmas there, as the neighbours are wonderful. The final goodbye will be tough, I will admit, but it's time to let it go.'

The conversation moves on quickly. Patricia isn't a secretive lady, just very private.

Once the meal is done and the table is cleared, Patricia asks me if I could give her a tour, so she can see the recent changes. As we pull on our coats, she reaches out to touch Nico's arm as he's walking past us.

'Could you join us, Nico?'

He immediately flashes her a smile. 'Of course, Patricia. Give me a moment to grab my jacket from the cloakroom.'

Stefan walks over to hand her something rather discreetly and she slips whatever it is into her pocket. Then she curls her arm around mine and we step outside.

'Is everything all right, Patricia?' I ask as we loiter.

'Yes,' she replies and turns to watch Nico as he walks towards us. 'Before I get to see all the wonderful changes, I have a little present for you, Nico. It's in the back of the motorhome, if you'd be so good as to help me to retrieve it.' She pulls a bunch of keys out of her pocket and hands them to him, as he stands there looking puzzled. 'A little something to thank you for the wonderful experience I had here at a time in my life when what I needed was the company of some kind people. And, of course, I met Stefan.'

Oh, my goodness, my instincts were right – Patricia's husband, Fred, must have passed away.

Nico flashes a concerned look in my direction, but as Patricia pulls away from me, I give him a quick shake of my head, indicating he should say nothing.

Unlocking the side door to the motorhome, Nico swings it open and steps back. Patricia indicates for him to go inside.

'It's the parcel strapped to the table,' she calls out. 'It's rather heavy as Stefan did a wonderful job of making sure it would survive the journey. Maybe we could take it into the château?'

Nico returns with his arms around the enormous package and as we follow him, I glance at Patricia, but she's giving nothing away. We unlink arms as I swing back the heavy oak door for Nico to pass through, and we walk down the passageway, then on into the studio.

Very carefully, Nico stands the box against the wall and prises open the end. Reaching inside, he begins to lever it out and polystyrene strips fall to the floor. His face freezes. I return my gaze to Patricia, puzzled.

'The last painting.' Nico's voice is uneven. 'The collection is complete.'

I can see how overcome he is; the colour has totally drained from his face.

'You guessed that Nico had taken me into his confidence, but how did *you* know about the painting, Patricia?' I ask.

I throw my arms around her, drawing her close as she begins speaking. This is a truly incredible moment, but I wonder if she understands quite how wonderful.

'My husband, Fred, bought this for me many years ago from a little gallery in Covent Garden. We were on holiday and he saw how taken I was with it. He said a work of art is an investment, not an impulse purchase. Well, that's how he convinced me we should buy our first piece. After that we bought a number of paintings and just a couple of years ago we purchased one by Nico Gallegos. We were on a month-long holiday, driving down through Spain.'

Nico eases the painting onto one of the rails and we cluster around it. 'It's the orchard in our garden in Spain, in autumn,' he murmurs, his hand cupping his chin and resting on his arm as it's wrapped around his body. He's caught up in a plethora of emotions that I can't even begin to imagine.

'As soon as the painting arrived and we unpacked it, Fred realised it was by the same artist as this piece. The signature was different, but the vibrancy and brushstrokes were unmistakeable. It had life in it, something that reaches out from the canvas and makes your heart leap.'

Nico lowers his hands, resting them at his sides as he looks at Patricia, humbly. 'And yet you did nothing about it, knowing one of the signatures was false,' he replies, softly.

'We loved both paintings for what they were. Before Fred died, he wanted me to meet you in person, so I came here. I was in need of a break after many months of nursing him, alone, at home. The man who had contacted us a while beforehand told us that José's son was interested in buying the canvas, because he wanted to bring his father's collection back under one roof. We were, naturally, rather curious, as we were convinced they were both by the same person.'

The way Patricia says the word 'curious' implies that both she and Fred had done some research and knew a little about Nico's father.

'I suppose we wanted to know the truth, or the full story, if you prefer. For us, it didn't devalue the beauty, or the validity of the pieces, but if this was part of a scam, that would have been devastating. Not because of the value, but the integrity.'

I'm holding my breath and so is Nico.

She continues. 'It was very clear to me that Nico has put everything he owns into this place. He has assumed responsibility for a group of people searching for a home, bringing them together to make a difference. It was then that I knew the truth. I didn't need to ask the question, because it was irrelevant. I simply experienced what you had achieved with the retreat and now, The Haven. I went back to Fred with a happy heart.

'So, this is our present to you, Nico. It was Fred's dying wish, and while I am a little sad to let it go, it belongs with you. No one, including Stefan, knows anything about it. He only thinks I'm bringing you a gift to thank you for my time here and that's exactly how I'd like to keep it. A little secret between the three of us that goes no further.'

We are all in tears as we come together, hugging each other in Fred's memory. Nico and I are marvelling at the kindness of two wonderful and generous people.

The last piece of the puzzle is finally in place and Patricia and I hold Nico up as he sobs quietly, his body trembling.

Fate had a plan, after all.

My heart feels both empty and full at the same time. This is the end of years of torment for Nico and, as it turns out, I had a very small part to play in it. One I could never have imagined. And now it's over, but I don't seem able to visualise the moment when I drive away and return to my old life. A light is extinguishing deep inside of me, as if an icy blast has infiltrated my heart.

26

'Hi, Aiden, can you talk?'

I'm phoning on a flimsy excuse, because after an emotional day and then waving Patricia and Stefan off, I feel empty. Needy, even. Nico retired to his room early and there's a party going on in the day room, but my heart wasn't in it. It's nearly midnight, so early evening in Mexico. I'm propped up on the bed, with only the light from the moon outside filtering into the darkened room.

'It's fine. I've just arrived back. We're having a bit of a party here later tonight. It's been a tough week, though.' He sounds jaded.

'Same here. I'm not in a party mood, either.'

'Problems?'

He's more at ease tonight, obviously content to talk and I'm guessing wherever he is, he's alone for the first time in a long while.

'One of the first visitors I gelled with here, dropped in for lunch today on her way further down south. Her husband was ill, and she came to the retreat for a little respite, but he's since died. She's made a very generous gift on his behalf and it touched my heart. She was very good to me in that first week after I arrived, when I was feeling a little lost.'

'It must have been tough for you, I didn't quite realise—' Aiden clearly thinks I'm making a point.

'No. I don't mean it like that. She was kind and went out of her way to ease things for me. I, um, want to buy a bench to replace an old rotting one down by the lake. Something sturdy that will last for years and get a plaque with her husband's name engraved on it. What do you think?'

'No need to ask me. Just do it. It's a lovely gesture.'

'It will probably cost a couple of hundred pounds and I know you were a bit concerned about the kitty.'

He laughs. 'I've spent way more than you on this internship and I'll soon be off on my next adventure. I think you can splash out on a gift without putting yourself on a guilt trip.' He sounds almost dismissive.

'Aiden, if something was wrong at your end, you would level with me, wouldn't you?'

The silence is painful. The longer I listen to it, the more the sound seems to grow. How can silence sound so deafening?

'More wrong than the fact that I have no idea what's happening at your end? You're with a group of people with whom you are growing close, building relationships as if they are a part of your future. I'm not blaming you, it's the same for me here. But where do we draw the line?'

'Are we talking about me, or you?'

Suddenly I can hear his breathing and it's laboured.

'Well, I'm talking about Nico. From what Hannah said, you two are very close.'

Is he accusing me of having an affair, when all that's going around in my head is thoughts of him and Joss?

'He's my mentor, Aiden. That's all. Being here I've discovered a new side to me, the one I've never had time to explore. And I can tell your experiences are changing you in subtle ways, too. But I still love you with all my heart, nothing will change that.'

He groans. 'I'm a fool, ignore me.' He sounds sorry, but what are his words actually telling me? Is he a fool because he's slept with Joss? Or is he a fool because he thinks I've slept with Nico and he's jealous?

'Let's not torture each other, Aiden. This is supposed to be a year of adventure. Most people get that freedom before they settle down. We didn't, and fate sent us that windfall for a reason. You lived for your job and were so caught up in the people's lives it touched, that you just ran out of steam. I was—' I pause, desperately casting around for the right word.

'Happy and I upset everything.' He sounds dejected.

'No. Don't say that.'

'But it's true.'

Is he right? Was I totally happy, or living on autopilot letting one day follow another?

'Maybe I was in a bit of a rut. You know what a worrier I am and this has given me time to stand back a little and see things in a slightly different way. I feel that I'm a better, more rounded person for it.

'I've found interests I couldn't possibly have guessed at, including meditation. We are people in our own right, it's simply a case of letting that shine through. When we're back home together, I want us to be in a position where we can help each other to continue growing and be happy. Not just be people who say they're happy without it really meaning anything. We know a lot of couples like that and it's not living life to the full, is it?'

He snorts. 'No regrets and no *what ifs*.'

'And that's what you said at the very beginning, Aiden, remember?'

'Yes, well. That was then, and this is now.'

'Something has upset you and you're rubbish at hiding things, Aiden, you know that. We can talk it through.'

I wish I could give him the hug he obviously needs.

There's a long pause but something tells me not to break it, just to give him a little time to collect his thoughts.

'There was a gang fight and the eldest son of the family whose home I've been working in was knifed. He died before they could get any medical help. He was eleven years old, Fern. It made me realise how we take each day for granted. We wake up in the morning facing a new day, but what if it's destined to be the last one? An accident, a heart attack – whatever. One thing keeps going through my mind – *what have I done?*'

Anxiety? I'm the worrier, not Aiden. He's always been a man of action, rolling up his sleeves to get things moving and to do that requires a positive attitude.

'You need to talk to someone about that, Aiden. I'm serious. After an incident like that you need debriefing. Helping people in that situation was bound to take a toll and if you get pulled down, you won't be able function and you will make poor decisions. That doesn't help anyone, and it could harm you.'

He emits a huge sigh that pulls on my heartstrings. 'You're right. I'm getting bogged down and I'm not thinking clearly. I'll chat to Alistair; he handles staff welfare. I'm glad we talked. Sorry I've been so uptight. You don't deserve that, and I didn't mean to stress you out.'

It's a pattern that's become the norm. At the beginning of every call, I feel I no longer recognise the man I've loved forever, as if he's gone. By the time we're ready to say goodbye, he's back with me again, but it's fleeting. Each time we talk it takes a little longer to re-establish that link and I'm fearful.

'You're always in my thoughts, Aiden. That will never change.' It's true, but in my heart, I know something is different and I hope it's only the distance between us.

'You promise?' His voice sounds uneven; maybe he's missing home.

'I promise. The trip to Thailand will be amazing. The project you've been involved in has been so worthwhile, but your time there is almost done. You made a difference, Aiden, and that's something to be proud of, but now you should take a little time to chill out and relax. No pressures, just being a tourist, as if you're on holiday.'

'Hmm. But I'm not, because if I was, then you'd be by my side.' His voice is tinged with regret. The death of that young boy has hit him hard.

'Don't get depressed over the things you can't change, Aiden. You learnt that a long time ago, so try not to dwell on the negative. Life goes on no matter how tough some of the lessons are and you need to be strong to support the people who are grieving for their boy. They can't give up and neither can you.'

He takes a noisy breath in. 'Thanks, Fern. He just... I mean, he reminded me of a young Owen. You know, when we first met and he was – what – eleven years old? That big silly grin he wore most of the time because he was always fooling around and he was all legs and arms. You remember that phase?'

I smile to myself, nestling the phone between my cheek and my shoulder. 'Oh, I do. Whenever you came to the house, he always wanted you to play football with him and we just wanted to slope off and have some quiet time together. And he was constantly hungry. Mum used to make you both her infamous toasted cheese sandwiches.'

Aiden chuckles. 'Owen never said *no* to food, no matter what time of the day, or night, it was. In fact, I could murder one of your mum's specials myself, right now.'

At least he sounds brighter and it's a relief to know what was eating away at him.

'I miss not having you there to ease the humps in my day. Does that sound selfish?' he asks.

'No. Of course not. That's my job... well, not my job—' I halt, mid flow.

'I think you had it right first time. We've always been hard work, Fern – me, your family – but you always sorted us all out. I'm not sure I really appreciated how much effort that required. Losing your sister at a time when you should have been a new bride, enjoying the first days of happy married life. Adulthood has never been carefree for you, has it? Anyway, it's something I won't take for granted when we get back home.'

What a huge relief it is to hear him say that. I've been wondering if he's been quiet recently because our old life seems rather staid and boring by comparison. His eyes have been opened to so many things beyond our safe little world at home. Would the thought of coming back to me be enough?

'Funny, we're thousands of miles apart and you still know when I need you. Now that's love.' His words are full of emotion.

I can feel the tears just waiting to be unleashed, but I hold myself in check. *Deep breaths, Fern, end this on a high note.*

As we say our goodbyes and disconnect, I close my eyes, trying to remember what it felt like to be wrapped in Aiden's arms. I give up, wondering how I'm going to get through another six months like this, knowing the divide between us could grow and trying not to imagine someone else in his arms.

Any thoughts of Nico are now fading into the shadows as I accept the inevitable. Our paths were only ever meant to cross for the briefest of moments – one year in an entire lifetime seems forever when you are living it, though. When, eventually, I look back, all of this will seem like a distant dream and I know that I will be given the strength to get through it.

MARCH 2019

27

FACING ONE'S FEARS

The Haven is busy. Since Christmas, the weather has been very mixed; January and February saw several flurries of snow falling over a large area of France that didn't hang around for very long but were a nuisance. But it hasn't stopped the new arrivals and we've been full virtually the whole time.

The twentieth of March is officially the start of spring, but the beginning of the month has brought strong winds, interspersed with bouts of heavier than normal rainfall. The sort that permeates every little nook and cranny if you venture out, and leaves you feeling miserable. At least in the frosty weather, when there was a little crunch beneath our feet, we could wrap up and enjoy a long walk. But it's frustrating waiting for spring to really make its presence felt.

Even Bastien has been running indoor workshops, with only the odd session down in the barns. He's taken over the ground floor of the art studio in the courtyard, with Nico's classes now confined to the mezzanine. Bastien teaches tooling on squares of vegetable tanned leather. Visitors can make bookmarks, belts and wallets.

What I found touching is that, despite the weather, Taylor and Bastien designed and assembled Fred's bench for me. Made from solid oak I purchased from a local sawmill, it now has the most beautiful plaque inscribed with:

> In memory of Fred, beloved husband of Patricia.
>   Heaven is where you are now,
>   Inside the hearts of everyone whose lives you touched.

Patricia wrote the inscription and we were all affected by the poignancy of her words. For me, it was because I knew she understood how enormous a gift he gave to Nico. They both did. We thought that maybe visitors would read it and relate it to the setting, maybe sitting here to take a tranquil moment to remember loved ones they'd lost.

We're all looking forward to getting through March and anticipating the usual, milder weather April has been forecasted to bring with it. Our newest staff member will arrive in a week's time. Yann Bisson is a personal fitness trainer and I'm hoping to join in with some of his classes. Maybe that will finally shake off the winter blues which don't seem to want to go this year.

The place does have much more of a buzz these days and the visitors are responding well to the new facilities on offer. Every morning, the gym becomes the meditation zone between ten and eleven. I'm still assisting Pierce by being another set of eyes and ears.

Now I have a better understanding, I can sit down next to someone and demonstrate the correct sitting position. Some people find it hard to get comfortable and often it's a case of doubling up the mats to help. Occasionally, we might have someone with a knee problem which prevents them from sitting on the floor, so I try and find a suitable chair.

There are two ground-floor rooms in the cottage which are permanent quiet rooms, although I find even that too intrusive with people coming and going. Instead, I've taken to heading up into the attic space in the château when I need time alone. The bedrooms here are infinitely more private than the accommodation the staff now have in the courtyard buildings. The walls are thin there, and the rooms are smaller. I miss being here, close to Nico, too. But every evening is spent in the studio together and I treasure that time.

There's something about the transitional period when winter bows out reluctantly but the signs of spring are few and far between. I long to get outdoors, but the unusual amount of rain this year makes it difficult. If I was at home, it would be freezing cold, of course, and we'd still be spending our evenings in front of the gas fire in the sitting room.

We heard today that our paintings have arrived safely at the gallery in Seville and will be on display as early as next week, so I should be feeling elated, but instead I'm deflated. Maybe it's because I'm a little under the weather; I've had a sore throat and a headache off and on for nearly two weeks now and this virus doesn't seem to want to leave me alone.

After waving off the last batch of visitors, I welcome the start of the weekend with a sense of lethargy. Nico is treading carefully around me, concerned that I'm not my usual self. He thinks I'm homesick, but it's more than that. I've been so worried about how I've been feeling that I even mentioned it to Pierce yesterday.

'We talked briefly about when you lost your sister and I don't want to labour this, Fern, but I really do think some of your anxieties stem from that. Your level of worry over the people you love is, at times, a little excessive. Do you feel you are in control, or is it getting out of hand?' he'd asked, and I'd shrugged my shoulders, unsure of how to answer him. That's all I needed, something new to add to the burden of worries.

'If this continues, then we ought to sit down and talk it through properly. I can't believe you didn't have counselling at the time. I suspect there's a link between a sense of loss you've never recovered from and your reaction to being apart from your family. Not getting a proper night's sleep is a red flag and that in itself can lead to a depressed state, as well as fatigue and moodiness. I'm here, Fern, and it's what I do. But you need to be ready to open up and accept that there could be deep-seated issues at play.'

His concern was real, and maybe he was right. Losing Rachel like that, without warning – without being able to say goodbye – left me feeling empty and powerless. I was angry that someone so vibrant could be snatched away from us because of an accident. It was supposed to have been a dream holiday with her two best friends. Why is fate so cruel at times?

Naturally, I cling on to the people I love now, because I don't ever want to lose them. Obsessive, maybe, but perfectly understandable surely. I'm not ready, yet, to unlock that box, even if I'm fooling myself that I can handle it without seeking help.

However, I feel guilty that it is Nico who has to suffer as my mood plummets late in the day when I'm tired. Listless, irritable and this damn temperature of mine is up and down all the time, making my skin itch. He tries hard to distract me.

As we paint, sometimes we talk, and he tells me stories about his life; mainly happy little memories from his early childhood living in a Spanish village. Other times, we work in silence. Like tonight.

The wild splashes of crimson, as I repeatedly swipe my brush on the canvas in front of me, invoke an anger that has materialised, seemingly from nowhere.

Suddenly, Nico is at my shoulder.

'What is it, Fern? What is really troubling you?'

He throws an arm around my shoulders, easing the brush out of my hand. Then he pulls me into him, holding me tightly until my anger subsides, only to be replaced by tears.

'I feel that nothing will ever be the same for me again and I don't know if I can stand that thought. The weeks are flying by now. When it's time to leave, I'll be different, too. In the last eight months, I've never felt more alive in some ways, although in others I feel incomplete, because I know something is missing. My family. But here it's easy to just take each day as it comes. People come to the château to relax and have fun learning new skills, so they're happy and they're healing themselves. But this isn't real life for me, Nico.'

The truth is that tonight I'm utterly exhausted. I haven't had more than a couple of hours sleep each night for the last two weeks now, and it's taking a toll. Feeling a little feverish, my mind is conjuring up all sorts of imaginary worries.

'What else is going on in that head of yours? You've coped perfectly well until recently. What has tipped you over the edge all of a sudden?' He leans forward. Our foreheads are almost touching as he stares deeply into my eyes, a worried frown wrinkling his brow.

'It's obvious Hannah's having problems at uni and losing heart. Something has gone wrong and she doesn't want to worry me, so her texts and calls have dropped off. Which is worse, as I keep going over what it might be. Maybe she's quit, who knows?' I sniff, pulling a tissue from my sleeve. 'Owen is flying out to take part in a NATO exercise in Norway and that's scary. His texts will be few and far between; the reality of his world is beginning to fill me with dread.

'And it was Aiden's thirtieth birthday on Thursday. I couldn't get hold of him, so I texted and then emailed him. I know it's silly as we'll have a party later in the year, but I wasn't with him on a land-mark day in his life. I hope he was on a high, exploring Thailand, but he's about to move on again. Last time we spoke his plans were vague and he wasn't his usual self. He's becoming more and more with-drawn with each week that passes. He's been travelling almost continually for over a month now and a break that was supposed to re-energise him is leaving him feeling exhausted.

'Even Mum and Dad don't seem to be around much, and I have no idea what's going on with them. I feel cut off from everyone; I'm not used to that – we usually discuss everything.'

'They aren't shutting you out, Fern. When they need you, or they have some real news, they'll be in touch. Why are you torturing your-self like this?'

'Because we should be united as a family and we aren't.' It's a battle to restrain the terse edge to my voice because I know how I sound. Possessive, needy.

'That's nonsense,' Nico says, forcefully. 'It's life and you can't bind the people you love to you, as if they are too fragile to venture out into the world on their own. It's wonderful to love someone without reservation, but you can't lead their lives for them. All you can do is be a safety net. That's the bond families enjoy and that's special; the feeling that no matter what happens there's always someone who cares enough to listen and help when you need it.'

I can see that he's speaking from the heart.

'You didn't have that, did you? Well, not with your father.'

He shakes his head as he gently releases me. He turns, still talking as he begins to pack up for the night. 'My mother was the rock in our family, but her life was hard. It's a long and sorry story.'

'Is it too painful to share?' I ask, gently, and I can see from his stance a moment of hesitation.

'Yes... No... I don't know is the truth because I never have.'

After a few minutes spent tidying things away, we head towards the attic without saying another word. Nico has arranged two old armchairs, facing each other just three feet apart and positioned so that we can lie back and stare up at the heavens. It's become a special place for us both.

Once we're settled, I look at him, frowning, giving him time to think about where to start. He takes a few minutes to compose himself and when he begins speaking his eyes are directed upwards, so I lean back and do the same.

'My father's family were olive farmers, but his heart wasn't in it when eventually he inherited the farm. He tried for a while because he knew they would have been bitterly disappointed in him, but in fairness it was a bad time, economically. I was a young boy and all I remember is that my parents rowed incessantly as his dependency on alcohol grew. By then he spent his days painting, veering from heights of great joy to the depths of despondency. My mother had no choice but to employ two local men, as my father lost interest in everything else around him. I spent my time avoiding him and trying to help out when I wasn't at school.

'He drank when he was happy, and his work was going well, then he drank when one single brushstroke seemed to ruin it all for him. Those were the times when his disappointment would overwhelm him. Sometimes he'd drink for several days at a time, and I learnt how to make myself invisible. My mother had enough to cope with, worrying about paying the bills, as well as making sure my dad didn't end up setting fire to the house or falling down the stairs and breaking his neck.'

The imagery in my mind, as I stare up at the darkness, is powerful. For a young boy that must have been frightening; for a mother, a desperate situation when her options were clearly limited. They were all prisoners in a hell that Nico's father had created.

'There were good times, but increasingly they became few and far between. My mother wasn't happy when I, too, first picked up a paintbrush. I'd always drawn. But when my father was in a good mood and he encouraged me into his personal space, I can remember the feeling of tremendous excitement, so vividly.

'He used traditional oil paints, so the smell of the linseed he mixed with it to help the drying process and the turpentine, which he used to clean his brushes, was prevalent. To a young boy, it was an exciting environment; the smells alone were heady. It was a place where beautiful things were created.

'I longed to express everything I was holding back, deep inside, and wanted to be given free rein. There was this need in me to have my passion acknowledged, but it never was by my father. Even today, walking into my own studio invokes a wide range of emotions, but I use that to fuel my creativity.'

'How old were you when you started painting?'

'I started with watercolours at school; I was probably around eight years old. My art teacher recognised an inherent talent within me and eventually she persuaded my mother that it was wrong to inhibit that. You can imagine that was a tough thing for her, as it was destroying my father before her very eyes. It brought him less and less satisfaction, but she could see that indulging me allowed me to escape for long periods of time. I was prolific, excited to experiment and see where it took me.'

There's great positivity in his voice, as if he's reliving that time and experiencing the lift it gave him.

'Suddenly I had a sense of purpose,' he admits.

'What effect did that have on your father?' I ask, hesitantly.

He stops looking upwards and our eyes meet. 'I was only allowed to paint in a loft, in one of the barns, out of sight of him. It was a couple of years before he realised what I was doing. He never visited my school; my mother went on her own as he was too wrapped up in himself to show any concern over what was going on around him.'

I swallow hard, feeling sad for a young boy expressing his talent and yet having to hide it.

'One day he was desperate for a drink. My mother and I had just returned from a shopping trip and were carrying boxes through to the kitchen. I went out to get the last few things, while my mother moved the pickup truck. As I walked back inside, he was combing through the boxes. Wine bottle in hand, he discovered a bag with tubes of watercolour paint my mother had purchased for my birthday. At that time, it was all she could afford, and we made up the canvases together, because it cost very little.'

I can't help but suck in a deep breath as I can see he's in the moment, transported back more than twenty years. I don't want to move, or make a sound, fearful of breaking his train of thought.

'He looked at me as if I was a traitor. The wine bottle slipped from his hand, splashing droplets of the rich red colour and tiny pieces of glass over our feet. He grabbed at one of the tubes, angrily, and made a fist, crushing it until the side fractured and I remember the stain of Prussian Blue as it forced its way between his fingers and started to drip onto the floor.

'He screamed at me "You want this?" as he unclenched his fist, holding up his paint-splattered palm. "Then you are more of a fool than I took you for, Nico. It is destroying me, and it will destroy you, too; a foolish father begets a foolish son." He spat the words at me.'

My heart feels crushed for that young boy.

'The farm was losing money and when my mother's parents passed on it was decided we should move to France and take possession of the château, rather than sell it. She said there was no point in trying to keep the farm going and she was tired of it all.

'When we were packing up, that's when my father discovered my canvases. Many had paintings on both sides and my passion had grown to the point where I did odd jobs for neighbours in order to buy more materials.

'He said nothing at the time and when we first arrived in France, we unpacked everything, and my paintings were brought up here to languish. It was several years later that I discovered what he was doing, by accident, really. By then I had my own little studio in one of the old stables. Sadly, it had to be knocked down when I began the renovations. I had graduated on to oil paint and I was signing my work. My mother was actively encouraging me as she could see that I wasn't the weak man my father was and art was my destiny. We set up the market garden to generate some additional income to keep us going and things were working out well. She was as happy as she could be, given the circumstances.'

Nico's face shows the shadow of a haunting smile as he thinks of her. Instinctively, his whole body shifts, discomforted by his thoughts. Placing his hands firmly on the arms of the chair, he turns his head once more, heavenwards. The silence is peaceful, but the sadness is tangible.

* * *

I have no idea what time it is when I stir, realising that Nico has touched my arm to awaken me. He leads me very gently back downstairs and into his bedroom, easing me back onto his bed and covering me with a blanket. My eyes are so heavy, and my head is full of a dream about a field full of yellow flowers; a picnic with my parents when we were young; Hannah merely a toddler. The sunshine is warm on my face and I welcome it as I drop back into a deep sleep.

When I stir in the early hours of the morning, my head feels so much better and the fever has left me. Nico is asleep on the chaise longue in the corner of the room. The instant I open my eyes, even in the gloom he calls out to me, softly.

'Everything is fine, Fern. Go back to sleep. It's time to let your mind relax and get some rest.'

28

THE INTRODUCTION

Feeling much more like my old self this morning, I decided not to join the others on their Sunday morning walk. Aiden didn't Skype yesterday because he's travelling. Again. But I'm hoping that little icon will pop up on my phone sometime today. I can't believe he's unable to find a quiet corner and a decent enough Wi-Fi signal for a quick chat – even to reassure me that he's okay.

Is it out of sight, out of mind? I wonder. Or is this more about what he's choosing to hold back? The question that's like a fire in my stomach is where's Joss? Is she always lurking somewhere out of sight when he does take time to make contact?

Stop it, Fern, I silently berate myself. It's normal to get caught up in things and the day flies by, so imagine being on the road and constantly moving from one place to another. I know I'm being unfair, but even his texts are few and far between.

Today I'm in the studio and facing a blank canvas. Jittery with anticipation, I squeeze the first colours onto the palette, ready to begin mixing. It's a thrill, that first brushstroke, but it's also nerve-wracking. I have a pile of sketches from a session down by the lake and now that the new bench is in place, I want a permanent memory of it. Something I can glance up at every day when I'm at home and remember my time here, fondly.

I've experienced a lot of little flashbacks as I've stared out over the rippling waters; sometimes alone and other times in the company of people who have touched my heart in so many different ways. When I return home, there's a little part of me that I will be leaving behind, because it doesn't fit into my old life.

I fleetingly think of the portrait of Nico's mystery woman and I understand that it isn't just a tribute to his mother as I thought, but to womanhood. He longs to capture the beauty of a woman, in a setting that she loved. To him it's a way of immortalising that special bond any mother has with her child; he saw her as an angel, the person who fought hard to keep them all together. Is that why he asked me to sit for him?

The sudden click of the door catch opening is a surprise, as Nico is in the day room with Pierce. They're looking at options for further expansion. I know that Nico isn't keen to convert the attic space in the château, so they are costing out a bespoke building in the court-yard which would add another eight double bedrooms with en suite facilities. We're getting a lot of enquiries coming in for twin-bedded rooms and Pierce thinks it's a worthwhile investment.

So, when I glance up and a total stranger is standing there, I'm caught off guard.

'Fern?' she asks, and when I nod my head, she walks towards me, smiling. 'I'm Isabel. Nico said I would find you in here. Sorry to intrude, but my visit was a surprise. A little detour on my way to a gallery in Nice.'

So, this is the Marquesa de Casa Aytona. Nico's Marquesa.

Her hand is outstretched and we shake as her eyes sweep over me. My hair is probably sticking out here and there after pulling my T-shirt over it. I stare at her in dismay at what she must think. She's beautiful, slim and elegant. In chic, skinny black leggings with a pale blue, soft leather jacket cropped at the waist. It offsets those piercing hazel-brown eyes to perfection. Chin-length, glossy, chocolate-brown hair, cut in that windswept, choppy look that only a very expensive, top hair stylist can achieve; she also smells heavenly. As I withdraw my hand, I find myself checking it quickly, hoping I don't have any paint smears on it.

'Don't worry.' She laughs and even that's a soft, musical tone to the ear. 'Paint is not a problem. And you are about to start a new canvas. Hopefully, soon I will have news as I have someone already interested in one of your pieces. So, this could be another one for my gallery, yes?'

I'm hoping to create something that will be a permanent reminder for me, every time I glance up at it on my wall at home. But I don't feel comfortable admitting that yet, so I simply shrug my shoulders.

Her eyes are so full of life, they sparkle. Everything about her is a little bit larger than life. I notice that she wears a wedding ring, and I'm not surprised. A woman like this could have any man she chooses, and her husband must be a very special man, indeed.

'Nico said you would show me some of your other canvases? Is that possible? Or should I not disturb you? I know that Nico would have already thrown me out at this point. He hates being disturbed when he's working.'

She reminds me of the actress Penelope Cruz; that sultry, slightly breathy way she speaks is beyond charming. I'm totally thrown and realise I need to pull myself together or risk looking like a complete fool.

'I'm sorry, Isabel. This is such a surprise and I'm a little speech-less. I'd be delighted to show you some of my other work. It would be my pleasure and thank you. Um, having... I mean, just knowing my paintings are displayed on a wall in a real gallery is such an honour, it really is!'

My rambling makes me wish I hadn't opened my mouth at all, so I decide to shut up and Isabel follows me across to the storage cupboard. As I slide the first door across, I ease out the trolley storing over a dozen of my canvases. I tilt the first one forward, so Isabel can view the second standing behind it.

'Oh, wonderful. And all of these you have done since coming here?'

I nod. 'Yes. Please, take your time. I'll just give my hands a quick wash.'

I leave her to leaf through, eager to check out my hair and my face for signs of paint in the mirror above the sink. I'm also conscious I need to pop the lid on my palette, so it takes a few minutes, which is enough time to compose myself.

'Can I take a picture?' She holds up her phone and points towards one of the canvases.

'Yes, please do.'

Snapping away at several of them in turn, I try not to watch her every move, but she's one of those glamorous people who mesmerise you because they look so flawless, it's jaw-dropping. If I saw her photo in a magazine, I'd swear she'd been airbrushed. No one should look that good.

'This is exactly what I was hoping for, thank you. The man I've been talking to is a big investor, always looking for a new artist. He loves to make money and that's why I need to keep discovering new talent.'

I don't quite know what to say to that, so I smile.

'He thinks you are a good investment. We must make sure we price you correctly. It must be win-win, no?'

I nod. I can't even believe someone would hand over money for something I've painted when I'm still learning. I'm hardly an artist, more of a trainee.

'So, you keep Nico company here when he paints late?'

'Yes. It's peaceful when everyone else is asleep.'

She inclines her head. 'And how long are you here, Fern?'

I have no idea why she's asking that question, but I feel uneasy.

'Another seventeen weeks. The time has flown.'

'Ah. And things have changed, yes? Nico, he worked hard to build this, but he is a painter first. And you? What happens after you go home?'

She doesn't seem edgy about my being here as I'd feared for a moment, but she is curious.

'I will still paint, but my family will be surprised. It will be nice to all be together again, as we're rather spread out at the moment.'

Did she want to hear that, or not? I wonder.

She's glancing around and now her eyes are on Nico's work. She saunters off, lifting the corner of the muslin covering the painting of the woman by the lake.

'Ah, still not finished,' she exclaims, sounding frustrated. 'He must focus. This is his past and it will haunt him until it is done. He never listens to me, so why I bother, I do not know.' She isn't talking to me but out loud to herself and I watch as she wanders down the room.

Nico has his current work in progress and two others drying, although they could probably be put away now.

'This, I want,' she says, standing back to admire another of Nico's beloved paintings of the garden in bloom. She spins around, directing her attention back to me. 'What if when you go home you cannot paint? What if your inspiration is here?'

Is she challenging me and my commitment? Or is this about Nico?

It catches me off guard. Does she think Nico is my inspiration? A voice looms up behind me and I see the reaction on her face. It softens, instantly.

'Fern doesn't need a château, or France, to inspire her. But she will be needing a studio.' Nico stands there, his eyes sweeping over my face for an instant before settling on Isabel.

A studio of my own. I haven't had time to think about what happens next with regard to my painting. More worrying to me at this moment is what if Isabel is right?

* * *

I dress with care for dinner, wanting to create the right impression for some reason I can't really explain, as you can't undo a first impression. It's vanity, I suppose. Isabel is in a different league to me and we both know it. But she's a businesswoman and, of course, I want the heady feeling of knowing that someone in the business thinks my paintings will sell, because it's validation.

What if when I leave here and return home everyone around me thinks I've lost my mind and I'm chasing an impossible dream? I don't know anyone else who paints and most people I know buy their art from a chain store, or IKEA. It's a sobering thought.

As I approach the dinner table to take my seat, Nico is talking to Isabel in Spanish. There is a lot of hand gesturing going on, but their eyes are firmly on each other and the interaction between them indicates she's on his case. He ends the dialogue by throwing his hands up in the air in a defeated gesture and they both laugh.

'She wants the painting of the roses, Fern. The one I do not want to sell because it belongs in the château. Letting it go is like ripping off my arm.'

His face is dramatic, but she's laughing at him. It's good to see the rapport between them. I thought he had no one, but now I'm not so sure of that.

'It's beautiful, Nico, that's why Isabel wants to display it in her gallery.'

'If you refuse me, then you will be in my debt again. You must come in the summer. You have not been to visit for a long time and I will throw a party in your honour. Come anyway, it will be good for business.'

If Isabel was simply reading out a shopping list, she'd still make every syllable sound sexy with that musical, halting quality to her voice.

'I'm needed here!' Nico exclaims, and now everyone around the table is listening to the back and forth between them.

'But you sell more paintings if people see you, meet you in

person. You know that. It is time for a trip home.' Her tone changes and I can see she's serious.

Nico glances at her, frowning. 'This is my home now, Isabel. I'll think about it. Now, let's eat. I'm starving.'

Margot's cassoulets are wonderful, and I can only hope that Isabel isn't a vegetarian and she likes rabbit.

I glance her way a couple of times throughout the meal and she seems happy enough. I have Kellie on one side of me and Dee-Dee on the other, so I end up being party to two very different conversations.

Once everything is cleared away, people drift off to do different things. Nico and Pierce end up playing cards and I'm left sitting opposite Isabel, so I feel obliged to go and sit next to her. She's wearing a soft pink cashmere jumper that clings to her slender body like a second skin and a beautifully tailored pair of black trousers. Simple, but she still stands out above the crowd. Next to her I feel *rustic*. As these thoughts are going through my head, I begin to laugh and she looks at me, startled, as I lower myself into the chair next to her. Rustic? Or boring?

'Sorry, my head was somewhere else for a moment, there. Nico is very fond of the rose painting,' I explain. 'He thought it would brighten the entrance hallway during the winter months.'

I don't know why I feel it's necessary to fight his case for him.

'As may be. He will be paid handsomely for it. An artist cannot get sentimental and some pieces will sell more easily than others.'

Even when she's delivering what could be regarded as a rather curt message, her warm Spanish accent seems to take the sting out of the words.

'I have a lot to learn,' I admit.

'Nico's paintings can command the middle range of five figures and within five years it will be six figures if he continues to listen to me. But we need to release the right paintings at the right time. Now you,' she looks at me pointedly, 'different market. You are more commercially viable. I hope you intend to be prolific. People like to impulse-buy but at the right price. They look for colour, the brighter the better. A statement piece to set off their beautiful room as an accessory, rather than an investment. Do not be offended by that because in time, who knows? Maybe they make a huge profit, too. But the demand is high, and I will give you my card. Is good for you, is good for me. Yes?'

I nod. 'Thank you. I don't really know what to say.'

'Don't say anything, just paint,' she says, leaning in conspiratorially.

It's the first time I've felt a connection with her, as if she has been trying to suss me out and now she's come to a conclusion.

'With regard to Nico, you help convince him to come to Spain this summer? He needs the exposure and he has been away too long. Things run well here and it's possible?'

I look across at Nico and Pierce, oblivious to the fact that we're watching them. Isabel has no idea what Nico has been hiding from her. At least he is finally free of the worry, but is he ready to go back to a place where the memories will seem even more real?

'Now Pierce is here, I'd say it's possible. But whether Nico wants to go, I'm not so sure, Isabel. Just recently he's been dwelling on his childhood, things I think that he'd rather forget. Going back might unsettle him further.'

She's watching me, watching him.

'You seem to understand him. I do not push for no reason, Fern. I came here solely for this purpose but will not admit that to him. I have a lot of wealthy clients. The sort of people who, when they buy an artist's work, it sends a little ripple through the market. The right message. Nico has been so cautious in the past, but now it is holding him back. We have history together and I have invested time in him out of our friendship. But this is business and I need him to step up.'

I can see her point. She's concerned that he's only content to bury his head in the work but isn't interested in the equally important task of establishing himself as a name people can recognise. If she knew about his father's deception, maybe we wouldn't even be having this conversation. I have no idea how strong their friendship is but, even so, there's nothing more I can tell her – this is between the two of them.

'It probably won't make a difference whatever I say, but I will tell him that I think it's a good idea. Because it is, for several different reasons. Not least because a change of scenery would be good for him. It's time he received the recognition he deserves in person, from people he respects. He should step away and let his team prove that they can take care of things here.'

'Good. We are like-minded. I want only what is best for him. I suspect you do, too.'

I try not to react to the loaded look that Isabel flashes at me and return it with a polite nod of my head.

29

A SENSE OF RELIEF

As the evening moves on, eventually Nico gravitates back to be with his guest. I change seats and it isn't long before Kellie appears, looking pleased with herself.

'I have some news,' she announces, discreetly, and nods in the direction of the kitchen.

Swinging open the door, she glances around to check we're alone.

'I've been talking with Pierce and Ceana. The Haven is going to pay for me to attend a couple of courses. The first one is a Crystal Healing Practitioner Diploma, which I'll be doing online. If I pass that, then I'll be going to Wimereux, on the coast, to attend the first module in Reiki Practitioner training. Isn't that just brilliant?'

I can see that she's buzzing. I can't help wondering whether she's told her parents, though. Considering they were so worried about her, they never did come over to see for themselves the sort of environment she's in. But either way, she's happy.

'That's wonderful news, Kellie, and you deserve it. I'm thrilled for you!' I hug her, and she's dancing on the spot.

'Taylor thinks it's the right thing for me, too. When we shut down for the three-week break next Christmas, he's going back home, and he's asked me to go with him. I said yes.'

Nine months is a long time, but I have a good feeling about the two of them. Age is just a number and in their particular case, it's the tough life experiences they've managed to survive which puts them on an equal footing.

Suddenly she bursts out laughing, unable to contain her excitement. 'My parents will freak out when I break the news. But I don't care. My future is here, Fern, and I know that now.'

At that moment, Taylor's head appears around the door and he shoots me a smile.

'Hey, Fern. Kellie, I thought we were shooting off to grab our guitars and do a session?'

She pulls a face. 'Oops, sorry, I forgot. Catch you later, Fern,' Kellie says as she traipses out through the door, leaving me feeling ecstatic for her.

It's wonderful to see her blossoming into a woman who is more self-assured and believes in her own worth. When good things happen to good people, it leaves such a warm feeling in your heart. Pierce gets things done, but it's only now I'm beginning to understand why Nico brought him on board.

Nico treasures his time in the studio, but he needs to contrast that with the company of people around him. To become isolated is his worst fear because I sense a part of him connects that with his father. The slide into self-destructive mode which, sadly, can sometimes sit alongside great talent.

His artistic temperament makes him feel things to the extreme and while it doesn't manifest in a temper, I often see it in his eyes. He holds on to things – memories, old hurts and a hint of fragility that sits uneasily alongside that tremendous strength and willpower. Lying just beneath the surface, it never leaves him and threatens to pull him down. Two very opposite sides of a man who works hard to keep himself on an even keel.

I walk back out into the day room, searching for him, but he's not there. Neither is Isabel. I'm not in the mood to sit and chat, so I say goodnight and head off to the studio. It's in darkness and as I switch on the lights, I feel a sense of contentment. I love this room.

Swapping my jumper for a loose, painting T-shirt, I stare down at it. Every little blob and smear is like a badge of honour. What I didn't show Isabel is the little pile of canvases that will never see the light of day. Rolled up ready to take home, and languishing in the back of the cupboard, they are an important reminder of my journey. Days of exasperation, followed by Nico's very patient tutoring as he guided me through the pitfalls of my learning curve. Treasures, in one way, because they chart my development, but there's always that feeling you could have done better. That's when I knew I was always meant to be an artist and I began signing my canvases.

* * *

'You're still here?'

Nico enters just as I'm about to begin clearing up. It's shortly after one-thirty in the morning and it's been a very productive, satisfying session.

I glance at him, wondering where he's been, because he doesn't look tired. More wired.

'Isabel has just gone to bed. She's leaving early tomorrow morning.'

He sounds apologetic for some reason. I don't know why.

'You're not starting work now?' I remark.

'No. I saw the light was on and wanted to check you were okay.'

As I wipe my brush on a rag, I focus on what I'm doing, avoiding his gaze.

'You need to tell her everything, Nico. She's trying to help you move up to that next level and yet she feels you aren't committed. Her loyalty to you is now in conflict with the business side of her. You can't have it both ways if you keep her in the dark. You owe her that, at least.'

When I do look up at him, he hangs his head.

'You're right. I know that. But I've lived in fear for so many years that it won't leave me. I'm not ready to tell her, but I will consider planning a trip to Seville at some point this summer.'

Argh! He's so stubborn at times.

'Nico, she's here, now, and you need to do this face to face. You can't wait another three or four months. A lot can happen in that time and Isabel will be working hard on your behalf, building your reputation and getting your name out there. She's putting a lot on the line for you; you owe her the truth and once she understands—'

His eyes blaze. 'No one understands. I worked for Isabel's father doing menial jobs around their property to earn enough to buy the supplies I needed to paint. I helped their gardener, raking leaves in autumn and deadheading flowers in the summer. It's bad enough she knew of my father; thankfully, my mother was well-loved and respected for her kindness and sense of community. But even she became reclusive and stopped inviting people into our home. This is one step too far for me, Fern. You must leave it alone.'

We're facing each other, and I can see he thinks I've overstepped the mark. He's angry with me.

'I know you don't want to hear this, Nico. But I'm begging you to reconsider your decision. It will clear the air and restore Isabel's belief in you, that you can rise to the challenge. This isn't solely about putting you on display and I don't know why you can't see that?'

His face is stony. 'I came here to escape all of that. Maybe it's a price I'm not prepared to pay.' The icy tone is a warning.

'Then you're not the man I thought you were, or who Isabel believes you to be,' I point out as I finish putting away my brushes. 'I can't decide whether you're being petulant, or arrogant – neither is warranted, or even appropriate. There are plenty of artists who would give anything for the opportunity you are turning down without so much as a passing thought.'

'You think it's that easy? There's so much you don't know. Isabel wears the wedding ring of her dead husband five years after he's been gone. He turned her from a warm-hearted young girl into a cool-headed businesswoman. If I tell her everything, she will walk away and that will ruin my career. Even the merest whisper of an association with fraudulent activity in the art world means doors would be slammed shut forever. For her and for myself.'

I look at him, horrified. 'Isabel is in love with you, Nico. How can you not see that in the way she looks at you? The way she's been prepared to sweep aside her concerns and support you regardless of what her head is telling her? What you are doing by keeping this from her is wrong and unfair, Nico.'

'Unfair?' He turns, shaking his head as he walks towards the door. 'You can't even begin to understand the meaning of that word, Fern, trust me.'

30

WORDS, WATER AND WISDOM

Guilt. Five little innocuous letters that when strung together can destroy hopes, dreams, relationships and, ultimately, lives. Nico is feeling guilty for not facing up to his demons. I'm feeling guilty because he matters to me. But then, so does everyone here.

Does guilt serve a higher purpose? I wonder. Is it designed to make us stop and think before we cross an imaginary line? A sort of inner alarm system that some people choose to tune out, while others are stopped in their tracks?

It might be paranoia, but everyone around me seems to be battling with it at the moment. Kellie is making commitments to tie her future to Taylor and France for a long time to come, by the look of it. But as each day passes, she keeps putting off making that call home.

And my family – well, this week the contact has been noticeably absent, yet again. I can't even begin to grapple with what's going on with them all at the moment. Of course, when they ring everything is wonderful, which it never is, and that's what is making me suspicious.

People think they are sparing you the angst, but now they're avoiding me and that's worrying.

I can't seem to let it go and it's time to reach out to Georgia.

'Hey, neighbour, remember me?'

She shouts down the phone in excitement, 'Fern! How are you?'

I yank it back away from my ear, pressing speakerphone.

'Sorry I haven't been in touch. Steve's had shingles and what a pain he's been.'

I can't stop myself from smiling. Georgia isn't big on sympathy.

'Ouch, I hear that's painful.'

'Yes,' she replies, forcefully. 'Poor me, it's been an absolute nightmare. It's lovely to hear your voice, though. You have no idea how much you've been missed.' The way she says it sounds meaningful. Worryingly meaningful.

'I'm missing everyone, too. I thought I'd call and find out if things are really ticking over well at that end? You know what it's like, everyone is busy. If it isn't battling with a poor signal, it's a timing thing. I'm missing out on so much. Is the house still standing?' I laugh, good-naturedly.

She hesitates for a second or two and when she does begin talking, her voice is unnaturally bright.

'Of course, everything is fine. You're worrying about nothing. We all think we're indispensable, but they manage without us, don't they? I mean, when they have to.'

Now, that's odd. 'I suppose so, but I'd rather know if something had gone wrong.'

This time she jumps in way too quickly. 'The roof is still on, so you can take a deep breath and get back to work. I hear it's going well for you in France.'

So she's spoken to one of them at least, then.

'It's very different and no two days are the same. There's no time to get bored, that's for sure,' I reply, truthfully.

'You can't worry about home, Fern. Just enjoy your little stint of freedom. I would.'

Georgia is hiding something from me.

'So, there's nothing I should be concerned about at the moment?'

'Nope.' Well, her tone infers she's not prepared to give anything away, so I might as well give up and pretend I believe her. 'Good. Great, in fact. How are the kids?'

That sets off a whole twenty-minute long monologue about wishing she didn't drive as all she is these days, is a taxi service. With Steve off sick and unable to get behind the wheel, Georgia is feeling frazzled. I'm glad I called, just because she needed a listening ear, but I don't feel reassured in any way.

With this week's arrivals due to fly home later this afternoon, I have to head off shortly for this morning's experimental workshop. One of the courses Pierce has run in the past with great success, apparently, is a Self-Awareness course. Twelve of the attendees are taking part, which surprised us all.

It's something he usually runs over two full days as it's aimed at gaining a clearer understanding of one's strengths, weaknesses, inhibitions and overall motivation. He says it's really about establishing *a path to happiness*. Learning to *unlearn* things which hold us back or threaten to stifle our ability to think outside the box. All very thought-provoking stuff and interesting.

There's one exercise from the second day of the course that he feels will work particularly well here as a debrief. A good way, he thinks, to spend the last morning when there's a lot of goodwill in the group now they have gelled and bonds have been formed.

Pierce asked Yann and me if we'd join in because it works best with a larger group, but, in addition, he's looking for feedback. He's expecting us to write a little report about how well it's received by those taking part.

'Right. If everyone can grab a sheet of paper off the easel and write their name in the top right-hand corner.'

There's a flurry of activity as we are all curious about what we're going to be doing. It's a fairly mixed group in terms of occupations, but age-wise there's probably only a ten-year span, which is unusual. Maybe that's why everyone has bonded so well this week, and it's only the artsy contingent, as someone named them, who are closeted away with Nico this morning.

'Good,' Pierce concludes, his voice rising above the chatter. 'Now, I want you to write two words in the centre of the page. Like this.' He flips the lid off his marker pen and lays his own sheet on the floor. He writes his name in the corner and then in the centre he draws two clouds. In one he writes the word *intense* and in the other *altruistic*.

He stands, and we all gather around him.

'I want you to come up with two words – one reflecting your strength and the other your weakness. Words that you feel best describe your personality in a way that sums you up. Yes, I'm *intense* which isn't exactly negative, but it's something about which I need to be wary, so it doesn't put people off. And my main motivation in life is *altruistic*, because in my line of work if I can't help other people to feel better about themselves, then I'd better shut up shop.'

Everyone starts laughing.

'Are you all happy with that?' There's a lot of nodding heads. 'Spread the sheets out over the entire floor space in the gym. I want you all to wander around and think of a couple of words that you're comfortable adding to each person's sheet; based solely on your perception of them this week. There's no rush and we have half an hour for this part of the exercise.'

It's actually quite fun. For some people, words instantly pop into my head, but for others, I find myself having to stop and think. Maybe I didn't get to spend much time in their company, or it takes me a few minutes to find the right word. It certainly focuses your attention and it's not as easy as it might appear at first.

As I walk around doing my bit, what surprises me is the wide variety of adjectives used. But I studiously avoid glancing at my own sheet as I mingle. It's gone from quite noisy banter to almost total quiet. People are taking this really seriously and suddenly I feel uncomfortable.

Glancing at Yann, he's on his knees and I wonder what he's doing because it doesn't take that long to write a word and draw a cloud, and then I realise some people are adding personal little messages. At that precise moment, Ceana steps into the gym.

'Sorry, everyone, I've come to grab Fern. We have a burst pipe and need an extra pair of hands. Lunch will be a little late, I'm afraid.'

I cast around apologetically and run to catch up with her.

'Nightmare,' I say, as I double my strides to meet her pace.

'Poor Margot is standing in an inch of water. The electrics have been turned off, but we can't move the stopcock. We need to mop up the floor before it begins to pour into the day room. Fortunately, the last batch of bread is already cooling so we're okay for lunch.'

As soon as we step in through the door, I glance across at the kitchen and see a mound of rags and old towels forming a barrier between the two rooms.

'If you can grab a broom and help Taylor and Dee-Dee, that would be great, thanks, Fern.'

The three of us work in a line across the large room to drive the water out through the back door.

'It would have been easier if the floor didn't slope back into that corner,' Dee-Dee complains.

She's right. As fast as we sweep, some of the water keeps running back.

'We need suction,' Taylor says. 'Keep brushing, I'll be as quick as I can.'

If it wasn't so dire, it would be comical. Dee-Dee and I decide to work in tandem, rushing forward so the water starts to gather speed like a wake in front of our brushes. But by the time we get to the back door, it's disappointing how little ends up trickling down the path.

Margot and Ceana are traipsing back and forth, moving everything needed for lunch out into the day room.

Several minutes later, Taylor returns with additional help and a wet and dry vacuum.

'Well done that, man!' I applaud, as Kellie and Odile take platters from the fridge.

'We need some more towels in the doorway,' Ceana calls out over her shoulder.

Taylor is the other side, plugging in the machine. 'Kellie can you grab something large, like one of those throws on the sofa? I can't stand in the water as I can only suction from the dry side. I need you to stop this ingress.'

'Sure. I'm on it.'

Bastien appears with a large wrench in his hand.

'Is it under the sink?' he asks, and Margot nods. Six strides and he's lying on his back, taking the full force of the finger-like jets of water spurting out inside the cupboard. The seconds pass and nothing happens, then there's a little cursing.

'I got the sucker,' he calls out eventually, sounding jubilant.

'Whoop!' Dee-Dee endorses, delighted that at least the pond won't get any bigger now.

With all the brushing action and Taylor's suctioning power, it takes us forty minutes to end up with a damp, rather than wet, puddle-free floor. The old floor tiles were at least sealed, but it's going to take a while to dry it out completely.

Bastien opens the windows wide and we can at last stand back and appraise the situation.

'Everything we need to serve lunch is now on the table. Fern, can you tell everyone to give us half an hour? The day room is fine, just a little soggy in the doorway. Dee-Dee, if we can drag these wet things out into the garden, that will help.'

'Great teamwork, everyone,' Margot acknowledges, gratefully. 'My skirt is soaking wet and my feet are like ice!' She laughs.

Kellie heads off to the laundry room to find some towels for Margot. I text Nico as I head back to the gym, to make him aware that lunch is slightly delayed. My shoes are squelching as I walk, so I push open the door and lean in.

'Sorry, guys. Another half an hour and lunch will be ready. I have to go and get some dry shoes, see you all in a bit.'

I wish I could say I'm sorry to have missed the end of the exercise, but the truth is that I was way outside my comfort zone with it. For some reason I can't even begin to explain, I didn't want to read what was written on my sheet while everyone was watching my reaction. Saved by a burst pipe. It must be my lucky day.

* * *

'Fern, I have something for you,' Pierce calls out, slipping his backpack off his shoulder to unzip it.

I stop and turn. We've just waved off the coach and because of the upheaval this morning, a late lunch turned into an afternoon of chatting and general socialising.

'It's your piece of paper,' he says, holding it out to me. 'I thought you might like to read the comments. It was obvious you weren't very comfortable and I'm sorry if I misjudged the situation. I'd rather hoped you'd find it a positive experience, but it isn't right for everyone. When you have a quiet moment, take a look. It sends a very powerful message and I've seen a lot of these over the years, enough to know this one is rather special. Anyway, thanks, Fern. Your help this week has been much appreciated, as usual.'

I watch as he walks off across the courtyard. Staring at the paper in front of me, I have no desire to unfold it. Some people love feedback; I'd rather not know what people think about me. I know I'm not perfect. I know I worry too much. I'll never change, because it's who I am.

As I walk into the studio, Nico suddenly appears behind me. There's still a tension between us and I hate that.

'I thought I'd join you. Unless you want to be alone. You look upset.'

I shake my head. 'No. Not upset. Unsettled.'

'What's that?'

He points to the folded sheet of paper in my hand.

'It's from Pierce's session this morning. We all had to describe ourselves in two words and then everyone else added their thoughts. It was a bit too uncomfortable and intense for me.'

'You haven't read it?'

'No.'

He strolls down to his end of the studio, pulling his plaid shirt over his head and grabbing his work T-shirt. I don't look away and he seems oblivious to the fact that I'm watching him. Physically, he's a strong man and I've seen him coming out of the gym early in the morning. You don't maintain a physique like that unless you work out. He's also a man who is very disciplined. The type of person who probably does a hundred sit-ups before breakfast. He replaces what's missing from his life with regime and that's what keeps him together. I can't help feeling it's a little sad.

He looks up and I look away.

'Can I read it?'

Is he checking on Pierce? I hope he doesn't think I'm being negative in any way.

'If you want. It's just not my thing, that's all.'

I place it on the shelf behind me, next to some of Nico's art books, then pull my working shirt over my head. In that few seconds, Nico has crossed the room and is staring at the unfolded sheet held aloft in his hands.

I watch his expression.

'It's very you. Except the two words in the middle. I'm assuming those were your words?'

I nod.

'You need to look at this, Fern.'

He holds the sheet out to me and when I don't take it, he gently lowers it, face up, onto the floor.

'You're good at giving me advice. My advice to you is that you need to read this and take it on board.'

He walks off and disappears into the workroom.

The paper is upside down, but it's covered in clouds – more clouds than there were people, so most have written more than one word. And in between the clouds are lots and lots of little messages written in much smaller print.

Inspirational. Kind. Thoughtful. Caring. Compassionate. Genuine. Determined. Positive. Motivational. Gracious. Gentle. Warm. Sympathetic. Empathetic. Kind-hearted. Fit! Engaging. Affectionate. Sociable. Cheerful. Approachable. Supportive. Welcoming. Talented. Outgoing. Trusting. Loving. Encouraging. Understanding. Sunny. Forgiving. Attractive. Cool. Selfless. Enthusiastic. Reassuring. Hopeful. Role model.

The two words in the centre, my words, are *Worrier* and *Sensitive*.

The wave of positivity that floods over me is undeniable. I begin to read the personal little messages until tears obscure my vision.

Thank you for listening to me, it meant a lot.

I will most certainly be taking your advice, lovely lady!

No one knows about our little late-night feast, right? Heh! Heh! J x

I will always miss Spook, but when I get home, I'll head to the pet shop, I promise, Fern.

So glad I gave pottery a go, as you suggested. Dirty nails, or not lol.

MAY 2019

31

WHAT PRICE A MUSE?

It's unsettling when your gut instinct is trying to grab your attention but you keep pushing it away. The warning is hard to ignore, but I don't quite know what to do about it, and that's the dilemma. All day, Nico and I have been avoiding each other after I managed to upset him again without uttering a word.

Since the Marquesa's visit, the rift between us has never really closed, maybe because Nico knows I saw the connection between them. The one he constantly tries to ignore.

Isabel rang earlier and, unfortunately, I was in the room when he took the call. I couldn't really catch any of what was said as it was all spoken in Spanish, but his body language told me they were arguing. When he turned, he caught me looking at him and I could see the anger in his eyes.

'What have I done wrong now? She wants what she can't have. There's no more to say.'

'Except the things you are keeping back, Nico. Why are you so afraid to admit that you are in love with her?'

He spins around on his heels, his back taut. Then he remembers something and his voice softens. 'Isabel says you have sold your first painting and another one has been reserved. She will be in touch.'

Now my mind is whirling. There are only eight weeks left before I head for home, and Nico and I are becoming increasingly subdued in each other's company.

I should be happy, my heart soaring because the Marquesa was so complimentary about my work and it's going so well. This is truly wonderful news. I can sense that Nico is angry with himself because he realises how important this moment is to me, but his anger has overcome him.

The pressure is on now, as I need to finish as many canvases as I can while I'm here. I have no idea how long it will be once I get home until I can paint again. Isabel is a woman who thinks with her head first, her heart second. She's all about the business and that's what makes it all so incredible for me, and significant.

It's important that I arrive home feeling confident in my abilities and determined to somehow incorporate this into my daily routine. None of this would have happened if it wasn't for Nico. But he's in no mood to be thanked tonight.

With no one around me at home who will understand that I need to express my artistic side, I fear I'll become disillusioned. Or, worse, pine for my place here.

There have been moments when I'd wondered how honest Nico's appraisal of my work had been. One's mentor is bound to nod enthusiastically and gaze appreciatively at the brushstrokes you lay so lovingly upon the canvas. But I wondered, even doubted him, in the beginning. And that's unfair of me. He's never given me any reason to disbelieve his intentions. Our feelings, well, that's another thing entirely. You can control what you choose to do, but not what your heart dictates.

My heart tells me I will always care for Nico. Always. And there is nothing I can do about that. But what if it's something more than that? What if when I arrive home, I yearn to come back because this is now where I belong? I can't even contemplate that, because my heart would shatter if this wasn't simply about the passion for expression.

Tonight, the mood in the studio is tense. We've kept well away from each other, almost as if we're in the middle of a row – which is ridiculous. Eventually, I realise I'm just faffing around, not really achieving anything much, but I can't just begin my clean-up and walk out. I don't know what I'm going to say to Nico when, eventually, I head out the door, such is the unspoken tension between us. Throwing down my rag, I put the cover on my palette and turn, thinking it's probably best to say nothing at all.

'Don't go.' His voice breaks the awful silence.

Reluctantly, I spin back around.

Nico eases himself up from his stool and walks over to partially dim the overhead lights. I gaze at his every move.

'Sit for me, Fern. Please.'

Fear grips me. But fear of what? I wonder. I watch as he walks past me to the cupboard, opens the door and pulls out a rolled-up rug. When he unfurls it in the centre of the studio, I want to turn and run, but my feet feel as if they are attached to the floor. He disappears into the workroom and returns with a folded, silky black robe which he places in the middle of the rug. Then he turns, heading back into the workroom, softly closing the door behind him.

I glance at the window, the moonlight streaming in like a shaft of light illuminating just that one spot and it draws me to it. Surrounded by inky blackness, which is like a cover blotting out the whole world, nothing seems to exist beyond this inner sanctum. I'm safe. I know that. So, without thinking, I gradually begin to peel off my clothes and drape the soft, flowing robe around me.

Nico's painting is etched on my brain, so I sit in the same pose, one leg tucked up beneath me, the other bent in front of me. Her hand lingered on her knee, her chin resting on her hand.

When he returns, he shows no emotion; no surprise. Instead, he's looking at me with appraising eyes as one would any model. He dims the overhead lights even further, then approaches to slip the gown off my shoulders, exposing my breasts. Nico then adjusts the angle of my leg just the slightest fraction. The touch of his fingers on my skin is strangely comforting. I'm no longer Fern, I'm the form he needs so desperately to capture. I can see the intensity of his desire to do just that, as he grabs his sketch pad and pencils, and I know I made the right decision.

Then he begins to work. His eyes flicker over me constantly and it's a gaze that I've never seen before. He's in the zone and every little nuance matters. My fear that I would feel awkward is unfounded. The only fear I have is making sure I don't move and become a distraction. Every little detail is dear to him and his brow is furrowed as he works, such is the level of concentration required. Each stroke of the pencil is crucial, as if it's indelible and cannot be redone. He knows this sitting is my gift to him. It's a night of intimacy I never expected to share with any man other than my husband.

Something deep within me, from my soul, connects with Nico in a way I cannot deny. It's a feeling that I have never experienced before. I love Aiden and I'm loyal, but my feelings for Nico are confusing. I feel sorry for him, for what he's been through, and I'm grateful for the way he's inspired me as a mentor. But somehow in my head it's all getting mixed up and I know it's time to walk away.

* * *

Slowly buttoning up my shirt, the words begins to flow.

'I can't stay, Nico… it's—' I falter as my voice trembles. 'My future isn't here, and I think we both know that. The Marquesa is in love with you, but she senses that you've been holding back, misunderstanding the reason for that because you won't tell her the truth. I've said it before and I'll say it again: that's not fair and it's not right.'

His face is ashen and his look pained as his eyes search mine. We're standing several feet apart now, but the pull between us is still electric. Two paces and this time I might not be able to walk out that door. I can see by the look in his eyes that he's fighting the same battle.

'You are my muse, Fern. Your presence changes everything for me and that goes way beyond love. With you here, my brush flies across the canvas, because you make my spirits soar.'

A solitary tear trickles down my cheek and I swipe at it with my sleeve as Nico watches, unable to move. The one thing I have to remind myself is that, without him I doubt I would have had the resolve to take myself seriously as a painter; let alone think of myself as an artist. Whether that makes him my mentor, or my inspiration, I don't know, but this man touches my soul.

'It's not enough, Nico. I'm not some sort of angel, I'm just a woman with flaws and anxieties.'

'And a big heart.'

I shake my head, sadly, as I look away. That haunted look of desperation on his face is too much to bear.

'A heart that belongs to someone else,' he acknowledges. The words hang heavily in the silence between us before I walk away for the last time.

32

A NEW DAWN, A NEW BEGINNING

Turning the key in the door, I bend to lift my suitcases and step inside. Instantly, the familiar seems to wrap itself around me like an old blanket. Comforting. Reassuring.

Finally, I'm home. Nearly eight weeks early, but at least it will give me time to readjust. After my journey of self-discovery, I need to emotionally detach myself from a world in which I was merely a visitor passing through. Now it's time to begin embracing the things I want to take forward and be grateful for this new lease of life it seems to have given me. I feel more alive than I have done in a long time. But there's a lot to process and it's a relief to know I don't need to rush myself.

Kicking the door shut behind me with my heel, I walk through the hallway, gazing around as if I'm seeing it for the first time. It's smaller than I remembered, I smile, but it feels so good to be home again. Placing the cases gently down on the floor, I wander into the sitting room, my eyes eagerly taking in every little detail. Nothing has changed, I'm relieved to see.

Mum's been in regularly and the framed photos capturing those most treasured of moments – our wedding day, anniversaries, Christmas and birthday parties – are dust-free. I pick up the most recent one; the party we had here in the house before Aiden and I set off on our adventures. Steve from next door stood on a chair and marshalled us all into a tight group so we didn't spill out of the shot. So many smiling faces, so many people with their arms wrapped around each other as he kept shouting 'closer, closer'. This is my life, I reflect, feeling more like a voyeur picking up someone else's photograph.

Mum's taken care of this house in the way that I do, keeping it ready for our return in the belief that we'd get through it. I will admit, though, that for one moment there even I began to have my doubts.

My favourite photo stares back at me from the bookcase, making my heart constrict. I caught Aiden sitting out on the patio, reading a report he'd brought home from work. He's in side profile and had no idea I was watching him.

It's not the same when you're not here, my inner voice speaks to him. *I'm scared that I'm not the same any more and I won't know for sure until you come back to me.*

A loud click makes me turn around, anxiously staring into the doorway. Suddenly, Owen appears, and I wonder if I'm daydreaming.

'F... Fern?' he stutters.

'Owen. What are you doing here?'

'I was about to ask you the same thing.'

My heart starts to thud in my chest as I notice he's wearing a sling.

'What have you done to your arm?' I demand, attempting to hug him while trying to avoid the plaster cast.

'A war wound,' he declares, as he flashes an annoyingly cheesy grin. I burst out laughing, despite my concern. Then I scowl at him, wondering when exactly he was going to tell me about his accident.

'So, how did this happen?' I indicate to the cast poking out of Owen's sleeve.

'I tripped over my own feet, but it's only a broken wrist. The embarrassment and heckling I got from my mates was way worse than the injury. Another week and the cast will be coming off.'

'But why are you staying here and not with Mum and Dad?'

'It's a long story and I'm not sure what to tell you first. The thing is, you can't get mad. Promise me that, because this was a family decision.'

'A family decision? Without involving me? I want to know exactly what's been happening, *now*.'

He nods in the direction of the kitchen and I let him walk on ahead, following behind in a daze. Pulling out a chair, I sit down heavily, berating myself for not pursuing my concerns that something wasn't right at home.

'Okay. I'll tell you everything and then we'll get everyone together. Hopefully by then you will have calmed down.' I can see he's still in a state of shock at seeing me here. 'Where should I start?' he tips his head back and a little sigh escapes from between his lips. 'First off, our little sister is pregnant.'

'She's *what*?'

'Calm down. It's all going to be fine,' he looks mortified by my reaction.

My hands fly up to my head as if it's about to explode and I jump up, pacing back and forth.

'Hannah didn't want you rushing back, but she really needs her sister right now. She's had to drop out of university. Mum will tell you all about it. Hannah has this hyper gravida something or other, which means she's sick most of the day.'

I stop pacing and stare at him.

'And no one told me? The decision to come back was mine, Owen, and you shouldn't have hidden this from me. Poor, poor, Hannah.'

My head is buzzing.

'Fern, stop right there. If we all pull together it's going to be all right.'

'Really?' He avoids my steely gaze and continues.

'The plan is that Liam will sell his flat and they're looking for a modest three-bed home they can buy reasonably cheaply and fix up. I thought we could all give them a hand once you and Aiden got back, and my wrist has healed. I have leave I can take before I head off again.'

He sounds so blasé about it. 'I can't believe this.'

'Well, I will admit that I had to fight the urge to turn and run the moment I saw you,' he replies with a grimace. 'We thought we had more time to get things... sorted.'

I realise I was the last person he was expecting to see when he opened that door. But I still don't understand why he's staying *here*. Slumping back down onto the chair, I turn to stare at him while in a daze.

'There's more, isn't there?'

He nods, and I feel myself sag.

'Dad set their kitchen alight when he left a frying pan on the ring while he went to answer the phone. They spent the best part of two and a half months living here while their kitchen was gutted and refitted.'

My heart sinks in my chest. I should have been here and not... what? Having fun in Provence?

Owen frowns, and I hold my breath. 'To tell you the truth, it's been total chaos since the day I arrived back. But we all pulled together, trying our best to hide what was going on so you didn't just jump in the car and head for home.'

'But that's my role, Owen. If I can't be there for you all, then who am I?'

'Someone who deserves to take a little time for themselves, that's who. We're all so proud of you, Fern, and for once we all wanted to put you first.'

'Proud?'

He lets out a deep sigh. 'You've carried us all in one way or another, Fern. Guess we wanted to make up for that. Aiden told us that you'd sold some paintings.'

'*Aiden* told you?' My question goes over his head.

'I did tell them you'd be upset, but Mum, Dad and Hannah were adamant. When I arrived home, the timing was unfortunate, as Mum wasn't talking to Dad because the kitchen fitters had messed up and he didn't notice. Sorry, Fern, but you just seem to sense things and it's too hard talking to you and... trying to keep things back. So, it was easier to say nothing at all. Why did you come home early, though?'

I came back to figure out who I am now and what is left of the old me, if anything, before Aiden gets back.

'I came home because even though I thought I'd be here on my own, this is where I feel closest to you all. And now – am I going to have to check into a hotel to get a bed?' I ask, half joking.

'Dad has had to paint the entire house due to the smoke damage, so I hope you don't mind me staying here. I didn't want to get in his way, seeing as I wasn't able to give him a hand.'

I can't laugh at his ridiculous question, because now my eyes are welling up. 'I'm going to be an aunt,' I whisper with incredulity.

'I know. It still hasn't really sunk in. I'm going to be an uncle; that's surreal,' Owen agrees. 'Once Hannah and Liam got over the shock, they were ecstatic about it, Fern. And we've all been dying to tell you.'

I nod. There are worse things happening in the world and I know that Hannah and Liam will rise to the challenge.

'And now you have a chance at a whole new career, Fern. We're all excited for you.'

'But how did Aiden know? I didn't tell him two of the paintings were sold.'

A sudden movement in the doorway attracts my attention and my jaw drops as I see Aiden standing there.

'It'll mean sorting you out a studio, of course. I was thinking about one of those smart log cabins in the garden. Your own space, what do you think?'

I stare at Aiden in total disbelief, then turn back around to look at Owen, who shrugs his shoulders, uncomfortably.

'I think it's time I made a swift exit and left you guys to it,' he says, rather sheepishly, and within seconds he's gone. Aiden, hasn't moved a muscle.

'Well, I thought I knew you as well as I know myself, Fern. You think after knowing someone for, what, thirteen years that you've seen it all. But you proved me wrong, my very own artist. Keep those surprises coming, babe, life was boring without you and that's the truth. Welcome home, Fern.'

We're staring at each other like strangers, but seconds later our arms are wrapped around each other. Aiden's hug is so tight, I can barely breathe through my tears. It's several minutes before either of us can talk and when I look up at him, his confusion is heart-wrenching.

'What made you come back early?' he whispers, his voice hoarse.

'I needed to reassure myself this life still existed,' I admit.

He groans and suddenly he pulls back a little. What I see is a momentary look of fear in his eyes. A cold feeling runs down my spine like a trickle of icy water.

'And what are you doing here?' I question him, frowning. I thought he was heading for Bangkok.

I can see how troubled he is – I was right to be scared because something is wrong here.

'I've been back for six weeks, now. Work is busy, and they were struggling.' He pauses, nervously. 'The truth is that it wasn't the same without you by my side, Fern. I wasn't the same person.'

Aiden releases his hold and his hands seek out mine, grabbing them both tightly as he leans back to gaze at me. It's a look of such intensity that it's as if he's trying to see into my very core, but his anxiety is tangible.

'Why didn't you tell me? Why didn't anyone talk to me about what was happening here?'

'Because I arrived back when everything was kicking off and none of us wanted you to come back until you were ready. I went

along with it because I needed some time to get my head together.'
His look is earnest, regretful – pained.

'But... but it was you who wanted this year of discovery, this time
to find yourself. It wasn't about me, Aiden, it never was.'

'I know. And unwittingly my stupid little life panic put me in
danger of losing everything we have. All I've discovered is that
without you I don't make good choices. I've seen some wonderful
sights, Fern, but it made me question everything and I messed up.'

Closing my eyes, I take a deep breath in. I've been living in dread
of this moment and what I might discover about myself, and Aiden,
when it finally arrived. But I thought I'd have some time here alone
to gather my thoughts before he returned. To discover that he's been
here, facing the same dilemma, is too much to comprehend. What
have we done to ourselves?

'I put *us* in this position, babe, and I realised, too late, it had
turned into a test. One that could go either way. The temptations out
there—'

My heart feels like a leaden weight inside my chest.

'We need to be honest with each other.' I stare up into Aiden's
eyes and he leads me into the sitting room and over to the sofa. As
we sit side by side, I'm glad I don't have to look directly at him.

'I'd hoped we'd simply fall into each other's arms and everything
would be back to normal, but the old normal wasn't working any
more, was it.' It's an admission, more than a question.

Aiden has been the centre of my life since I was sixteen years old.
I thought I knew him inside and out, but as I turn to glance at him, I
have no idea what he's thinking any more. Is it the same for him as
he stares back at me? I wonder.

'This is a new beginning for us, then. If that's what you want.' I
will my voice to sound strong, positive and not desperate.

'I slept with Joss,' he blurts out, and his head droops forward. He
stares at his hands as he laces his fingers together, his knuckles
turning white.

'Did you think I didn't know that?' I mutter, my voice barely audible. I thought if I kept pushing my fears away, it would make them less real, but deep down I knew what was going on.

'I'm sorry, Fern,' he says in a half-sob. 'I didn't mean for it to happen and I know that's a lame excuse. Joss gave me an ultimatum and I walked away. It's like I stepped outside my life for a while and I wasn't thinking. I hoped that coming back here would help me make sense of things again.'

'And has it?'

He launches himself back into the cushions, turning to look at me. 'The moment I heard your voice and then saw you sitting there, I suddenly felt... safe again.'

'Safe? What does that mean?' I try not to sound angry or disappointed, but I am – a little of both.

'I wasn't sure you'd come back. Hannah told me all about this artist guy of yours and the thought of how closely you were working together has been eating away at me. He was a stranger and yet he saw something in you, something I missed. You don't get to exhibit in a gallery and sell paintings unless you have real talent. How ironic that I was the one feeling trapped, but you were the one suffering in silence.'

I almost recoil in shock. 'That's crazy, Aiden. I knew that someday I'd set aside time to explore my interest, but I had no idea it would go anywhere. And how did you find out about the gallery?'

'Look, it wasn't Hannah's fault, but after she mentioned his name, I looked him up online. I wanted to find out more about the guy who was spending so much time with my wife.'

I'm disappointed that it's only jealousy that has made Aiden stop and think. 'But you never said you were uncomfortable about my being there. I didn't think you were that interested, to be honest.'

He grunts and gives his head a little shake. 'Jealousy is an ugly emotion and it's not something I wanted to admit had begun to consume me. Particularly, when... well, when I wasn't feeling very proud of myself.'

It's hard not to give a rather terse retort, but I remain silent.

'One of the links that came up was to a gallery in Seville. His work was good and that made me relax a little, but then I saw your name in the sidebar listed as a new artist *coming soon*. I called Owen to ask if he knew anything about it and he was as surprised as me. I didn't mention it to Hannah, or your parents, because I felt awkward about it. Shouldn't I have known what was going on? And then I realised I'd been holding things back, so who was I to complain? But a few days later Owen emailed me to say your paintings were up and Fern Wyman was officially an artist. I think he shared the link with everyone we know. And since then it says two of them have been sold.'

I've always been the one supporting everyone else and now they're all supporting me. Even though it can't have been easy for Aiden, in particular, not to voice his fears.

My life seems to flash before me. After losing my sister, I felt I had to step up to help fill the hole she left in our family. Mum leaned heavily on me, while Dad simply shut himself off for a while. But I kept a close eye on him whenever I felt his courage waning. It was a time when Owen and Hannah really began to look to me, to save worrying our parents. It's a role I never handed back, until now.

As for Aiden, well, temptation comes in all forms and while I wasn't unfaithful, I knew it was too dangerous to stay. When you find yourself caring enough to want to save someone from themselves, there is a connection – even if you don't want to admit it.

'So, where does this leave *us*?' I ask, and Aiden looks away, shrugging his shoulders.

APRIL 2020

33

FACING UP TO THE TRUTH

'How are you feeling? Sad? Angry?' Hannah's voice is low as the baby is in bed asleep.

'I'm fine, really.' It's not a platitude, because when something ends amicably, it's more of a relief. Like working your notice in a job and it's the last day; you are finally moving on. There's a little tinge of sadness for what has gone, the friendships and the memories you are leaving behind, but you know that the time has come to say goodbye.

Divorce is no different. When the passion has gone, the period spent unpicking your life together is like tipping water out of a bottle. Once it was full and as it gradually empties, it becomes just a hollow vessel.

'I'm sorry, sis. I know how hard you both tried and Aiden didn't mean to hurt you. I just wish he hadn't gone off like that. He owed you a proper explanation after messing you about.'

I know that it's been hard for them all as Aiden was a part of this family for such a long time. How can you not miss someone you thought would always be there? For Mum and Dad he was like a son, to Hannah and Owen he was a brother.

'Sometimes the things that people choose not to discuss, or

share, aren't important. And sometimes they are, but they don't need to be said out loud because it won't change anything. Aiden and I both knew that within a short time of being back together. I hope he is with Joss, but a part of me also doesn't want to know for sure. Silly, isn't it? You accept that you don't want someone any more and yet it hurts to think of them with someone else. Above all, I do want him to be happy.'

I can hear Hannah's tiredness in her sigh. 'Some people have a party and a divorce cake to celebrate their new-found freedom. Guess you aren't out partying tonight, then?'

'I'm alone, sipping coffee at the bed and breakfast. At least I have two blissful weeks in Canterbury, sketching and painting while I get to know Rosemary, my potential new business partner. I'll soon know whether it's the right thing to do, but it's scary buying into an art gallery and the thought of giving art lessons. But with a sizeable bank balance from my share of the house and the sale of over a dozen canvases thanks to Isabel, I have capital. But now I've given up work I will need some sort of regular income. Everything in my life is decidedly lacklustre at the moment. Committing to the next step feels like an impossibility because my emotions are all over the place,' I admit.

'Did you open the letter the Marquesa gave you?' Hannah's gentle probing tugs at my conscience.

'No. It's still in my bag, but I can't bring myself to open it.'

'That's silly, Fern. Read it and then maybe you can really get on with your life. It's not like you to be so indecisive. Buying into that gallery in Canterbury is a great opportunity and if you keep putting off making a decision, someone else will step in and you will regret it.'

I know she's right. 'I have a deadline. Two weeks, but it's scary, Hannah. What if I never sell another piece? The money I have could dwindle and I will have thrown it all away.'

'Hey, you've done well so far and the Marquesa is supporting you every step of the way still. She wouldn't do that if she thought someone else's work would sell better. It's time to have some self-belief, Fern. And that's an order. Love you and get some rest, for goodness' sake. And long, head-clearing walks.'

I start laughing. Since when did my little sister start mothering me? As I put down the phone, I decide the time has come; grabbing the letter and my thick jacket, I saunter out onto the balcony. There's a slight chill on the breeze and in the fading light I'm overcome with a sense of loneliness. Happiness seems like a distant dream these days, something I once had but may never have again.

Pulling my collar up around my ears, I sit at the little bistro table with the letter in my hand. The wind almost whisks it away and I grab it firmly, turning it over to stare at my name, handwritten on the front. Nico's writing is purposeful, and each letter is carefully crafted. Little curlicues on the tail of the F and the N look like tiny flowers. It could almost be a wedding invitation, except that if it were the case, I know Isabel would have told me before she handed it over.

We met up in August of last year when she came to London for an important art auction. She invited me to go with her and afterwards insisted I accompany her to an exclusive reception in one of the local galleries. I wasn't keen on going, but she'd been so good to me and I didn't want her to think I was ungrateful. She had no idea I was going through a painful divorce. Aiden was rarely contactable as he was trekking in the Himalayas, I presumed with Joss. But I couldn't be sure, seeing as he didn't leave a note the day he left. That broke my heart; it wasn't that I begrudged him a new start, but the fact that he'd put up with the constraints my hang-ups had forced on him. He'd never complained, but stifling his yearning to travel must have made him unhappy. As unhappy as I would be now, if I couldn't paint. Aiden had loved me once, I know that for a fact, as I had loved him. The unknown, was when exactly that love had started to fade and die.

'You should read this,' she'd said as she handed over the envelope and we'd hugged goodbye. 'I have no idea what's in it, but I can tell you that Nico was adamant I deliver it in person.'

'Has he finished the portrait?' An image of his face filled my mind as I recalled the night that I posed for him.

'Yes. He has captured you perfectly. It's rather beautiful.'

I'd looked at her, shocked. Captured *me*? 'You've seen it?'

She'd nodded. 'Of course.'

I remember feeling the colour draining from my cheeks as I'd stared at her in horror. Nico had betrayed me; betrayed my trust and my good intentions. I would never have sat for a nude portrait, but I was prepared to sit for him so he could finish the painting that tormented him.

And now, as I stare at the envelope between my fingers, I realise it's time to read what he has to say. Without Nico's tutoring, I may well have spent time drawing at some point in my life but might not have been bold enough to discover what I was really capable of doing. He was my inspiration, whether I like it or not.

Tearing it open, I slip out the single sheet of paper and stuff the envelope into my pocket.

My dear Fern,

The night I locked the door of the studio, as you sat on the rug with the robe half draped around you is etched in my memory forever. As we were bathed in the soft light, I was a man transfixed by the beauty of my muse. As an artist, I directed you into the perfect pose and my pencil greedily filled page after page. My soul soared in celebration of something that transcended physical beauty; something I still can't quite explain.

Your inner beauty and goodness permeated through the glow of your naked skin as I strived to capture every little nuance, every sensual curve. I believe I came to understand how close passion can be to insanity that night. For I realised that I was insanely in love with you.

You were my beautiful angel and always will be. But I know that angels are meant to be ethereal and that, sadly, you could never be mine in the real sense of the word. Not least because I am undeserving.

For one night, though, you were mine and mine alone – to capture on paper.

My fingertips touched your shoulder for one brief moment as I slipped down the robe. We didn't share a single word the entire time. Yet it was to become the most exquisite night of my life. One that will never leave me until I take my final breath.

I know how dear your family are to you; everything you do is for them, and as a man who is often selfish in his moodiness and sense of regret, I found that truly humbling.

Have a long and happy life, my darling Fern, for you deserve it. Be happy, keep painting and let your artistic soul soar. You touched my life briefly and for that I will be eternally grateful.

Your portrait is the first thing I gaze upon each morning before I begin my day and the last thing I see at night. I am a happy man indeed and I wanted you to know that it's because of you I was able to finally let go of my past demons.

I will never forget your kindness. You will always be an angel, to me.
Nico

I too remembered so vividly the moonlight shining in through the expanse of glass, covering my body in soft shadows. Nico made me feel beautiful, truly beautiful, that night. In a way that I had never done before – revered, flaws and all. Time seemed to stand still for us both, as if it wasn't real, but merely a dream.

I sit for a while, my mind in a whirl. Then I pick up the phone and dial Hannah.

'Sorry it's late, but I did as you suggested and I finally read Nico's letter.'

She stifles a yawn and I realise I've woken her; I only hope I haven't disturbed anyone else.

'Was he begging you to return?' she asks, suddenly alert.

'No. But he's saying he was in love with me.'

The seconds pass and I think Hannah is as stunned as I am.

'You must go to see him, Fern, before you decide what you are going to do next. He has no idea what has been happening, or that you're a free agent now.'

I close my eyes for a moment, blocking out the view of the twinkling lights in the distance, which seem to be dancing around in the darkness. Or maybe that's just the effect of my tears.

'I walked away from him because Aiden was waiting for me, Hannah. Throughout my life it's been about love, duty and responsibility. I always thought those three things went hand in hand. I had no idea love could change; that it could wane and become friendship. With Nico it's different. We never talked like lovers do because that wasn't the nature of our relationship; our connection was on a more spiritual level. If he's saying it was more than that, then he was lying to me all along.'

'And how about you, Fern? Were you being honest? Is it possible that you couldn't allow yourself to admit your true feelings? There's no shame in that; you didn't hold a grudge against Aiden with regard to Joss. These things happen and none of us can pick and choose our feelings; it's instinctive when we're drawn to someone.'

I think it's time I told her my guilty secret, but I'm scared that putting it into words will sound damning.

'Nothing happened between us, Hannah, but I allowed Nico to paint me in the nude. Oh, my reasons were genuine because I thought... well, it's a long story, but it was supposed to allow him to finish off a painting of a woman sitting by the lake. It was beautiful, hauntingly so, but he wasn't meant to be painting me, I was merely a model. In his letter he says it's *my* portrait he has hung on the wall and I would never have agreed to sit for him if I'd realised that was his intention.'

'I'm sorry you feel he used you, but if he is in love with you, can't you forgive him? Why was it so important to him, anyway? I'm sure artists don't finish every painting they begin – I know you don't.'

It's not easy talking about this as where do you start when Nico's story isn't simple to tell. It took me a long time to understand him.

'His father never recognised him as a true artist, Hannah. Their styles were very different. For Nico to paint a portrait in the style of the old masters is about validation. As successful as he has become, losing both his parents means that a form of recognition he longs for will never come. Instead, he's anxious to prove something to himself – that his father wouldn't have found him lacking.' I let out a long, slow sigh. 'Nico wasn't in love with me; he was in love with a muse and that's what he's holding on to.'

'And now you're understandably angry. It sounds like he has betrayed your trust, Fern, and that must hurt. Go back and demand that he take your portrait down. You have always been a very private sort of person and clearly he doesn't know you. If you genuinely feel nothing for him other than compassion, then this is your last hurdle – jump it. If you want me to come with you on this trip, just say the word. Little Rae loves being in the car, although her things will probably fill the boot. But even a feisty Spaniard will quake before two angry women and a wailing baby.'

I smile to myself. It doesn't seem all that long ago that I was fighting my sister's battles for her and now here she is, rolling up her sleeves for me. A new mum is not to be messed with and our darling little Rae has brought out Hannah's protective instincts, fuelled by hormones and that rush of motherly love. She looks like she could take on the world and win.

'You're right. It's time to pay Nico a visit, but I need to confront him alone. He wouldn't have done it to upset me, his letter is proof of that, but he doesn't understand how hurtful this is, or how disappointed I am at what he's done. Isabel said it's beautiful, but that's not the point. The point is that I did it for one reason only, because I thought it would help him to heal and it wasn't never supposed to be a portrait of me.'

There's a gasp. 'You already knew the painting was on general display for everyone to see?'

'Well, hopefully not *everyone* but on a wall in the château, yes.

Isabel told me when I met up with her in London. I was caught up sorting things out after Aiden's abrupt departure and it seemed the least of my worries. But thinking about people looking at my naked form, even if it is the work of an awe-inspiring artist, that isn't me, Hannah. The very idea makes me want to curl up in a ball and hide myself away. I've just been pushing it to the back of my mind, but I hate feeling so exposed, so vulnerable. And Nico has done that to me, seemingly, without a second thought.'

'Oh, Fern, I'm so sorry. This is the last thing you need right now.'

I know. What had become a rather magical memory for me, is now shattered beyond all recognition. How could I have been so naïve?

'I'll see if I can get a tunnel crossing tomorrow. With one overnight stay to break the journey there and back, and one night in the village close to the château, five days will do it and it will give me plenty of thinking time. I've not been able to settle since I arrived here, because I've been avoiding this and, deep down inside, I knew that. It's like the last piece of the puzzle, which means I can then start afresh. When I return, there will be nothing left to clutter my mind and I can press forward in peace.'

'Finally!' She exhales, loudly, and I ease the phone away from my ear a little, trying not to laugh at her exasperation. 'Travel safely, be firm and try to relax and enjoy the road trip. Springtime in Provence is lovely, I should imagine.'

Ironically, this time last year I was also at loggerheads with Nico, trying hard to convince him to listen to Isabel's advice. No doubt, she's steering him carefully forward in the right direction and now he's able to 'let go of his past demons' there's nothing to keep them apart. Unless he's using me as an excuse in some ridiculous, self-destructive attempt to deny himself happiness. Art appreciation aside, if she understood the reason I sat for Nico, then she would most certainly agree he had over-stepped the mark.

I don't like confrontation, but I won't be used. And, yes, it will be nice to spirit myself away for a spell on the road; driving along with a little music blasting out and feeling the breeze through my hair might be just what I need while I rethink my life. Fortunately, I have many memories of wonderful times spent in France and I'm not going to let one little upset spoil that for me.

It's time to let Nico know that his actions have broken any trust we had between us.

34

WHERE ANGELS FEAR TO TREAD

It's raining when I finally pull into the car park in front of the château. As I glance up at the windows my heart begins to pound inside my chest. The anger that was my companion for most of my journey seems to have disappeared and now I feel... vulnerable. It's hard to make out anything as the windscreen wipers can't cope with the torrent of water. It's the sort of rain that falls like steely rods, relentless and seemingly never-ending. It matches my mood as the last part of the journey has given me a headache from the constant swoosh, swoosh of rubber against glass.

Well, I'm here now and as nervous as I feel, it's time to right a wrong. But what also became clear to me with every passing mile of the journey is that I need to stand, facing Nico and feel nothing. Then I'll know I'm right and this was never meant to be. As I reach back to grab my jacket off the back seat, suddenly the passenger door is flung open. Ceana stands there, shielding me from the slanting rain with one of the retreat's colourful umbrellas.

'Well, this *is* a surprise. What on earth are you doing in this part of the world? Oh, I can't believe it!'

She looks overjoyed as I squeeze into my waterproof and ease myself out of the seat to join her, trying my best to stay under cover.

'Mind the puddles,' she points out, staring down at my trainers. It wasn't raining when I left Dijon this morning. With each passing kilometre, my anxiety levels continued to rise and now I feel slightly nauseous.

We link arms as we dodge the little dips where the water congregates and my mood begins to lighten.

'Why didn't you let us know you were coming?' she asks, giving me a quizzical look.

'It's a short visit. I rang Isabel yesterday to check that Nico was here and not at the gallery, or at a function. She wasn't around but her assistant confirmed Nico wasn't there.'

'Isabel?' Ceana gives me a curious look as she steers me towards the day room.

Once inside we hang up our coats to dry and head into the kitchen, where Ceana pops the kettle on.

'I assumed they spend a fair bit of time here these days. I couldn't imagine Nico wanting to be away for prolonged periods.'

Ceana's back is towards me as she grabs two mugs from the cupboard. Talking at me over her shoulder, her answer isn't quite what I expected.

'To my knowledge, she's only seen Nico twice since you left. Once when he took a trip to the gallery for some big exhibition she'd arranged. And she came here to check up on him, I think it was late July last year.'

She hands me a mug and we take a seat at the breakfast bar along the back wall.

'But I thought they were together?'

Ceana raises her eyebrows.

'Really? All I remember is that when she was here, they had a big row. He's not painting as much as he did, and she wasn't very happy about that. But our new IT guy set up a separate website for Nico's art classes and he's started a programme for emerging artists. There are already plans in the pipeline to add another accommodation block next to our newest addition.'

Well, that's an unexpected twist. But at the moment I can't get past the eerie silence around us. 'Where is everyone?'

'Off on a coach trip to Nice. There have been a lot of changes around here since you left. We've had several new people join the team and things are much better organised, thanks to Pierce.'

'Is Nico with them?'

'No. He's in his studio, I think. Why don't you wander over to say hello? The others won't be back until around nine-thirty tonight. This is going to put a big smile on a few faces, I can tell you. You are staying overnight, I presume?'

'No. I'm... taking a little road trip, so my stops have been pre-booked.'

She screws up her face. 'That's a real shame. Now you're here we won't want to let you go that easily; we have a lot of catching up to do. How is Aiden and the family?'

I finish my coffee and take my mug over to put it in the dishwasher. It's hard to look Ceana in the face right now.

'Aiden's fine. He's travelling. We decided to call it a day, actually. Owen and Hannah are doing great, but always busy these days. So much has happened in this last year.'

Even from the other side of the kitchen, I can sense her reaction – she's shocked. The sound of a stool scraping on the floor makes me turn and suddenly Ceana flings her arms around me.

'I'm so terribly sorry to hear that, Fern. I did wonder when you went very quiet. Those early text messages were quite upbeat and then suddenly, well, it was obvious something wasn't right. So, this is a little holiday then?'

We step back and her eyes flick over me as if she's looking for answers about the real reason for my visit.

'Sort of. A road trip to allow me some time to think. I'm considering going into partnership with another artist who runs a little gallery in Canterbury. It's time to make some big changes in my life and leave the past behind.'

'Well, I'm jolly glad you were able to at least pop in for a few hours on your trip. Nico will be delighted to see you. He had a real dip after you left, but Pierce had a plan. Pierce always has a plan,' she laughs, good-naturedly. It's good to hear her sound so content and optimistic.

'So, he's doing okay, then?'

'Yes, I think you'll see a difference. He enjoys running the courses. The set-up is much more focused and the people coming through are artists who already have some experience. It's more structured and runs as a separate part of the business. He joins in a lot more with the group things in the evenings, too, and that was the reason for Isabel's trip, I think, to try to put pressure on him. I thought she was being a little unfair; it's nice to see him more relaxed, and happy. If that means less paintings to sell, then so be it. Money is no longer the issue it was and teaching seems to invigorate him.'

Relaxed and happy, well, that's something.

'Great. I'll walk over and see what he's up to,' I reply, rather awkwardly. Why did I ever think this was a good idea?

She leans in to give me another hug. 'I'm sad for what you've been through. That must have been tough.'

'It was, but I'm over the worst. See you in a bit.'

'Take the umbrella,' Ceana calls out as I grab my coat and slip it on.

The umbrella is huge and as I step into the car park a sudden gust of wind turns it inside out.

'Damn it!' As I fight to stop it being ripped out of my hands, my hood blows backwards and the rain begins to fall in rivulets down my face. Suddenly a voice looms up, carried on the wind. Still struggling to turn the umbrella the right way out, two arms reach around me to grab it and I loosen my grip.

Nico stares at me, frowning, and I stand looking back at him as the clouds above continue to empty themselves with fervour. My hair is already plastered to my head and no doubt my mascara is leaving black tracks as it slides down my face. Clearly the umbrella is beyond repair and he shrugs, throwing it out of the way and pointing in the direction of the château.

'I saw your car. I couldn't believe it,' he shouts over the noise of the heavy rain, as we walk as quickly as we can. It's too slippery to run.

'I'm on holiday,' I yell back at him, and he looks up at the heavens and then shrugs.

'When I saw your car, I thought I was imagining it and I had to check. Everything is all right, isn't it?' He leans forward, pushing open the heavy oak door to usher me inside.

I do a grand impression of a rag doll as I stand there arms straight, pointing down towards the floor with my body rigid. The water runs off my coat, puddling around me as I slip out of my squelching trainers.

'Yes, well – I'm not sure. Sorry about the mess.' I look back at him and see he's even wetter than I am, as he wasn't wearing a coat. Just a navy shirt that is now stuck to him as if it's been glued onto his body. He looks even fitter than the last time I saw him. I was expecting… what, after hearing he's not with Isabel? A broken man? Even more broken than he was when I first came here, maybe. Well, that's definitely not the case and if I didn't believe what Ceana was telling me, I do now.

'Come on through to the studio. I'll grab some towels.'

This is surreal, to say the least. As we walk along the corridor, a whole host of memories come flooding back in a surge. I gaze at the place where a drunken Nico slipped out of my arms and almost collapsed to the floor. I remember the excitement I felt each time my feet trod these old, oak floorboards late at night, my stomach tied in knots over whether my brush strokes would be good enough. Or was it as much about the excitement of working alongside Nico? I push that thought aside. I'm here for one thing only and I'm not going to be put off by a bunch of random thoughts, even if they invoke some strong emotions within me.

The moment I walk in through the door to the studio, the surge of memories turns into a full-on tidal wave. The familiar smell is heavenly and short, sharp images shoot across my mind in quick succession. Things I don't care to remember with such intensity and I'm glad Nico has left me alone. I expected to feel a little nostalgia, but not this.

A sense of panic begins to rise up through my core and settles in my chest. I can feel my heart beating way too fast.

As Nico hands me the navy-blue hand towel, I give him a nod of thanks, momentarily unable to speak.

'It's so good to see you, Fern,' he mumbles. He makes no attempt to dry his hair, he simply stands there watching me as I wipe my face and try to soak up some of the water that has seeped inside the neckline of my jumper. 'Are you well?' he enquires, anxiously.

'I'm good, Nico, thank you. You'd better change your shirt.'

He looks down at his body as if he wasn't aware he was soaked to the skin and he smiles.

'Of course.'

As I watch him walk down to the other end of the studio to grab one of his T-shirts off the rack, it's like turning the clock back one whole year. Surreptitiously watching him out of the side of my eye as he slips the shirt off, he exposes a body that reflects how hard he's still driving himself. Muscles he pushes to the limit each morning before he begins his working day. He told me once it was important to his mental health. I didn't understand until he explained it to me.

'I'm not my father,' he'd said. 'He was a man of excesses that destroyed his body and eventually his mind. Sure, I inherited his fierce passion and a sense of compulsion, but I'll use it in a positive way. My body reflects my determination, but it's easier to control the body than it is what's going on inside my head.'

I remember thinking how sad that was and yet it was another thing that endeared Nico to me. We both understood what it was like to have a compulsion. No one chooses to become a worrier and having that acute sensitivity is a burden. How can you not worry when you look at someone and see what many don't?

'There. I'm dry. You're not cold, are you?' Nico's face is full of concern.

I hand him the soggy towel, shaking my head. 'My hair's a bit damp now, that's all. Nico, I'm here because of your letter. When I sat for you, I thought I was... I thought it was in order for you to finish the portrait of the unknown woman by the lake. In your letter you referred to the portrait of *me*. That wasn't our understanding, Nico, and you know that.'

He looks away. Suddenly he begins to wring his hands, nervously.

'I'm sorry, Fern. I shouldn't have sent that letter. There were things buried deep inside of me that needed to come out and that was the only way I was ever going to let you go. As for the portrait... I no longer dream about the woman at the lake and that canvas has been reused.'

'So you decided to paint *me* without even considering you should have asked my permission, first? And you hung it on the wall and showed it to someone else.' I'm finding it hard to suppress my annoyance, not least because what I'm feeling should be disgust for his betrayal, not love. Instead, I want to throw my arms around him and bury my head on his chest. I want to hear the beat of his heart and feel the warmth of his body next to mine. And now he's telling me *he* has moved on.

'I'm sorry. I never meant to offend you,' he looks at me, dismayed by my reaction. 'Your presence in my life opened my eyes to so many things. It was tough knowing that you had a loving family to go back to and I had nothing to remind me of you. My intention was never to alienate, or use you, Fern, please believe that.'

'But you said in your letter that you loved me. But I think you're confused, because you don't love someone simply because they inspire you. And what about Isabel?'

He shakes his head and I hear a sigh escape from his lips.

'Can I speak freely? Or have you simply come to vent that obvious anger. Anger I don't think I deserve, by the way.'

I stare at him, unblinking.

'I came here to confront you. You were my mentor and I trusted you. All I want is the truth.'

'And that's what you'll get.' Now I've angered him. 'I never hid the fact that I was close with Isabel, but she knows I can't return her love. *You* didn't want to believe that because it eased your conscience when you walked away. But you and I, we hadn't done anything wrong, Fern. It's not a crime to fall in love with someone.

'Isabel and I have history stretching way back; we argue and we do business together, but that's it and I've always been honest with her. There's a side to Isabel with which I simply can't connect. And now I know what true love means, I could never settle for less. You saved me from being talked into something for all the wrong reasons, Fern.'

Is he right? When I left, was I running away from my own emotional turmoil? Were there feelings I didn't want to acknowledge because that would have meant I was giving up on my marriage. And now it's too late, the moment has passed.

'It's irrelevant, Nico. The damage has been done and I just want to see the painting you dared to share with Isabel, without my knowledge, or consent.' I'm tired and confused and I just want this to be over before I say something I'll regret.

'It's hanging in the attic.'

* * *

Isabel is right. It's beautiful. I'm standing in front of an easel, wearing my favourite T-shirt that ended up being a homage to at least three of my canvases. Almost as colourful as the paintings themselves. My arm is extended and the look on my face is one of pure concentration.

'You approve?'

'It's wonderful.' I gulp down the most enormous lump that has risen in my throat. 'I look like an artist,' I whisper, more to myself than to Nico.

'You are,' he enforces.

'This wasn't what I was expecting at all.'

He frowns, crossing his arms as he surveys every inch of the canvas.

'I thought it was perfect. A modern take on a classic portrait. I wouldn't change a thing; it brings me such happiness every time I stand in front of it. Maybe a flaw isn't the worst thing in the world, after all. And I say that with pride.'

As I turn to look at Nico I can see the love he has for me reflected in his eyes. How could I have fought the truth? Shame, maybe? Horror of realising that I could love another man in a way I was supposed to love my husband? I thought what I felt for Aiden was an all-consuming love, but how does anyone really know if they have nothing against which to compare it?

The love I feel for Nico touched my soul, before it touched my heart. With Aiden, it had been lusty, young love. All hormones and long spells apart to fuel those wonderful and passionate weekends together in between studying. The thought of love was exciting and everything we experienced together was new. Getting married, buying a house, putting down roots.

With Nico, the passion that connected us was on another plane. If it had been purely physical, it would have meant little to me. I would have seen it for what it was and dismissed it lightly. But the intensity of what was sparking between us was scary and I had to be strong to fight it. That's why I left. And now I can see that's why I came back.

'You aren't wearing a wedding ring,' Nico says, softly.

'No.'

'I want to be truthful, Fern. When I brought Isabel up here last summer, I needed to know if I had done you justice. She stood here gazing at the painting and do you know what she said? She accused me of being in love with you. I wasn't expecting that; I simply wanted her to cast her expert eye over it; to confirm that the muse lives on, not simply because my heart melts every time I look at it. And I was shocked to the core by her reaction. Was it that obvious? Well, it was to her. I admitted that I had never spoken to you about love; how could I, given the circumstances? Isabel called me a fool.'

I move closer to the painting, in awe of the subtlety of the brush-strokes.

'That was harsh, but it must have been tough for her, given how she feels about you.'

He nods. 'She'll find someone when the time is right, of that I'm sure. She doesn't trust many people and I'm her comfort zone in many ways, as few know the truth about her first husband. There's a thin line between an unhealthy obsession and cruelty. He straddled that line. So, Isabel and I are well used to talking openly and I wasn't offended. I told her that before I met you, I hadn't realised how much loving someone could hurt. Then I came to appreciate that it was a form of divine ecstasy. The real pain would be in never knowing that truth.'

Nico is a man who feels things deeply and this is what makes him an inspiring artist, but that sort of sensitivity doesn't come without its drawbacks.

'She made you write the letter?' I ask, trying to keep my voice on an even keel.

'Yes. Reluctantly. What right had I to unsettle you? But the more I laboured over what to say, the more I came to understand that it isn't wrong to tell someone you love them, even if they can't love you back. After all, that's true for Isabel and me. We're not speaking at the moment as I'm spending more time teaching than painting. That annoys her, but she will forgive me as our friendship has endured much worse.'

I was expecting to stand here, demanding the painting be destroyed. Instead, what I'm feeling is an overwhelming sense of longing. And belonging.

'And you are happy?' I ask, tentatively.

'As happy as I can be. I am no longer tormented by my dreams. Occasionally, just occasionally, I allow myself the indulgence of glancing through those sketches and it's clear to me my dreams were a vision. You were the woman I saw, but our paths hadn't yet crossed. You were meant to save me and you did. You gave yourself to me in the only way you could. And that meant everything to me.'

When I throw my arms around Nico's neck, he holds me to him so gently that my heart feels like it's going to explode.

'I'm not an angel, Nico,' I whisper into his shoulder. 'I'm just a woman who thought she knew what love was, only to discover that I knew nothing.'

DECEMBER 2020

35

TWO PEOPLE, ONE LIFE

It's been a busy day and as I head for Nico's studio, a canvas is calling me. Tonight I hope to put the finishing touches to one that Isabel has been pressing me to complete ready for her next exhibition.

But when I swing open the door, to my utter surprise the room is dotted with the tiny flickering flames of a myriad of tea lights. Nico is seated in amongst a pile of cushions scattered over a rug. Next to him is a wine cooler holding what looks like a rather interesting bottle of wine and a hand-tied posy of electric blue, winter-flowering irises. I raise one eyebrow as I look at him, a tad disapprovingly.

'What's going on?' I demand, as I walk towards him.

The teasing look in his eyes is enigmatic. The Mona Lisa's sardonic smile has nothing on him when he's up to something.

Nico jumps up and as I lean forward to kiss his lips very briefly, I have no intention of getting sidetracked. He slides his arms around me and one kiss turns into two, then three. The trouble is that he's irresistible and he knows it.

'Hmm. You taste good. Sweet, even. Have you been eating cake?'

I laugh as he pulls back, accusingly. 'I might have been tempted by something Margot wafted under my nose. Unfortunately, she left the plate next to me as I helped unload the dishwasher.'

'Well, that explains why you're late. Okay, you need to sit here. In the middle of the rug.'

I screw up my face. 'On the floor?'

'On the floor.'

'But I need to work.'

'Work can wait.'

The flickering light is soft and relaxing. He grasps my hand as I lower myself down and begin to make myself comfortable.

I glance up as he towers over me. 'Will you please sit down. You're making me nervous. Am I going to get a glass of that non-alcoholic bubbly, or is it only for show and you're going to whip out a sketch pad?'

Suddenly he drops down on one knee. 'Fern Emilia Slater, will you marry me?'

I start laughing as he pulls a little box from his pocket. The look on his face is priceless.

'No. But this is a vast improvement on your first proposal. The packed day room wasn't the best idea, was it?' I chide him.

His face drops a little. 'Ah. Well, no, I guess it wasn't. But I rather hoped I was upping the bar a little.'

'Good try,' I admit.

Nico hauls the champagne bottle out of the cooler and reaches out to grab two glasses. 'That's a definite no, then?'

'It is. And is that stuff going to taste anything at all like the real thing?'

He sits down next to me, popping the cork, and we laugh as it flies across the studio, as impressively as if it's the finest champagnes. Holding out the glasses in front of him, he begins pouring.

'Probably not. The alternative was orange juice. How's the bump doing?'

'She's fine. Although we'll struggle a bit when it's time to get me back up off the floor again.'

'Sorry. I thought it might be romantic, you know, reminding you of the night you posed for me. Naked. With no clothes on. And I resisted the temptation to take you in my arms and show you how much I was in love with you.'

'Now that's sort of romantic. But being seven months pregnant, all I want is to paint for an hour or two and then get my feet rubbed, after a long soak in a warm bath.'

Nico looks disappointed.

'The upside is that when you ask me again, we can have real champagne to toast as I turn you down.'

His smile grows, as we chink glasses. A quick sip confirms it doesn't taste quite as bad as I thought it was going to, but it's an acquired taste, for sure.

'I really thought you'd humour me and say *yes* this time around.'

'You keep asking and maybe one day I might. Anyway, are we decided then – we're going to call our daughter Olivia when she puts in an appearance?'

Nico nods as we glance at each other and my heart begins to pound in my chest. Every single time he looks at me that way, I feel as if I'm drowning. The look in his eyes takes my breath away. I don't want to formalise what we have and I know Nico doesn't, either. He's just making sure I haven't changed my mind with the baby on the way. Our love is deeper and so much more than a marriage certificate. Instead of joining hands and having a blessing in front of a gathering, we stood by the lake one sunny afternoon and declared our love for each other.

I'd learnt that a piece of paper means nothing and Nico understood that, and I loved him all the more for it. I never wanted him to be the second husband because our union isn't just a marriage, it's two souls coming together as one.

As we begin each new day together, we pledge that it will be a renewal of our continuing love and commitment. And every time he asks me to marry him, we both know that I'll say *no* because it reminds us that we colour outside the lines, as well as *inside* of them.

Being different sums up who and what we are. Two people brought together against the odds. A match made in heaven.

When the time comes and our daughter is old enough for other people to ask her why we never got married, we know we'll have done a brilliant job if she simply shrugs her shoulders and smiles. 'Because they'd been blessed already.'

DOES 'THE END' EVER LEAVE YOU WANTING MORE?

I always feel that the ending of a story merely signals the beginning of the next chapter in each of the character's lives. But even as I type those words, my mind is asking me, *But what happened next*? Because I'm always curious and always reluctant to let them go.

By now you know them every bit as well as I do and probably have your own ideas about what the future held. But if you can't resist the temptation to see where my imagination led them, then read on.

Life is a mixed bag, and there isn't always a nice, neat little happy ending, but sometimes there is...

NICO AND FERN

Nico did, eventually, paint Fern sitting in the long grass, gazing out across the lake. It sold, many years later, to a London art gallery for well in excess of one hundred thousand pounds. Entitled: *The Angel of Love*, the beauty Nico Gallegos had succeeded in capturing enthralled the eye of the beholder. It was his tribute to the woman he had fallen in love with from the very first moment he saw her.

Fern once confided in her daughter that when she eventually admitted to herself that she was in love with Nico, she felt she was seeing everything for the first time. Suddenly the world was bigger, brighter and exciting. And it was, every single day they spent together. Many thought her happiness was due to the success she achieved as a prolific and very popular artist, but looking back on her life her words put everything into perspective: 'It was only ever the icing on the cake. Nico and my beautiful daughter, Olivia, were the twinkling stars that lit up my little heaven on earth.'

ISABEL, THE MARQUESA DE AYTONA

The gallery in Seville brought the Marquesa continuing success and elevated the careers of many artists, including Nico and Fern, to whom she was not simply a business acquaintance, but a good friend.

But imprinted forever on Isabel's mind, was always that eight-year-old boy, Nico, chasing her around the orchard of her family home, as she shrieked at the top of her lungs. They were children, as yet untouched by some of the harsh lessons life had to teach them.

For Nico, his father was about to go into decline and the effect would scar his life for many years to come. Until he finally met his muse.

For Isabel, her scheming mother and then a controlling husband would influence the way she looked at everything. Everything except Nico, the first real love of her life and one never forgets that feeling.

Would Isabel have swapped her success and her fortune to have Nico by her side and be the one to heal his wounds? Yes, of course. But she could see that Fern was his true soulmate. To accept that someone isn't destined to be yours is painful; however, that little flame of selfless love deep inside of Isabel's heart softened her as the years passed. It made her a better person. It inspired her not to give up on love and, eventually, she met and married a very successful businessman, some fifteen years her junior.

People who knew her saw only a strong, independent woman whose fabulous lifestyle was often in the tabloids. No one really knew of her sacrifice in loving someone so completely that she was prepared to let him go. Encouraging Nico to write that letter to Fern had been the first step in sealing the destiny of two kindred souls.

Everything happens for a reason.

AIDEN AND JOSS

After several years of backpacking, mainly visiting various dive sites as Aiden and Joss trained to become scuba diving instructors, they finally made the Cayman Islands their home. Thanks to Aiden's share of the lottery win, they bought a small diving business run from Aiden's pride and joy, his boat, *The Sea Spirit*.

They lived a simple life together on the west side of the Grand Cayman and were often found strolling Seven Mile Beach early each morning, or late at night. Their modest bungalow was far away from the bustle and luxuries of George Town, and to them it was paradise.

Joss knew that Aiden followed the rise of Fern's career online, but she tried her best not to let that make her feel second-best. After all, she was the one who was able to give Aiden the life he'd longed for but hadn't had the courage to grab. She convinced him that life was too short not to follow one's dream. Aiden told her once, that when he was swimming with the stingrays in the crystal clear waters, it felt like heaven on earth. It made her heart feel full.

TAYLOR AND KELLIE

Sometimes people heal themselves; sometimes two people can heal each other. And that's what happened with Taylor and Kellie, but it was a slow process.

When Taylor introduced Kellie to his family, she immediately realised that he had cut himself off as his penance. His penance for being a survivor. All she could do was to get to know them and, after they both returned to France, encourage him to keep up regular contact.

It took four years, during which time Kellie studied hard on her journey to becoming a trained Psychological Well-being Practitioner, before Taylor asked her to marry him. She said *yes* on one condition and that was that they would start their life together back in the States.

While it was a sad upheaval leaving behind the love and support of their family at The Haven, Kellie felt it was time for Taylor to let go of his guilt. Going home represented a fresh start for him; he faced his worst fears and realised they were all in his head. The lesson he'd had to learn was acceptance.

Taylor set up his own carpentry business, building bespoke kitchen and bathroom units. Two years later, Kellie gave birth to their daughter, Alicia, and later found a part-time job in a private clinic while continuing her training.

Over the years, her relationship with her parents dwindled further and they had little to do with their granddaughter. However, Kellie came to realise that you can't let other people define who you are, or drag you down. Her personal experiences actually made her a better practitioner and she went on to help many, many people over the years. But her biggest triumph was seeing the confident man Taylor eventually became. Their daughter grew into a strong and determined young woman, whose love of nature and animals led her into a rewarding career as a veterinarian.

CEANA

When her father died several years later, Ceana moved back to Scotland to look after her mother. She continued to keep in touch with both Nico and Pierce for many years and made two trips back to visit her old friends.

While she never found love in the form of a companion and soulmate, Ceana ended up becoming a short-term foster carer. Taking in children requiring emergency placement, she found her true vocation. Eventually, she also offered respite care to parents and families with a disabled child. She was an active fundraiser for a local charity supporting the cause and was well respected by the community at large for the work she did.

At the age of seventy-eight, Ceana was awarded an OBE. She was quoted as saying it was 'Very nice', but the only thing that mattered to her was being able to make a difference. The love she received in return from people of all ages was reward enough and she considered herself to have been blessed with a rich and happy life.

PIERCE

Pierce recruited a new deputy manager after Ceana returned to Scotland. Sadie Marchant knew she had big shoes to fill. But she didn't just achieve that, she also stole Pierce's heart. They became not only a strong management team but also husband and wife.

Their twins were born five years later and they asked Nico and Fern to be godparents. Whenever Karl and Kyla disappeared, everyone knew they would be in Nico's studio, paintbrushes in hand, daubing away. Throughout their lives, they remained close with Nico and Fern's daughter, Olivia, and often reminisced about their childhood and the wonderful times they had shared at The Haven.

DEE-DEE AND ODILE

When a very special relationship began to grow between these two very different ladies, no one was really surprised. They had much in common after all; both were talented in what they did and inspired many visitors to continue on after their first experiences of working with textiles and clay at The Haven.

But Dee-Dee was always the over-the-top personality and Odile the quieter one. As time passed, they formed a bond that would one day see them living as a couple and becoming firm favourites with visitors of all ages.

They eventually retired to a little cottage on the outskirts of the Bois-Saint-Vernon, where they lived quite happily until their deaths, some six months apart.

PATRICIA

When the love of your life dies, nothing is ever quite the same again, but Patricia knew that Fred was with her always. Her fate was to live until the age of ninety-one.

Stefan remained by her side, although they were only ever friends. They travelled far and wide together in that smart, shiny black motorhome.

For more than ten years, every August they returned to The Haven for a week's stay and their word-of-mouth endorsement helped a lot of people discover it for the first time.

Patricia died peacefully in her sleep, just one month after Stefan died of cancer. In the final moments before her eyes closed for the last time, a smile flickered around her mouth. The two men whose lives she'd felt privileged to be a part of were waiting for her. The next chapter was about to begin.

BASTIEN

No one knew Bastien's story until after he died, unexpectedly, from a heart attack, twelve years later. Always the gentleman, kind-hearted, he was the proverbial gentle giant. Arms like steel, he was never happier than when the forge was fired up and the almost unbearable heat reddened his skin.

Among his personal effects were some letters and Pierce made contact with someone he assumed was a relative. A woman named Ana.

Ana turned out to be Bastien's estranged wife of many years. Their only son had drowned in a pond in the back garden of their home when he was three years old. Unable to cope with his loss, Bastien disappeared one day and it was years before he contacted Ana again.

She wanted to see where he'd been living and made the trip from Vittel, in the north-east of France, accompanied by her sister. When she stood in Bastien's room, her eyes swept around and immediately alighted on the black, wooden crucifix hung on the wall. Her religion had saved her sanity, but as a devout Catholic she had feared for Bastien's soul when his faith lapsed. She stood and cried, as she lifted it down and hugged it to her body. The relief was immense and she thanked God for looking after the man she had never stopped loving.

MARGOT

When Sadie took over from Ceana, the first initiative she implemented was the *visitor's wish list*. A little form they completed after dinner on day one. It encouraged guests to focus on what they wanted to achieve during their time at The Haven. She tied this in with Pierce's end-of-course wrap-up, on the final day. The *word cloud*, as it came to be known rather affectionately, was a huge success, but Sadie's idea was clever, too. As everyone ticked off the items on their wish lists, they were encouraged to give feedback and make suggestions.

It turns out that Margot's occasional cookery demonstrations were becoming increasingly popular. When she was asked if she was willing to become a tutor, running three sessions a week in the evenings, she was delighted.

Pierce and Sadie realised she'd need help, so Margot drafted in her daughter, Yvette, and a long-standing friend. And what a team they made. Margot prepared the menus and oversaw dinner in the evening. Her demonstrations turned into more of a hands-on class, with people invited to work alongside her. It became a firm favourite with the visitors and eventually a new, bespoke facility was built. *Le*

Havre de Cuisine was born and throughout the year, places were offered for Margot Bressan's five-day culinary courses.

Margot was delighted with her enhanced role and, before long, the new kitchen was also producing a range of The Haven's own jams and sauces. A little *industrie artisanale* had been born.

HANNAH AND OWEN

Hannah went on to have four children within a period of six years.

Eventually, once the children were all at school, she trained as a teaching assistant and her home and working life revolved entirely around kids. She'd found her calling.

Owen's army career ended up spanning twenty years and he rose to become a Warrant Officer Class 2, responsible for the training, welfare and discipline of a company of more than a hundred men.

When he left the army, he took a year off to go backpacking around the world and Fern feared he was going through a mid-life crisis. However, he ended up meeting his future partner, the woman he married in Las Vegas only six months later. Returning home for good, he and his wife set up an outdoor activity centre in the Forest of Dean. From paintballing to archery, the business grew and Fern was relieved that at last her brother was finally settled and had found his soulmate.

Every year at Christmas when The Haven was closed, Fern's family hired a minibus and Owen drove them to Provence. It was bedlam, but it reminded them all that there's nothing so comforting as having family around you. It was the highlight of the year for each and every one of them.

Not everyone is lucky enough to have a family. That's the way life is and sometimes the family you have isn't the family you need. But everywhere around the world, groups of people, as with those at The Haven, are drawn together by an invisible, cosmic design. All with a common cause, need, or altruistic goal. And that's a very powerful thing.

When we stand alone, we are an island;
  when we join together, we become a force.

ACKNOWLEDGMENTS

It's time to give a shout out to my amazing editor, Sarah Ritherdon, who is a real pleasure to work with and a tremendous support. You are an inspiration, lady!

And to the wider Boldwood team – a wonderful group of inspiring women I can't thank enough for their amazing support and encouragement.

A hug to my wonderful agent, Sara Keane, for being there for me every step of the way on this exciting journey.

There are so many friends who are there for me through thick and thin. They suffer periods of silence when I'm head down, writing. I hide myself away to spend my days with characters who become very real to me and I'm sad when a story draws to a close. But when I pop my head back up it's like I've never been away and no one refers to the fact that I'm such an erratic friend!

As usual, no book is ever launched without there being an even longer list of people to thank for publicising it. The amazing kindness of readers and reviewers is truly humbling. You continue to delight, amaze and astound me with your generosity and support. Without your kindness in spreading the word about my latest release, your wonderful reviews to entice people to click and download, or pluck my book from a shelf, I wouldn't be able to indulge myself in my guilty pleasure... writing.

Feeling blessed and sending much love to you all for your treasured support and friendship,

Linn x

MORE FROM LUCY COLEMAN

We hope you enjoyed reading *Summer in Provence*. If you did, please leave a review.

If you'd like to gift a copy, this book is also available as an ebook, digital audio download and audiobook CD.

Sign up to Lucy Coleman's mailing list for news, competitions and updates on future books:

http://bit.ly/LucyColemanNewsletter

A Springtime to Remember, another glorious escapist read from Lucy Coleman, is available to order now.

ABOUT THE AUTHOR

Lucy Coleman is a #1 bestselling romance writer, whose recent novels include *Snowflakes over Holly Cove*. She also writes under the name Linn B. Halton. She won the 2013 UK Festival of Romance: Innovation in Romantic Fiction award and lives in the Welsh Valleys.

Visit Lucy's website: www.lucycolemanromance.com

Follow Lucy on social media:

facebook.com/LucyColemanAuthor

twitter.com/LucyColemanAuth

instagram.com/lucycolemanauthor

bookbub.com/authors/lucy-coleman

ABOUT BOLDWOOD BOOKS

Boldwood Books is a fiction publishing company seeking out the best stories from around the world.

Find out more at www.boldwoodbooks.com

Sign up to the Book and Tonic newsletter for news, offers and competitions from Boldwood Books!

http://www.bit.ly/bookandtonic

We'd love to hear from you, follow us on social media:

facebook.com/BookandTonic

twitter.com/BoldwoodBooks

instagram.com/BookandTonic

Made in the USA
Monee, IL
04 November 2020